The Woodcarver of Krakow

The
Woodcarver
of
Krakow

Rachel Clare

The Book Guild Ltd

First published in Great Britain in 2020 by
The Book Guild Ltd
9 Priory Business Park
Wistow Road, Kibworth
Leicestershire, LE8 0RX
Freephone: 0800 999 2982
www.bookguild.co.uk
Email: info@bookguild.co.uk
Twitter: @bookguild

Typeset in Adobe Garamond Pro

Printed and bound in Great Britain by CPI Group (UK) Ltd, Croydon, CR0 4YY

ISBN 978 1913208 769

British Library Cataloguing in Publication Data.
A catalogue record for this book is available from the British Library.

MIX
Paper from
responsible sources
FSC
www.fsc.org
FSC® C013604

For my brother, Gareth
For always being there for me.

"As the family goes, so goes the nation
and so goes the whole world in which we live"

– St John Paul II.

Prologue

Off the Netherlands' coast, March 1945

I am dying.

My breathing calms and slows as I find myself powerless to continue my struggle. The silence enfolding me in its embrace; my spirit ascends beyond the canopy of stars, silver pinpricks in the infinite black universe. All I have to do is submit. Then let go. But while my brain recognises how easy this would be, the braver part of me fights to cling to life.

Adrenaline catapults me back into my body and I manage several shallow breaths. The high-pitched wailings of the distressed engine pierce my eardrums and my muscles tense taut as parachute strings; ready for action as my survival instinct kicks in. Grasping the metal gearstick in my padded glove, its coldness seeps through to my skin and relief floods through me that I am still alive. Reaching up, I try to open the hatch. But it is no use.

As the plane nosedives beneath me, I register every sensation: sweat pooled around my throat, hot breath trapped in my mask, petrol fumes flooding my nostrils. Plummeting through the sky, I am like one of the acrobats my grandfather, Dziadek, took my brother and me to see when the circus pitched up on the field next to ours the summer when I was seven and Jacek was eleven. Licking sweet ice creams topped with tart bilberries, the three of us sat side by side on wooden benches, enraptured as the gymnasts tumbled, their multi-coloured costumes arching through the balmy air like rainbows.

The cold pierces my body like a thousand needles as my plane plunges into the heaving waves of the North Sea. Momentarily, I am taken back to the day I fell into the Dunajec River, how my brother rescued me from its fast-flowing waters and the promise I made to him. As the sea drags me downwards, I can only pray that God grants me the chance to keep it now. The black waters overwhelming me, my last thought is of her.

1

In a sunlit corner of my grandfather's workshop, I perched on the chair he carved for me from elmwood six summers ago, studying the intricacy of his craftsmanship in the backrest. A revered woodcarver in the traditional Podhale style, the old man depicted a dozen scenes from the fairytales he used to tell Jacek and me before bedtime. I remembered how we'd burrowed beneath warm furs listening intently as he'd told us tales of bears and eagles and princesses, the flickering candle on the windowsill illuminating the old man's animated face and keeping the darkness at bay.

Although the chair was too small for me now as I folded my sun-warmed legs beneath me, I knew I could never bear to be parted from it for as long as I lived. As I committed the details of Dziadek's carvings of the Bear in the Forest Hut, the Frog Princess and the Good Ferryman and the Water Nymphs to memory, I hoped that one day I would be able to pass the chair down to my children and grandchildren and they would sit attentively while I recited the stories to them, known to me by heart. The aroma of resin cloying in my nostrils, I coughed suddenly and Dziadek looked up from his current piece, his grey eyes as kind, his beard as bushy as St Nicholas's, who rode on his sleigh through the ancient streets of Krakow every December 6th giving gifts to the gathered crowd of excited children. Happiness coursing through me, I returned Dziadek's smile, realising that he was my very own St Nicholas who took care of me all year round, not just for one day.

Indeed, Dziadek and my brother, Jacek, were like a comfort blanket wrapped around me and the only family I had, as Mama was long dead while Tata was a general in the army, a distant figure whom we saw just a couple of times a year. Dziadek once said Tata stayed away because my brother and I reminded him too much of Mama in our looks and mannerisms, something too painful for him to bear. Eager to please Tata in order to gain his love, Jacek planned to follow in his footsteps with a military career, whereas my creative talents were always closely affiliated with Dziadek's. Unlike me, Jacek never showed any interest in our grandfather's workshop, nor did he have the same bond with him that I did. The old man was just too quiet, too otherworldly for a boy with Jacek's lust for life. Even with me, Dziadek had always been a man of few words. But that had never bothered me, in fact, if anything it had strengthened the bond we shared.

Last January, when snowdrifts closed our school for weeks on end, I witnessed Dziadek carve a relief of the Last

Supper to hang on the wall of our local church, dedicated to Our Lady of Częstochowa. First, he let me choose the wood from the vast selection of panels propped against the wall of his workshop. As I sorted through the linden, the oak and the cherry, he explained that hardwoods were more difficult to shape but had greater lustre and longevity, while it would be easier to carve the finer details of the figures in the softwoods, though these were prone to damage. After much deliberation, I opted for a sturdy oak, envisaging this would be a special piece of Dziadek's, one which I and others would want to behold for years to come, unaltered by age. We then secured my chosen panel onto his workbench with a huge vice before setting out his tools in a neat row, the worn, wooden handles almost touching, but not quite. There was his carving knife, a specialised tool used to pare, cut and smooth the wood while he would remove any extraneous chunks with his coping saw. His gouge, whose curved blade he would use to fashion hollows and rounds before embarking upon the sweeping curves of the figures in the Biblical scene. His chisels, which he would employ to create lines and clean up flat surfaces and, finally, his fluter, with which he would score the deepest gouges before adding the finishing decorative cuts to the piece.

As Dziadek completed his preparations, he allowed me to experiment a little on the surface and that was when it became apparent that the oak panel I had decided upon was equally strong in all directions, thus somewhat limiting the complexity of his carving. But I stuck with my decision and I immediately found the wood's grain, the direction in which the panel was strongest. Pleased, the old man told me he would arrange the more delicate parts of the carving of Jesus, His disciples and the table with the bread and wine along the grain rather than across it.

Dziadek explained that since it was an elongated design, he'd have to carve some of the details on the end grain, a prospect which would prove challenging even for such an experienced woodcarver as himself. In his deep, authoritative voice, he stated that if we failed to adhere to these fundamental rules it would almost certainly result in inferior work and that anything he subsequently added across the grain, such as a face, a glass of wine or a piece of bread, would eventually break away. "The skill of a good woodcarver is to allow the wood to reveal to him what is already there within it, rather than foist his own ideas onto it, Tad," the old man said with a wry smile.

"But how will I know what is hidden in the wood?" I asked, puzzled, looking into his serious eyes the shade of storm clouds.

He laughed. "*Kochany*, I can't tell you that. But trust me, it's something that comes with experience, with knowing and understanding the wood. Such a thing can't be taught. It's inside you already, Tad. You just have to ease it out over time." He patted his chest with his hand, which was as brown and gnarled as the wood I'd chosen. Then, lowering his head, he turned his attention to the piece, a gesture which signalled that our discussion for the day had reached its end, even though I had a dozen and one questions hovering upon the tip of my tongue. It was the wood that bound Dziadek and I, not words and conversation.

Entranced, I watched him set to work on the shaping of the piece as he used his largest gouge to painstakingly remove portions of wood. Then, turning the implement to its cutting edge, he scooped out smaller sections as smoothly as if he was removing the pink-yellow flesh of a peach and he soon became lost in his own world with just the wood and his thoughts for company. For the remaining weeks of my enforced exile from school, I marvelled as Dziadek transformed the scribbled figures which looked down from sketch papers pinned on the walls into a vivid scene on that flat panel of wood. In his studio, infused with lilac light reflected from the snowdrifts outside, Dziadek bevelled away until the table and the Biblical figures assumed lives of their own, the details appearing in harmony with the growth of the wood. The speed with which his elegant fingers worked bewitched me as he chiselled and gouged, often requiring his mallet to drive his implements through the unyielding wood to create the exact imprint he wanted.

As the thaw melted the snow to slush, I rushed home from school in the twilight, eager to watch Dziadek work with his fluter to give expressions to the faces of his figures, while simultaneously seeming to breathe life into their lungs. Once he'd completed the finer details, we sat in silence together, studying each nuance of the carving before Dziadek set about finishing the surface. He didn't consider a smooth one appropriate for this particular piece, as he thought it would drain away the essence of the animated dining scene, and I agreed. So, discarding his rasps and rifflers onto the stone floor beneath his bench, he abandoned his plan to polish, preferring to emphasise the rough texture left by his gouge on the carving's surface.

As the first snowdrops pushed their way through the frozen ground outside his workshop, Dziadek sealed and coloured the wood with walnut oil, which also acted as a protection from dirt and moisture. A few weeks later, studying Dziadek's completed tableau of the Last Supper positioned below the west window of our family church, I understood how his skill and meticulous work had come together to create a masterpiece. From his selection of implements, to carving with the grain, to the oil he'd chosen to impart a delicate sheen on the wood, I saw the piece was far more than the sum of its parts. To my untrained eyes, it was perfection.

The tableau still hangs in the church, inhabiting its silent world untouched by daylight during the week, to be looked upon and admired every Sabbath day by the congregation.

2

Blackpool, August 2020

Sarah Farland's eyes were drawn to the horizon, where sky and sea met in a blue line smudged by the heat haze of the afternoon. Emerging from the corner of her mind was a memory of her first visit to the beach when she was just three years old, her father's huge hand enveloping her tiny one. Despite his stern warnings of catching a chill, her strong will had eventually persuaded him to let her remove her shoes and socks so she could feel the sand beneath her feet, wet and cold, as the tide had gone out only minutes before. Forty years later, the beach was still her safe haven where she came to mull over small dilemmas and get her head around seemingly insurmountable events like her dear dad's death and her daughter Bella's birth, the seagulls' piercing cries often a welcome distraction from her swirling thoughts.

"Look, Sarah, it's heading our way." Her mother's high-pitched voice drew her out of her reverie. Sarah looked skyward just in time to see the Lancaster Bomber dip its nose to the amassed crowds on the promenade, its dark grey body and wings giving it the appearance of a gigantic bird, wings spread wide. The fearsome rumble of its great engines rushing in her ears, her eyes followed the aircraft as it raced out to sea before disappearing from sight. For a few moments, the holidaymakers and locals around her seemed to hold their collective breath before the World War II plane roared back towards the sizzling sands to take its final bow.

"They've done such a good restoration job to keep her airworthy for shows like this," Bella commented, her blue eyes squinting in the strong glare of the late summer sun.

"It gives me such a thrill each time I see it," said Sarah, recalling how the Blackpool Air Show on the second weekend in August had been a red-ringed date on her calendar since she'd worn gingham dresses and knee-high socks. In those early days she'd come with her grandma, Eirlys, whose back had begun to stoop from arthritis, and her mum, Anna, whose hair had reached down her back like a golden veil in the style of the seventies.

Looking up, Sarah saw that her mother was morphing into how Eirlys had looked in her later years. Her once-long hair now steely grey and cut short, there were fine lines around her eyes. Although Anna's weight had crept up in the few years since her husband's death, Sarah had to concede that she'd inherited Eirlys's interest in fashion and still looked good in stylish clothes. But whereas her grandma had possessed a self-confident air about her, Sarah knew her mother had always been inhibited, a trait which had only got worse with age.

Sensing her daughter's eyes on her, Anna turned and smiled before glancing down at her programme of events, which fluttered as a gust of warm wind caught its pages. "The Spitfire is up next." She hooked her hand around Sarah's arm, taking the weight off one foot then the other.

"And then the pièce de résistance, the Red Arrows. My all-time favourite," Bella squealed, forking her fingers through her pretty chin-skimming bob. Looking at her daughter's attire of a stripy red and white vest beneath dark denim dungarees which clung to her shapely figure, Sarah couldn't help but smile. Despite growing up as a bit of a tomboy, eschewing 'girls' games' for football and building dens at the bottom of her garden with the boys, not to mention her less-than-ladylike dress sense, a subtle change had come over Bella since she'd turned eighteen in April. With her high cheekbones, sapphire eyes bordered with long, dark eyelashes and silky, white-blonde hair, Sarah saw that there was more than a hint emerging of the striking woman into which she was slowly transforming. She supposed her daughter took after Anna in that respect who, in her younger years, had also been considered a beauty.

Despite her decent height of five foot nine, the good looks of her grandmother, mother and daughter seemed to have bypassed Sarah. She had always been more than a little self-conscious about her too-pale skin and mysterious sea-shaded eyes, which, depending on the time of day and the season, shifted from blue to green. But it was her wavy shoulder-length dark hair which had always been the bane of her life, too unruly to style effectively. As a result of these insecurities about her appearance, Sarah had always sought to blend in with the crowd with clothes in a stylish monochrome palette. She kept herself slim enough to wear black trouser suits and white fitted shirts to work, which, along with her deep voice, gave her an air of authority when delivering lectures and tutorials to her students. This formality of dressing even extended to her holidays and today her fitted cream linen dress complemented her tall figure. What she didn't realise, though, was that far from being inconspicuous, whatever she wore, her statuesque build drew looks from men and women alike.

Her attention was diverted by a dark dot bobbing on the horizon. Getting bigger and bigger, Sarah made out the wings, head and tail of the Spitfire as it rushed towards the excited crowd. "That is pretty incredible, though, I have to admit!" Bella yelped, holding her iPhone in her perfectly manicured hands, clicking a series of photos to capture the plane's sleek shape as well as its motion across the seafront. After some clever antics, the Spitfire was joined by the Lancaster Bomber and Hawker Hurricane for the Battle of Britain Memorial Flight, a fitting finale to the first part of the air show.

"It makes me feel incredibly patriotic," Anna sighed, stretching her legs which had turned to lead. "Thinking of what those lads went through in order to safeguard their country eighty years ago. If it hadn't been for the RAF's victory in the Battle of Britain in the summer of 1940, the Allies would have almost certainly lost World War II and the world as we know it would be quite different."

"I just can't imagine the boys in my year at school having the bravery and the get-up-and-go to risk their lives for their country," Bella commented, admiring the intricate ironwork of the ochre-coloured Blackpool Tower which soared into the sky.

"Just as the lads did in World War II, I think if our country was in danger again you might be pleasantly surprised about how the youth of today would react," Anna said. "Even though I know some people refer to yours as the Snowflake Generation."

"How do you know about that, Gran?" Bella teased, the sea breeze ruffling her immaculate hair.

"I have eyes and ears. I read the newspapers and eavesdrop on the conversations of the college students on the bus," Anna smiled, "and I think, given the opportunity, nine out of ten young people would fight if their country and freedom were under threat. Not having the opportunity to show their true colours is another thing entirely."

"If you could drag them away from the iPhones for five minutes," Bella sighed, before adding, "but, yeah, Gran, I think you have a point. Ah, here comes the Turbulent Team."

Their conversation was interrupted as six planes entered their line of sight from disparate directions to make a rendezvous ready to fly in formation. The subsequent stunts of the wingwalkers – which could only be described as death-defying – were met with rapturous applause from the crowd. "Wow! I wish I had the opportunity to do something like that," Bella commented, emerging from the performance which had kept her spellbound – and surprisingly mute – for well over five minutes. "That must be the ultimate adrenaline rush, Gran."

"Maybe for you, Isabella, but a little hair-raising for me!" The old woman laughed, her heart pumping a little slower now that the wingwalkers were safely back inside their aircraft. "I can understand, though, why someone would want to fly a plane. Imagine the weightlessness of being up above the clouds! It must be heavenly. Balancing on the plane's wing with the wind's G-force buffeting you about, however, is beyond my comprehension."

"Gran, you always play things so safe!" Bella laughed to reveal perfectly white, perfectly uniform teeth, painstakingly achieved by wearing braces for the greater part of her teenage years.

"Yes, and it has got me to seventy-four relatively unscathed! I don't know where you get your adventurous spirit from, sweetheart. Certainly not from your granddad's gene pool! He was the most cautious man who walked the earth, God rest his soul."

Bella smiled as she fondly remembered her Papa George with his big, black eyebrows and throaty laugh. Never having met her biological father, whom her mum had split from before Bella was born, this old man had been like a surrogate dad through her childhood, a positive male influence in her young life which had been painfully cut short by a fatal heart attack while out walking his elderly beagle, Flora, two Christmases ago. "I miss Papa George so much," she sighed as a breeze mussed up her tidy bob.

"I know. Me too." Sarah put a comforting arm upon her daughter's shoulder as they turned their attention back to the show and its traditional thrilling Red Arrows finale.

The red, white and blue smoke trailing behind them like party streamers in the sky, the women followed the prom to the state-of-the-art glass building of Blackpool's trendiest and probably most expensive bistro. Although a pretty tearoom where she could enjoy a nice pot of tea and slice of Victoria sponge was more up Sarah's street, and her mother's too, Sarah could see from Bella's expression that she was desperate to try out the Beach House Bistro Bar. So she relented, knowing her daughter would probably spend that evening uploading photos of the swanky, sleek restaurant to her Facebook page with clever captions to show off to her friends.

Anna gratefully accepted the cool rush of air conditioning which came her way as a waiter in his late twenties held open the door for them. Dressed in a smart black-and-white uniform, he led them to one of the stylish chrome tables in the window which offered a three hundred and sixty-degree view of the packed promenade and the central and north piers jutting out into the Irish Sea, the waters sparkling like emeralds in the sun.

"The view's not at all bad here," whispered Bella, smiling unashamedly as the waiter pushed the plush white leather seat beneath her before taking their order and retreating to the bar.

"Isn't he a bit old for you, Isabella? Anyway, I thought you were dating Harry? He's such a nice boy," Anna said, finding the sea view calming after the heat of the hectic promenade.

"Broke up last week," said Bella matter-of-factly as she flipped through the screens of her iPhone to check for incoming text messages or emails. "He was 'nice' but I think that was the problem, he didn't give me butterflies in the pit of my stomach. And besides I don't want to date anyone from school now I've left. I feel as though I've outgrown it and all the guys there. They are so immature!"

Anna stifled a smile. "Well, you did the best thing then, sweetheart," she said as seriously as she could. She felt a little out of place as she glanced around to see she was the only person in the restaurant the wrong side of fifty, never mind seventy. "You're better off just enjoying yourself for now, going out and having fun. You're far too young to have a serious relationship yet."

Bella watched as her mother shifted awkwardly in her seat. Despite never having met him, Bella knew that her father was called Bradley Ledge and was American. That, like her mother, he'd been a junior lecturer in the English Department at Lancaster University when they'd met. That they had shared a fling or 'dalliance', as her grandma liked to call it, which had lasted the duration of the hot summer of 2001. That, at the start of September, his sabbatical year had come to an end and he'd headed to the University of Charleston to do his doctorate where she presumed he still was. That, by the time her mum had found herself to be pregnant that October, they'd both moved on. That, although Bradley had diligently sent child maintenance cheques over The Pond for the past eighteen years, his curiosity at being a father hadn't quite peaked enough to propel him across the Atlantic Ocean to visit or indeed have any personal contact with Bella. Once Sarah had joked that even if he'd shown an interest in Bella, theirs had never been destined to be a long-term relationship, not least because of her necessary name change to *S Ledge* if they'd married. "I never wanted to share the same moniker as a piece of wood which people use to whizz down hillsides at twenty miles per hour on their backsides," she'd quipped, and they'd both laughed, even though the situation was far from a joke for either of them.

Bella had one small picture of Bradley. With his jet-black, gelled-back hair, he looked nothing like her, but rather like Elvis Presley. When her mother had described his 'slow as molasses' southern accent, Bella had uploaded some Elvis videos to her iPhone, imagining Bradley singing lullabies to her in a similar way. Over the years, Justin Bieber had slowly replaced Elvis in her affections as Bella had tried to convince herself that none of the business with her father impinged on her life, the person she was or would become. There were plenty of other kids in her classes at school who had ended up having absentee fathers, after all. She almost considered it was more painful for them, growing up with their dads who'd shared their everyday lives as a family and then all of a sudden, their father's affair or something else had caused their relationship with their mother to hit the rocks. The child caught up at the heart of all that anguish and hurt. She counted herself lucky that hadn't happened with her father and somewhere in the dark recesses of her mind, she still harboured the hope of meeting up with him one day.

Bella's other great regret in life, though, was not having a sibling with whom to share her happiness and sadness, her successes and failures, and her hopes and dreams. However, she could not lay the blame for this at Bradley's door. She knew her mother had been happy to concentrate on raising her and progressing her career these past eighteen years, pushing away any man before he had the chance to get close to her. Setting their tea and cakes onto the table with a smile, the waiter provided Bella a welcome diversion from her rather doleful thoughts.

"I used to love swimming in the sea," Anna said later, wistfully looking out of the Beach House's window to the pier, its sturdy, iron legs fearlessly striding out into the choppy waters. "Of course, I did all my serious training for the competitions at the Derby Baths."

"Wait a minute, Gran!" Bella absently twisted a strand of hair around her index finger. "You took part in swimming competitions when you were a girl?"

"Yes, when I was a teenager. I felt such freedom whenever I swam, as though I'd shed my skin along with my clothes." She smiled. "I was the Fylde Coast champion in the butterfly stroke category in sixty-one, two and three. Of course, George insisted I give it up once we were married." Anna fell silent as she looked out at the waves ricocheting off the pier's girders. "We should make this a regular outing. This carrot cake is to die for."

"It's certainly the place to come and relax," said Sarah, sipping her tea, "overlooking the sea with such an amazing view. And the Mediterranean menu here is so healthy. Perhaps we could try a meal next time?"

"Wait, back up a minute! You were swimming champion of the whole of the Fylde Coast?" Bella clarified as Anna nodded. "And, Mum, you knew about it? Why wasn't I aware of this? It's such a big deal. If you were a teenager today, Gran, an achievement like that would be in pride of place at the top of your Facebook page."

"Yes, well, all this new-fangled technology makes me glad that I'm not young in this day and age. I don't think I could keep up!" Savouring her final mouthful of cake, Anna took a deep breath before digging into her black patent handbag to retrieve a small box wrapped in pink paper, a white bow adorning the top. "Isabella, this is a small token to let you know how proud I am of you for studying so hard for your A-level exams."

"But Gran, I haven't even got my results yet! I'm pretty confident I'll get good grades in Art, Design Technology and Maths, but English… I'm not so sure." She pulled a face.

"I have every belief in you, Isabella!" A kind smile lit up Anna's face as she pressed the present into her granddaughter's palm.

"But you already gave me all that money for my eighteenth," Bella protested, noting from her grandma's use of her full name that this must be something serious, "for when I finally decide what I want to do with my life."

"That'll have to be sooner rather than later." Her mum swallowed a mouthful of cake to cut in. "Next year's university intake will be making their applications in the autumn so you need to make your mind up soon or you'll miss that boat as well."

"I think, Isabella, you just need to take some time to decide. In the meantime, why not open your present?" Anna's eyes gleamed with excitement as she gazed at the box lying in her granddaughter's hand. With one rip, Bella peeled back the paper to reveal a brown, rather dog-eared cardboard box with some strange writing on it in a language she didn't recognise. *Kocham Cię*.

"What does it mean?" Bella tucked her long swept-over fringe behind her right ear, a subconscious gesture she did whenever she was feeling caught off guard.

"It's Polish for *I love you*," her grandmother said simply. Without waiting for further explanation, Bella opened the box and took out an angel, every detail from her long hair to her flowing robe, her smiling face to her closed eyes, her halo to her praying hands, carved in the palest of blond wood.

"But you've had her on your bedside table for as long as I can remember." Bella brushed her fingers over the bevelled roughness of her wings. "I've always thought she was protecting you, Grandma. I can't take her from you."

"Yes, you can. It's true she's very special to me, but I know you'll take good care of her. She was passed down to me from my mother." Her grandmother paused, choosing her words carefully. "My father gave it to her during the war. Isabella, I've been thinking about this for months and now you've turned eighteen, I want you to be her next custodian until you pass her to your children..."

Bella sat the wooden figure in her palm, studying the angel's beautiful face, hair and wings, each carved with the most exquisite detail, saying, "I always thought she looked a bit like you, Gran."

"I suppose she does, before I got all these wrinkles." Anna paused. "Isabella, I decided to bring you to the air show today because it felt like the right time to give you the angel, the right time to tell you about my father and where he came from. Where *we* come from." Bella saw her grandma's eyes were shimmering with unshed tears behind her glasses.

"But I don't understand, I always thought Great-Granddad was in the RAF?" Bella looked at her mum and grandma with wide eyes. Just as her dad had not been a topic open for discussion with either of them over the years, neither had her great-granddad.

"During World War II, Blackpool was a debriefing station for Polish flyers who had escaped Nazi oppression in their homeland." Anna blinked back tears. "Such men did their basic training at Squires Gate before being assigned to the famous 303 Squadron, which was formed in the town. Mother always said the Poles were so brave and gallant and very popular with local girls. And she fell for one of them, my father, Tadeusz Lewandowski."

3

I was born in my grandfather's cottage, nestled in the frozen forest to the north of the town of Zakopane in the dying hours of January 31st 1920. It was an inopportune night to be born, as the icy roads were too treacherous for a midwife or doctor to brave. So, with Tata away on army manoeuvres and Mama having had no contact with her overbearing mother-in-law since an argument had forced her to leave the Lewandowski city mansion the previous autumn, it was left to my maternal grandfather, Mateusz Nowakowski, to bring me into this world.

With the snow falling faster and faster and the wind howling against the windowpanes like an angry wolf baying to be let in, it soon became clear to my grandfather that the birth of his daughter's second-born would not be quick and easy as her first son's had been.

The cottage having just two rooms, Dziadek made my mother comfortable in his bedroom, where, with no one to assist him, he managed to safely deliver me. My brother told how I was blue and silent and, remembering how he'd once watched our grandfather breathe life into a new-born kitten which had appeared lifeless, so Jacek put his small mouth to mine to blow air into my lungs while rubbing my chest. Then he held me next to his warm skin, enfolding me in his cardigan and jacket until my face turned pink and I started to cry. But while my brother brought me to life, the old man fought in vain to save his daughter as her lifeblood seeped away. Jacek said he brought me to lay me on the pillow next to our mother and that is how she died, smiling at her baby, regretting everything she would miss.

My father was a career soldier, an honourable and brave man. The middle of three sons, Konrad Lewandowski was born into an aristocratic Krakow family, whose palatial magnolia and white family villa sat proudly at the foot of Wawel Castle. Its grand gardens washed by the waters of the Vistula River twisting through the ancient royal city of spires and palaces like a scene from a fairytale, my father enjoyed a privileged childhood there, with everything he could ever wish for served to him by the household of servants. His grandfather and father before him having had distinguished army careers, it was little surprise when, aged twenty-one, he too enlisted for officer training. Handsome and fair-haired, he not only looked the part in his uniform but he always came top in his class, proving himself to be of excellent soldiering material.

My mother, Krysia Nowakowska, meanwhile, was raised by her loving parents, Mateusz and Zosia, on their farm seventy miles south of the city. But Krysia's idyllic childhood came to an abrupt end when she was just seventeen and her beloved mother died from pneumonia. Inconsolable, the young Krysia barely left the cottage during those winter months and, concerned for his daughter's wellbeing, Mateusz thought a move to the city would help her to get over her grief in the company of younger members of the family. So that summer as she turned eighteen, he arranged for her to stay with some distant cousins of his who lived in a grand apartment in the heart of Krakow overlooking the Planty Park. Initially, city life agreed with her. Befriended by the youngest daughter, Ola, whose beauty and kindness, my father always said, somewhat compensated for her lack of brains, Krysia accompanied her cousin on her many dinner dances and theatre visits during those sun-soaked months.

It was at one such soirée in the ostentatious ballroom of Wawel Castle in July 1914 that Konrad first laid eyes on the bewitching country girl. As Krysia danced in his arms, he saw beyond her porcelain-white skin, her luscious brown hair and entrancing blue eyes to the fierce intellect and passion which burned in my mother's soul. Without the full approval of his parents, who were dismayed at the prospect of their son having an unsophisticated bride, my father, used to getting whatever he wanted, was determined to have Krysia for his own. Just before Christmas that year when he managed to get a few days' leave, they were married in a candlelit ceremony at Bazylika Mariacka in central Krakow, the Madonna and Child immortalised in Veit Stoss's altar carving looking down upon them, blessing their union. Theirs was a fairy-tale romance with a joyful wedding; the only thing it lacked was its happy ending.

With my father returning to his regiment in the New Year, soon afterwards my mother discovered she was expecting a baby. That summer, as she became heavy with child, she loved to sit in the gardens which surrounded the Lewandowski mansion sketching the imposing turreted castle above or else depicting the greens and blues of the river in watercolours. When she gave birth to my brother Jacek in late September 1915, my father managed to get a few days' leave home and had Mama's room filled with vases of chrysanthemums in an array of autumn shades, simultaneously a 'thank you' for his beloved first-born son and a 'goodbye' as he was due to return to his regiment on the first of October.

In those early days, my mother received a letter from my father almost every week as he poured out his love for her on paper. But Jacek wasn't an easy baby and as winter turned to spring, my mother grew restless trapped within the confines of her gilded cage. She was also beleaguered by the constant interferences from her mother-in-law Matylda Cristiana, an imposing woman who, having borne three sons, felt well-qualified to offer advice on every aspect of her mothering skills. And so, my mother soon found herself longing to inhale the fresh mountain air and the wood resin of her father's workshop once more. As the spring blossom swirled around the trees along the riverbanks like pink and white spun sugar, against the wishes of Matylda Cristiana, she took my brother to introduce him to the place of her childhood, not returning until the following October.

And as the years of the Great War dragged on, so the pattern continued. My mother spent the snowy winters in Krakow, kicking her heels in the draughty Lewandowski mansion, counting the days until the thaw set in when snowdrops and tulips pushed up through the new grass, heralding that it was time to return to the mountains once more. There, she and her young son spent idyllic months, tending to the sheep, pigs and horses, bringing in the harvest, and watching her father transform pieces of wood into animals, birds and people, before the fall of leaves signalled their return to the city to spend quiet, contemplative days waiting for my father's return.

Then, five autumns after my parents first met, the armistice was signed and Konrad came home to Krysia. That Christmas, they enjoyed a belated honeymoon at the lovely lake of Morskie Oko getting to know each other again as they relaxed in the calm solitude of the Tatra Mountains. As the cherry trees bloomed the following May, my mother discovered she was pregnant once more and she basked in the happiness of family life. But when summer turned the city air sultry and the arguments with her mother-in-law escalated, she began to feel like a prisoner once again. So that autumn, when Konrad rejoined to his regiment, he agreed that my mother should stay with her father to see out her confinement in the fresh mountain air.

My father blamed himself for being away when I was born and my mother died. But even if he had been there, Dziadek and Jacek assured me there would have been nothing he could have done to save her. Devout Catholics, they said Mama and I had been in God's hands on that night and He had decided to take her to heaven and leave me on this earth. While my brother and Dziadek were able to transfer the love they felt for Mama onto the new-born, the one she had given her life for to safely enter this world, my father wasn't that type of man. With his privileged upbringing, from a young age nothing had ever been denied him. So the grief he felt at losing Krysia, his beloved and brave wife, extended far beyond the realms of anything he'd ever expected to experience or had been prepared for. He was never cruel to me and I know he loved me in his own way, but seeing me grow up as a constant reminder of losing his wife must have broken his heart piece by piece. So, Father willingly gave himself up to the army, its rules and routine a godsend as he sought to restore some semblance of order to his shattered life while leaving Dziadek and Jacek to raise me with the love he was incapable of giving.

And so it was that Jacek and I became as thick as thieves. Despite being almost five years older than I, my brother had a young, exuberant spirit, his thirst to experience new things seemingly unquenchable. Wearing Mama's silver crucifix around his neck like an amulet to protect him, he was a boy who never saw the danger in situations, only the endless possibilities. Whether it was because I was brought up under the watchful influence of Dziadek, or as the old man said, because I possessed an old soul, I don't know, but I was far more cautious than my brother.

Jacek once told me of Mama's soft, brown hair which he loved to smooth between his fingers while burrowing his face into the silky folds. With the voice of an angel, she'd sung soft lullabies to get him to sleep. He also recalled the time when she'd been pregnant with me and they'd both been filled with such hope, excitement and anticipation of my impending arrival. Her stomach a growing mound, she'd told Jacek to put his ear up to it and had giggled when I'd given my brother-to-be a sharp kick. And then one day, Jacek had a little brother and his mother had gone.

One of my earliest memories is of bringing in the harvest with Jacek. It was the autumn I was six, my brother eleven. I recall dutifully following him up and down the rows picking the wheat, my fingers chafing as I carried out his instructions, careful not to disappoint him. It felt as though more than those five years separated us as Jacek was a big, strapping boy with a broad back, straight hair the colour of the ripened wheat and eyes the brilliant blue of a summer sky. He already possessed strong arms and legs, bronzed after hours of work on the farm beneath the blaze of the summer sun. He was like a Greek god to me, a Zeus or Apollo where I was his polar opposite. Apart from sharing the same blond hair and blue eyes, my scrawny body was as yet untouched by early adolescence as his was and so in his presence I appeared even younger than my years. But I didn't begrudge or envy Jacek; it only made him more magnificent in my eyes. With every breath I took, I aspired to be like him, venerated as he was for his sporting prowess by the other boys in the village school we attended. As the sun set that late September evening, bathing the fields in its rosy light, Jacek showed me how to load the wheat onto my back before we carried it to Dziadek's barn. The following Sunday, after church, Jacek brought out Dziadek's pestle and mortar and demonstrated how to grind the ears of wheat to turn them to flour before we made it into bread. Eating the warm bread with cheese by the fireside that evening, it seemed to me there was nothing my brother couldn't do.

The bread-making foray gave Jacek an inspired idea; he decided to teach me how to forage, something he'd learned from Father and a necessity for living in the countryside where food and medicine weren't always readily available, especially when the winter snows blew in. Surmising Father would never be around to impart his knowledge to me, my brother assumed the paternal mantle himself. Our foraging ventures were of course determined by the seasons. In early spring, our hands protected with four pairs of thick winter gloves, worn over the top of each other, we picked stinging nettles, Jacek instructing me to select those with the pale green tops. We handled them with care, cooking them to remove the sting before making the most delicious soup I've tasted. By late March, it was time to forage the wild garlic which carpeted the back of our land, the white and green swathes falling down to the river. This time, my brother showed me how to select the young leaves, returning a few months later for the little white flowers to add a gentle flourish to summer salads the three of us enjoyed while sitting out on the porch on warm evenings.

In mid-May, the appearance of elderflower in Dziadek's garden marked the transition from spring to summer. With the white flowers Jacek and I made a delicately flavoured cordial, which refreshed us after hot days spent working on the farm, while Dziadek experimented with elderflower vodka, which he reluctantly allowed us to try one evening. Despite waking up the next morning still out on the porch, with sore heads and chattering teeth, I think it was worth it! The early summer saw Jacek and I leave the cottage before dawn to collect wild rosehips in the woods to make into syrup, which gave the most deliciously delicate flavour to cakes and breads. Indeed the countryside was at its most bountiful at this time of year, with tiny wild strawberries and bilberries, redcurrants and loganberries ready to pick and eat. After gorging on fruit, we'd stagger back to the farm, our bellies full, our fingers and mouths stained with signs of our weakness. However, we always made sure there was enough for Dziadek to preserve in his ice cellar as the coming winter months would undoubtedly be inhospitable and food scarce.

Come the autumn months, Jacek and I picked purple mountains of blackberries, which Dziadek made into sumptuous pies, served with soured cream to cut through the fruit's sweetness. We also accumulated stores of wild nuts, the squirrels often beating us to the hazelnuts, meaning we had to make do with the sweet chestnuts, which we made into stuffing to accompany Dziadek's legendary winter stews or else we simply scored and roasted them and ate them steaming hot, our fingers burning. Though I enjoyed collecting our provisions, Jacek impressed upon me that the most important thing was to be one hundred per cent sure that what I was picking was what I thought it was and he took great pains to explain which plants I should avoid like the plague. He pointed out that while wild chervil was a delicious herb, it also looked almost identical to hemlock. "That's a deadly plant which would send you out of this world much faster than you entered it!" he told me on more than one occasion. The same applied to mushrooms, which were always plentiful on the forest floor; some were delicious fried with butter, while others were highly poisonous, but Jacek taught me to spot the difference.

Sometimes, during those lazy summer holidays when Dziadek was occupied with an all-consuming carving of his own or else one requested by someone else with a tight deadline to meet, Jacek and I didn't return home for days on end. We lived like our primal ancestors, surviving off the land and our wits. We often played games, our favourite being human airplanes. We darted in and out of trees as fast as we could, our arms splayed out at one hundred and eighty-degree angles. "Try and keep up, Tad!" Jacek shouted, making the loud roar of the aircraft's engine.

"Slow down then!" I replied, my voice hoarse.

"No, you need to catch me up." He laughed, turning his face, a ripe, red strawberry.

"It's not fair! Why can't I be as tall and fast as you?" I struggled to keep up with him.

"You can, little bro." He winked, waiting for me. "One day, you might even outrun me!"

Every August, feeling like intrepid Amazon explorers weighed down by our heavy haversacks, we walked a mile or so into the forest on the lookout for a spot to build our den. Jacek always found us a patch of grassy land, avoiding slopes and dips, as neither of us fancied rolling down a hill or ending up soaked in a puddle in the middle of the night! With a perfect place to pitch, my brother then took out his compass to position the doorway to face south to ensure our dwelling had as much sunlight and warmth as possible.

Having located a tree with a low enough branch to act as a roof support, Jacek enlisted me to collect some of the old branches which had naturally fallen from the trees.

We finally set about constructing our den and assembled the frame around the tree before weaving several sticks through it to give it extra strength, with Jacek insisting we build it small as it would not only be warmer as the temperature dropped in the night but also stable and less likely to be damaged if the wind picked up. Although I begged to make a tipi, imagining us scoring our faces with berry juice to play American Native Indians who had featured in many stories I'd read, Jacek's practical nature meant that we opted for a lean-to which sloped from the entrance to the ground just as he made sure the back rather than the front faced the wind. We finished it off by covering the frame with the leaves, ferns and moss, stuffing them into every space we could find.

Once my brother had checked the structure was sound, he entrusted me with the task of lining the floor with the remaining soft ferns and leaves as an extra layer of insulation while he went down to the stream to collect stones and water in pails. Returning, Jacek built a small fire from the stones at the den's centre before making a fire-starter from tree sap using dry scraps of dead wood as kindling. In those early days, we'd stay in the den for a week or more, returning to the farm now and again to check on Dziadek and fetch provisions. But as the years passed, Jacek taught me to fish and hunt and shoot animals, to gut and cook them and to eat off the land, and so the two of us became separated from civilisation throughout those summer months, content in our own company.

Although I idolised Jacek and had wanted to be just like him for as long as I could remember, it was during our den-building escapades that I came to realise what a good team we made. I'd been wrong to wish to emulate my brother, something I could never have done, however hard I'd tried. Jacek wasn't the type to have deep and meaningful conversations but he always listened to my suggestions and so we worked well together as he helped turn my fanciful ideas for our den into reality.

Gazing up to the stars, we'd talk long into the night about a whole spectrum of subjects. Our profound love for our homeland, for its rivers and mountains, for its animals and people, for our father and grandfather bound us tightly together. But while I always wanted to share my hopes and dreams with my brother, too, Jacek was a practical boy who preferred to talk about new skills in building, hunting or preparing meals in the wild, garnered that day. Jacek's down-to-earth nature extended to dismantling the den when it was time to return home for the start of school as he insisted on restoring the forest floor to the way we'd found it. He said leaving the den standing would result in the structure becoming unstable and therefore a danger to any living creature who might stumble across it. So, at the end of each summer as the leaves started to brown and crisp, we returned the materials to nature to rot away to nothing.

Although Jacek was a self-sufficient boy with much more of a practical nature than I could ever hope for in two lifetimes, he was also a lot of fun with a daredevil streak which sometimes took him to within inches of serious danger. The summer when I was eight and Jacek twelve was sultry, as the countryside shimmered in intense heat for well over three months. Even Dziadek's weekly bath turned into a daily affair while Jacek and I slept on the forest floor at night, as the cottage was the temperature of an oven in which we were scared of being cooked alive.

The heat dictated that we spent many of those listless days fishing between the villages of Ochotnica and Krościenko. We'd lay patiently in wait for our catches in a quiet kink in the river well out of the way of the white-water rapids, fast deep troughs and rocky outcrops. Surrounded by the silent solitude of the scenic mountains and forests, the fish was plentiful there. We caught brown trout, averaging twelve to twenty-four inches, grayling and bullhead, which Jacek taught me to skin and debone before we cooked them on a campfire in the smoky open-air. That was also the summer we went rafting on the Dunajec River. Under Dziadek's watchful eye, Jacek and I spent weeks assembling our raft from the strongest off-cuts of wood the old man had discarded around his workshop, which we nailed together before securing the construction with lengths of rope. Then one morning in early August, we loaded the contraption onto his delivery cart and the old man drove us through the villages past traditional wooden buildings, which were often decorated with red and white flowers to celebrate weddings, popular throughout the summer months.

Eventually the landscape became more rugged, rising into the Pieniny Mountains, the setting for many of the folk tales Dziadek had told us and at lunchtime, we finally reached the Dunajec River, a blue-green snake slithering along in the heat. On the riverbank, the three of us shared a picnic of sausages and bread while watching the guests of the nearby Niedzica Castle enjoy their raft excursions. Dziadek explained to us it was a picturesque trip beginning in the village of Sromowce Wyżne-Katy before ending in the town of Szczawnica and following the seven loops of the gorge in-between. But as we watched them advance at a snail's pace, I hoped our raft ride on the river would be a little less sedate.

After lunch, Dziadek helped us lower our raft into the water, but with his food lying heavily on his stomach, he said he needed a short rest on the riverbank before he'd be in a fit state to supervise us. He soon fell asleep, his newspaper perched on his protruding stomach while water lapped his ankles. Very soon and very predictably, my brother's patience ran out and after an unsuccessful attempt to awaken our grandfather, Jacek suggested that we just try sitting on the raft, 'pretending' to sail it. At first we barely moved, but propelled by a slight breeze and the strengthening currents in the Dunajec River, we eventually began to pick up speed.

It all happened so quickly. A strong current catching the helm, the brute force of the water wrestled me under, its iciness consuming my body. I thrashed my hands in a vain attempt to find the raft or anything solid to catch hold of so I could pull myself back. But I could not. The fast-flowing river would not allow me as the weight of the water pressed me downwards, pouring into my ears, eyes and mouth. Although I could feel the pebbles beneath my feet on the riverbed, as I tried to upright myself and walk, the currents dragged me along, claiming every inch of me. It was then I realised I was going to die.

Fear paralysed me, as there didn't seem to be any air left to breathe. All I knew was I had to get out, but I couldn't move as I was rendered immobile by the crushing power of the water. As I felt myself losing consciousness, I reached out my hand, willing my brother to take it…

It was at that moment I felt Jacek's hand grab mine. I tried kicking my legs and gasped as we ascended through the blackness, our heads breaking through the water's surface. "I've got you, Tad! I've got you," Jacek shouted, pulling me to the safety of the riverbank. Then, holding me closely to him, he rubbed my icy body back to warmth just as he'd said he'd done the night I was born. And I realised that, for the second time, Jacek had brought me back from the edge of death. "You saved my life, Jacek," I spluttered.

"Ah, you'd do the same for me, little bro." He laughed as we collapsed on the grassy bank, both of us spent. Although I smiled in relief as I laid there, a crowd of concerned faces hovering over me, I vowed silently that I would do just that, one day, in whatever way I could. Of course we both had to face the wrath of our grandfather for our exploits that afternoon. Ordering us to dismantle and burn the raft, as well as grounding the two of us for a week to do jobs around the house, seemed an appropriate punishment for our behaviour.

Another important lesson Jacek taught me was to stand up for myself. Being scrawny and underdeveloped compared to other boys my age made me into a prime target for the school bullies. One February evening just after my eleventh birthday, I encountered a brutish boy called Antoni and his gang as I walked home. Antoni was tall and thickset for his age and never normally bothered me in school, I suppose because he knew Jacek was my brother and would beat him to a pulp if he ever laid a finger on me. But on that slippery path hidden by the surrounding forest, he and the others pushed me, ripped my clothes and called me the most awful names before leaving me lying there bloody-nosed. Struggling to get up, I heard hurried footsteps behind me and my stomach lurched with fear that the boys had decided to come back to finish the job. But instead, Jacek hauled me to my feet.

"Are you okay, little bro?" His voice was concerned, his cheeks the colour of cherries. "I saw they gave you a bit of a mauling."

"You were watching?" I said as he mopped blood flowing from a gash above my eye with his handkerchief. "Why didn't you help me?"

"Because it would have made it worse for you, Tad. You need to learn to defend yourself against bullies like that," he smiled, brushing dirty snow from my shoulder, "and I will show you how."

So, over the coming weeks, Jacek taught me how to box in Dziadek's workshop as the snowstorms precluded us from venturing outside. Suffice to say, the next time Antoni and his gang accosted me in the forest, it was him and not I who returned home nursing a bloodied nose. After that I continued to box with Jacek, which built up the muscles and strength in my arms, and as word got around school of my prowess, neither Toni nor anyone else challenged me to a fight again. My new-found fame also gained me two friends, Antusz Kozol and Marek Simonowicz. Always at the bottom of the class in tests whereas I came out on top, they were no-nonsense, physically strong boys. With the same boot-black hair and wiry bodies, they were often taken for brothers as we went on escapades together. Although I was the third person in the friendship, they always treated me with kindness, showing respect for my academic achievements and, as we progressed through senior school together, the three of us forged a deep bond.

Two things I loved about the harsh winters of my childhood were the snow and ice. I sat for hours in Dziadek's workshop, hypnotised as snowflakes flurried past the window, covering the surrounding woods and fields in a white blanket purifying everything beneath. Jacek and I would get kitted out in woolly jumpers, thick socks, coats, boots, gloves and hats, and leap through the powdery snow, laughing with delight. Although my balance wasn't the best, my brother also managed to teach me to ski on wooden skis fashioned by Dziadek. My skill not being on a par with Jacek's, I never managed to fly down mountains as he did. But we enjoyed cross-country skiing together, slaloming through woods, the swish of our poles in the snow the only sound to break the silence.

Another experience I looked forward to was the Krakow Christmas market. Every December, the day after school broke up for the Christmas holidays, Dziadek loaded his cart with the wooden decorations he'd spent the autumn months carving. He then drove us to Krakow where we stayed with a distant cousin, Ola, and her family in their spacious apartment for three weeks. Beneath the candlelight of the huge Christmas tree which dwarfed the magnificent cloth hall in the city's main square, we set up our stall with Jacek and I arranging Dziadek's painstakingly carved angels, nativity scenes, stars, holly wreaths, robins, snowflakes and crucifixes as artistically as two boys could! There we spent day after day selling our wares, soaking in the festive atmosphere and wishing all our customers "Merry Christmas" as they went on their way.

I made sure I stuck close to Dziadek, interested to hear him explain the carving techniques he'd used to his fascinated customers, while Jacek always seemed to be off elsewhere in the market, scouting our competition or else chatting to other stallholders. From his trips, my brother brought us back an array of edible treats, from chocolate-covered fruits to roasted chestnuts, his charm ensuring that he'd acquired them at a reasonable discount. In the evenings, we returned to the warmth of Ola's apartment and hospitality, and, after a home cooked meal, our cousin told Jacek and I stories of our mother. It was always a magical time of year for Dziadek, Jacek and I, which I never wanted to end.

Then, when Jacek was sixteen and I eleven, things changed. My brother fell in love with a girl called Alicja, who lived with her father, Pan Kowalski, on the neighbouring farm. With a sunny disposition, Alicja was a country girl through and through with a love of walking and outdoor pursuits who suited Jacek's down-to-earth nature. On her seventeenth birthday, my brother gave her Mama's ring, which no one else knew of apart from me, Alicja wearing it on a chain around her neck hidden beneath her clothes. A delightful raven-haired girl with porcelain-white skin, ruby-red lips and an hourglass figure, I have to admit to having a crush on her as I approached adolescence, even though I knew she merely saw me as Jacek's slightly introverted, slightly annoying younger brother.

The first time I met Alicja to talk to was one bitterly cold January morning when we were to go ice-skating. In the summer the surrounding forest gave the shallow lake a pretty aspect, making it a popular haunt for families and couples to enjoy a picnic on its banks before cooling off by taking a paddle in its waters. But I'd always preferred it in the winter when Jacek and I claimed it for our own, so it felt odd for me that day to share our special place with a girl. My brother's sweetheart looked like a perfect Russian doll in her fur-trimmed green cape and red hat as Jacek drove Dziadek's cart down to the shore. Snuggled up in rugs, we chatted and sang folk songs, our breath hanging on the cold air. When we arrived, however, Alicja hung back with Jacek, making it clear she'd rather not have me as a chaperone, even though Pan Kowalski had made it clear that was a stipulation if she was to go at all. Weighed down by my skates, which hung by their laces over my shoulder, I rushed on ahead, nevertheless, eager to see whether the freeze was deep enough to bear our weights while Jacek and Alicja trailed behind me, whispering and giggling together.

Wending my way through the trees, their bare branches intertwining like black lace overhead, I was stopped in my tracks by the scene before me. Like something from a half-remembered fairytale Dziadek had once told me, the clustered trees gave the lake a magical quality as though an enchantress had cast her spell over it, seemingly cutting it off from the outside world. I gazed at the mirror-like surface of the ice as it reflected the changing hues of the sky, moving from white to the palest of blues as clouds scudded overhead. Alicja and Jacek eventually caught up and, to warm ourselves up, we bought hot chocolates, served by an enterprising young couple who'd set up a small, woodburning stove under the trees.

"Come on, race you to put your skates on," Jacek challenged, and I skidded through the powdery snow to the lakeside where I secured the skates over my boots, my knuckles raw with the cold. Alicja did the same before carefully adjusting her crimson velvet beret which had been a Christmas present from Jacek. Then my brother took our hands and heaved us both to our feet before pulling us onto the ice. Dziadek had specified to keep to the edge as the ice would likely be thicker there, but I had no chance to heed his warning as Jacek propelled Alicja and me to the middle of the frozen lake. Wincing that every sudden movement might result in a crack, I found myself abandoned at the centre while Jacek took Alicja in his arms and they wheeled away from me, like graceful ballroom dancers with perfect poise. For the next few minutes I stood rooted to the spot, all my momentum lost as I feared putting one foot in front of the other, lest the ice would crack, swallowing me whole.

"Jacek," Alicja's shrill cry pierced my thoughts, "my hat."

Looking up I saw that her head was now free of the red beret she had so prized but also her black curls, which had bounced on her shoulders on our way to the lake, were gone. As my brother wheeled away to retrieve it from the ice, I was just in time to catch her as she burst into fits of hysterical laughter.

"I sewed the curls into my hat." She laughed. "I thought it would impress Jacek."

At which point I laughed too and we were still giggling when my brother returned, out of breath and his cheeks flushed from skating so quickly. "Your hat and your hair, Madam." He handed them to her with a flourish. As Jacek led us around the lake at a more sedate pace, I saw from his expression that Alicja had no need to make an effort to catch my brother's attention. He was already smitten by her.

On occasions, however, the fun took a serious turn as, while it was in my nature to be cautious, Jacek had a reckless streak and often took unnecessary risks, especially when there was a girl to impress. One blisteringly hot summer's day a few months into his courtship with Alicja, he suggested we venture down to the river at the back of Dziadek's property to cool down. Following my experience with the raft, I didn't even like getting water in my eyes when I bathed but, agreeing it would bring effective relief from the stuffy humidity, I resolved to keep to the shallows and out of harm's way.

To be fair to my brother, he realised I didn't possess his bravery so he was happy for me to linger on the riverbank with Alicja, where we dipped our toes in the water while he stripped off to the waist to reveal his tanned torso before diving in. Eventually emerging from the murky waters, he broke into a fast crawl, his muscled arms pushing back the water as though it was weightless when I knew just how heavy it truly was. Our attention was focused on Jacek as he dived down, so deep the rippling waters became still and silent. After a few moments when he failed to re-emerge, consternation creased Alicja's young face, though I had no such worries for my brother's wellbeing. For, after my accident at the Dunajec River, Jacek had spent many hours teaching me how to hold my breath until I'd surpassed the two-minute mark, trailing in his wake by some forty-two seconds. As Alicja dashed down to the riverbank, shouting my brother's name, he emerged from the water, reeds and algae tangling in his hair, a makeshift crown for this king of the underwater world. Scampering up the riverbank, he caught her in his strong arms.

"You frightened me." Alicja laughed, droplets of water from Jacek sparkling on her bare arms like temporary tattoos. Normally having such a laid-back nature, I noticed that her body was taut with tension as my brother held her.

"I'm invincible." He smiled before covering her face with wet kisses, Alicja responding by drawing her body into his as I watched from a distance.

Just a fortnight later, though, my brother wasn't so lucky. We'd gone down to the river once more, but the skies glowered grey and, as Jacek was recovering from a cold, he didn't want to risk getting further chilled by taking a swim. So, instead he attached a rope from an old oak tree whose strong branches overlapped the river's edge, from which he intended to swing like Tarzan of the Jungle. His first few attempts went to plan as Alicja and I watched him swoop across like an enormous eagle, beating his chest and hollering as he did so.

I didn't notice whether it was Jacek's fault or just an unfortunate accident. One minute, his brown body was flying through the air, outstretched and as graceful as the trapeze artists I'd seen at the circus, the next he lay in a crumpled heap on the riverbank, his hands clasped to his mouth, blood pouring through the cracks in-between his fingers. Propping him up between us, Alicja and I brought Jacek back to Dziadek, and the three of us spent the next few hours cleaning him up and easing his pain. Although Jacek hadn't broken any bones, his pride and his good looks were injured that day, as he'd knocked out two of his teeth on impact. Patched up and sedated later that evening, I watched him from the threshold of the bedroom as he took hold of Alicja's hand, whispering, "It is a good job I have a childhood sweetheart. No girl would look at me twice now."

That night I woke startled from a dream in which Jacek had been falling and, trying to save him, I'd grabbed his arm. But, unable to sustain his substantial weight, pain had ripped through my fingers until they'd released him, letting him plunge into the darkness. Beads of sweat clustering at my throat like a choker, I sat bolt upright in bed until my breathing eventually calmed. I had learned a difficult lesson that day: that my heroic brother wasn't immortal or untouchable as he'd led me to believe. Jacek was just as vulnerable as the rest of us.

Then, in 1934, there came a day I had been dreading – Jacek leaving school – for I knew that it would mean he would go to university in Krakow, leaving me behind. As we walked home together that rainy July afternoon, I told my brother I would visit him in the city as often as Dziadek allowed me.

"But I'm not going to the Jagiellonian this autumn." He smiled. "I've decided to postpone it for a year or so. As you know, Tad, Pan Kowalski has been laid up since he fell off his cart in November as his leg has failed to heal properly and so I've promised Alicja that I will help run the farm. It will be Alicja's inheritance after all and her old man had been running it into the ground even before his accident. I want to build it up, I need to be able to provide for any children we might have one day and, of course, you're still young. Who would look after my little bro if I went to live in the city now?"

"Oh, I'm so pleased you're staying! It also means you will only be a couple of years ahead of me at university when you finally go, Jacek. We will be students together. We could rent a city apartment…" I smiled, but my brother offered no further comment. We were always as close as brothers could be, but the dark clouds of war would soon cast a shadow over us and millions of people across Europe and beyond the sea.

4

Blackpool, August 2020

Anna's elegant terraced house was situated in a leafy suburb far from the bustle of the amusement arcades and kiss-me-quick hats of the promenade. Built in the early 1920s with fourteen rooms spread over three floors, it had been in the family for three generations, with Anna's grandmother running it as a guesthouse in the 1930s before, along with many other Blackpool hotels, it had been requisitioned to accommodate the RAF personnel who'd flooded into town during the war years. Anna remembered with fondness sitting on her grandma's ample knee listening to her stories of the polite young men – and some of the more rowdy ones – who, after a day's intensive training, had enjoyed her cooking as it had reminded them of home. Despite only staying a matter of weeks before they'd been moved to a southern airbase in readiness to join the war, they had evidently made a lasting impression on the old woman.

Then, in the resort's heyday of the 1950s, the house had reverted back to being an upmarket B&B and Anna could remember the long summers when they'd been full to the rafters, meaning she'd had to give up her bedroom to sleep in the 'chalet' in the back garden. With the door wide open to let in the cool night air, fragrant with the scent of honeysuckle, she'd fallen asleep cuddling her teddy bear, mesmerised by the silver stars in the night sky as she'd pictured her father in his plane, wondering whether he still flew it in heaven beyond. Then on Anna's marriage, her mother had passed on the reins to her and she had brought up Sarah there while running the B&B business until her husband George's death. His substantial life insurance policy meant she could now live out a comfortable retirement without bothering with the increasingly troublesome guests attracted by the emerging stag and hen parties in the town.

Even though the house was much too big for her nowadays and she had to employ a cleaning lady once a week to help keep it up to her usual standards, Anna couldn't bear to be parted from it. She always swiftly rebuffed Sarah's suggestions of moving into somewhere smaller, saying that the house held all her memories of her family life as well as being close to the peacefulness of Stanley Park with its Art Deco cafe, Italian formal gardens and boating lake. Having spent many happy times in the park with her daughter and then granddaughter over the years, which always started with feeding the swans and ducks, and ended with a little treat in the cafe, Anna still regularly liked to walk up there to reminisce about old times.

Bella had a thousand and one questions burning in her mind on arriving at her grandma's house later that afternoon. As she'd grown up with just her mother and grandparents and no extended family or knowledge of her paternal side, she had never found the need to enquire about her family history. So being hit with a thunderbolt that she had Polish ancestry had stirred up a melee of emotions within her and a curiosity to discover more about Tad and his roots.

Bella paused for a moment in the front garden before following her mum and grandma up the path to step into the shadow of the porch. As her grandma unlocked the door, Bella's attention was attracted, as always, to the magnificent stained-glass. The door itself depicted a pretty pastoral scene with a turreted castle in wine-red and gold glass surrounded by a forest in a spectrum of dark greens, the sky above in shades of azure. But she was most drawn to the two side panels which portrayed huge bunches of purple grapes while stretching across the top was a long panel of geometric Art Deco design in vibrant yellows and oranges. Almost too majestic for the modest B&B forming as it did the end wall of the hall, she'd spent many hours of her childhood sitting on the staircase attempting to capture the essence of the door's design on paper. However, she'd always been frustrated that she had never been able to translate the way the sun hit the glass, refracting a rainbow of colours across the pale wallpaper. As the door swung back, she followed her grandma and mum down the long hallway, resolving to have another attempt with her watercolours very soon.

"Sarah, would you mind putting on tea? There's a curry and naan bread I made earlier that need heating up," Anna asked as they entered the back sitting room. "I'm going to take Bella upstairs to look through all the stuff that has accumulated over the years," she added, slinging her bag onto a leather-backed chair, which looked out of place in the pretty room but which Anna couldn't quite bring herself to throw out as it been George's favourite.

"Sure, Mum, I will, but can you wait for me?" Sarah switched on the hob and oven. "I'm as dumbfounded as Bella about this revelation about your father!"

Although Bella hadn't pressed Anna into revealing anything more about Tadeusz on their walk home from the air show, she knew that her astute grandma had gleaned from her silence that she was, in fact, very interested. The back bedroom on the third floor had a closed-in smell as they entered and Bella immediately opened the window to let out some of the stale air. Her grandma sat down with her back to the dressing table, sorting through a shoebox of photos balanced upon her knee while Bella sprawled on the double bed. Cardboard boxes were strewn on the white candlewick bedspread while a further three had been laid on the faded carpet.

"I forgot you could see the tower from here," Bella remarked, remembering, when she'd been little, her mum's hands nipping her armpits as she'd held her up to peek over the rooftops to see the illuminated top in all its glory. Bella had always insisted on being suspended in mid-air to watch the stick at the top of the tower light up again and again. "I bet it is well over five years since I last came up here."

"Probably is. Right, I think we'll make a start looking through these while we wait for your mum." Anna pressed a sheaf of photos into Bella's hand. Scrutinising the pictures, there were some Bella had seen before, one of her great-grandma Eirlys dated 1937 in which she was about the same age as Bella was now. But that was the only similarity she could make out as she studied the black-and-white photo. Whereas Bella had a sleek, white-blonde bob, Eirlys's hair was a mass of dark unruly curls resting in line with her shoulder. Her eyes were clearly dark to Bella's bright blue ones and, while Bella was tall and slightly awkward, she could see her great-grandma was petite, her pretty summer dress enhancing her classic curves.

"I wish I looked more like her. She was stunning," Bella sighed, her eyes drinking in every detail of the photo. "And what's that building behind her? It looks like Art Deco with its streamlined elegance."

"Yes, the Derby Baths were built in the twenties. I think the RAF might have even used them during the war. They were huge, the main pool being Olympic standard, but then they were pulled down in the name of progress," Anna sighed, moving her attention to Eirlys's young face. "My mother was indeed beautiful and always proud of her appearance. Even in old age she would never be seen without her smart outfits, neat hair and, of course, bright lipstick!"

"I've looked at this photo of her many times." Sarah entered the room, having twisted her hair up in a butterfly clip. "And I've definitely got Grandma Eirlys to thank for my dark, untameable hair!"

"She was considered a striking woman," Anna countered, cupping her daughter's heart-shaped jaw in her fingers as

Sarah sat on the bed in front of her, "and so are you, if you'd only believe it."

Bella was looking intently at Eirlys's face in the photo. "She looks so vivacious and full of life, as if she is on the verge of something wonderful."

"That's what it must have seemed like then, but things worked out differently for her," Anna sighed. "Never marrying the man she loved affected her deeply."

"Just hang on a minute, Mum. You led me to believe my grandma was a war widow like her mother before her," Sarah said.

"In a sense she was, Sarah. Mum only told me the truth about Tad just before she died. As you were heavily pregnant and unmarried, she was worried that you had enough to cope with, so she asked me not to tell you that she too had raised a child out of wedlock, something which still carried its own stigma for a woman of her age. She was so upset I promised I wouldn't say anything to you or your dad, but now circumstances have changed. Your dad's dead and…" Anna paused as tears collected in her daughter's eyes. "Oh, I've wanted to tell you about my father, about our Polish heritage for such a long time, but I could never seem to find the right moment to do it."

Anna clasped Sarah's and Bella's hands. "Of course, in wartime, whirlwind marriages, even those resulting in a child, were commonplace. So after my father died, all Mum had to do was wear a wedding ring and assume a married title, taking her mother's maiden name. As we had no close family it was an easy thing for her to do and because of the stigma of illegitimate births it was necessary to preserve Mother's reputation and my legitimacy."

"Fortunately things had moved on by the time I had Bella," Sarah reflected, brushing away a tear which had escaped down her cheek.

"Yes, luckily so," Anna sighed. "Meeting Tad, my father, was the single most exhilarating experience of Mum's life. She had a sheltered upbringing, which in no way prepared her for her relationship with my father and its aftermath. Growing up in mainly female company with her mum and her schoolgirl friends made her incredibly naive. Initially, she was reticent to get close to Tad because she knew from her mother what it was like to lose your beloved during a war, but her feelings for my father were too strong to be denied. From what she told me, Tad and hers was a typical wartime romance; sweet and innocent at first. She said my father made her feel loved and protected in a way that she'd never been before or ever felt again, for there was never another man in her life after he died. During their brief time together, she provided emotional support for Tad too, who was naturally distraught for his family living under Nazi occupation in his defeated homeland." Anna paused, flipping through the photos.

"Oh my God, I haven't considered that! Thinking of some of the terrible things that happened in Europe, especially Poland, under Nazi rule, I expect Tad must have been out of his mind with worry," Sarah said as Anna nodded grimly.

"Great-Grandma Eirlys must have been terrified too that the love of her life was in constant danger flying in the Polish Air Force," Bella added. "I can't imagine how she coped with it."

"With great difficulty, Bella, I think. After the news that Tad's plane had crashed came through, Mother said her days were a living nightmare as she reluctantly came to an acceptance that she'd never see my father again. She told me once of the unimaginable terror and pain she felt as she awaited confirmation of his death. Of course, it had always been her greatest fear that the war would claim Tad after her father, Edward, had been killed at the beginning of November 1918 on the final assault of Mons, four months before her birth. She said that my grandmother, Louisa, had never got over his death, sleeping with my grandfather's photo beneath her pillow for the rest of her life." Anna paused, reliving the painful memory. "Anyway, back to my father. In late April 1945, a brother officer, whom my mother had met several times the previous summer, made the trip from RAF Northolt to Blackpool to tell her that Tad had been reported missing, believed killed over the North Sea. Picturing the crash, Mother told me it played over and over in her mind like a cinema reel left on by a forgetful projectionist. Her nights were punctuated by dark dreams of Tad's final moments plummeting into the icy waters of the North Sea as she thought of how she would manage without him. A month later, she received the devastating confirmation from Tad's colleague that the wreckage of his plane had been located off the Dutch coast. Having only just had her suspicions confirmed that she was pregnant, it was a further heartache that she would never get the chance to tell Tad he was going to be a father, that he never knew about me."

"That must have been terrible," concluded Bella, looking down at her great-grandmother's smiling carefree face cradled in her hand, "for such a young woman to come to terms with."

"Yes, I think she bore the pain by constantly looking for ways to escape. She went for long, solitary walks on the beach right up to her later years when arthritis made movement difficult." Anna paused.

"What a tragedy," said Bella, "to think nowadays, we just throw so much away. I've known girls to dump their boyfriends by text or on Facebook. It just feels like such a waste for two young people who were so in love for it all to end so abruptly and finally."

"At least she had those months with Tad when her future was awash with dreams and possibilities," Anna said philosophically. "My father was such a special soul, like no one she'd ever met, and Mum always said she felt blessed by God that she'd had him in her life, albeit for such a short interlude. She once told me that every time she looked at my face she saw his, which she found to be a consolation."

"She would have taken some comfort in her memories of him and, of course, you." Bella's eyes lingered on Eirlys's face in the photo.

"Yes, she devoted the rest of her life to being a good mother." Anna smiled. "She wanted to fill the void in her heart vacated by my father and, of course, she was frightened of letting him down. But she needn't have worried. She was the best parent I could have hoped for."

"She sounds so sad." Bella couldn't take her eyes from the black-and-white image of Eirlys.

"She was, I suppose. But she threw herself into running a successful guesthouse to support us both and, even when she hit eighty, she still insisted on helping out with the cooking. But I sensed there was always something missing from her life, always a closed part of her, which even I could never reach. Losing Dad before I was born affected everything she did, who she was," Anna said, sorting through photos before pausing, a wistful look crossing her face. "Ah! Here he is."

Bella's eyes widened as her grandma placed her great-grandfather's black-and-white photo into the palm of her hand. Although his expression was grave, she saw Tad was undoubtedly an extremely attractive man, with strong cheekbones and brooding eyes which seemed to look right into the heart of her. Beneath his air force cap, his hair was sleeked back off his forehead, but even with Brylcreem, it was evidently fair like her own. He proudly wore a dark tie, white shirt and uniform with shiny buttons marking the epaulets and pockets, which Bella guessed to be air force blue. Pinned to the left of his collar was a badge which looked like a bird.

"I've seen this photo many times, but surely this is an RAF uniform?" Sarah quizzed. "Although, of course, I wasn't looking for anything else."

"It has one important difference: that's the Polish eagle on his cap badge and his collar." Anna pointed to the shoulder. "Look, it says PAF which stands for Polish Air Force. It distinguished the Polish squadrons from the others in the RAF."

"No wonder Grandma Eirlys didn't want to date other men! He is gorgeous." Bella studied this face she'd never seen before but which already felt familiar.

"Along with the little wooden angel which she had on her bedside table, Mother kept this photo close for the rest of her life." Her grandma peered over her granddaughter's shoulder, drinking in her father's face as though for the first time.

"I can see you, Grandma, and me in his features and pale hair," Bella said, a lifetime of not knowing which branch of her family she'd inherited her high cheekbones and pale, almost translucent skin colouring from, solved in an instant. She mused what else she had in common with this man she'd not known existed before today but who was slowly coming to life before her very eyes.

"Yes," Anna smiled, "before my skin crinkled and my hair turned grey."

"You're still beautiful, Grandma," Bella said, tracing her fingertips over Tad's fine Slavic features in the dog-eared photograph. Her Polish great-grandfather.

"Recently I've started to dream about my father; it's always the same one. That Mother and I are walking on the beach and suddenly he appears a little way ahead, racing towards us, arms outstretched. But on each occasion he never manages to reach us, and when I look up and down the beach he isn't there, only the trail of his footprints left behind in the sand. Ah, this is something I once asked a Polish man to write for me." Anna unfolded a yellowing piece of paper. "I used to know it by heart. *Jestem twoją córką i przez całe życie czekałem, aż wrócisz do mnie.*"

"What do the words mean, Grandma?" Bella asked, the soft syllables of the Polish language like a melody in her ears as her grandma whispered them.

"I'm your daughter and I've been waiting my whole life for you to come back to me." Anna carefully refolded the paper along the deep creases as a tear traced its way down her cheek. "But I never got to say them to him."

*

"This is delicious," remarked Bella as they sat at the table in the corner of her grandma's sitting room later that evening, the Tiffany lamp throwing arcs of blues and reds across the lacy cloth. "It has a distinctly Middle Eastern flavour."

"Yes, I only learned how to make it on my cookery course last week and, if I do say so myself, it's come out surprisingly well. I like the sweet and savoury combination." Anna mopped up the remnants of fruity lamb curry with a homemade naan. Since George's death, she'd attended a number of evening classes at the local college, enhancing her skills in needlework, cooking and cake decorating while meeting an array of interesting people along the way.

"Quite healthy, too, Mum. I like it." Sarah smiled. "It's a shame we never knew your dad was Polish, that we have Polish ancestry."

"I know, as I said, Mum only told me the truth about him just before she died and, as you were nearing your due date without Bradley's support, she didn't want to inflict any further upset upon you. Up to that point, she'd just said Father had been in the RAF and she'd cried whenever I'd asked about him, so I'd long since stopped prying." Anna took a gulp of chilled Bordeaux. "In school, I remember there were girls who were half-Polish whose dads had survived the war and stayed in Blackpool. Their surnames were often shortened to 'Kay' because the teachers couldn't pronounce the Polish, but my mother couldn't face being judged for not having been married, I don't think, so she hid Father's identity from everyone, including me. Luckily, we had a frank conversation at the end and she told me everything she could even, though due to her failing health, her mind wandered a bit…"

"I know from my GCSE History lessons that Britain declared war on Nazi Germany because they'd invaded Poland on September 1st 1939, but that is as far as I can remember," said Bella, ripping her naan rather inelegantly with her perfect white teeth.

"I looked into what happened in Poland in detail in the weeks and months after Mother died," said her grandmother, taking another fortifying sip of wine. "The Nazis actually began their land-grab in September 1938 when the leaders of Germany, Britain, France and Italy signed an agreement allowing German troops to claim the Sudetenland in Czechoslovakia. But a year later when Hitler's army invaded Poland, due to a protection pact, her allies could not stand by and so they declared war on Nazi Germany."

"I didn't know the UK had a pact to protect Poland?" Bella said.

"From what I recall from my A-level History, the allies gave Poland little support and it became known as the 'phoney war'. Within a fortnight, the Polish Army was defeated and the country under Nazi occupation, including the cities of Warsaw and Krakow," Sarah countered. "In the meantime, the Soviets invaded Poland to the east and many experienced Polish soldiers went underground, taking it upon themselves to fight a covert war against the Germans. It must have been a time of fear and uncertainty for the young Polish men who were called up and ordered to report to the Third Reich, either for military service or forced labour."

"Is it possible Tad was one of those men called up?" Bella pondered aloud.

"Yes, it's possible, but I can't say for certain. However, I remember my mother telling me that, following his brother's advice, Tad decided his only option was to escape," Anna added. "So his situation must have been very grave."

"Imagine having to leave your own country because it is more dangerous to stay?" Sarah mused and they fell silent for a few moments, considering. "It's unthinkable."

"I know his brother, Jacek, and their father, Konrad, were both in the Polish military when the war broke out," said Anna, "but my father was a student at the university in Krakow."

"A student? God, he really was just my age!" Bella savoured her final mouthful of curry. "So how did all these young Polish men manage to end up in Blackpool?"

"After the fall of Poland, thousands of men who had been in the air force and army chose to escape rather than fall into the hands of the Nazis," her grandmother explained. "Blackpool was the debriefing centre for such men, where they were assessed and enjoyed some rest and recuperation before beginning their training. It was here that the famous 303 Squadron was formed. After what they'd been through, the days the pilots spent here in the town were a relief and a respite. In fact, they nicknamed the UK the 'Island of the Last Hope'."

"Possibly a touch of black humour there," chipped in Sarah, sipping the chilled wine.

"Quite. Mother said the Poles had to prove themselves to be skilled pilots in order to be accepted by the British. But with most having already fought in the Battles of Poland and France, they were actually among the most experienced in combat," Anna continued. "In fact, the 303 Fighter Squadron made one hundred and twenty-six kills in the Battle of Britain, the greatest number of any of the Allied Hurricane squadrons engaged in combat in the summer of 1940. The head of RAF Fighter Command, Air Chief Marshal Sir Hugh Dowding, said that had it not been for the unsurpassed gallantry of the Polish squadrons, the outcome of that vital battle would have probably been very different."

"Wow, and actually that might have changed the course of the war." Bella crinkled her nose.

"Yes," Anna nodded, "I think that because the young Polish men had already lost so much and had witnessed such dreadful events in their homeland, they must have hated the Nazis with a passion. They simply had nothing left to lose."

"Yes, I can see that. A lethal combination." Bella fell silent, considering. "You never learn any of this at school, Gran."

"No, it's because they have largely been written out of history," Anna continued. "In fact, in May 1945, the Polish flyers weren't even permitted to take part in any of the VE parades around Britain."

"That's disgusting. To think that those pilots had risked life and limb fighting for the allies when they didn't know what was happening in their country or how their families and friends were faring under Nazi rule, only to be swept aside once the victory was won," Sarah sighed. "I can't begin to imagine how they managed to reconcile that."

"I know, it's dreadful," Anna added. "From what Mother told me, my father missed his family awfully, especially his grandfather and his brother, Jacek."

"The fact that his father and brother were in the military probably motivated Tad's decision to come here and become a flyer?" Bella said thoughtfully.

"Yes, I got the feeling he always looked upon his older brother as a hero. Tad showed Mother a photo of Jacek once and she said he was a tall, good-looking boy who bore a strong resemblance to his brother."

"But he wasn't with Great-Grandfather in Blackpool?" said Bella, trying to fit the indistinct pieces together to create a cohesive picture.

"He definitely never came to England, no. But Mother said Tad worshipped the ground his brother walked on and, if I remember rightly, she once mentioned that Jacek had a wife and child in Poland." Anna paused before continuing, "but whilst my father missed his brother, he also made the most of his time here. I know that Tad was captivated by Blackpool. So very different from where he came from, he hardly believed such a place could exist in wartime."

"You know, Bella, Blackpool has been a popular holiday resort since Victorian times," Sarah added, noticing her daughter's eyebrows arch in surprise. "You can see its grandeur reflected in the architecture of the Winter Gardens, the Grand Theatre and, of course, the Tower Ballroom has chandeliers fashioned from the finest Austrian crystal. It was the height of luxury, which was accessible to the working class for the first time ever."

"Yes, I can see how it would seem so. To dance in the Tower Ballroom must have been the treat of a lifetime for people who worked in factories or else down mines," said Bella. "We'll all have to go sometime. I've heard the afternoon tea dances are legendary."

"I'll have to treat you both! Anyway, to continue… Mum told me the summer of 1939 was a poor holiday season in Blackpool as the winds of war blew over to Britain," Anna continued. "Everyone in the town was issued with a gas mask, while cardboard coffins were stockpiled and thousands of air raid shelters sprung up, the largest slap bang in the middle of the prom ready to house eighty-five thousand people in the event of bombing raids on the Lancashire coast. Men enlisted and, on completing their National Service, they were sent to Europe to try to hold back Hitler's army or else to defend the outpost of the British Empire in the Far East. Everyone prepared for the worst."

"It's hard to think of war right here on the doorstep," Bella said, listening intently.

"Yes it is, sweetheart, but everyone had to adapt quickly. Women were put into jobs like driving the town's trams as more and more men left," Anna sighed, pulling a photo from the pocket of her cardigan. It was of a young Eirlys in overalls, her dark hair tied back with a scarf. "Mother got a job working on the production of Wellington Bombers at the Vickers Armstrong Factory at Squires Gate, which was one of the largest aircraft manufacturers in the country during the war."

"Wow, I can't imagine her assembling plane parts," Bella said, staring at the delicate-looking woman in the photo. "It must have been completely alien for her."

"At the start, I think that was the case. But she soon got used to it as she, along with hundreds of other young Blackpool women, churned out three thousand of the large, twin-engined bombers to operate in night raids, flattening places such as Cologne and playing a critical role in the Allied victory. Even though the carpet-bombing of German cities has been criticised recently, Mother was proud to do her bit and, of course, she hated the Germans as her father had died at their hands in the final days of the First World War," Anna said. "As a result, she worked herself to the bone under stiflingly hot and noisy conditions and in her later years, suffered from partial deafness, which she attributed to working in the factory."

"And, I suppose it was a dangerous place to be," Bella mused. "If the Nazis had learned of the factory's location, they would surely have bombed it to bits?"

"Well, after the war, evidence was uncovered that the Germans knew about the runways and factory buildings here in Blackpool, which you would have thought would have made it an ideal target for Nazi Bomber Command. But in fact the site was only attacked on one occasion when a lone German bomber tailing a night fighter let its bombs loose on the central runway. Mother was working her shift and recalled flying glass cutting her face as windows smashed while the surrounding streets suffered bomb damage," Anna explained. "But otherwise Blackpool escaped a deliberate bombing raid."

"I remember reading a newspaper article a few years ago about some documents found in Germany," Sarah added. "They stated that Hitler himself ordered that Blackpool was to be left intact with the idea that when Nazi Germany defeated Great Britain, they would use the resort as a 'people's playground' as well as a cog in their propaganda machine."

"How?" asked Bella, intrigued.

"The plan was for German paratroopers to capture the resort undamaged and celebrate by goose-stepping northwards up the promenade, the swastika fluttering from the top of the iconic Blackpool Tower for all the world to see." Sarah grimaced.

"Yes, have you seen the famous shots of Hitler strutting like a peacock beneath the Eiffel Tower after Paris fell?" Anna looked at Bella. "Thank God that never happened here, that's all I can say!"

"Although the documents explain the reason the Nazis didn't bomb Blackpool, I doubt we'll ever really know what Hitler's full plan for the town was," Sarah mused.

"It must have been such a terrifying time for the people here," Bella said. "I can't imagine living in such fear and uncertainty."

"Mother also said dozens of evacuees streamed into the town from cities such as Manchester, which put a strain upon the local services. But Blackpool was a place where people could escape and forget the war, especially in the entertainment halls." Anna gathered their dirty plates to soak in the sink before fetching a trifle from the fridge. "A little treat for you, Isabella."

"Thanks, Grandma, just what I need to cool my mouth down a bit!" Bella helped herself to a substantial wedge of the dessert before sprinkling hundreds and thousands on top, the colours bleeding a rainbow into the whipped cream. "So what happened to the Polish airmen in Blackpool, Gran?"

"Well, new arrivals were registered at the Goodwood Hotel before they were billeted in boarding houses around the resort while they undertook their training. In fact the Lansdowne Hotel became the headquarters of the Polish Air Force."

"Can we visit these places?" said Bella, suddenly wanting to find out everything she could about the experience of this Polish flyer, Tad, who'd piqued her interest and who hadn't been much older than she was now when he'd left his country to fight on a foreign shore. "Tomorrow?"

"Yes, there's no time like the present." Her grandmother smiled.

5

The summer of 1937 was one of hot days and sultry nights. With my friends Antusz and Marek occupied helping on their fathers' farms, I spent all my days with Jacek and Alicja. We'd set off early in the morning with our haversacks filled with bread and cheese for lunch, which we'd supplement with wild strawberries picked on the lower slopes of the Tatras. Warm from the sun, their sweet, sticky juice trickled through our fingers as we ate them. We'd swim in the rivers and hike in the mountains until we reached the plateaux. Refreshed by the cooling breezes at the higher altitude, we'd rest while gazing down to the lush valleys far below. As dusk fell before we returned home, we'd build a little fire and huddle around it telling ghost stories. Those were halcyon days that I never wanted to end. What I did not know then was that I would never recapture that blissful existence ever again. On the final night in July as the three of us watched fireflies dart and dive in the encroaching darkness, Jacek dropped a bombshell which would alter the course of all our lives forever.

"Little bro, I know this will come as a shock to you but I've been considering my future for a while now and…" he paused for a moment, pushing his floppy fringe off his sweat-beaded forehead, "I've been accepted into the cadet flying school in Dęblin, *kochany*."

Alicja and I sat dumbfounded until I finally found some coherent words to say. "Join a flying school? What are you talking about, Jacek? I thought we were both going to Jagiellonian University next year?"

"The Jagiellonian? It's one of the most prestigious universities in Europe, they would never accept someone with my grades." He turned back to me, his mouth quirking in amusement. "Book-learning just doesn't interest me as it does you, Tad. I need to be doing things, not reading about them. And Father is not impressed that I've been working on Pan Kowalski's farm since I left school, despite all my efforts to persuade him that I'm building something for my future with Alicja." He looked at Alicja, whose face was creased by a frown. "Father's been putting pressure on me every time I see him to pursue a military career and I want to make him proud. It's been nagging at me for months because I've never been interested in following him into the army. But then it came to me! You remember we used to play airplanes as kids?" I nodded as Jacek continued, "I've always been fascinated with flying. Imagine careering at speed through the air, thousands of feet above ground with just a small plane to hold you up! I can't think of anything more exciting than learning to fly. Can you?"

"I've never actually thought about it," I conceded, not wanting to admit that the thought of sitting in a steel box thousands of feet up in the sky terrified me somewhat. Seeing such enthusiasm and excitement on my brother's face, though, I feigned it too and slapped him on the back as he drew me into a celebratory hug. But as I felt his strong arms tighten around me, I saw the expression on Alicja's face mirrored my own feelings of loss, fear and something else I couldn't quite put my finger on. I considered how, over the years in Father's absence, Jacek had become a kind of father figure to me and I knew that Alicja, having an increasingly distant father, preoccupied as he was after his wife's untimely death with the demons of drink and his lame leg, had come to rely on my brother's down-to-earth practicality in a similar way. To be honest, on that night, I didn't even make the leap to think about the implications and potential dangers of Jacek joining the military, if indeed war was on the horizon. I just thought about the void my brother's decision would leave in all our lives. Selfish, I know.

Returning to Dziadek's after midnight, my only concern was locating Dęblin on the faded map which entirely covered the south wall of the old man's workshop. Observing all the colours marking the different territories, I was at first drawn to the vast blue swathes of the Austro-Hungarian Empire vying for dominance with the pink of the British Empire which was dotted here and there in both the northern and southern hemispheres. Refocusing on the red circle I'd drawn long ago to mark the city of Krakow, my eyes moved away to the north-east, almost reaching Warsaw. My heart hammering in my chest as I finally found Dęblin, I wondered how I could bear for Jacek to be so far away from me.

After Jacek's surprise announcement, things progressed very quickly as he left to begin his basic training at the flying school. Following his three months' mandatory training and a Christmas vacation with Dziadek, Alicja and I, which passed by in the flicker of an eye, he was gone again. As the New Year dawned, I accompanied him to Krakow Główny railway station, waving him off as he made his way back to Dęblin. Standing there saying our goodbyes, we were jostled by crowds of people loading their cases onto the waiting train and I noticed the admiring looks the young ladies gave my brother. Gazing at his tall, handsome figure, proud in his smart uniform, not for the first time in my life – or the last – I wanted to be just like him.

To my profound disappointment, I barely saw Jacek for months after that, except for a few short weeks at Easter. So, I began to spend more and more time with Antusz and Marek as we shared fishing and hiking expeditions together most weekends. Although the boys could never replace my brother in my affections, they filled the void left by him as, being physically strong, no-nonsense, outdoor sorts, they reminded me of Jacek in different ways, making his absence slightly more palatable.

Although my brother was far away, he took care to brief Dziadek and me in his weekly letters as he filled us in on the details of his training, his pride palpable that he was the first in his year to qualify as a fighter pilot. The only thing he bemoaned was how the bitter cold of the east seeped into his very bones, before signing off as cheerful as ever with how he loved and missed us all. Jacek's graduation was such a wonderful occasion, made even more special by Father's attendance as he looked on proudly. His first-born son, so like him. Of course I knew Father would never see me that way, nor did I want him to. Jacek was my idol; that honour was for him alone.

After the ceremony, we left Jacek to celebrate with his fellow graduates as Dziadek, Tata and I moved onto an inn for dinner. As Tata sat opposite me, sipping his borscht in a gentlemanly fashion, I couldn't help but think how much he'd aged since the last time I'd seen him, almost two years before. Resplendent and smart in his dress uniform and hat at the ceremony, studying him more carefully now, I saw that his short hair was completely grey, his features somehow sharper as if pared down to the bone.

"I've been accepted by the Jagiellonian to study Architecture and English," I announced halfway through the main course, wanting to impress him, as always.

"It's an illustrious university. Congratulations, son." A half-smile raised his mouth slightly before being swallowed by a frown. "But I doubt you'll ever finish your degree, Tad. War is coming. This year or next, I don't know, but it is coming. And then there'll be no need for building. Fighting to preserve what we have, that is what we all must do."

I wanted to tell him that architecture was about designing not building. I wanted to tell him that I dreamed of travelling to America one day to develop the skyscrapers of the future. I wanted to ask him why he'd never been there for Jacek and me when we were boys. I wanted to ask him whether he blamed me for Mama's death. But the words lodged in my throat. It was all too late. Instead we finished our meal and outside the inn, we shook hands and said goodbye. And as his imposing figure receded from Dziadek and me, I knew that if what Father had said was true about war coming to Europe, I might never see him again.

That autumn, despite the wrench of leaving behind the countryside where Jacek and I had fished and hunted and walked, I moved to Krakow to begin my degree at Jagiellonian University. A country boy through and through, my impressions of the city up to that point had been limited to our brief visits to the Christmas markets. Now, looking with the eyes of a student of architecture, I couldn't fail to be impressed by the beautiful, medieval buildings, starting with my entrance into the city through the thirteenth-century St Florian's Gate, through which future kings of Poland traditionally walked on their way to be crowned in the city's basilica.

Of course, when we were young boys Dziadek had told Jacek and me the tale of the Smocza Jama, the dragon's cave on the banks of the Vistula River. The story went that long ago, when people first came to live in the kink of the river, King Krak built his castle atop Wawel Hill, not knowing that far below a dragon resided in an underground cavern. Dziadek said that when peasants decided to graze their cows and sheep on the riverbank, the noise awoke the dragon and he began helping himself to their animals, sometimes taking their young women too. His townspeople frightened, King Krak offered his daughter's hand in marriage as well as all his wealth to whoever could kill the beast. Scores of knights perished trying to defeat the creature until a young shoemaker took the challenge, preparing sheepskins with mutton fat and sulphur to help him with the daunting undertaking. The clever shoemaker placed the bait at the entrance of the cave which, on waking, the dragon ate. With a fire burning in the pit of its stomach, it drank and drank from the river to try to quench the flames. However, the dragon consumed so much water that it exploded and so the cobbler won the princess and the kingdom. "The city has fire in its belly," Dziadek had told us both, "as you boys must."

On my first morning, I strolled around the city's main square, the stalls in the splendid one hundred-metre-long Sukiennice, a reminder of the vital role trade had played in Krakow since the thirteenth century, vying for my attention with Bazylika Mariacka. A Gothic church with its two mismatched towers soaring above the city's skyline, I took a peek inside at its high altar fashioned by the renowned sculptor Veit Stoss. With its rich colours and carvings in several folding sections, the oak and limewood altar featured around two hundred gilded and painted figures, mostly relating to the life of the Virgin Mary, but it was the faces I found most intriguing as they were said to be those of Krakovians Stoss met in life.

I was able to do some further sightseeing during those first few weeks, but my initial joy at living in such a vibrant city came to an abrupt end on October 1st 1938 when the German army rolled into the Sudetenland in accordance with the Munich Agreement. Three weeks later, Ribbentrop summoned the Polish ambassador to Berchtesgaden to present him with Hitler's plans regarding the Polish Corridor and the free city of Danzig. Ambassador Lipski refused and three days later, the first mass deportation of Jewish Polish nationals from Nazi Germany began. The situation escalated in mid-November with the Kristallnacht attacks in Berlin and other cities, in which thousands of Jews living and working in Germany who held Polish citizenship were packed onto trains headed for the Polish border and German concentration camps.

In early December, Jacek and Alicja visited me in my university digs to tell me their news. Having been granted forty-eight hours leave, Jacek had come to Krakow to obtain a special licence so they could be married at Bazylika Mariacka. The three of us having grown up so closely together, in the end, Jacek's wedding wasn't the wedge between us that I'd feared. Instead of losing my brother, it felt as though I was gaining a sister, as the gentle girl who'd been part of our lives for many years became part of our family. Standing by Jacek's side in the candlelight of the cathedral as he stood next to the woman he adored, promising to love and protect her for the rest of his life, I thought of our parents saying the same vows many years before and it made me hope for a similar love, one day, too.

A few days later, I returned home to Zakopane to celebrate Christmas with Dziadek. We tried our best to enjoy ourselves, but with Jacek away and having heard no news from Tata, it was difficult to enter into the festive spirit as a general air of tension hung over the town. In January, though, we had a short respite from the gloomy predictions of war as the Nordic and Alpine World Ski Championships came to Zakopane, bringing a much-needed lift to everyone. Watching the cross-country skiers brought back memories of when Jacek and I had slalomed through the very same forests, albeit with a little less skill and speed while the ski jumpers entranced their audiences, flying through the air like elegant birds before making miraculous landings.

The political situation seemingly deteriorating by the day, I rarely ventured beyond the ancient walls of Jagiellonian University that spring. While Jacek wrote me letters of his daring flying escapades, I could not have found a quieter setting than the Collegium Maius where I was studying for my architecture degree. The place was steeped in tradition, Kazimierz the Great having founded the Krakow Academy in 1364. Some forty years later, Queen Jadwiga gave her crown jewels to fund a university with King Władysław II Jagiełło donating buildings to house the lecture halls. I loved to just walk around, imagining the history of the place seeping through my skin into my very bones, a necessary distraction from my studies and everything else going on beyond the safety of the walls, I'm afraid. My days punctuated by the musical clock in the courtyard which played the university's song, 'Gaudeamus Igitur', on the hour, I quickly found a home from home.

I discovered my true place to be in the grand library, with its beautifully painted ceiling and walls crammed with shelves of books, and in the neighbouring room dedicated to the astronomer Nicolaus Copernicus, who'd studied at the university at the end of the fifteenth century. In those early days of my course, I saw that Krakow was a city with many faces, its medieval, beautifully restored buildings mixing effortlessly with its young and vibrant student population to ensure that it moved with the times. The streets of the old town barely changed since they were laid out in the thirteenth century, behind ancient wooden doors were cafes secreted in courtyards and cellars where I met with my friends to discuss all manner of matters.

Probably my best friend from that time was Jerzy Wozniak, a fellow architecture student, who had the most brilliant mind and came out top of the year whenever we had tests and examinations, even beating me. A Krakovian, Jerzy was fair-haired with intelligent, alert eyes, a city boy through and through; his childhood spent with indulgent parents in a grand house in the picturesque surroundings of the Planty far removed from mine. Meeting a boy like Jerzy was a whole new experience for me, as my close friendships up to this point in my life with Marek and Antusz, and of course Jacek, had been built on shared experiences and values as well as the same moral compass. Whilst Jerzy was different in this respect due to his privileged upbringing, our profound interest in architecture made us firm friends from the moment we met after the opening lecture of our degree course. From that day onwards, we spent hours walking round the city streets, sketching cupolas, gables, balustrades, porticos, arcades and buttresses of the buildings we passed, discussing the styles and materials used. To Jerzy, although everything was familiar, I helped him see it anew as we talked of the intricacies of the designs and how we could incorporate what we saw into our own work, one day.

But Jerzy's intelligence wasn't one-dimensional, as he possessed voracious debating skills and fierce views on all manner of current politics. He looked uneasily upon our German neighbours and warned of Adolf Hitler and his National Socialist Party. His opinion was shared by many of our fellow students but I, at this point, while interested in hearing them debate, felt that the political situation was not relevant to me. Was I really that naive to believe that it wouldn't touch us all?

Instead, during those early months I was totally preoccupied with my studies. I felt honoured and humbled to study in a place where so many esteemed scholars had walked before me. In the library, I often found myself marvelling at the collections of rare books on all manner of subjects, running my fingers over their leather spines and covers before sliding one from the clutches of the others in a cloud of dust. On every walk I took outdoors, the imperial history of the city bore down on me, but I soon became aware that modern-day politics had great implications for the future of my country. Immersed in my studies and with lively discussions with my friends in the city's public houses occupying my leisure time, I assimilated into life at Jagiellonian University and my freshers' year flew by in a heartbeat. Doing well in my end-of-year exams, I had it in mind to do a master's degree when my course came to an end. But then, a few days before I was due to return for my second year, things took a different turn. Hitler's Germany invaded Poland.

6

Just after midday, Anna glanced up to the cloudless blue sky above the redbrick former Eagle Club, noting that the late summer heatwave showed no sign of ending just yet. Not having visited for a couple of years, she studied the building, registering the familiar details and subtle changes. The central section resembled the narrow canal houses in Amsterdam, with its steeply gabled roof which rose to a point before descending to the main body of the building on either side. Projecting out onto the ledge above the main window, the gigantic white stone eagle caught her attention as she recalled how, in the weeks following her mother's death and revelation about Tad, she'd walked past it every day, mourning the loss of them both. Looking at the 'Future Focus' sign, she saw the one-time community hall of the old Polish Club now housed an energy firm. The irony wasn't lost on her that not only had she no idea of what that was, but neither would many of the elderly Polish people who still liked to walk past the place to reminisce about the good times they'd spent within its walls.

"So Tad, I mean, Great-Granddad, would have come here during the war?" Bella asked. Seeing that the building had plenty of character, she carefully positioned her iPhone so she could fit the majestic Polish eagle sitting above the 'Eagle House' sign into her shot.

"No, I've been reading up on this." Sarah shook her head, tucking an escaped dark curl behind her ear. "The Eagle Club didn't open until 1950, when it served as a social club for former airmen who, having married local girls, settled in Blackpool after the victory. And of course, it soon became a meeting place for the growing Eastern European community which flourished in the resort after the war."

"Some girls in my school whose Polish fathers stayed in Blackpool in '45 used to come here and enjoy their country's food, singing and dancing. Of course, at the time, I didn't know anything about Tad," Anna said, regretful that despite regular invitations, she'd never gone along with her schoolmates. "Come on, shall we see if we can have a look inside, girls?"

Bella followed her grandmother as she strode purposefully up the steps, under the watchful eye of a CCTV camera, to press the buzzer. Just as they were beginning to think their trip was destined to be fruitless, the door swung open to reveal a middle-aged man with a ruddy complexion dressed in a dark business suit, his ID card identifying him as Mike Jenkins. Suddenly at a loss as to how to explain their presence, Anna let Sarah take control. After briefly filling in the details of Tad's story and how Anna, his daughter, wanted to find out more about him, they were met with a positive reaction from Mike, who smilingly ushered them in. "You're lucky, most of the staff are on their lunch break, so I'm holding the fort, so to speak!" he explained. "I would be more than happy to give you all a little tour of some of the areas which I think might interest you."

As he spoke he led them into a corporate-looking hallway which didn't give them any hope they would find anything left from the time the Polish Club had first opened. "Now let's see what we can show you ladies." Mr Jenkins smiled, tapping the plastic card which hung from a royal blue lanyard around his neck to open the first door they reached.

They followed him through a mercifully air-conditioned, open-plan office, the computer stations either side temporarily vacated by their owners. Along a short corridor and up a narrow flight of stairs, he ushered them through a set of double doors into another room, sub-divided into small office areas and in dire need of refurbishment. Yet the room's proportions, its fine plasterwork, ceiling and beautiful parquet floor spoke of some special past of its own. Turning around to meet their confused expressions, Mr Jenkins waved his hand theatrically. "Ladies, you are now standing in the centre of the club's former ballroom. It's difficult to picture how it used to be, I know," he smiled, his dark eyes crinkling at the corners, "but we have a collection of photos taken in the fifties and sixties somewhere; you will be able to see how splendid it was then."

"It's definitely seen better days," commented Bella, nevertheless clicking a dozen or so photos of the peeling paint and fading ornamentation on the ceiling.

"I'm afraid so. The White Eagle Officer's Club held its final party on New Year's Eve 1999. As the new millennium dawned, it was consigned to history, as is the way with many things nowadays." Mr Jenkins stepped back, giving the women space to look around.

"Yes, if I recall correctly, my next-door neighbours at the time attended." Anna turned to Sarah and Bella. "Diana and Barry? Do you remember them? They said the Polish Club's dinner dances were always great fun and they also came for a meal here most weekends."

"The Sunday lunches were legendary here." The man frowned as though sorry for the sad state of repair now as he saw the room through their eyes. "Actually the building has just been sold, so perhaps the new owners might restore it to its former glory?"

"Hopefully," mused Anna, her breath catching as she followed the others up yet another flight of stairs.

"It's sad that it closed after being here for fifty years as a place where fellow Polish people could meet up," commented Bella, skipping up the steps, "perhaps keeping their language and traditions alive."

"It is." Mr Jenkins nodded solemnly. "There was a great sense of community here, but it all came to an end when the three remaining Polish war veterans retired, I'm afraid. It was their indomitable spirit that kept this place going. I was privileged to talk to them on a few occasions after the sale of the building to the present firm. What they all said was how welcome they'd always felt in the town. One recalled how, at one point of the war, there were so many Polish flyers in Blackpool that all the signs in the Pleasure Beach were translated into Polish." He laughed throatily as they climbed the final few steep stairs.

"I hope they felt valued," said Anna, struggling to keep up as Mr Jenkins opened the door to the boardroom. With a dozen padded leather chairs seated around a huge, highly polished oak desk, it was very plush. As Mr Jenkins poured Anna a glass of cooling water from the dispenser, Bella's eyes were immediately drawn to the half a dozen models of planes. With Polish flags painted alongside Union Jacks on their wings, they sat in pride of place on the desk. Studying them in turn, Bella estimated each one to be a metre long.

"These are like the ones we saw at the air show," she said, attempting to photograph them from every conceivable angle to capture their sleek shapes.

"Yes, that's right… Leon Jastrow, an Auschwitz survivor, who settled on the Fylde Coast and opened the Eagle Club, had them made specially to display downstairs. They hung suspended from the ceiling in the bar until it closed its doors for the final time on January 1st 2000." Mr Jenkins pointed at them one by one. "There's a Spitfire, a Hurricane—"

"And a Lancaster," Bella butted in, snapping it from as many angles as she could. "They are so intricately made."

"Very impressive, young lady. The final thing I have to show you is this." Mr Jenkins stepped away from the wall to reveal a large gilt-framed watercolour depicting the gabled building, the white Polish eagle luminescent against the deep ochre of the Blackpool brickwork of the Eagle Club. "Leon had it painted in 2000 so that, although the Polish Club has been consigned to history, both it and the people who came here will never be forgotten."

7

On September 1st, Dziadek and I were at the Friday market in Zakopane, pushing through the throng of people to purchase the scant provisions available. The autumnal air was thick with whispers and rumours as neighbours sought information when a disturbance down the road heralded the arrival of a man dressed in traditional mountain garb. It was an unusual sight which grabbed everyone's attention. With an anxious crowd gathered round him, he yelled that German troops had crossed the border that morning and the advancing soldiers had obliterated the neighbouring village of Czarny Dunajec, the houses pillaged and set alight, their inhabitants killed. Abandoning our shopping expedition, I shook in silent rage as I remembered the carefree days my brother and I had spent rafting on the Dunajec River, our little piece of paradise brutalised by an invading, foreign army.

There was optimistic news, however. Fortuitously, the Polish Air Force had the foresight to move their aircraft to secret locations and, obscured by an early morning mist, the Luftwaffe had only succeeded in shooting-up empty airfields, giving me some hope that Jacek had survived. But our commanders had also made some fundamental mistakes. The decision to concentrate Poland's air defences over the grey skies above Warsaw had inadvertently given the Luftwaffe superiority in the air everywhere else, so allowing the Germans to stop our army from mobilising. To compound this, our leaders had ordered sporadic raids on Nazi columns advancing on foot, which had not only been a grossly ineffective use of our planes but had forced many of our pilots to retreat into the heartland with no access to fuel. This had resulted in a complete breakdown in communication between units. With our country's air force and army in disarray, reservists were called up, but they could do nothing to stem the tide of Nazi armed vehicles swarming eastwards like a storm of stinging wasps. A proud citizen of our ancient land, I could only watch in horror as all this unfolded in front of my eyes, powerless to stop it.

Following the invasion, Hans Frank, the Nazi governor of the newly christened Third Reich's Distrikt Krakau, set up his headquarters in Wawel Castle. Returning to Krakow in early October in expectation of the commencement of the new academic year, I decided to take a walk by the river one Monday morning. I was enjoying the autumn sunshine when I looked up to the castle, as I always did, and the gold dome of Zygmunt Chapel glinting in the sun. But what I saw next filled me with revulsion and horror.

Crimson flags with evil black swastikas flying triumphantly from the castle's turrets, defacing and sullying the ancient building from which Polish kings had ruled for centuries. Retching, I dodged behind an ancient oak tree, where I was violently sick. Overnight my homeland didn't feel it was mine anymore.

I'd never held any ambitions of being a soldier, as I'd known from an early age that Jacek was more suited to that profession, with his fearless nature and athletic build, than I, his younger, scrawny brother. But seeing the Nazi occupation of my city become a reality compelled me to action, so I signed up to the Army Auxiliary Service. However reluctant I was to fight, I felt it was my duty to be ready if needed. At the nearby Nowy Targ airfield, I learned basic infantry drill, including how to use weapons, something I kept from both Dziadek and Jacek because I knew that, fearful for my safety, they would try to prevent me. In those early days of war, I noticed that street signs began to appear in the German language as the occupiers used propaganda to rewrite the thousand-year history of my city. But far more menacing than that for me was the Nazis' posting of an armed guard on Floriańska Street, the medieval gate which had always protected the city from invasion. Their machine guns poised, it was yet another visible reminder that Krakow itself no longer belonged to the Polish people.

During my first year at university, Kazimierz, the old Jewish part of the city, had become my favourite quarter to explore. Strolling down those quaint, narrow streets, there seemed to be something intriguingly new and unexpected at every turn. I'd regularly taken early-morning runs, hungrily inhaling the wonderful smells of freshly baked breads and pastries emanating from the many Jewish bakeries as dawn broke in the east. During my evening forays, I'd enjoyed eating and drinking in the cafes, engaging in friendly conversations and lively debates, punctuated by the mournful notes of klezmer music playing in the background.

But as a chill enveloped Krakow in the autumn of 1939, fear of the intentions of the Nazi occupiers pervaded, keeping people off the streets, particularly in this part of the city. I found myself venturing into Kazimierz less and less and on each occasion I did, I noticed seemingly half a dozen more shops boarded up, half a dozen more windows smashed, the word *Zyd* daubed on scores more doors whilst men, half-hidden beneath their wide-brimmed black hats, scurried home from the synagogue or the shops, eager to beat the night curfew. I knew from high-school history lessons that Jews had lived in Krakow for over six hundred years, making it one of the oldest such townships in Europe. Yet suddenly the Nazis had marched in, deeming them no longer welcome. It made my blood run cold pondering who they would next decide was unwelcome in the city.

Lectures failed to restart at Jagiellonian University and instead October was a feverish time of discussions and speculation of what the war would bring. I attended meetings in cramped airless cellars with Jerzy, my closest friend at university, who filled in some of the void left by Jacek's absence. Everyone was issued with ration cards, but even the staples of meat, fruit and vegetables became scarcer by the week. The windows of the upmarket shops on Grodzka Street were empty, a pattern repeated on streets all over the city as supply and demand plummeted. Over time, it became part of daily life which we got used to, along with all the other hardships we were forced to face.

But alone at night, all I could think of was my brother and the dangers heading his way now war had been declared. Then, late one evening, I was on my way to my digs, absently kicking through piles of dead autumn leaves, the Bazylika Mariacka bells muffled in the distance, when I felt hands grab me from behind. My heart pumping furiously in my chest, I clenched my right hand into a fist, poised to hit my assailant and make my escape. Spinning around, however, I saw my brother's face emerge from the shadows, our mama's crucifix glinting in the moonlight. "Jacek, what are you doing here?" I said, remembering how smart he'd looked in his uniform at his graduation and noting that he was wearing a rather shabby coat and a cap pulled low over his eyes.

"Tad, we have to get off the streets." He spoke quietly. "Is there anywhere safe we can talk?"

We hurried to my garret in time for the nightly curfew, not a word passing between us. But once I shut the door to the world, Jacek pulled me into a hug, joyously slapping me on the back as I thanked God he'd survived the invasion. Holding him, I noticed he was much leaner than I remembered. Evidently his fitness training at flying school coupled with a dirth of Dziadek's wholesome stews and dumplings over the past years had whipped my brother into shape. "Jacek, what are you doing here? You must have taken a terrible risk to come here; the city is crawling with Nazis."

"I had to see you, Tad," he started, his face agitated. In the candlelight, I noticed his skin had a greyish pallor, his eyes edged with dark rings. "I've just taken Alicja back to Zakopane, to her father's farm, and I had to make sure you were safe. I only have a few hours here, as I must leave the city before daybreak."

"Where are you going, Jacek?" I said, my heart thumping in my chest. "Surely you'd have been better lying low in Zakopane too?"

Fear gripped me as my brother nodded his head. "During the battle, I was separated from my squadron, but witnessing what I did, I can't just give up. I'm going to try to find other survivors and locate an operational airfield from where we can launch our fight back."

"But Jacek…" I began to protest as he raised his palm to halt me.

"Tad, I've been waiting my whole life for a moment such as this." As he hurriedly detailed the rigours of training over the past few years and his redeployment to a specialist flying corps in the east, his mercurial attention flitting from one subject to another, I sat back and listened intently. I knew the futility of trying to persuade my brother to take the easy way out; it wasn't in Jacek's nature.

As he drew to a close, I told him about the dire situation at the university before we relived happy memories of times together. I warmed up some vegetable soup, which we mopped up with hunks of stale bread, my brother eating his with such gusto I wondered whether it was the first meal he'd had that day. Deep into the night, we talked of our camping and rafting escapades, of Dziadek and the mountains, but as the new dawn streaked the sky blush and red, our conversation became serious once more.

Clearly fearful my neighbours would hear, Jacek lowered his voice which was etched with worry. "Tad, I know you never wanted to be in the military like Tata and I, but the situation is so grave I fear that young men like you will almost certainly be called into action."

I nodded once more, knowing full well that I would be conscripted very soon and cognisant of the dangers facing me. "I have heard such things from my friends."

"Just promise me you'll be careful, little bro." My brother whispered beneath his breath, his blond fringe sticking to his forehead, which was shiny with perspiration. "Don't be brave or do anything foolish. Poland is a precarious place for all of us now."

"But I want to fight," I asserted, having made the decision some time ago to embark on this path. "I love my country too as you do, Jacek. Surely, I have the right to defend it as well?"

"Don't you understand, *kochany*? Krakow is a dangerous place now and things are not likely to improve. If you have the chance, run. Run and don't look back. All you can do now is save yourself, Tad. The war in Poland is lost. Lost," he whispered, pushing his wheat-coloured hair back from his forehead in that so familiar gesture. Hearing the despair in my brother's voice sent a chill through my body. I wanted to argue with him, tell him he was mistaken, that this couldn't be the case, but he sighed so wearily that I didn't dare take him on.

"What a place, what a time to bring a new child into the world." His eyelids flickered as though it was an effort to keep them open.

"Jacek, you're going to be a father," I said, incredulous as the mention of new life seemed incongruous in the very moment I'd realised all was lost for our great country.

"Yes, so you see, I have no choice, I have to fight for my wife, for our baby, for the future of our homeland." He smiled, the lines around his eyes crinkling, making him appear much older than his twenty-four years. "And I will try with all of my being to see that no harm befalls them. As Alicja's husband I must do my upmost to safeguard her and our unborn child. But you, *kochany*, I fear I won't be there to protect you as I've always tried to do up until now."

Seeing the unshed tears glisten in my brother's eyes, the seriousness of what he was saying hit me like a physical blow. I knew Jacek wouldn't heed his own advice and flee with his family while there was yet time. I saw that in battle he would be a fearless warrior who would fight until the very last for his country, for his people, and for his wife and child. Although I said nothing, for the first time in my life I knew I would defy my brother. I had to fight too.

With dawn breaking in the eastern sky, Jacek and I parted, my brother glancing behind him as he descended the dark stairway. "We'll meet again one day, never fear, Tad." As the shadows swallowed him, I could only pray to a god I wasn't certain was listening anymore: *Please God we do. Keep him safe.*

For me, November 6th was the darkest day in Krakow's history to date. Luckily I was at my lodgings nursing a heavy cold or I might have found myself caught up in the horror of what passed just a few metres away. Having fallen asleep as my body fought the virus, at around midday a loud commotion stirred me. Hearing the ominous rumble of trucks on the cobbled street below, I peeked between dishevelled net curtains in my attic garret and a terrible sight greeted me. I saw the black-uniformed soldiers, the blood-red flash of the Nazi insignia on their arms as they alighted a dozen or so trucks and rushed into the old halls where my lecturers resided. Half an hour or so passed, my heart thumping in my chest as I stood looking down on the deserted street, waiting for something to happen, imagining it would be horrific and yet being unable to drag my eyes away.

Then I saw them leave one after the other, eminent professors whom we'd all esteemed and in whose footsteps we'd hoped to follow. With blood pouring from gaping head wounds, their shirts and jackets torn and glasses smashed, they stumbled along, herded as though they were cattle into the waiting trucks. Waves of nausea pulsing through me, I turned and vomited into the coal bucket in the corner of my room. Swilling my mouth out with cold water, against my instincts, I felt compelled to return to the window to bear witness to the horrors unfolding on the street where I lived.

When the packed trucks eventually pulled away, I sat motionless on the floor for the rest of the afternoon, unable to make sense of what I had just seen. University professors arrested and battered on the elegant streets of Krakow. I shook my head vigorously in the hope that the image of the elderly learned men, their faces bloody from being kicked and punched, would dissipate from my memory, so that in a day or two, I would begin to doubt whether that was what I'd actually seen unfold. But I knew it was no use; such events were the reality of life under the occupation of a brutal regime.

I spent that evening with Jerzy in the hushed backstreet bars of the city, my friend, who'd been caught up in the thick of events that day, repeating his dire warnings about Hitler to anyone and everyone who would listen. There were so many rumours it was hard to keep up but by the end of the night, even my vodka-soaked brain noticed a common thread running through many of the stories. Earlier that day, the Gestapo chief in Krakow, SS-Obersturmbannführer Bruno Müller, had commanded the university rector, Professor Tadeusz Lehr-Spławiński, an unassuming but charismatic man whom I'd heard speak on a number of occasions, to require all professors to attend his lecture for Nazi Germany's plans for Polish education. Thus, at noon, all the university's academics had gathered in lecture room fifty-six in nervous expectation of what was to follow.

But according to a third-year student, who had hidden in the corridor outside, no lecture took place and instead Müller told the lecturers that the university did not have permission to start a new academic year. The SS-Obersturmbannführer then informed them it was the Nazi view that Poles were hostile toward German science and acted in bad faith. The assembled men were then arrested by armed policemen, frisked and escorted out with some senior professors being kicked and hit with rifle butts, which went someway to explain the appearance of those I'd seen from the safety of my garret. The student then told us that our teachers had been incarcerated at Montelupich Prison, but he so was severely inebriated by that point I didn't really know whether to believe that part of his tale or not.

One thing that I did know, as I sat staring out of my window into the impenetrable darkness of the night which cloaked Krakow, was that I had to get out of Poland. Jacek was right, the fight was over here before it had begun, my city lost to the Nazis.

The situation was changing on a daily basis and later that month, Hans Frank created the Judenräte – the Jewish Councils. They were to be run by Jewish citizens for the purpose of carrying out orders for the Nazis, which included the registration of all seventy thousand Jewish people living in the area and the collection of taxes. Things worsened still when the Nazis commanded that all Jews of twelve years of age or older were required to wear an identifying Star of David on their clothing. The fight was indeed lost here for everyone. Discussing the matter with Jerzy, we came to the conclusion that we had no choice but to leave Poland, to attempt to make our way to some other country where we could regroup and prepare to fight back. To reclaim what had been taken from us.

8

The sky was a watercolour of muted greys, the road as slick as sealskin as Sarah pulled up in front of their Victorian terraced house, just a stone's throw from Lancaster city centre. Exiting the car, she was proud that her garden stood apart from the others on the street. Without exception, the neighbouring houses were rented by students from absentee landlords and their gardens all rather unkempt. Being only nine by seven feet, Sarah had used her space well, her green fingers always on top of the pruning and weeding necessary to keep it neat. It was dominated by a sapling cherry tree which she'd planted the previous spring, while along the little wall separating them from the overgrown lawn next door, she had planted chrysanthemums which gave the garden some much-needed colour on days such as this. Bright splashes of yellow and orange acted as an instant mood-lifter every time

Sarah stepped through the gate into her quiet little haven away from the rest of the world.

"It feels we've been away longer than just the weekend. The air has definitely turned autumnal all of a sudden," Bella remarked, clomping through the open-plan downstairs with its shabby-chic flowery settee and mismatched green velvet chairs. She skirted the low, pine coffee table strewn with large hardback books and old Sunday supplements to switch on the numerous lamps, shedding light into the corners of the living room and book-crammed alcove by the window, before making her way through to the modern kitchen with its surrounding stainless-steel units.

"Yes, I think the late heatwave has well and truly burned itself out," Sarah sighed, securing her car keys onto their hook before taking a cursory flip through the accumulated mail. But it was more than the summer's not-so-subtle shift towards autumn occupying her thoughts. With her mother's revelations about Tad and Eirlys, it felt something had moved in their lives too. Sarah unpacked their overnight bags and loaded the washing machine while Bella arranged their toiletries in the bathroom. Twenty minutes later, they sat on the high stools at the breakfast bar, Bella having changed into a comfy grey tracksuit tucked into Ugg boots in the same shade. There, they hugged steaming cups of tea accompanied with some softening shortbread they'd brought back from a brief break to the Scottish Highlands to celebrate the end of Bella's A-level exams in June.

"It's weird," Bella said after a while, "but how many times have I walked up the hill from town past the Church of Our Lady Queen of Poland and I had no inkling that we had Polish ancestry?"

"I know." Sarah nodded, dunking her biscuit into her tea to make it slightly more palatable. "I always assumed my granddad was in the RAF and neither Grandma nor Mum ever dissuaded me. As we know, the efforts and contributions of the Polish flyers in World War II weren't recognised until decades after the war and there would have been a stigma growing up as the illegitimate child of one so that will be the reason they kept it all hush hush. I can see why Grandma Eirlys only told Mum about Tad on her deathbed and I understand why Mum kept that to herself until now, not even telling my father." Sarah paused.

"He wouldn't have approved?" Bella frowned, sipping the hot tea.

"No, not your Papa George!" Sarah smiled. "Even when I told him of my pregnancy, he made me feel I'd gravely let him down. Being an old-fashioned type, he never reconciled himself to the fact that I'd had a child outside marriage. He loved you dearly, but I always felt his disappointment in me which I deeply regretted."

"It's all so sad," Bella sighed as Sarah looked up at the inscription on the black and white clock which dominated the wall opposite. *To every thing there is a season and a time to every purpose under the heaven.* She must have read it thousands of times but paused now to ponder its meaning before her thoughts were interrupted by Bella. "In the years since Granddad died, Gran's obviously decided she wanted to share it with us, a different generation. All I can say is I feel incredibly honoured and humbled to be related to such a brave man as Tadeusz."

"I'm still getting my head around having Polish ancestry but, you know what, I'm really proud of him, too." Sarah caught hold of her daughter's slender hand, each finger adorned with the narrowest of silver rings.

"Since Gran told us about Tad, I've decided I'd like to find out more about him," Bella said, sliding off her stool to retrieve a packet of chocolate digestives from the cupboard. "Ooh! These are much better. Soft biscuits just aren't biscuits in my book."

"I agree." Sarah dropped the ripped, red tartan packet with the remaining shortbread into the pedal bin and reached for a crisp chocolate biscuit instead.

"So what do you think about trying to discover more about Tad?" Bella persisted, wiping the scattering of crumbs from her top. "I'll have oodles of time to research him once you're back at uni."

"You're serious about this?" Sarah said, feeling the sweetness dissolve on her tongue. "His story has really captured your imagination, hasn't it?"

"Listening to Mike Jenkins at the old Polish Club talk about the bravery of the airmen just brought it home to me; what they gave up to come here, how driven and fearless they were. And to think we are the direct descendants of one of them! It's such a big deal!" Bella paused to savour the final bite of her biscuit. "I would like to find out, if I can, what made Tad leave his family and country behind to fight alongside Great Britain and her allies."

Sarah smiled at her daughter's eager face. "I don't want you to get your hopes up that you'll find anything specific about Tad. You might discover his name on an official document or something, if you're lucky, Bella! It was all such a long time ago."

"I can at least try. Learning we're connected to such a courageous young man makes me ashamed that I barely paid attention in my GCSE History classes or on the trip we took to the Imperial War Museum North. My friends were busy taking selfies with the ceramic poppies which had been on display at the Tower of London while I was more concerned trying to capture the sleek curves of the building than I was with listening to the guide. She might have even mentioned the Polish airmen and what compelled them to escape their defeated land to continue their fight thousands of miles from home, I don't know. Tad was only a couple of years older than me when he left his homeland and some of the men would have been my age! Boys, really…"

While Bella was talking, Sarah fired up her laptop and opened a search engine. Seeing her daughter was serious about discovering more about Tadeusz, she thought acquainting themselves with the background details a good place to start. "So, as we know, Poland was defeated in September 1939, right at the beginning of the war," she began. "Shortly afterwards, their commander-in-chief General Sikorski met with the British and the French to discuss how best to use what remained of his country's armed forces. The Poles, being no fools, wanted to re-establish their air force in the UK because we had superior aircraft to the French and, in turn, the UK was happy to take hundreds of PAF airmen to make up the shortfall in the RAF."

"Wait a minute. So although France and the UK didn't come to Poland's aid in her hour of need, they soon decided their trained soldiers and airmen could be of great use to them?" Bella pondered, biting the top of her pen. "Have I got that right?"

"Yes, but we can't place any judgements on that. In war, governments always look after the interests of their own countries," Sarah said, easing her arms out of her chunky knit, olive-green cardigan. "And it was a beneficial arrangement to all parties, the French and British assisted the Poles in their escape from a perilous situation while getting much-needed reinforcements."

"So many of the Polish airmen escaped south and reached Romania through a clandestine network? Over 90,000 of them ended up in transit camps there," Bella read over her mum's shoulder.

"But there were also thousands who fled north to neutral countries like Latvia and Lithuania, too. Their evacuation sounds as though it was a well-planned operation, right down to providing civilian clothing, visas and passports," Sarah mused.

"After their perilous journey it must have been a relief for the men to set their feet on British soil," Bella commented.

"Unfortunately those who arrived in the UK were often treated as second-class citizens. In the early days of the war, the Polish airmen were only allowed to join the Royal Air Force Volunteer Reserve and were obliged to wear British uniforms and fly British flags as well as taking two oaths, one to the Polish government and the second to George VI."

"That must have been humiliating for what I'm learning are extremely proud and patriotic people," Bella sighed. "Look, it says here that to begin with all Polish pilots were given the lowest RAF rank of pilot officer, regardless of their previous experience and they were only allowed to fly with a British counterpart. That is truly shocking, Mum!"

"Extremely demeaning." Sarah nodded. "But they quickly proved their worth. The Polish and British governments signed an agreement to form the 300 and 301 Bomber Squadrons and the 302 and 303 Fighter Squadrons. The Polish Hawker Hurricane Squadrons fought effectively in the Battle of Britain in August 1940."

"Yes, it says that Polish pilots were regarded as fearless and their success rates were very high in comparison to the less-experienced British pilots. In fact, as Gran alluded to, the 303 Polish Squadron became the most efficient RAF fighter unit at that time." Bella smiled, nodding in satisfaction to herself. "I like the sound of that. When Gran showed us the photo of Tad, I got the feeling he was brave and courageous. Look, it says here that an American called Ralph Ingersoll reported in late 1940 that the Poles were 'the talk of London' because of their victories and such pilots returned with a girl on each arm. He wrote that the girls could not resist the Poles, nor the Poles the girls." Bella laughed at her feeble attempts of an American accent.

"Yes, if they all looked like Tad I'm not surprised for he was extremely good-looking." Sarah smiled. "But from what

Grandma Eirlys told Mum, Tad wasn't like that. He was a quiet country boy who missed his family desperately."

"But wait a minute, Tad wasn't a military man at the outbreak of war, he was a student, wasn't he?" Bella raised her eyebrows in question. "I wonder what prompted him to make the decision to leave his family and country?"

"Maybe he had witnessed some of the atrocities the Nazis had committed and wanted to fight them on a level playing field? Of course they rounded up, beat and imprisoned many of the lecturers at the university in Krakow. I remember seeing it in the film *Sophie's Choice*," Sarah mused. "Maybe Tad knew some of them?"

"But I thought it was just the Jewish population whom the Nazis persecuted?" said Bella, furiously scribbling notes.

"The Final Solution was undoubtedly their worst atrocity, but the Nazis also had a twisted logic that they had to erase Polish history and culture before imposing their own on the country. It was classic expansionism and so, at the start of the war, they imprisoned intellectuals before moving onto the Jews later on."

"I think that makes it understandable why men like Tad would leave their country in order to fight," Bella nodded. "I'd imagine a boy like him would be consumed with anger and unable to sit back, waiting for his fate at the Nazis' hands."

"That's right! You need to try to put yourself in his shoes. He was a young man whose country had been savaged by the enemy. He was intelligent, idealistic and God knows what had happened to his family," her mum said. They then sat in silence for a few minutes while Bella pondered Tad's possible reasoning and Sarah closed down her internet search.

"Have you given any more thought to your university applications? I know you don't know *exactly* what you want to do, so why not just carry on where you left off with your A-levels? You could apply to study one or more of your A-level subjects as a single or combined degree," Sarah asked, logging off her computer.

Bella's heart sank. This was a conversation they'd repeated many times but, still not sure what she wanted to do, she didn't really feel like another full-blown discussion and analysis. Her interests lay in design, but she knew that her mother, being a university lecturer, wanted her to get a degree in an academic subject, perhaps followed by a qualification in teaching. This prospect horrified Bella, who was adamant this was a career she would never pursue.

"A degree in a core subject like Maths or English would open up your options. I've often seen students change their mind or decide what they want to really do halfway through their degrees." Sarah paused. "They end up having to change courses and repeat years because the scope of their initial choice was too narrow. It wastes time and money."

"Yes, I see how that could happen," Bella commented with a sigh, wondering how she could curtail this conversation as soon as possible.

"How about I set up meetings with some lecturers at the university to give you some advice and help you make your decision, then?" Sarah added.

"Aren't we jumping the gun a bit?" said Bella. "I think we should wait until I get my exam results."

"Maybe you could make a list of your interests then? That might help you to decide." Sarah averted her eyes to the ground as Bella stayed silent. Realising she sounded like a pushy, over-ambitious mother and knowing Bella was resisting her attempts to focus on her future, she decided to back off for the time being. "Just remember how proud I am of you. Always." She hugged her. "But you do need something to occupy you these next few months, Bella. There's a temporary library job going at the university that might suit you for now."

"Yes, and it would give me an income." Bella nodded, restarting the computer. "I'll take a look!"

*

In the event, Bella achieved better A-level results than she ever could have imagined, being awarded As in all her subjects. To celebrate, her mum treated her to her favourite meal of cheeseburgers and fries, followed by ice cream sundaes at Frankie & Benny's. But whilst Bella's stunning performance opened up her options of universities and degree courses, the proliferation of choices before her now only seemed to make her decision what to do next with her life that much more difficult.

9

Poland, Winter 1939–40

Following the Nazi invasion, my hometown of Zakopane became a hotbed of activity for resistance groups, who took full advantage of the difficult mountainous terrain to launch attacks against our occupiers. In response, the Gestapo established a unit in the grand building of the sanatorium and, unsurprisingly, whenever I visited Dziadek that autumn, apprehension pervaded every street of the town, the air iced with tendrils of fear. Women, children and the elderly stayed at home, afraid to venture out, while many of the young men who'd lived in the area 'disappeared' in those first few months of occupation, taken God knows where by the Nazis. Even when people were brave enough to attempt to stand up to the evil which overshadowed our land like a dark thundercloud, they whispered behind cupped hands and arranged covert assignations behind closed doors as suspicion gripped us all.

As the first frosts laced the fallen leaves, the war began to inflict physical as well as mental wounds upon my neighbours. The Nazis responded to lone shootings of their soldiers by resistance units with reprisal killings of dozens of villagers, which they carried out with relish. Even the surrounding forests where Jacek and I had played as carefree kids were not spared as the Nazis, under instructions to chop down trees for timber needed to build hangars and barracks in labour camps, desecrated our childhood haunts. Life as we'd known it stopped as we just fought to survive each day.

But winter passed and, as is often the way, my neighbours began to slowly adapt to this new state of affairs thrust upon them. Although the Nazis largely succeeded in suppressing the covert activities of the area's main ZWZ resistance unit, fortunately the Home Army had the foresight to enlist mountain guides to act as couriers. These were men who were well acquainted with operating in the complex network of trails and caverns across the Tatras to the high peaks of the Carpathians, while the SOE also managed to forge secret routes through the mountains.

After my chance meeting with Jacek that night in Krakow following the outbreak of war, I put my Army Auxiliary Service training to use, joining the ZWZ Zakopane unit along with Antusz and Marek. Although fragmented and without any central co-ordination, the movement's exploits during those first months of the war were nevertheless determined and brave, ranging from espionage and assassination through to smuggling, disinformation and terrorising our Nazi occupiers. All noble activities we were proud to be part of but still, it wasn't enough for me to operate from the sidelines. I had to get out of Poland, as Jacek had warned me. I had to fight back.

So it was, as darkness fell on February 14th 1940, I was forced to leave Zakopane. With just immediate supplies in my haversack and my late mother's brooch pinned inside my jacket pocket, it was imperative I make my escape, as the previous day, the Gestapo had arrested a member of our unit and were hell bent on hunting down the rest of us. I recall Dziadek sitting by the fire watching me, his wise eyes unblinking as I safely stowed my *kennkarte*, the identification card we had been issued with shortly after the Nazis had occupied our country, below my ten layers of clothing. I would need it in the unfortunate eventuality of being stopped by a German patrol in the environs of Zakopane. But if I managed to escape over the Slovak border, I planned to discard it immediately, knowing that my journey required much quick thinking and subterfuge if I was to make it across the patchwork quilt of Southern European countries.

"*Do Widzenia,*" Dziadek whispered. Pulling me into a hug, he slipped into my palm a little wooden angel that we'd once carved together in the palest of woods. "She has the face of your mother, Tad. May she watch over you and bring you back safely to me."

"*Do Widzenia,*" I replied. *Goodbye.* I wanted to say more but tears choked me, rendering me silent. Retreating from the old man's warm embrace, I thought it somehow fitting that in that moment of great emotion neither of us broke our habit of a lifetime of being economical with words. Walking down the dirt track away from the house where

Jacek, Dziadek and I had shared so much, I glanced back with tears obscuring my vision, wondering whether if ever I would see my beloved grandfather again.

The streets were deserted as I left my hometown that evening, people sheltering behind locked doors, deterred by the threat of Nazi patrols. But even then, I took care to pull my hat down over my eyebrows and my scarf up over my mouth so that I was unrecognisable as a young man, there being so few of us left. The only living souls I saw were several Goral women, clothed in traditionally patterned thick jumpers on account of the bitter cold weather Guessing from the interval between their ages that they were generations of the same family, I deduced they had most probably ventured down from their homes in the high mountains to sell their wares in town. I stopped briefly to purchase bread, cheese and milk from them which I packed into my haversack for my meals that evening, the following day and possibly beyond.

Walking down the streets where I'd spent my childhood, I tried to consign all the details to memory. The wooden houses, their steeply sloped roofs designed for the snow to slide off during harsh winters, clustered together as though engaged in clandestine conversations. The deserted storks' nests, portents of new arrivals in the spring. The farmers transporting winter fodder for animals to their barns, the sweet warm smell and steaming breath hanging on the cold air. The intricate carvings decorating the doors and windows of the houses I passed, each one a work of art. All these memories imprinted upon my brain to be brought out and cherished whenever I needed comfort in them. Despite knowing the countryside south to the border was sparsely populated, I remained vigilant at all times as, since the dawn of the New Year, Dziadek and I had heard stories of young men being taken for conscripted transports to the front.

Out in the open, though, I suddenly felt rejuvenated. Below me, my feet were taking unfettered strides after months of hesitant ones while cautiously peering over my shoulder. There was no one here now, either to stop me or call me back. Nevertheless, I took one final look back at my town and that was when the realisation struck me like a punch to the stomach. I wasn't coming back.

Knowing my escape was imminent, I'd hidden my skis in the forest and I retrieved them now so I could progress quickly through the beginning of the route, which was so familiar to me. Negotiating the remnants of winter snows, I managed to escape via the steep Circha valley, passing through woods and crossing streams where Jacek and I had played as children only a few years before. It seemed like another lifetime now, though, as I skied on, leaving it all behind, leaving behind a part of myself in the process, a part which would always belong to this landscape, these skies. Like thousands of other young men and women who had fled the country, I feared my escape would be perilous, as I knew I had Hitler's armies biting at my heels like angry wolves every step of the way.

I met up with Antusz, Marek and Jerzy at a deserted farm building, as arranged. We all had our different roles within the group, which seemed to complement each other. With his attention to detail, Jerzy was the one who'd planned the route, and I used the navigational skills Jacek had taught me to make sure we followed it while Marek and Antusz were both well-built farmers who employed their knowledge of the outdoors to great effect. Meeting them that day, my childhood friends had expressions of grim determination on their faces while Jerzy had fear in his eyes. In the months to come, I suspected that he hadn't told his overprotective parents of our escape plans and I pictured them waiting at the window of their fine house in Krakow, looking out over the parkland with the forlorn hope that their beloved son would one day return.

With the protection of the countryside, we made our way through the snow on our skis, carrying them over our shoulders when the terrain was unsuitable. Crossing one of the bridges over the frozen Dunajec River, I remembered how, all those years ago, my brother had powerfully pushed through the water as he'd dragged me to the safety of the bank and, carrying on, I said a silent prayer to God, asking Him to keep Jacek safe now, wherever he was. The temperatures that first night were so bitterly cold that we all feared we wouldn't survive if we stayed outdoors. Luckily for travellers like us, there were small wooden huts dotted at strategic intervals in the Małopolska mountain region which had provided overnight shelter to climbers before the war. Catching sight of one at just past 11pm, I thanked God that we would at least have a roof over our heads this freezing night. Once inside the relative warmth of the hut, we shared out our provisions, Antusz adding some smoked sausages and Marek beer to my bread, cheese and milk, while Jerzy had been able to procure some apples in the city. Not taking the risk of lighting a fire as the smoke might identify us to passing Nazi patrols, we snuggled into each other's warmth so we could rest and prepare for another day.

That second day, we climbed towards a large hunting lodge where people had enjoyed their summer holidays before the war. As we approached the top of the mountain, we came across three more of our countrymen trying to escape along the same route we were taking. In our eagerness to meet and chat with our compatriots we let our caution slip and with tree cover sparse we inevitably became a target for one of the German planes patrolling the area. Tracking us, the plane circled above us and, its machine guns stuttering, killed two of our new acquaintances. The rest of us managed to run to the safety of an outcrop of rocks where we waited a considerable time until certain the plane had gone and silence returned once more to the snowy landscape. This was the first of many times my survival relied on luck, providence, God's protection; call it what you will. After a mercifully peaceful night at the hunting lodge, we vigilantly set off once more, bartering for food from isolated woodland farmhouses, trusting the people who lived there not to turn us in.

We pushed on, our blistered feet causing us to slow down significantly. Our tiredness exacerbated by a lack of food, our progress was further hampered by the Nazis' previous bombing of villages and towns which made provisions hard to come by. Fortunately, along the way, we met with many acts of kindness by farmers and villagers. We were given bread, cheese and whatever meagre provisions these poor people could spare, often, we knew, at great personal danger to themselves.

We journeyed on. Negotiating loose stones and heading into a strong cross wind which brought driving snow slowed my progress as I lagged behind Antusz, Marek and Jerzy. Lessons learned from Jacek about survival in the woods, I focused my eyes on the ground in search of plants and berries and nuts, and anything else that could provide our supper that evening and the subsequent day. Presently, I smelt smoke and relief flooded through me that a house or farm was nearby, where we might find shelter and warmth in an outbuilding overnight. Careful not to let this promise cloud my judgement, I proceeded to the black hulk of the building with caution. Although there was every chance that there might indeed be sympathetic Poles living there minded to assist us in whichever way they could, they might just as well be people ground down by rationing and privation. People ready to betray escapees to the Nazi occupiers in exchange for extra food to see their family safely through the harsh winter. Whilst I couldn't condone such duplicity, who was to say what I would do if either Dziadek or Jacek was in trouble?

Bent double so we were safely below the window, we scurried to the vast barn at the rear of the farmhouse. With cooking smells emanating from the gap below a wooden door at the back of the cottage, I managed to eschew thoughts of a hot meal. Instead, we made ourselves beds from the profusion of hay in the barn where we feasted on my forest hoard, saving half of it for another day. Exhausted as I was, I fell into a deep sleep in my warm cocoon of hay, safely hidden from the world, knowing this would be my last night in Poland, for at least a while and maybe forever.

When I woke the darkness was all-consuming and I thought for the briefest of moments that I was back in my bedroom at Dziadek's, that if I peeped out of the window, I would see the flicker of candlelight illuminating his workshop as he worked deep into the winter's night. I mused how once a piece had captured his soul, it possessed his every thought, causing him to work all the hours God gave him as he industriously brought his vision to life, cut by cut, bevel by bevel. But then a finger of straw scratched my cheek and the picture conjured of Dziadek dissolved into the darkness of the barn. With a jolt I remembered exactly where I was and why.

Leaving before dawn, we made the most of the half-light to stride out over the open fields, knowing that we could hide quickly should a patrol come near. Though the temperature still hovered barely above freezing, the thick drifts of snow had melted and just a fine sprinkling covered the ground, a sign that spring was at last on its way. But while the worry of hyperthermia and freezing to death retreated from my mind, it was replaced by another more terrifying one as I pondered how the milder weather would doubtless encourage the Nazi patrols out of hibernation. We would have to be more vigilant than ever on our continuing journey. Despite our fatigue and the reluctance of our limbs to keep moving, we compelled ourselves to carry on.

After a few hours' walking, I heard the crunch of footsteps behind us, following the path ours had left in the snow. Antusz, Marek and Jerzy managed to dart into the trees, but I wasn't quick enough. Not knowing whether the steps belonged to a friend or foe, I stood stock still, holding my breath while my heart hammered in my chest. Glancing over my shoulder, to my intense relief I saw a red deer, its coat seeming to glow against the stark, monochrome winter landscape as it turned from me and strode majestically into the forest. Walking on, the staccato snap of twigs beneath our feet magnified tenfold in the forest, I heard a low rumbling. Barely discernible, I nevertheless felt the cold creep from my extremities towards my heart as the sound transported me back to the morning of the Aktion at Jagiellonian University. And I knew that Nazi trucks were heading towards me, once again.

10

Over the next week while her mum made regular trips to the university in preparation for the start of the academic year, Bella found herself at a loose end. September had always been a time of anticipation of what the new school year would bring, of buying pastel-shaded files and brightly coloured pens to fill a pencil case emblazoned with her current favourite reality TV stars. And then there had been the restart of school: sharing holiday stories with her friends and getting acquainted with her new timetable and teachers. Each year, she'd never had any trouble adjusting to these challenges and by the time the leaves had begun to turn and fall, and the bonfire had appeared on the recreation field opposite her school, she'd settled into her new routine.

Always having had a structured life, Bella was now finding it difficult to adjust to the prospect of filling the empty weeks which stretched out in front of her. She didn't even have anyone to hang out with, as her two best friends from school, Lulu Piper and Lily Simmonds, had gone off to Exeter and Bournemouth universities, literally as far as they could travel before southern England petered out into the sea. Even though they frequently contacted her via WhatsApp and Facebook, their excited tales of freshers' week, new friends and new experiences made Bella feel more isolated and cut off than ever. Although she'd applied for half a dozen jobs in addition to the library post, she'd received no letters as yet inviting her to interview, which she found disconcerting. So, in-between going for walks with her drawing pad to sketch the elegant Georgian buildings in Lancaster city centre, she decided to find out all she could about her own past. First of all she took out the few things she had relating to her father: a crumpled photo, a handwritten note to her mum and a guitar pick, and laid them out on her bed. In her mind, she'd always pictured Bradley to be like Elvis Presley, singing sweet lullabies to her in his slow, southern accent, but as she twisted the guitar pick in her hand, she conceded this to be unlikely. As she placed the meagre collection of mementos carefully back into the drawer, she worried that the idealised image she'd built up of her long-lost father in fact had nothing to do with reality after all.

*

Anna waited for Barbara at a table in a quiet corner of the Cosy Cafe, the windows annoyingly misted by the rain. She and Barbara had been best friends since they'd met forty years ago while picking up their daughters from primary school. Chatting at the gates at 3pm every day, they'd quickly formed a deep friendship based on their similar philosophies on life, as well as sharing the same wicked sense of humour. Over the years, they'd gone through the similar ups and downs of marriage and motherhood together and had been each other's crutch when their husbands had passed away two years apart.

Sitting with her back to the wall gave Anna a good view of the cafe, its tables draped with pristine white cloths and adorned with pretty vases of cream and pink roses. With its mismatched chairs and Eternal Beau crockery, it had the homely feel of a tearoom, which appealed to her much more than the proliferation of popular coffee chains which had popped up all over town in recent years. Who wanted an over-priced cinnamon-sprinkled choco-moco latte when a cuppa with two sugars sufficed? Looking up, Anna smiled as Barbara headed her way, the newly coloured blonde waves of her thick hair framing her face which was relatively line-free, her green eyes as bright as emeralds. Dressed in a tailored navy jacket, elegant cream slacks and flamboyant red boots, Anna realised her friend looked ten years younger than her, suddenly making her feel her age. She was glad at least that she'd made an effort today, accessorising her black knee-length coat, which she'd bought in the Wallis January sale, with a scarlet chiffon scarf.

"How are you?" Anna smiled at her immaculate-looking friend.

"Good, thanks. I have some news." Barbara sat opposite Anna, her perfectly made-up face lighting up as she excitedly tapped her pearlised acrylic nails on the table. "Sian's pregnant again!"

"Congratulations! So this will be grandbaby number six?" Anna smiled, finding it hard to keep up and hoping she hadn't forgotten anyone.

"I know, at this rate between Sian and Laura we'll have enough for a football team!" Placing their coffee and cake order, they spent some time discussing their respective children and grandchildren before Barbara leaned forward, her forehead furrowed in concern. "Are you alright, Anna? Only you look really pale."

"Just a bit tired, that's all, I've been feeling a little run down recently," Anna sighed, loosening her scarf.

"You should go to the doctor for one of those over-seventy check-ups," Barbara suggested, unbuttoning her jacket. "It gives you piece of mind if nothing else."

"Yes, I'm sure it does. But it's not just that. It's Bella. Her reluctance to make a decision on her future is driving Sarah around the bend." Anna paused, knowing her friend would offer her sound advice. "And Sarah being Sarah, she never stops harping on about it every time she phones. She just wants to see Bella settled, I get that, but I think she's going about it in the wrong way by pressurising her. My granddaughter is so strong-willed! But I can't say anything to Sarah about education. She knows best, I realise that, but I sense a full-blown confrontation between the two of them if this carries on."

"Tell me about it! Sarah's concerned about Bella and you're worried about them both. Being a grandmother is almost as difficult as being a mother, probably worse because you seem to spend all your time biting your tongue. Hopefully, one day Bella will just have an epiphany and find her direction, like our Bethany did. She's applying to do a veterinary degree, for pity's sake!" Barbara threw her hands in the air dramatically.

"Where did that come from?" Anna asked, bemused as Barbara's eldest granddaughter had always been stagestruck and had seemed more interested in her ballet than biology lessons, or so she'd thought.

"No one has any idea! As a child she was always scared silly of dogs; she even avoided walking past the gate where an Alsatian lived a few doors down!" Barbara paused, inspecting her nails. "My point is, Bella will find her own way in her own time. You and Sarah just need to give her a bit of breathing space!"

"Try telling Sarah that! At the moment, Bella's at a loose end and so she's found out all sorts of stuff about the Polish airmen in Blackpool during the war. She's got a bee in her bonnet about collecting all the information she can about my father." Anna took a tissue from her coat pocket to wipe her glasses which had steamed up.

"But you're a bit more reticent?" Barbara read the concern in her friend's eyes. "I know you were torn about telling them both about Tad this summer."

"Yes, I was but, actually, I'm glad I did. It's given Bella something to focus upon when otherwise her life seems pretty directionless at present." Anna bit her lip. "I'm just concerned about what she'll bring to light. I'm all for letting sleeping dogs lie."

"You need to warn her off a bit, Anna." Barbara's expression was kind. "You don't want her digging up anything too painful for you."

"I know. But I also don't want to dampen her enthusiasm either and that's been holding me back. Poor love, she has little enough family as it is with Bradley's Stateside disappearing act!" Anna tidied the laminated menus back into their holder. "But I will mention something to Sarah."

"Be sure you do," Barbara sighed, reading her friend's signals that she wanted to change the subject of their conversation. "Well, now that's all sorted, here's the big decision. Do you want the coffee éclair or the vanilla slice or shall we share them?" Barbara suggested as the waitress approached with their tray.

But it was far from sorted. As Anna bit into the creamy custard and flaky pastry, her mind rewound to her school days as she thought about the girls in her form whose dads had returned from the war. She remembered sitting in the lavatory weeping, knowing that she would never experience her own joyous reunion with her father. Long since having laid him to rest, she now had mixed emotions about what digging into the past would unearth.

11

Czechoslovakia, February 1940

As we approached the Czechoslovakian border knowing that Nazi patrols would be more frequent and vigilant here, Antusz warned that travelling in a foursome would inevitably attract their attention. Although I argued we would be better off staying together to pool our resources and knowledge, I was soon overruled by the others.

"Tad, you should go with Jerzy," Antusz sighed, his body lumbering with fatigue. "You have the knowledge and skills to endure this difficult terrain, while he is a city boy and wouldn't survive very long on his own."

"But Antusz, what about Marek and you?" I protested feebly, staring at the grey landscape but unable to spot a single living creature among the vast forests and mountains.

"We'll look after each other as we always have," Marek

said, pulling me to his body, a colossal bulk. "Goodbye, old friend. May God journey with us all."

So Antusz and Marek paired off while I went with Jerzy hoping to approach the border with minimal attention. Saying swift but heartfelt goodbyes, we wished one another well but, such was the perilous nature of the onward journey, we made no arrangements to meet up further down the line. Watching my friends whom I'd grown up with walk off into the distance until they became black specks before disappearing from my sight altogether, I felt more alone than ever.

After another two hours of trudging through the unrelenting snow, Jerzy and I stopped dead in our tracks, looking at the path as it twisted and turned upwards before disappearing into the grey blanket of mist obscuring the mountain's summit. As I peered into the swirling cloud, I realised that Dziadek, Jacek and I had never gone beyond this point on our camping holidays, partly because the High Tatras were difficult to cross on foot but mainly as the top of the mountain marked the border before descending into Czechoslovakia on the other side. I'd never had any cause to leave Poland before.

But as driving snow stung my face, I saw that the time of childhood games belonged to another lifetime which was irreconcilable with the dangers facing me in the present. So, with a heavy heart I headed up the rocky track with Jerzy until we reached the wooden hut on the mountain's crest marking the border crossing. Seeing it was manned, Jerzy and I each said a quick prayer before opening the door to face whatever waited for us on the other side. The Germans also occupying Czechoslovakia, I'd heard stories while in Krakow that the border guards had been trained to organise manhunts using bloodhounds, a fate I hoped would not be ours.

"*Dobrý večer!*" the middle-aged guard greeted us. Although my eyes were blinded by snow, I managed to make out that he was dressed in a dark overcoat and stooping over a stove in a vain attempt to keep warm. My ears muffled by my hat and scarf, I couldn't distinguish whether his tone was friendly or not. But luck was on our side that day. Despite the Polish, Slovak and Czech languages being distinctly different, they have enough similarities to understand one another's. So accordingly the border guard, Jerzy and I engaged in a fruitful discussion over warming cups of ersatz tea, although we were vigilant not to divulge anything personal about either ourselves or our families and I noticed the Czechoslovakian did the same. Presently, this pleasant interlude came to an end with the man doing a cursory check of our papers, patting us on the back and wishing us 'good luck' as we set out in the snow again.

Descending the other side of the mountain, mixed emotions about departing Poland inevitably conflicted in my mind as I tried to convince myself for the hundredth time that leaving my homeland was the right thing to do, that I would be better placed to fight for its freedom from a foreign shore. But it was cold comfort as I thought of Dziadek alone in his workshop, his loved ones far away while he might be in all kinds of danger himself.

In the event, my worries proved well founded as the journey across Czechoslovakia was the most dangerous we'd encountered yet, with an arduous slog over difficult terrain. The weather conditions deteriorated by the hour with high winds blowing snow into deep drifts, which made it difficult to walk or even see what lay before us. Our boots forever sinking into the frozen snow, it was exhausting just to put one foot in front of the other but, somehow, we kept going. Growing up in the mountains and forests with Dziadek and Jacek had set me in good stead, and Jerzy and I managed to cross valleys and forests intersected by river gorges, foraging what we could off a land in the icy grip of winter and camping in the least exposed spots as we swung south. In many places the route was dangerous, requiring great strength and stamina, but luckily Jacek had taught me survival skills which I put into good use now. Just as on that day when he'd pulled me out of the river, my brother saved my life over and over again during my escape from Poland, despite being miles away from me by then.

During that time, I lost my spare clothing and the little money I had on me when a patrol almost caught me trying to fill my water bottle from a stream. Luckily I managed to evade them by hiding under brushwood, such a narrow escape that, as the Nazi soldiers passed, I could have reached out and touched their boots. Whether it was being constantly wet and cold but, just over a week into the trek across Czechoslovakia, I began to feel unwell. Having faced the full fury of a snowstorm that afternoon with no choice but to continue over exposed grounds, my head thudded with wave after wave of pain. That evening Jerzy and I found a barn to shelter in and I knew that my survival depended on my ability to make a fire, so once again I turned to Jacek, following the methods my brother had taught me. Setting to work with branches and twigs we'd collected from the forest floor, I realised it was a difficult balance to keep the fire burning enough to generate the heat needed to keep us alive but to produce little enough smoke as to not signal our presence to either the people who lived here or passing patrols. Yet another thing my brother would make appear effortless, if he were here.

In the early hours of the next morning, I woke with a raging fever. The fire reduced to a pile of smouldering ashes, I lay on my straw bed sweating and shivering, a pain spreading across my chest each time I took a breath while seemingly every muscle in my body ached. Despite Jerzy's comforting encouragement, for the first time since we'd fled Zakopane, I felt truly terrified that I might die there and then in that barn in the middle of nowhere in a country that wasn't mine; that it had all been for nothing. That I would never see Jacek, Dziadek or my motherland again.

As the day dawned, although my aches had subsided somewhat (probably down to sleep rather than any abating of my illness), I still felt unwell. Overnight, I'd developed a rasping cough and I spent ten minutes on waking coughing up yellow-stained phlegm. Needless to say, I had no appetite, but Jerzy forced me to drink some of the ersatz tea the farmer (kindly this time) had brought for us along with some bread. That day was the most difficult yet as we pushed on, every mile a marathon for me as I struggled not only with the driving snow and the uneven terrain but also with the knowledge that every single step took me that little bit further away from my homeland and all that I loved. That night, as Jerzy and I took shelter in yet more farm buildings whenever I coughed, my phlegm was streaked with blood.

12

Blackpool, September 2020

"This is an interesting article, Gran." Bella glanced up from her laptop and out of the window to her grandma's neglected back garden. The flowers in the border, in Anna's favourite shades of purple and lilac, had died with the summer and were in want of a prune before winter set in. Meanwhile, the lawn needed a good mow and weeding, being strewn with dead plants and fallen leaves. Papa George had always been a keen gardener, a passion Bella's mum had inherited. Passing her interest down to Bella, mother and daughter made a habit of visiting their local garden centre most Sunday afternoons to pick up a plant or two and enjoy tea and a scone on the terrace in the walled garden there. Bella made a mental note to mention to her mum to do a little tidy up when she next came to Blackpool for the day. Up to her eyes with the new university term, Bella knew that an afternoon's gardening would help to de-stress her.

"What have you discovered, sweetheart?" Anna nudged away a pile of cookery magazines from the table to set down a tray laden with two cups of tea and a plate of freshly baked rhubarb and ginger scones.

"It says that when the Polish airmen first arrived in Blackpool, they were thought of as over-boisterous and unused to the reserved British ways of the time. Some drank too much, got into punch-ups and they were labelled collectively as trouble-makers." She paused to take a bite of her buttered scone. "Umm, delicious, Gran, these scones are sooo good."

"Thanks, Bella, it's a new recipe I'm trying out so you're my guinea pig!" Anna said, taking a delicate sip of tea as she gazed out at the garden. She winced to think how she'd let it go since George's death, but she simply didn't have the inclination or energy to do anything about it. Seeing her granddaughter was waiting for a comment about the Poles, she added, "But surely the fact many were combat veterans who had already seen action, as well as possessing a deep hatred of the Nazis, counted for something?"

"Apparently it was seen as a drawback rather than a bonus. Stiff-upper-lipped RAF types feared they would not be able to control the Poles because of what they'd witnessed and experienced at the Nazis' hands." She tucked her long fringe behind her ear. "Listen to this. One squadron leader actually referred to them as 'hurtling bolts of fury, beyond all reason and authority', saying that if the Polish men were to be of any use then they needed curbing of their dangerously suicidal temperament!"

"That's awful," Anna reflected, her teacup clattering as she replaced it into her saucer. "You'd think they would have been welcomed with open arms by everyone here for trying to help the Allies to win the war."

"Far from it." Bella shook her head vigorously so her pale fringe fell across her face. "In fact, in training, the Polish airmen were humiliated by being made to practise on bicycles until they could prove that, on command, they could wheel left or right in formation. Once in planes, they were closely marshalled too before being dispersed among British squadrons so they'd be sure to knuckle down."

"From what Mother told me, when many of them arrived they were actually sick and exhausted from their long journeys, which had been mostly on foot across Europe on escape routes to Britain. I've always felt that they were extremely brave," Anna said proudly, taking another drink. "I also know they became some of the most skilled and daring pilots in the RAF. They certainly proved the upper echelons wrong!"

"They did! Apparently to the surprise of the high-ups in the RAF, the Poles quickly fitted in well. They proved superb flyers, disciplined in the air, brave but not foolhardy at all, and popular with their British comrades." Bella smiled, reaching for another scone. "In fact, it says here that it is hard to overstate the impact the influx of Poles made on the backs-to the-wall mentality of Britain when they arrived here in the early years of World War II."

"And not forgetting their impeccable and old-fashioned romantic manners! I recall Mother telling me they were so polite and attentive, bowing from the waist and clicking their heels when they were introduced. In fact, my grandmother said she was enchanted the first time she met Tad as, when she went to shake hands with him, he bowed his head, took her hand and touched his lips to it. It's such a lovely, romantic custom, totally unacceptable with today's young women, though!" She looked at her granddaughter, who rolled her eyes. "Apparently, the English girls they met were bowled over by them. No wonder some 'put-out' British airmen took to stitching a 'Poland' label on the shoulders of their RAF uniforms when they went to dances in the hope of getting in on the action!" Anna chuckled.

"It wasn't just the Poles' flamboyance and obvious charm that was attractive, but also the fact that they were undaunted in the face of the dangers before them," Bella added. "Their nation had been crushed under the jackboots of the Nazis, but these men had resisted as best they could and, though beaten and exiled, they were never going to lie down. They were fighters, not quitters. And fight they did with great distinction and success."

"Yes, I think it was Tad's drive and determination as well as his kind nature which attracted Mother to him, as she definitely wasn't one for flattery." Anna fanned her face with her hand, suddenly hot. "She was always a very self-sufficient woman who knew her own mind."

"What exactly was Great-Grandma Eirlys doing when war broke out?" Bella asked, noticing her grandma's red face despite the cool temperature today. Perhaps her tea had warmed her up, as Bella knew she always drank it scorching hot.

"Well, it was quite sad because she went to the Girls' Grammar School where she did well enough to gain a place at college. She always wanted to teach, you know, but unfortunately her mother, having been widowed in the First World War, couldn't afford to fund her training and there were no grants in those days, of course. After she left school she ended up helping her mother in the guesthouse, effectively seeing her ambitions nipped in the bud before they'd had the chance to flower."

"Things were so different for young girls back then," Bella mused, brushing crumbs from her mouth. "Although I think perhaps we have too many options now! That's why it's taking me so long to decide what to do next."

"Yes, maybe you do! Anyway, when war broke out, Mother was twenty and in a strange way it was the most exciting time of her life. Of course, her job at the Vickers Armstrong Factory opened a whole new world to her," Anna said, her face animated as she spoke of her mother.

"Since you mentioned where Great-Grandma Eirlys worked, I've been reading up about the factory and it's a really fascinating place." Bella leaned back in her comfy chair. "In the Second World War, the site was called RAF Squires Gate."

"That's right, Bella, and the hangars were easily converted into the vast factory floors needed to assemble the plane parts. Mother said it was a huge complex." Anna drained her teacup. "So big she had to cycle around it."

"Yes, it was. They produced over three thousand Wellington Bombers there, twenty per cent of all Wellingtons manufactured during the war." Bella read from her laptop screen. "At its height, over ten thousand people worked on the site. Do you know whether Eirlys was on the factory floor?"

"Yes, being grammar school educated, she worked mainly on the switchboard," Anna added. "She said the working hours were very long and even the toilet breaks monitored! It was considered unpatriotic if you didn't work as hard as you possibly could."

"It must have been a complete culture shock for her," Bella commented, closing down her laptop, and the silence stretched between them as she put it into its case before tidying her notes.

"Have you had any time to consider your university applications?" Anna said after a few minutes, lifting her hands in a gesture of surrender as she saw the stormy look on Bella's face. "Okay, I admit your mum asked me to have a word, because she's worried and says you always seem to get into an argument every time she broaches the subject."

"I know. But it's difficult discussing it with her, as she spends all her time at the university where she's surrounded by academics who think that studying is the be-all and end-all. But I don't want to study for studying's sake. I need to decide what I want to do for a career and then work back and choose a degree that will get me there!" Bella said tetchily.

"Have you told your mother that?" Anna sighed. She knew her daughter hadn't accepted that Bella was fast growing up before their eyes but still saw her as a child needing direction. Bella, on the other hand, was clearly resentful of this fact and her refusal to cooperate was a form of protest, which if left to fester, Anna feared would result in a serious rift developing between the two, something she didn't know how she would bear.

"Not in so many words no," Bella said sulkily. "Mum isn't interested in what I have to say. I've got an interview for a temporary library job at the university, though, so if I'm successful maybe that will cheer her up?"

*

That evening after work Sarah drove down to Blackpool to take her mother and Bella around the illuminations, starting as they always did at the Pleasure Beach in the south and culminating with fish and chips in Bispham in the north. "Did you know that the Pleasure Beach remained open throughout the war?" said Sarah, as the three of them sat in the car which was crawling at a snail's pace down the light-festooned promenade. "Although from 1939, the lights didn't shine for a decade."

"I didn't know they switched off the illuminations during the war, but I suppose, thinking about it, it makes sense," said Bella, looking at the rainbow of lights reflected on the car window. "With the Luftwaffe bombing Merseyside down the coast, the seafront would have stood out like a beacon in the darkness."

"Yes, even though Blackpool was thought to be at low risk of attack compared to the east coast, they wouldn't have wanted to take any chances," said Sarah, looking up at gigantic chandeliers strung above them in silver lights.

"In response to the blackout, I recall Mum once telling me that my grandmother and many other Blackpool landladies had coloured bulbs installed in their front rooms to try to recreate the lights," Anna added, bewitched by

130

the greens and blues which mingled together overhead. "An attempt to bring a bit of cheer to those dark times, I suppose."

"A typical keep calm and carry on attitude," commented Bella, clicking away on her iPhone, capturing the animated tableaux and the golden tower soaring like a rocket up into the night sky.

13

Despite feeling desperately ill, I knew we had to keep pressing forward if we were to survive. Unfortunately, the journey became ever more perilous and, on nearing Czechoslovakia's southern border with Hungary, Jerzy and I lost our way in a snowstorm. Barely able to see to put one foot before the other, the snow blinded us, hiding trees so that we stumbled into them. These conditions and my illness meant I began to lose my grip on reality, as in my delirium I couldn't remember where I was or what I was doing there. The trees around me became those in the forest behind our cottage in Zakopane and through them I saw light from the windows spilling across the snow and I knew Dziadek and Jacek were there waiting to welcome me home into the warmth and comfort of the fireside. It was then I saw my brother and grandfather emerge from the snow:

Jacek smart in his ceremonial uniform looking the image of our father, standing proud; Dziadek dressed in the blue overalls and apron he always wore when he was carving, his boots lightly sprinkled with wood shavings. All I wanted to do was go with them into the warmth.

"Tad! Get up!" Jerzy's urgent voice pulled me back into the real world just as my friend hauled me to my feet. "You can't go to sleep in the snow – you will never wake up again if you do. We must keep moving, we are very near the Czechoslovakian-Hungarian border. Don't give up now!" Jerzy put his shoulder beneath my arm to support me and we walked like this for several minutes, my friend keeping me talking until I was fully back to my senses.

The blizzard had been so intense for all we knew we could have been walking around in circles but, after a short time, visibility improved and we spotted a border post in the distance. I knew this was going to be the most dangerous border to cross as, moving from occupied into neutral territory, the post would almost certainly be manned by German guards. However, on drawing closer, the flag flying from the hut filled us with profound relief. Red, white and green, we had somehow already left Czechoslovakia and entered Hungary, the whiteout having concealed our passage through the border. In celebration, Jerzy and I shared our precious last bottle of cherry vodka with the jolly Hungarian guard who took us into his hut where we warmed through by his fire. Our bellies full with the proffered soup, we carried on, and we were two of countless Poles who crossed illegally into Hungary that month.

Despite the deterioration of my health, reaching a country with a flatter landscape meant that we were able to make faster progress and so Jerzy and I travelled much more quickly, clinging to the cover of the trees. Although this remote countryside was only punctuated by a farm every five miles or so, we were, however, careful to remain on our guard at all times. I knew that the Germans were aware of this chain of escape, and that many of our countrymen had already been caught. We had no intention of being their latest victims.

As we trudged on into the night, heavy clouds gathered to the south, portending more snow. But that was the direction we were headed and so we had no option but to follow them, hoping that any snowfall would not be significant enough to hinder our journey. Continuing on, we were pushed back by the force of the wind, expending energy we could ill afford. I pulled down my hat and secured my scarf over my mouth so that only my eyes and the bridge of my nose were exposed. Looking skyward, the clouds shifted as though they'd been ripped apart to reveal a full moon, which glistened upon the snow-covered fields. Forging our way through the deep drifts, we followed the silver trail of moonlight, certain that God was leading us to sanctuary. Spurred on with renewed vigour, I was more determined than ever to reach a safe place where I could regroup and prepare to fight back.

Budapest was a city I'd read about in books as a child and had dreamed of visiting ever since. On my arrival, the Danube did indeed glitter in the sunshine as it flowed past the splendid Gothic parliament building in Pest adjacent to the Neo-Romanesque Fisherman's Bastion terrace perched resplendently on Buda Hill as though guarding Saint Matthias Church. But apart from that the reality was nothing like the dream as I barely had time to glimpse the architecture or the river as we focused on obtaining overdue medical treatment for what I knew was pneumonia.

At the beginning of the war, Hungary had declared itself as a non-belligerent nation and had refused to allow German forces in, making it possible for Poles like Jerzy and I to travel through the country. From Budapest we headed west, the mile upon mile of flat prairieland, although easier to negotiate, a constant reminder that we had left the high peaks of the Polish Carpathians far behind. Arriving at Lake Balaton at the start of spring, its wide, still blue waters were like a sea in comparison to the fast-flowing rivers of our homeland. In Budapest, we had learned that a Polish high school and college had been founded in Balaton by a local priest the previous October and that, under this cover, it acted as a transfer point for the evacuation of young men such as us to France. Here we were provided with false papers and it was Jerzy's and my intention to travel to France to join up with our compatriots. However, the war still snapped at our heels and in May 1940, just a few weeks after we'd arrived in Balaton, France fell to the Germans, closing that escape route to us.

With our goal still in mind of joining our fellow Poles to fight against the Nazis, Jerzy and I continued on to Yugoslavia, a country still mercifully flying the flag of neutrality. At the border, we encountered hundreds of Poles, some of them pilots who had been shot down during the invasion or who had been forced to abandon their planes due to a lack of fuel. I, of course, sought news of Jacek from everyone I could, but it was to no avail so I had no choice but to focus my attention solely on my own survival.

Entering Yugoslavia Jerzy and I travelled to the ancient city of Split, its mellow ochre rooftops contrasting with the dazzling turquoise of the Adriatic Sea. Despite being in the midst of a war, Split's Roman architecture was a feast to behold for students like Jerzy and I, and, during our sojourn, I penned the letters I'd written a thousand times in my head home to Dziadek, telling him I was safe. We stayed there several weeks where I was able to rest and recuperate, my symptoms gradually improving as, with daily hot food and drink, I began to feel stronger with each passing day. But as summer slowly gave way to autumn, the overcast skies turning the waters of the Adriatic a murky grey, we heard grim news of the political upheaval in Romania, our next destination. Like Hungary and Yugoslavia, Romania had declared itself neutral at the start of the war but since then its government had lost popularity and there were rumours of a fascist takeover, which would put the country firmly in the Axis camp, making it imperative that, if this was to be our escape route, we had to act quickly before another door was slammed in our faces.

So we promptly crossed the Romanian frontier from where travelled across the country, a vast, beautiful landscape whose hills and mountains reminded me of home. Making our way partly on foot and partly on trucks and buses, we eventually arrived in Tulcea, a town at the head of the Danube delta. In stories Dziadek had read to me, I'd always pictured this majestic river as the bright blue snake I'd seen twisting its way through Budapest, but the delta was a mosquito-infested swamp at odds with the idealized image in my mind. However, Jerzy, I and the other Poles who arrived alongside us, found ourselves billeted in comfortable barracks where the royal guards of the Romanian king had once lived and there we were able to regain our strength for whatever lay ahead.

With winter approaching and the possibility of Romania joining the Axis, I felt despondent. For the first time, I questioned whether what we had set out to do would ever come to pass. I thought how Jerzy and I, like thousands upon thousands of other Poles, had left behind everything that was dear to us, only to find ourselves living in constant fear of what would happen to us, of where we'd end up next. I often heard my fellow countrymen weeping in those lonely dark hours of the night, as they thought of everything they had lost. We had lost our country and, having no idea when or if we would ever be able to return, desolation soon spread among the refugees like an infectious disease.

We had to keep going, though, and decided our next move was to try to reach Bucharest to obtain papers. Cloaked by the relative safety of darkness one night, Jerzy and I managed to board a train. We paid the ticket collector, who, thankfully, asked no questions and we arrived in the capital city four hours later. Only the third city I'd been to since leaving Poland, I found Bucharest functional, with neither Budapest's finesse nor Split's stunning coastal setting. At the embassy, though, Jerzy and I were shocked by the numbers of dishevelled Polish soldiers wearing torn civilian clothes waiting in a queue which wound its way out of the building, skirting two blocks. Before joining the rear, I spent an hour and a half scanning the hundreds of worn-out faces, searching in vain for my brother's. Waiting in line, I talked to a boy called Jan, who I discovered was the same age as I and had lived on a farm near Zakopane. Jan and his friends had already been there four days and he told us they were staying in a nearby hotel and that we could bunk with them. I had such hope that night but, after three days of returning to the embassy queue, Jerzy and I realised we were frittering away our money on the hotel while getting no closer to obtaining papers. So we reluctantly returned to Tulcea empty-handed. It was at this point I felt as though our journey had hit a dead-end, that we were destined to travel in circles, getting nowhere fast.

14

October blew in with wind and rain. Soaked to the skin cycling to the university, Sarah began to include a change of clothes in her backpack. Although the weather thankfully soon mellowed to scattered sunshine and showers, she had little opportunity to enjoy it, being snowed under with seminar preparation and marking as she got into the swing of the new academic year. She was also anxious about Bella, hoping she would find something worthwhile to occupy her time. To combat some of the stress she was feeling, Sarah made sure she fitted half an hour's yoga into her early-morning routine to get her into the right frame of mind for the day ahead. An hour's run after work pounding the terraced streets near her home, past the sprawl of the Boys' Grammar School and out to the unspoiled countryside of the Trough of Bowland helped relax her at the end of the day. The wide-open spaces gave her a chance to think and breathe while counteracting her guilty pleasure of enjoying a scone and pot of tea at her favourite Victorian tearoom in town on Wednesday afternoons.

As the relatively organised chaos of the first few weeks of term came to an end, the freshers becoming accustomed to university life while her second- and third-year students resumed their studies, so Sarah settled too. The syllabuses unaltered, she spent the majority of her free periods rejigging old lectures and catching up with her colleague of the past ten years, Joel. His travels during the summer holiday read like a bucket list of the average Joe Bloggs. He'd already regaled to Sarah his adventures in the Philippines, Malaysia, Vietnam and, most profusely, India, which he was using for the setting of the thriller he was working on, *Death in Delhi*. When she'd told him about Tad, he'd mooted her grandfather's story might make a good debut novel for her. But Sarah had given him short shrift, insisting she didn't know enough about Tad to hide the real reason for not attempting such an undertaking – a lack of confidence in her own writing. An excellent creative writing teacher, actually producing her own work was another thing entirely.

"Need some sustenance?" Joel's friendly voice drifted into her consciousness as she looked up from her computer screen to see his well-built frame duck through the door with two steaming cups of coffee that Friday morning.

"I must have been sending telepathic messages to you next door." She leaped up to move a pile of files and papers so he could take a seat.

"Yes, or maybe it's just because it's the end of a very long third week back." He handed her a cup before settling into one of the red-padded, low seats used for tutorials as she took the one next to him. Seeing her office from this new angle, she noticed what a mess her desk was, heaps of half-marked essays vying for her attention with the mountain of administrative paperwork which was part and parcel of being a lecturer. Add bringing up a teenage daughter single-handedly into the equation, it was moments like this, exhaustion suffusing every part of her body, that she honestly wondered how she managed to fit everything into her overflowing life.

"Is it only the third week?" She smiled, flicking back a tumble of dark curls which had worked free of her tortoiseshell hairclip to take a sip. "Ooh, just what I needed."

"Caffeine? I don't honestly think I could live without it!" Joel said, casually folding his legs in front of him. "Do you want to go the whole hog with a chocolate digestive?"

"No, thank you," she said, laying her hand upon her flat-as-a-pancake stomach as she leaned back. "I don't want to negate the effects of my early-morning run."

"Oh yeah, your body's a temple. A bit like mine!" He patted his slightly protruding stomach, a grin spreading across his face. Sarah thought the smile made him seem younger than his forty-five years. With grey eyes and dark hair lightly sprinkled with silver, he was indeed growing old gracefully. After splitting from his wife the previous year, some of their colleagues had been intent on matchmaking them but they'd ended up disappointed as, despite enjoying Joel's company and his dry sense of humour, there was just something missing for Sarah. A spark, a connection, whatever it was. Maybe it would come with time, her old university friend and the only person she ever discussed her love life with, Cath, had told her. And as Joel sat in front of her, his expression intent, she pondered whether she should give him a chance in the romantic department after all.

"Got anything planned for tonight?" he asked, his expression turning serious.

"Marking and tidying." She indicated her disarrayed desk. Apart from her first edition of *Villette*, Charlotte Brontë's tale of a woman who had gained her independence by becoming a teacher, protected by a securely attached glass case, it looked like a bombsite; there was no point shying away from it. "Then some more marking tomorrow, then on Sunday—"

"Some more? You need to take a break, Sarah. There's a French film on at the Dukes theatre I thought you might enjoy, *Bonjour Tristesse*," he said, expectation audible in his voice.

"And what would you do?" she said, thinking how they often shared 'no strings attached' evenings together, beginning at Pizza Margherita and ending with a cocktail or two in the theatre bar. She'd been a good friend to him over the past months, giving him counsel through his messy divorce.

"Read the subtitles." He smiled, raising his dark eyebrows.

"I think I'll take a rain check tonight, Joel," she said, noting his slightly disappointed expression. "Bella and I've arranged a girly night in."

"No problem at all." Joel brightened, finishing his coffee in one slurp. "Well, I'll leave you to it, I don't want to be blamed for keeping your daughter waiting. Maybe some other time?"

"Maybe." Sarah smiled as he backed out through the door, hitting his head on the jamb before adding, "Enjoy your weekend, don't work too hard, Sarah."

Sarah winced as she finished the last of her coffee. Why had she said 'maybe', why not nip his hope in the bud, there and then? She should be cruel to be kind. But then the counter-argument came into her mind. Why not go out with him? He was attractive, intelligent and attentive, and Bella seemed so wrapped up in her own life these days to even notice, let alone care about her mother's. Why not have a little fun with a colleague? *Because it would all end in tears* came the answer in a resolute voice. *As it always does.*

Cycling home later that evening, the weight of her guilt at disappointing Joel lifted from Sarah's shoulders as she determined to make the most of the weekend. Genuinely too drained to go out for a meal and not wanting to resort to fish and chips this early in the term, she dropped by Booths where she bought some fresh ricotta stuffed tortellini, mascarpone sauce, ingredients for a salad, as well as a little treat of a bottle of chilled prosecco and tiramisu for dessert. Arriving home, Sarah snapped on the kitchen light and put the pasta and sauce into pans before setting up the breakfast bar for two and having a quick read of that morning's paper.

"Bella, tea's almost ready!" she shouted upstairs as she poured the wine before lighting the candle, the flame flickering in its jar and reflecting on the glasses. Truth to tell she didn't really like the breakfast bar, the black granite being far too modern for her taste, but the kitchen had just been decorated when they'd moved in three years before and she didn't have the savings to refit it in the pale Shaker style she wanted.

"Mum," Bella came bustling in, her white-blonde hair scooped back from her face with a gigantic pair of white headphones popular with Premier League footballers, her cropped orange-neon top and low-slung white jeans exposing her toned waist, "we'd better set another place – look who's here."

"Mum?" Sarah swept Anna into her arms, who was looking smart in a navy jumper embellished with pearls around the neckline and tailored trousers. "What's wrong? Why have you come up to Lancaster? Has anything happened?"

"Oh, spare me the third degree, Sarah. Can't an old lady visit her daughter and granddaughter if she feels the urge?" Anna looked conspiratorially over to Bella, whose face flushed with a somewhat sheepish expression as she laid out extra cutlery for her gran.

"Yes, but…" Sarah hesitated, seeing that her mother did indeed look perfectly well, "how did you get here? You didn't come on that interminable bus that calls in at every conceivable place between Blackpool and Lancaster?"

"I did, and actually it was quite a picturesque journey," her mother replied as they sat down and Sarah set about dividing the pasta into three portions instead of two. Luckily there was a garlic baguette as well as salad to pad out the meal. "I travelled up because Bella phoned me and wanted my help with something."

"With what?" Sarah eyed her daughter suspiciously.

"Planning a trip to Krakow." Bella raised her palm in a defensive gesture. "Oh, Mum, you know how I've been researching Great-Grandfather Tad on the internet; well, these past few days I've run into a bit of a dead end and I figured we could find out more if we actually went to Poland. Gran's up for it!"

"Oh, for heaven's sake, I hope you two are joking! Tad died seventy-five years ago, where would we even start? I bet you've given no thought to that, have you, Bella?" Sarah frowned.

"As a matter of fact, I have. We know from what Grandma Eirlys said that he was a second-year student at Jagiellonian University in Krakow when war broke out. They are bound to keep documentation of students, aren't they? We also know he had a brother, Jacek, so perhaps that's something we could look into? Maybe Jacek had a family of his own, meaning his descendants would be our cousins?" Bella offered, enthusiastically ripping off a piece of steaming garlic bread. "We might even be able to track them down!"

"Highly unlikely, and they would be very distant cousins!" said Sarah, nevertheless liking Bella's logical way of working all this out. Now she came to think of it, there were actually numerous avenues they could go down, potentially uncovering all kinds of facts. Surprising herself, she found the thought quite intriguing. She took a mouthful of pasta to give herself some time to consider before turning to her mother, who had an expectant smile. "You're sure you want to go to Poland, though, Mum? I know how Bella can be a persuasive little minx!"

"The truth is, Bella didn't have to twist my arm," her mother countered, sprinkling Parmesan on her pasta. "Since the air show I've been thinking about my dad a lot and I feel I owe it to him to find out what I can. And if it happened that there was nothing to discover, that I'd left it too late, I'd enjoy just seeing the sights in Krakow and connecting with the places he'd been. That's all I want to do. Sarah, you know your father never liked venturing beyond Scarborough or Skegness?" Anna paused as her daughter nodded before continuing.

"One year, I got really excited because he applied for passports, but it was only because he thought we needed them to travel to Scotland! Since his death, I've visited the Norwegian fjords and the Balearics, but I'd like to go abroad one more time before I die. And ever since Mum told me of my father, I've had a burning desire to visit Poland, to connect with his homeland."

"Oh, Mum, you're not going to leave us any time soon," Sarah slowly sipped her wine, "but I concede you both have a point. Tell the truth, Mum, I've been thinking about Tad since you showed us his photo and told us the part of his story you know, and I would be fascinated to discover more about him too. And I agree, there is no better place to start than Krakow!"

"I thought she'd go for it." Bella triumphantly clinked her wine glass against her grandmother's. "Mum's inquisitive, intelligent mind constantly whirring away, I knew she wouldn't be able to resist."

"Flattery will get you nowhere, Bella. But, okay, maybe we could go next summer? Then we could stay for a month and get a real feel for the country?" Sarah noticed her mother subtly shake her head.

"That's what I've been bursting to tell you." Bella couldn't keep it in anymore. "Grandma and I have been trawling the internet all afternoon searching for flights and hotels. We've found a hotel which is just a stone's throw away from the main square where the Christmas market is. We fly to Krakow on December 6th!"

"All booked and paid for!" Anna added with a glint in her eye.

"But that's…" Sarah stuttered.

"Your Christmas holidays, sweetheart." Her mother smiled conspiratorially at Bella. "We'll be spending Christmas in Poland, although you'll have to deal with all the e-tickets and emails. I can never seem to get my head around all those new-fangled computers. You recall your father was always the man for arrangements!"

"Yes, I do." Sarah remembered her chats with her dad in his home office where, after his retirement, he took care of the finances of their boarding house.

"Now, let's make some plans for when we get there! All I have to do is find a pen that hasn't been chewed to within an inch of its life!" Bella flipped open a notebook in the red and white of the Polish flag. "I won't have much time in the coming weeks now I've joined the employed of this world."

"Bella!" Sarah smiled. "You got the job at the university library?"

"Uh-huh!" Her daughter's cheeks turned crimson. "I went for the interview this morning. I didn't want to tell you and risk jinxing it."

"Well, congratulations!" Sarah drew her into a hug. "But I told you that I had every faith in you for good reason."

*

Bella's stomach churned as her mum drove her to work on her first day. But as their car wended its way past the tennis courts up the driveway to the campus, she focused on shafts of sun shining through the trees, which were resplendent in their autumn coats, and felt her gut calm. This was her first foray into adulthood and the world of work, and she was determined to do herself and her mother proud. Entering the vast library, she was struck by its silence and felt extremely self-conscious walking over to the vast enquiries desk, thinking she should have dressed a little less formally than the white blouse and black suit she'd worn for her interview.

"Hi, I'm Bella Farland. I've come to report for work." She smiled at the young woman behind the desk, having heard people say that line in movies.

"Bella." A tall man spun around from the other side of the desk. "I'm Will Beckett, pleased to meet you. I'll be showing you the ropes, so to speak."

For one of the few times in her life, Bella was rendered speechless. She had never met anyone like Will Beckett before. With a dark fringe flopping over deep brown eyes, casual pale blue shirt and smart jeans, he was like no boy she'd ever known in school. Estimating he was a good few years older than her, he exuded a sophistication which left her weak at the knees. "Just you lead the way." She smiled eventually.

"We'll begin on the top floor and work our way down," he said, his lip curling slightly as he nonchalantly threw the girl at the desk a half-smile. Walking to the lift, Bella kept up with his long stride, aware that they were turning the heads of female students left, right and centre.

15

But I'd come this far, leaving behind everyone who was dear to me, and I wasn't about to give up. Our next objective was to make the journey back to Bucharest in another attempt to obtain travel documents from the embassy. Travelling through Romania was becoming increasingly dangerous, making our escape imperative. We found out that a local bus travelled to the city every morning and so, before daybreak on October 31st, Jerzy and I went along to the bus station where the vehicle was due to start its journey. Mingling among women taking their produce to market, we offered to carry their crates of chickens and boxes of apples on board, help which was gratefully received while giving us something to hide behind when seated. A heart-stopping moment came when the bus was ready to leave and a serious policeman boarded, which I'd heard was common practice, to check whether there were any Poles on board. In response I dug my nails into my palms, deep enough to draw blood, while Jerzy sat on the other side, gazing out of the window. But luckily for us, the policeman merely had a short chat with the driver with whom he was evidently acquainted and then disembarked, and I breathed again.

Reaching the capital, we headed straight to the embassy, determined not to fail this time. Fortunately for us, there weren't any queues that day and so, in seemingly no time, Jerzy and I reached the desk and spent the next few hours answering questions on every possible aspect of our lives. Two days later we returned and, to our profound relief, were presented with passports and tickets for a ship sailing from the port of Constanţa to Haifa. We were informed we would be travelling with a group of Polish Air Force mechanics and given the name of the hotel where we would be staying in Constanţa. When we arrived we were to remain in our hotel room until the time came to board the ship.

The ship setting sail in early November meant the weather was inclement and unsuitable for a sea voyage. My fellow compatriots, including Jerzy, were terribly seasick and needed no persuasion to keep out of sight below decks. As for me, this was my first journey by sea and I loved every minute of it! Whenever conditions permitted, I stood on deck, bewitched by the ever-changing colours of the sea and sky. I watched as the continent already clouded by war retreated into the distance but knew that the conflict would no doubt follow us wherever we went; we were merely one step ahead.

Sailing past Istanbul, I got a glimpse of the Hagia Sophia, a truly glorious building with its soaring sixth-century dome, before we continued through the Dardanelles, where we saw the pinky-red dawn reflect on the heaving waves, the most beguiling sight I'd ever seen in my life. Stopping off in Greece to pick up more of our countrymen, it would have fulfilled a lifetime ambition of mine to see the ancient architecture of Athens, particularly the Acropolis, but we'd been through so much to get to this point of our journey, we couldn't risk leaving the boat. By the time we set sail for Palestine, the boat was full to capacity, the decks crammed with people. Jerzy and I now had to share our cabin with six Polish airmen, and we enquired whether any of them recognised Jacek's name or knew what had happened to his squadron. But they didn't know him and, in the chaotic situation in Poland, had no information on the fate of any of the squadrons.

The remainder of the voyage passed uneventfully and at last we reached our destination, the port of Haifa. Part of the British protectorate, it was in Palestine that Jerzy and I enlisted in the Polish Land Forces under British High Command. It was also there where I made the most momentous decision of my life so far. Up to this point, I'd just been driven by the need to fight back against the Germans but had no practical idea on how I would achieve this. However, talking to a boy called Michal who was a few years older than I who had trained in the same cadet school as my brother, I was drawn into his enthusiasm about flying. Of course while at university I had undertaken some basic military training at Nowy Targ but had really never wanted to enter into the army like Father. Suddenly, though, I knew very clearly what I must do. The decision I made that day to become a flyer was to change my life forever.

I spent that Christmas in Palestine. Looking up into the starlit sky on Christmas Eve, I was filled with a sense of peace and hope, despite the chaos of war that held the world in its grip. I was standing on the land where on this night almost two millennia before, my Saviour, the Prince of Peace, had been born in the humble surroundings of a stable. Feeling close to Him, I said my prayers, putting my trust in Him to give me the strength I needed to face whatever lay ahead.

From Haifa, Jerzy and I travelled to Egypt in March 1941. There, we trained and served in the Free Polish Brigade for the duration of the summer and into the autumn. The final leg of the journey to England took three months via South Africa before crossing the South Atlantic to the coast of South America to follow the Eastern seaboard up to Canada. The route was considered the least perilous, avoiding enemy U-boats and shipping, and the trip was thankfully without incident. From Halifax, Nova Scotia, Jerzy and I took the Bayano, a ship owned by Cunard White Star and we arrived in the United Kingdom at the end of January 1942 when we sailed into the port of Liverpool. I reported to the Polish Air Force Depot in Blackpool a couple of days later just in time to celebrate my twenty-second birthday.

Blackpool was like nowhere I'd ever been before. Jerzy nicknamed it a playground on the coast and, as I strolled around the town centre on my first afternoon, I marvelled at the ornate façade of the Winter Gardens and the iron fretwork of the tower. The Victorian and modern architecture sitting side by side each other was like nothing I'd ever seen before in the ancient city of Krakow and I found it truly beguiling. Dziadek would have been bewitched by it all, too, barely able to believe that such a place existed on this earth! And the people in the town were so hospitable, welcoming me into their homes as I walked their streets.

That first evening, Jerzy, I and two other Polish lads, Jan and Mike, whom we'd met at the debriefing centre, which was housed in an upmarket hotel I couldn't pronounce the name of, went out to a bar, where we were soon surrounded by a dozen girls wearing bright dresses and red-lipstick smiles. They made the country girls I was used to meeting in Poland seem very drab and dull. Flocking to us, I could tell they thought us handsome and brave men who had risked our lives to travel to Britain and fight to defeat Hitler. The young women seemed extremely taken by us and while the other boys took advantage, I found their behaviour a little unladylike, I have to admit.

The four of us were assigned lodgings in a former guesthouse on the promenade. Our landlady was called Mrs Matthews and her personality was as big as her ample behind. With her deep red hair and matching smile, she could have been anywhere from forty to her late fifties, it was difficult to tell. Whether there had been a Mr Matthews or any children, we didn't ask, but over the coming months this kindly woman came to look after us as though we were her own sons even though she was initially a bit reticent at having to manage a house full of airmen. She was, as she informed us on many occasions, more used to accommodating families from mill towns across Northern England as they enjoyed their coastal escapes. As well as us, there were also the RAF lads – Jock, Alfie, Tommy and Leslie– staying there. Whereas the Polish lads, Jerzy excepted, were country boys like me, the RAF lads had grown up in sophisticated cities like Edinburgh, Oxford and Warwick, and spoke with refined accents which we could barely comprehend. But they were friendly enough chaps who made us feel welcome in this foreign land far from home.

That first night on our walk back to our digs, we recounted our journeys from Poland, each one different, each one hazardous. It turned out that Jan had undertaken a similar route to mine and Jerzy's, escaping south via Czechoslovakia and the Balkans before taking a ship to Israel. Mike, however, had ended up in Morocco before completing the final leg of his journey to safety in England. As the moonlight filtered through heavy clouds catching the waves of the dark Irish Sea, Mike's face was animated as he described exploring the spice-scented alleyways of Marrakech and the main square, the Jemaa el Fna, with its snake charmers and wizen-faced purveyors of exotic medicines, before recalling his flight over the Atlas Mountains. But just as he was clearly rapt by the hullabaloo of the African market and the brown ridges of the mountain range beyond, all I craved was the market in Zakopane, the cool air from the surrounding snow-capped Tatras infused with aromas of dill and freshly baked poppy seed bread.

16

That Wednesday, Sarah had arranged to meet Bella for lunch at the Jolly Juicy Cafe, a friendly little place at the heart of the university campus decorated in a bright yellow colour scheme, the low sofas resembling giant bananas. Located on the south spine, it was a ray of sunshine sandwiched in-between the housing office, where people worked behind monochrome blinds, and the grey Students' Union building, which was adorned with slightly peeling posters advertising the Freshers' Ball and various university clubs. The Jolly Juicy Cafe had always been a favourite of Sarah's and, specialising in lush fruit smoothies and juice takeaways, it more than stood its own with the sprawling Costa Coffee opposite. Fortuitously, Sarah and Bella found a table for two between the newspaper rack and computer charging station, where a fraught first-year student was hammering his keyboard in what appeared a desperate attempt to finish his essay before its deadline.

"That could be you this time next year." Sarah picked at her chicken salad baguette. She tried to sound as casual as she could, even though she was getting a bit neurotic about her daughter actually sorting her life out instead of just going round in circles talking about it or else dodging the issue altogether.

"Nah, I'd get my essays submitted with time to spare." Bella smiled as she demolished her sun-dried tomato and mozzarella panini. "I've been taught by the best!"

"Any further ideas on what you might actually be studying?" Sarah tried to hide the exasperation in her voice, but it was becoming increasingly difficult. If Bella missed that year's university applications deadline, it would mean another twelve months of procrastination and changing her mind with every whim that took her fancy.

"Not really," Bella shrugged, "just that I want to do a degree which will enable me to get a really interesting job. I know what I don't want to do, though."

"What's that?" Sarah smiled at two girls from one of her first-year tutorial groups before turning her attention back to Bella.

"Teach. I mean, I wouldn't know where to start working with children and as for lecturing… I think you need to have a certain presence that commands respect." Bella slowly sipped her strawberry and blackberry smoothie. "You've definitely got that but I'm not sure that I—"

"I had to work at it, Bella. I don't consider myself a natural-born teacher," replied Sarah. "Any career worth having takes a lot of work and dedication, as does studying for a degree. You just have to make a decision, once and for all, and then stick to it."

"I know, Mum," Bella sighed, her exasperation audible, at which point her mother changed the subject.

"How's the job going?" Sarah took a sip of her passion fruit and guava smoothie.

"I think I'll be reciting the alphabet in my sleep soon! And my arms are aching from all that stacking," Bella smiled, "but Will's been really good showing me the ropes."

"I bet he has!" Sarah paused to choose her words carefully. "Bella, just watch him. I know Will Beckett is charm personified, but, well, he's twenty-six and you are eighteen—"

"I can take care of myself," Bella said sharply, sheepishly glancing around to check no one else had heard. Her mother made her feel about five years old sometimes.

"I know but… Well, this isn't like school. And I've heard stories about Will having a bit of a thing for freshers, even though he's into the third year of his PhD. Just take care, that's all, Bella. I know you're a sensible young woman, but men like Will… Well, his reputation goes before him—"

"Thanks for the heads-up, I'll bear it in mind," Bella said. Evidently miffed at her mother's interference once again, she stuffed a stack of crisps into her mouth to prevent herself from saying something she'd regret later.

After depositing Bella back at the library, Sarah hugged the sides of Princess Alexandra Square as dark clouds glowered overhead, portending rain. Turning off the square, she followed the north spine which was thronging with students, their giant rucksacks resembling turtleshells as they veered off in different directions through doors into various faculty buildings. Making the final few steps to the new state-of-the-art grey and green building which housed the English and Creative Writing departments, the heavens suddenly opened. Soaked to the skin in seconds by the torrential downpour, she arrived back at her office looking like a drowned rat and every bit as miserable as she felt.

"Here, let me get you a towel." Joel rushed to his feet, taking in her bedraggled appearance, her dark, wavy hair dripping wet, her shirt sticking to her skin as though she had just stepped out of the shower. "Nice lunch?"

"No, it was dreadful," she said, tears springing to her eyes as she slumped in her chair. "It's just so hard being a mother sometimes. I feel as though I can do nothing right."

"Here you go." He diligently wrapped the towel around her shoulders. She sensed he had the impulse to enclose her in his arms but knew this would be inappropriate and awkward. Besides, she had made it more than clear that she didn't want a relationship with him, or any man. "Too much baggage," she had said. Knowing romance was off the cards, having secured the towel, he retreated to the door. "If you ever want to talk about it—"

"Thanks Joel." She managed a smile. "You are such a good friend."

*

"Hi, partner in crime!" Will greeted Bella with a friendly smile. Dressed in designer jeans, a blue shirt open at the neck and his hair carefully arranged to look casual, he assumed that nonchalant air of his. "Nice lunch?"

"No, it was awful!" She stifled a sob. "Mum just won't let it drop about my university applications. I'm sick of having the same conversation with her over and over again; it's getting a real pain in the arse. I feel like Bill Murray on Groundhog Day!" She glanced shyly at him, taking care not to mention Sarah's characterisation of him as the university's resident Don Juan.

"Then give it a break." He smiled, lightly massaging her shoulder, which she found bizarrely soothing despite all the pent-up frustration bubbling inside her. "Come out with me to see the firework display next week?"

"Okay, yes I will," Bella blurted out, although by the time she said goodbye to him at five-thirty that evening, she still wasn't sure whether she'd agreed to Will's suggestion because she wanted to go out with him or if it had been a tiny act of defiance against her mum's dire warnings about his reputation.

17

Blackpool, February 1942

There were things we hated about those first weeks in England. The weather, for one, as strong gales whipped in from the sea, bringing mountainous waves which at high tide deluged the promenade, so very different to our cold and snowy winters back home. After a time, however, I found myself enjoying bracing walks along the beach when the tide went out, breathing in the fresh sea air which was so invigorating.

English food was quite a different matter, however, to which I will never become accustomed. Rationing was cutting deep and although it seems ungracious to mention it, I found some of the food unpalatable. Jan was so appalled by the glutinous yellow sludge called custard our landlady served us that he point blank refused to eat it. The RAF boys seemed to enjoy it, though, heaped on stodgy puddings with bizarre names like 'roly-poly' and 'spotted dick', with Jock joking that it surpassed anything served up by his mother, who he declared was the 'worst wee cook in Scotland'. It irked me that someone could speak of his mother this way, but I soon learned that it was part of the self-deprecating British humour which came with being a confident and strong nation.

On my journey north from the busy port of Liverpool, I'd heard talk of Blackpool being a coastal town and a popular holiday destination. As we'd travelled through Lancashire towns, the grey smoke which billowed from factories reminding me of the time Dziadek took us to the industrial town of Katowice to visit distant cousins, my anticipation grew at what we would find at our destination. Apparently Blackpool was somewhere quite different to anywhere else in the UK. More than a century ago, it had developed as a playground for the people of the industrial north, an escape from the drudgery of their working lives and it had enjoyed its position as the UK's premier holiday resort until war had broken out. Even amidst such trying times now, it didn't take a long leap of imagination to see why.

Seeing it for the first time with its beautiful tower seemingly rising out of the sea, it surpassed each and every one of my expectations. Feeling the sand scratch my bare feet as I walked on the beach, I enjoyed the peace of the place, counting my lucky stars that I'd landed in such an oasis. I soon discovered for myself that the seaside town's wealth was reflected in the grandeur of the lavish architecture of its formal buildings and magnificent hotels on the promenade. Making enquiries as to why the interiors of the public ballrooms were so extravagant, I found they'd been designed to give working-class people a taste of what would normally only have been experienced by the rich. I found myself warming to the town immediately.

But it was equally obvious that war had given the town a new role, the RAF having already requisitioned many hotels and guesthouses for billeting their personnel. So it also became the depot for Polish aircrew prior to being despatched to stations for training and operations. We new arrivals were sent to Goodwood Hotel in Hornby Road for debriefing and registration prior to assignment to our units. In the aftermath of Dunkirk, British forces had been left short of equipment and in pretty poor shape and, with the country understandably on invasion alert, the Poles were expected to fit in where we could. I have to say that some of my compatriots regarded the duties assigned to us as tedious and quite demeaning, resenting the fact that the nearby social club was reserved for officers only and not for the likes of us. But after all the turmoil and hardships I had been through, I just wanted a little normality restoring to my life.

On our third afternoon there, Jerzy and I decided to explore the town a little more. Wanting to thank God for my safe arrival on Allied shores, I asked an officer for directions to the nearest Catholic church. With its brick building situated on a busy road, Sacred Heart Church could not have been further removed from the wooden church surrounded by woodland where I'd worshipped all my life thus far. But as soon as I stepped through its doors, entranced by its exquisite pews and pretty stained-glass windows reaching up to the roof, I knew that I had found a new church many miles from home, where I could come and pray. That afternoon and every Sunday afterwards, I lit a candle there and prayed the rosary for my brother, my father, my grandfather and all my fellow countrymen.

Afterwards, Jerzy and I walked down to the seafront where I sketched the tower, which appeared to me to be standing vigil over the town scanning the horizon for danger. Walking around freely was an odd feeling, though. After our often-dangerous escape from Poland, it seemed bizarre that we had landed in this famous holiday resort, a place for rest, relaxation and fun.

On my seventh night in Blackpool, I was standing at a bar with Jerzy and a group of RAF boys enjoying a second round of beers, when, out of the blue, a man in his fifties approached us, shouting, "Polish scum, get back to your country!" I had no time to prepare myself for the full force of his fist as he punched me square on the jaw and I felt myself falling weightlessly through the air before I hit the floor, breaking the skin on my hands.

"Get a wet cloth!" I heard a young woman's voice cry. Opening my eyes cautiously, I focused on a pair of sparkling eyes and a lovely face lit by a kind smile. "Are you alright?" this vision whispered.

Truth to tell I had never felt more alright in my life apart from the ache in my jaw and stinging hands where the skin had broken. Despite her slight frame, the young woman helped me to my feet and, leaning on her, I managed to stumble outside, desperate to breathe some fresh air. As the cold night air cleared my senses, I was able to take a good look at my rescuer. I gauged her to be about my age, maybe a little younger, her dark hair pinned up in flattering folds and her brown eyes, while undeniably beautiful, also radiated intelligence and good humour.

"Thank you very much for helping me," I said in my careful English, hoping I had got the words right. "I'm Tad."

"I'm Eirlys." She smiled. "It means 'snowdrop' in Welsh."

I shook my head as I did not understand all of what she'd just said, apart from her name, which was just as lovely as she was.

Shortly after, Jerzy came out of the pub, casting a furtive glance behind him. Noticing a line of red cuts punched along his knuckles, I concluded he'd given the man who'd floored me a taste of his own medicine. We were soon joined by a group of girls, who were obviously with Eirlys and impatient to leave as one took her arm, saying, "Come on, Eirlys, it's getting late. Your mother will be so worried."

I smiled at Eirlys, noticing her hesitation which reflected my own reluctance to part. I wanted to see her again but, my head throbbing, at that moment I couldn't find the words I needed. Then I had an idea. I pointed up to the tower, then to my watch. "Three o'clock tomorrow, here."

"I'm not sure, I…"A frown clouded her expression before dispersing. "I can just about get here from Squires Gate when my shift ends." She smiled as I took hold of her hand and kissed her silky-soft skin before letting her leave with her friends, while Jerzy quickly led me away before the military police arrived.

That night, listening to the soft shush of waves coming in through the open window, I could not drift off to sleep for thinking of her. I rolled her name, 'Eirlys', off my tongue again and again before remembering she'd said it meant 'snowdrop'. Clicking on the light, I scrambled around the room for my Polish-English dictionary before settling back in bed, smiling. *Przebiśnieg. Snowdrop. Eirlys.* It seemed an appropriate name for her. At the start of each spring, Dziadek had always encouraged Jacek and I to spot these delicate, white flowers in his garden, saying their appearance marked the end of winter, that they were symbols of new beginnings. Instead of falling asleep, I sat up with my dictionary on my lap for hours, attempting to learn as many new English words as my brain let me in preparation for seeing Eirlys again. After that, I slept spasmodically. At 5am I dressed and headed out to the beach to walk in the darkness, the soft squelch of sand beneath my boots unfamiliar and yet somehow reassuring. Silver stars still pinpricked the sky, glittering upon the blackness of the water below. The push and pull of the waves comforting in my ears, I tasted the salty air on my lips and tongue. I said the new English words I'd learned over and over to myself as I anticipated seeing Eirlys again. She was a snowdrop not just in name but a sign of hope for me, spring following winter. For the rest of the day everything seemed to pass in a blur – breakfast, training, lunch, training – my thoughts overflowing with Eirlys.

Having dropped by at my lodgings to wash and spruce up, I reached Blackpool Tower at just after half past two, the redbrick circus building below skirted by dozens of sandbags in preparation for the predicted coastal bombings. Too nervous to anticipate whether Eirlys would show up and what would happen between us if she did, I turned my attention to study the tower in more detail. Standing directly below it, I appreciated just how big it was, soaring upwards as far as my eyes could see as I'd always imagined skyscrapers doing in New York. Attracting the attention of a group of young girls, I smiled back as I might do to a neighbour's daughters back home, only to see their mothers avert their eyes and hurry them away. And then Eirlys was there and everything else faded into the background. She'd left her hair fall towards her shoulders today in reddish-brown waves while her dress was forget-me-not blue.

"Hello," I smiled, "shall we take a walk?" Jerzy had taught me that phrase on our walk back from the pub the previous evening and it seemed to meet Eirlys's approval.

"That would be nice." She smiled, and we crossed the road, dodging a green-and-cream-painted tram. Safely on the pavement which ran alongside the beach, I felt Eirlys's fingers brush mine, the softness of a woman's skin unfamiliar to my touch. The only hands I'd felt before were Dziadek's, Tata's and Jacek's, all much bigger and coarser than mine. Aware this was new territory I was entering now, I hesitated.

"You can hold my hand, Tad, if you like," Eirlys whispered, her voice as sweet and soft as honey. Silently I slipped my hand into a loose clasp, my fingers intertwined with hers. And in that moment, thousands of miles away from the mountains and Dziadek's wooden cottage, the sea gently shushing in my ears, it felt I'd come home.

"You speak much better English than the other airmen," she observed.

"I learned it in school and at university." I paused, pondering what had happened to all the other boys I'd studied with, whether they were still in Krakow, whether they were still alive. But I didn't want to think about that with Eirlys by my side. "The air is so fresh here. I'd never even seen the sea before until a few months ago," I said, smiling as the wind whipped her hair off her face.

"I've been down to the beach almost every day of my life. It's never the same, it's changing constantly with the tides and the light." Eirlys smiled. "I love making sketches here and transforming them into watercolours when I get home."

"So you're an artist?" I replied, somehow unsurprised at her disclosure.

"Not really," she shrugged her shoulders, "I paint by candlelight when the rest of the house has gone to bed, when everything is still and silent and I can escape into my imagination."

"Yes, I know what you mean," I said, as suddenly memories transported me to Dziadek's studio, the air heavy with resin as he'd let me finish off an intricate carving of a deer. Looking up, I saw Eirlys was waiting for me to continue. "I was remembering Dziadek, he taught me to work with wood."

"Dziadek?" The Polish word sounded strange as she pronounced it.

"Grandfather," I said, and the word felt formal on my tongue. "He is a true artist and there is certainly nothing he doesn't know about woodcarving. It fills me with wonder when I see something he's carving appear from the wood: a figure, a face, an animal, a scene."

"Art is just a hobby for me. I'm not good enough to make a career out of it. For now, I have my job at the factory, but only until the war is over." She smiled, looking out to sea as though there was something waiting for her just beyond the horizon.

"You work at Squires Gate, you said?" I asked, it suddenly dawning upon me that we worked in close proximity with one another.

"Yes, at the Vickers Armstrong Factory where Wellington Bombers are assembled. Blackpool has a long aviation history, with the airport hosting Lancashire's first powered flight in October 1909. Over two hundred thousand people attended, flying flags. My mother told me it was a sight to behold," she replied proudly. "Anyway, the factory produces over one hundred planes a month for the RAF as well as the Free French, the South Africans and the Polish. It takes sixty hours to build a plane, with all parts of the bomber manufactured on site. We have the very best of drilling apparatus, metal lathes and riveting machines."

"It sounds like hard work," I replied, hoping that I didn't sound condescending, but, luckily, she didn't take it that way.

"It is, and long hours too. But it's well paid, and more importantly it makes me feel I'm contributing to the war effort. We are constantly reminded that the faster we work, the faster we will win the war and maybe there is some truth in that." She smiled. "Over ten thousand people work at Squires Gate."

"Yes, it's quite a sight when the shift changes and thousands of bicycles pour onto the roads," I replied, wondering whether she had cycled past me on her way to or from work.

"It is. More people seem to arrive every week from all over the country to meet the increasing demand." She looked out over the vast sands. "A few months ago over three hundred bombers had to be stored here on the beach awaiting the installation of propellers, as nothing is permitted to slow things down at the factory. It was a most peculiar sight!" She grinned.

"I would like to have seen that!" I smiled. "It seems like you enjoy working there?"

"I find it very rewarding, doing my bit for my country, for the men fighting, so to speak. I would never have got the chance to do anything like that if it wasn't for the war." She paused and watched as an oystercatcher puttered a few feet away, burrowing its bright orange beak into the wet sand in search for food. "What did you do before you came to England?"

"Before the war, I was studying architecture." I looked at Eirlys to check whether I was boring her but saw genuine interest in her eyes. "But my true love is woodcarving. My grandfather's been teaching me all his techniques since I was a small boy. It is a very old tradition in the Podhale region of Poland where we live."

"It sounds wonderful." She considered for a few moments. "To create something beautiful from an idea only you can see must be truly thrilling, Tad!"

"Yes, it's a curious mixture of precision and imagination." I wondered whether I had found the right words but Eirlys nodded and took my arm as we carried on walking south, leaving the main promenade, which was crowded with people, behind.

We walked in companionable silence for the next hour, each of us making brief comments about the weather and scenery. It was as though we both decided we didn't want to discover each other's life stories on this second meeting, that we wanted to get to know one another first through the shared experience of the present. As we left the buildings and bustle of Blackpool promenade behind, the compact, well-trodden sand of the beach was replaced by little hillocks of loose sand. Shifting beneath my feet, I struggled to walk, but Eirlys just laughed as seagulls cawed above before swooping down as though sharing her amusement. "These are the sand dunes." She laughed.

"They're so hard to walk on," I replied, my boots slipping and sliding on the unstable ground.

"You think so? Before the war, Blackpool's football team came here to train every day; running up and down the dunes kept them fit! I sometimes used to watch them play before the war stopped the football league schedule."

I shook my head, not completely understanding what she had just said. "Come on, I'll race you," she shouted, and suddenly she powered away from me, her dress a blue streak trailing like a streamer through the air. I ran after her, but I had no chance of catching her on this ever-shifting surface, my chest still weak from pneumonia.

"What?" She stopped, looking back, her hair windblown, her cheeks rosy.

"You're so fast for a—"

"For a girl!" she hooted. "Don't let my friend Maggie hear you say that. She was the school cross-country champion and I came a close second! We still do a three-mile run on the beach at 5am every day if you want to join us?"

"I'll have to decline," I said. "I think that sand is so strange to run on. My feet give way on me. A neighbour of ours visited Gdynia on the Baltic Coast a few years ago, so I had an idea from him of what a beach was and then, of course, I got my first taste of one in Split, but these sand dunes are like nothing I've encountered before. It is almost as though they're moving of their own accord."

"I've walked on them all my life." She smiled. "Did you know that sand dunes form over long periods of time, changing from flat beaches to high hills? A fisherman once told me that the sand is originally trapped by an obstruction on the beach, either by something natural like a plant or patch of seaweed or else a discarded piece of rubbish. It slowly builds up, but over time it usually collapses."

Recovering my breath, I grabbed her hand and ran up one of the dunes, pulling her along. As if to prove her point, the ground beneath our weight gave way and we fell through the air together. As we hit the yielding sand, I pulled Eirlys on top of me and she didn't resist. "My mother warned me what you airmen are like," she whispered, her face so close to mine that I felt her warm breath brush my cheek.

"Well, maybe she has a point with some of the RAF types," I smiled, thinking of Jock after a couple of pints, "but we Polish are polite, chivalrous and well-mannered."

"Not too polite, I hope." She smiled, leaning in to kiss me lightly on the lips. As I responded, she pulled back, her expression one of amusement. "Well, my mother may have been right after all." She stood, shaking the sand from her dress. "Speaking of which, I must be getting back to help her with tea."

I fought hard to disguise my disappointment. Was Eirlys underwhelmed with our kiss and, seeking to bring an end to our date, had made an excuse to leave? But as I got to my feet, she flashed a smile so bright that it felt like the sun had emerged from behind a dark cloud. "Same time tomorrow, beneath the tower?"

18

Bella admired the green-glazed vase sitting on the polished coffee table in her grandma's living room which was filled with an artful arrangement of coppery-toned chrysanthemums. "Gran, this is amazing work. You are so creative, it's a shame you were never able to cash in on your artistic flair."

"Thank you, sweetheart, but I don't think people would actually pay for my work! I'm just lucky to have a good pottery teacher." Anna sipped her tea. "Unfortunately, he looks more like Brian Blessed than Patrick Swayze, but we can't have everything in life, can we?"

"You've always been too modest, Mum." Sarah smiled. "You should have gone to art college when you left school, and don't give me the excuse about not getting the opportunity! It is up to each and every one of us to make the most of our talents." She glared pointedly at Bella, who, equally pointedly, was now looking out of the window at the garden.

Feigning deafness to yet another jibe, Bella was admiring the fruits of her and her mother's labours that morning. Her grandma's borders were now neat and tidy, pruned back in preparation for their winter sleep and the lawn looked in much better shape after they had swept it of its covering of fallen leaves. Her grass-stained jeans were a sacrifice worth making, as she'd enjoyed being out in the fresh air working with her mum, the conversation about her future being avoided for once. Bella hoped it could become a more common occurrence between them; that they would have more to agree on than disagree when her mum's voice suddenly broke into her thoughts.

"How about I run us all up to Sacred Heart Church this afternoon? That's where many of the Polish airmen worshipped during the war. Considering how devout you said Granddad was, there is a good chance he would have attended some of the services there."

"Yes, I'd like that. I remember I went along a few times when I was Bella's age and even considered converting to Catholicism." Anna smiled. "As an impressionable teenager, I was taken in by the beauty of the church's surroundings, the carved Stations of the Cross and the statue of Mary, not the right reasons for conversion at all!"

Following afternoon tea with Anna's homemade cinnamon scones and apple butter, Sarah drove them the mile or so to Sacred Heart Church near the centre of town, the windscreen wipers working furiously to keep the sudden squall of autumn rain at bay. The road and buildings indistinct beyond the misted-up window, Bella felt cut adrift in the back of the car and used the quiet time to imagine her great-grandfather and his friends walking this same route all those years ago. They were literally following in Tad's footsteps, she thought, as her mother brought the car to a stop outside the church, its bricks mellowed to yellow through time. "Here we are then, Bella," Anna announced excitedly.

Stepping inside, Bella had never visited a church like it. Strolling around, she saw the chairs were arranged to mirror the octagonal red-painted ceiling, which was Chinese lantern-like in appearance. Positioning herself beneath it, she gazed up at the deep-brown wooden supports, substantial and sturdy enough to hold in place the hundreds of ruby slats which made up the main body of the roof. Looking higher still, she noticed how these in turn rose to some delicate white and blue fretwork before reaching the window at the top, which gave the roof the effect of disappearing into the blueness of the sky. Taking a seat, she continued gazing out of the high windows to the heavens above before turning her attention to the Stations of the Cross finally focusing upon a marble effigy of Mary, her hands clasped in obedient prayer.

"I didn't know this church existed, even though I must have been in the vicinity loads of times," Bella remarked as her grandma quietly sat down beside her, "with the North Pier just at the end of the road, as well. The roof and the architecture are just exquisite, aren't they?"

"Indeed they are, Bella. Maybe now you can understand what an effect they had on an artistic teenager like me, my dear," Anna said, softly taking hold of her hand.

"I was just thinking how the interior of this church is so ornate, so inspiring I could look at it all day. But it doesn't fit with the outside at all, which is rather ordinary Victorian in its appearance." Bella closed her eyes, picturing the airmen such as her great-grandfather, smart in their uniforms, sitting in this space, saying the Mass in Latin every Sunday.

"No, I've always thought that its colourfully decorated interior doesn't look like it belongs to an English church somehow," her grandmother said, seeing how the pulpit jutted out to enable the priest to stand amongst his congregation. "That maybe churches in Poland were like this and that is why it appealed to these brave men like my father, as praying here reminded them of home."

"I like that idea." Bella smiled, thinking how the faith of these young men must have brought them strength in times of fear and loneliness. "I'm eighteen, near enough the age a lot of the flyers would have been, and I can't even decide what I want to do next year. Putting myself into their shoes, I just can't imagine how it must have felt to have to leave their country and their families, not knowing whether they would ever see them again, not knowing whether they'd even survive. Ever since you told me about Tad, that's the one thing I can't seem to get out of my head. It's incredible to think that he might have once sat in these pews and prayed here."

"Yes, it is." Anna stared at the beautiful effigy of Mary and wondered whether Tad had once gazed at her too. "I think we owe a great debt to men like my father, more than you or I will ever know. I deeply regret not going on this journey before."

"Grandma, try not to feel that way." Bella took her grandma into her arms. "You're doing it now, and that's the important thing, and Mum and I are here to help you along the way."

"Mum, Bella." Sarah's excited voice broke apart their embrace. "Come over here. I think you will both want to see this."

Bella held her grandmother's hand as their footsteps clattered on the stone floor over to where Sarah was standing. On the wall before them just above their eyeline, they beheld a sizeable plaque. Made from a dull stone which looked like black slate, Bella took in the bronze etchings in the four corners, the images of some sort of medals carved in the top two and the Polish colours of red and white in the bottom left corner, whilst an eagle holding a laurel leaf sat in the bottom right corner. There was also the Polish Air Force crest, flanked by the dates 1940 and 1945. Below that, Bella carefully read the inscription.

This plaque is to commemorate the efforts, sacrifices and victories for which the foundations were laid at the Polish Air Force training centre at Blackpool. It was here also that the everlasting links existing between Polish airmen and the most hospitable citizens of Blackpool were forged.

"What a beautiful inscription. Since I first read it many years ago, I've loved the idea of everlasting links of friendship between the airmen and the people of the town; it makes it very special," Sarah said, brushing away a tear from her cheek as she thought of its personal significance now.

Anna put one hand on her daughter's shoulder and the other on her granddaughter's. "And the three of us are here today because of the bravery of one of these men."

After some deliberation, Bella sighed. "It is amazing to think that, Gran. But I still want to find out more about him. I think we owe it to Tad to try to piece together what we can of his story and bring him back into the family." She smiled as her grandmother nodded in agreement, the old woman's bright smile belying her worries as to whether they were emotionally prepared for what they could potentially discover about him and about themselves.

Getting out of the car at Layton Cemetery half an hour later, the rain had been replaced by a damp autumnal chill. Across the road Bella noticed a cluster of unremarkable shops: a bookies, bakers, off-licence, dog-grooming parlour and, turning away, she pulled her scarf firmly round her neck and dug her hands deep in her anorak pockets. Entering through black, wrought-iron gates, they took the long and winding lane to the right, which ran alongside a row of redbrick houses and was overshadowed by a wall high enough to block out the sunlight even on the brightest summer day. Two men in blue council uniforms were using leaf blowers to clear the graves, the thrumming buzz of their machines competing with the uncarthly screams of swooping seagulls. To the left of the path were vast swathes of tall graves, obelisks and impressive-looking monuments which reflected the importance of some of the people buried there and their prominent roles in the town's history. There were old, weathered graves, made taller by the crosses and angels perched on top. There were black plinths with urns or else busts of men, faithful likenesses of how they had looked in life, carved in stone, preserved. After walking for a short time, their eyes were drawn to the huge cross, standing erect and formidable at the cemetery's centre.

"I saw some like this when I visited the First World War battlefields in France," said Bella as her mum walked on ahead. "I think the guide told us they're called crosses of sacrifice."

"Yes, that's right. The Commonwealth Graves Commission placed them in cemeteries where there were a great number of war graves," said her grandma, threading her arm through her granddaughter's as they approached a tree bent double by the wind but still somehow managing to stand. "Maybe one day when we have time we could go and find some of them here, as they are scattered around. Look, there's one here belonging to a young officer in the Lancaster Regiment. He will have made it back to England before dying of wounds, that's why he's not buried in France or Flanders."

They followed the path round until they reached a neat, perfectly manicured plot with twenty-two uniformly white war graves, the green grass cut neatly around the edges. They resembled those Bella had seen in the Somme cemeteries, except where those had had curved tops like crescent moons, these ones were pinched to a point. At the base of each stone, red roses and white heather had been planted; the colours of the Polish flag. Bending forward, Bella saw each of the graves had *Polish Forces* inscribed on it above a carving of the Polish eagle, proudly beginning to unfurl its wings as though ready to take off and fly.

Remembering that on the French excursion, her history teacher had told her class to read as many names as they could to remember the soldiers and the sacrifice they had made; this is what Bella did now. Making her way down the rows, she lingered on each name: Plt Z. Witczak, T.T., 24 Feb 1945, Age 28; Kpl K. Frackiewicz, 307 Sqn, 17 Feb 1941, Age 24; Kpl W. Gandurski, 307 Sqn, 10 Jan 1941, Age 25; Sierz O. Pudrycki, 306 Sqn, 5 Dec 1941, Age 30; PPLK L. Pamula, 8 Aug 1940, Age 41; PLT H Noga, 316 Sqn, 29 Jul 1945, Age 24; DCHOR R. Zywicki, 610TU, 15 Apr 1945, Age 31. Just a rank, name, date and age, nothing more personal than that.

The graves were nestled around a brown stone memorial, which stood at around eight feet tall with red glass perpetual lights glimmering on the three stone steps leading up to it. On the second step was carved *ZA NASZA WOLNOSC I WASZA*, which Bella quickly typed into a Polish translator on her iPhone. "It means for our freedom and yours," she said, squeezing her grandma's hand. The three women then stood in silence as they read the English inscription. *We Polish airmen gave our souls to God, our bodies to the British soil and our hearts to Poland, 1940–45.* With her mum and grandma absorbed in their thoughts as they stood before the memorial, Bella noticed Blackpool Tower poking out of some trees in the distance, anchoring these men to the town where they'd once lived.

19

Training began in earnest at the beginning of March. Our drill sergeant, a veteran of the Great War, was a burly man with a ruddy complexion and a handlebar moustache who barked out orders to us like a fearsome Alsatian dog. Some of the recruits were afraid of him, but nothing he could have ever done would have been on a par with the brutal actions of the Nazis I had witnessed that day they had arrested our professors at the Jagiellonian. The wet weather at this time of year, however, was a different matter entirely, as we had to do most of our physical training and marching practice on the Golden Mile, more often than not, lashed by unforgiving winds which blew straight off the Irish Sea. But somehow I got through it all, regaining the fitness and strength I'd lost during my journey from Poland and my brush with pneumonia while learning to adapt seamlessly to the rigour and discipline of military life just as my father and Jacek had done before me. Wanting to improve my basic English so that I could have meaningful conversations with Eirlys, I took advantage of the language lessons offered to us Poles and Czechs too. I supplemented this by borrowing books from the library until I was confident enough to express my thoughts and feelings to her.

The promise of meeting Eirlys kept me going through those difficult days. On fine mornings when I managed to get out of bed early enough, I joined her and her best friend, Maggie, a girl with a greyhound-like physique, on their 5am run on the beach. As time passed, I got rather used to pounding the sands, even though more than my fair share of coarse grains congregated between my toes, despite wearing socks and running shoes supplied by the RAF! At 8am, I'd head down to training at Squires Gate where the stiff breeze blew straight off the sea despite the cluster of over two hundred buildings which should have acted as a substantial windbreak. These included four large metal Bellman hangars to house the planes safely, arms and bomb storage facilities, air raid shelters and a Naafi, as well as a large air traffic control tower in the centre of the airfield.

Most days, Eirlys and I found that the meeting time of three-thirty suited us both fine, as it gave me time to have lunch after my morning training and briefing while she completed her shift at the factory. One afternoon, as we were strolling along the beach, the waves breaking gently on the shore, I told her my story. Closing my eyes, I explained I was neither a hero nor an experienced man of the world. I was just a country boy, caught up in a war.

"I escaped Poland to fight the Nazis on equal terms. After witnessing their treatment of the people of Krakow, including my own professors and fellow students, I was desperate to respond to such unprovoked and unjustified brutality." I paused, inhaling the cool air which instantly relaxed me. "My homeland means everything to me; it makes me so angry to think that the Germans feel justified in taking what doesn't belong to them!"

"That's perfectly understandable, Tad. I often wish I was a man so that I could join up and really fight," Eirlys frowned, "but in any case I'm all Mother has so I have to be content with what I contribute at the factory, building planes, which will hopefully help us win the war."

"My brother is a career soldier like Father, and when Poland was invaded he told me to leave my country." I hesitated, grasping Eirlys's hand tighter. "Every night, I question whether it was the right thing to do."

"You think you should have stayed?" she said, her huge, dark eyes full of anguish as she looked solemnly out to sea.

"Sometimes, I feel I'm fighting someone else's war," I replied bitterly. "I'm just so far away from my family and my grandfather is all alone. He could be in great danger, as the Nazis occupy the nearby town and patrol the surrounding area. I don't know what is happening there now, but I worry that I will never see my grandfather again, that he has no one to look after him. He brought up my brother and I, so I saw him almost every day of my life and it is hard not knowing if he's well or even alive. All I can do is focus on the job I have to do here."

Eirlys nodded, her expression one of sympathy. "That's all any of us can do, Tad."

Anger rose within me once more as I told Eirlys in detail of the brutal acts I'd witnessed in Zakopane and Krakow during those first few months of the war. But far from flinching at my hate-fuelled rage, she merely nodded.

"But you wouldn't have been in a position to protect anyone if you'd stayed. You'd just have been in terrible danger yourself. We all have choices to make, Tad, especially during a war, and I'm sure yours were made in good faith and for sound reasons. And I will be grateful until the day I die that you came here and found me." She paused, before taking a deep breath and continuing, "A German soldier killed my father in the Great War, Tad. When I was a little girl, I used to lie awake at night searching for both their faces in the darkness. As time went on, my father's face became hazy and less defined and I hated the German even more. But still I couldn't see this unknown man's face to pin my anger and sorrow upon; he wouldn't reveal himself to me. Night after night, I berated his cowardice, willing him to step out of the shadows and meet me face to face so I might exact my revenge. But of course he never did. And so my hatred for his cowardice extended to his country..."

I nodded, taking her hand in mine. Neither of us wanting to break the silence, we stayed this way for a long time, not speaking. The effect war had already had on both of us was yet another thread which bound us tightly together.

"I heard that our planes bombed Lübeck last night. Apparently it is an ancient city, or was an ancient city. Part of me mourns for the inevitable loss of innocent life," she said, her anger audible, "while another part of me thinks of what the Luftwaffe did to Coventry, obliterating hundreds of years of history in just one night."

I nodded solemnly, grateful that the fate of that majestic medieval city wasn't Krakow's. I went on to tell her what I knew of my mother, that she was called Krysia, that she was the kindest woman my father had ever met, that she died giving birth to me, that Jacek had once told me that he'd laid me on the pillow next to her just as she'd drawn her final breath. "When I was younger, I raged at God in my prayers every night for letting her die, for denying me the chance to meet her, to love her, to be looked after by her. It ate away at me," I said, "so in the end I had no choice but to let her go."

"I always regretted being an only child," Eirlys continued after a minute or so. "My father died a couple of days before the Great War ended. With the Armistice already in preparation, he was shot on the outskirts of Mons. That's what makes me so angry, that after four years' fighting, why couldn't he have just survived those final forty-eight hours when the war was practically over? Witnessing the effect losing my father has had upon my mother made me quite angry with him, isn't that awful?"

I found myself unable to speak as I tried to take in the enormity of what she had just said. In a way I realised I'd always felt angry too that my mother had died when I was born, that she wasn't in my life at all and Jacek's only briefly. Until this moment I had never acknowledged that this was how I'd felt towards her all these years. But I sent a silent prayer now that she would forgive me.

"You're lucky to have a brother, Tad. My mother once told me she and my father had always planned to have more children and I've always wondered what it would have been like to grow up with a sister or a brother, sharing things with them, not being alone."

"I know I'm lucky, my brother is wonderful." I pulled out the photo I always carried in my breast pocket. "He's the good-looking one."

"Yes, I can see that." She laughed mischievously, instantly lightening the mood. "Your brother didn't escape with you?"

I shook my head. "No, Jacek would never leave Poland." I saw from her expectant expression that she was eager to find out about my family. "He is married with a child and he'd never abandon them."

"Lucky I met his handsome single brother, then." She put her arms around my neck, pulling me to her, and her kiss transported me away from the pain in my heart.

She wanted to know about my journey here. So as not to alarm her I chose my words carefully, omitting all the dangers I'd faced and the possible arrests we'd narrowly managed to avoid. Instead, I described all the countries I'd travelled through: Czechoslovakia, Hungary, the Balkans, Romania and, most wonderful of all, the Holy Land at Christmas. I told her of the many simple kindnesses shown to us on our journey which had helped restore some of my faith in human nature.

"You've been to so many places, Tad, places I can only imagine. I've never even stepped foot out of England. Well, I suppose that's a lie." Her laugh was soft and instantly lost on the sea breeze. "When I was younger, my mother and I went on a bus trip to Scotland. It was the first time I'd ever visited mountains and I thought I'd never seen anything so majestic. The lavender and lilac-shaded heather was truly beautiful."

"I imagine it was! I love my Tatra Mountains," I said. "They are part of my soul. It would be wonderful to take you there one day, Eirlys." I held that image in my head to keep at bay the reality that I may never see them again myself.

"Yes, I would love to do that with you, Tad. My hobby is collecting old postcards from different countries, mainly in Europe. I scour antique shops for them. I think most of my mountain ones are of places in the Alps, though, rather than the Carpathians. I've always wanted to see them since I first read *Heidi* when I was seven. I also have postcards of the Norwegian fjords, the Spanish and Greek coastlines, and, of course, the elegant Italian cities," she added dreamily.

"Anywhere in particular?" I asked, intrigued, thinking how I'd always wanted to visit Tuscany to see its rolling hills and its ancient hilltop towns.

"Well, Rome and Venice are the two you'd expect me to say," she teased, "and of course one day I would like to see the Colosseum, where once gladiators squared up to one another, or else sail down the Grand Canal, admiring the fading palaces."

"Who wouldn't?" I smiled. "But I've always found something very appealing about the architecture of Florence. I think it would be fascinating to see buildings in Renaissance, Gothic and Baroque styles side by side one another."

"Oh, Tad, Florence is the city I most want to visit in the entire world! To feast my eyes on Botticelli's paintings in the Uffizi Gallery and then stroll over the Ponte Vecchio which arches over the Arno. That is my idea of heaven!" she enthused.

I nodded, a grin spreading across my face, as in that moment I was struck by the notion that her pretty, slightly flushed face perfectly resembled that of a Botticelli angel. "It's my idea of heaven, too," I added, looking into her eyes. Our discussion about places we wanted to visit when the war ended naturally moved onto talking of our hopes for the future. Eirlys told of how, for the moment, she was content with her work at the factory because it gave her time to pursue her art in the evenings. Although she had aspirations to train to become an art teacher when the war was over, her mother was pushing for her to marry, to see her happy and settled and provided for financially so she wouldn't have to worry about her struggling to make ends meet as she'd been forced to do as a single parent, following her husband's untimely death.

Eirlys then asked about my hopes for the future. I repeated that when war broke out I'd been studying for an architecture degree at Jagiellonian University. To my surprise, she knew of its prestige as one Europe's oldest universities. I told her that I planned to continue my studies when my work here was done, that it was imperative we win the war or else Poland would be swallowed by Nazi Germany, erasing our thousand-year-old history in an instant. I pulled out a crumpled photo of Jerzy and I, the magnificent Copernicus globe in the background.

"It certainly looks grand, like the pictures I've seen of Oxford and Cambridge universities." She handed it back after a moment, studying me. "You must be extremely clever, Tad."

I felt I should fill the silence with something but, being a modest young man, at that moment I didn't know what to say. Luckily, I thought Eirlys believed my unpractised English was to blame and that I was unable to find the right words. I was happy to go along with her surmising as we walked hand in hand down the beach before we parted, Eirlys catching a bus home while I returned to my digs.

Jerzy was waiting for me when I arrived back, his face creased in consternation. Out of the gloom of the room stepped another man who I didn't recognise for a few moments. "Marek?" I eventually registered his gaunt, haggard appearance.

"Yes, Tad, it is me! I took a little longer than you, but I got here in the end!" he said, pulling me into a hug.

"Where's Antusz?" I glanced behind him, looking for our friend's thick mop of black hair, his wide smile, but there was just the dark wallpaper.

"Dead," he answered, the word inflicting physical pain, which caused me to flinch. "When we left you, Tad, we made it over the border into Czechoslovakia, but that night a German patrol came upon us and shot Antusz in the back while we were trying to escape over a field. I had no choice but to leave him there or they would have killed me too. It's so hard to live with the guilt; I often see him lying on the ground in my dreams, calling for me."

"You couldn't have saved him, Marek. You can't blame yourself," I said calmly, knowing I would feel exactly the same guilt if it had been Jerzy and me. I also realised how easily I could have suffered Antusz's fate, but he'd turned to go one way while I'd turned to go the other and it had led me all the way to Blackpool. It brought it home to me just how precarious life was, especially in times like these.

"No, I suppose not," Marek reflected, sighing deeply. "I'm sorry, Tad, Jerzy, I'm exhausted. I think I might have a short sleep before I report back to base. I'm being deployed south tomorrow, I can't recall the name of the place, something 'Hill'."

"Of course, old friend." I watched him as he lay down, thinking how strong and carefree he used to be when he worked on his father's farm, how he had aged in the months since I had last seen him. I tried to imagine the hardships he must have endured after Antusz had been killed and my heart bled for my old friend.

*

On our date the following Saturday afternoon, Eirlys suggested we get away from the seafront to visit her favourite spot in Blackpool, Stanley Park. As we entered through the ornate gates, I had to admit that I'd never seen nature so formalised and ordered in my life, accustomed as I was to living in the wild countryside with craggy mountains and raging rivers forging their own divergent courses. But walking around, I noticed the park was a fusion of interesting contrasts. Eirlys told me it had been laid out in the 1920s by an architect called Thomas Mawson who'd wanted to design a park where everyone could find different things to enjoy. Whether it was the peace and beauty of the flower gardens and lake where people could sit on sunny afternoons listening to the band playing in the pretty bandstand or else stroll along meandering paths through the trees. There were also areas where the more energetic could enjoy sporting activities too and, as we passed the tennis courts, I spotted some of my friends from the base playing a game.

I waved and shouted, "*Dzień dobry!*" to which their reply about Eirlys made me blush.

"What did they say, Tad?" she asked.

"Just that you're very pretty," I extemporised, hoping she hadn't noticed that my translation was very much shorter than what the boys had said!

Eirlys smiled. "How about we have a cup of tea in the cafe? You'll love the Art Deco there, being a trainee architect!"

The tearooms were indeed beautifully decorated in classic Art Deco style. As Eirlys and I walked through the stained-glass doors, I admired the greens, blues, azures and aquamarines of the glass depicting two peacocks facing each other, proudly posturing. The wooden tables and chairs were less ostentatious, however, and more in keeping with the wartime austerity which was apparent all over the town. We found a corner table by the window and Eirlys ordered us tea, which came in a pretty china teapot which she expertly poured into matching teacups.

"Do you like it?" Eirlys enquired as I dug my fork into the cake she'd insisted I try. It was a light, vanilla sponge sandwiched together with jam and cream, and I found that it melted deliciously in my mouth. "It's called Victoria sponge cake after Queen Victoria. Apparently the Duchess of Bedford, a lady in waiting to the Queen, created the

British tradition of afternoon tea, and it has become a bit of a national treat to enjoy. It is an extremely popular cake which everyone makes at home. It's my favourite sponge, although I think my recipe has a slight edge on this one!"

"I'm sure it does, but this is very nice," I replied, the tartness of the jam cutting through the sweetness of the rest to create a perfect balance.

"Do you have anything similar in Poland?" She smiled sweetly as she daintily lifted her cake fork to her mouth.

"Not a cake, but we do have pierogi." She looked confused and so I proceeded to explain. "They are small dumplings which we fill with fruit jams, bilberries, strawberries and blueberries."

After we'd finished our tea and cake, we strolled arm in arm down the steps and into the gardens, the formal beds radiating from an Italianate fountain at the centre. Also placed at intervals were statues and stone columns, the flowerbeds empty as yet as spring had not fully taken hold. "It's so lovely here in the summer, with the vibrant colours of the flowers planted in patterns," Eirlys said, and I wondered whether we would have the chance to come back and see it together. Beyond the gardens was a wooded area, where I felt more at home, with twigs snapping beneath my feet while birds fluttered in and out beneath the canopy of branches and emerging leaves.

"I sense you have found your place in the woods." Eirlys looked thoughtfully at me but I didn't quite grasp her meaning. "That you feel at home here."

"Home," I said to myself, although it felt so far away from me at this moment, a distance not merely measurable in miles. I was grateful when a squirrel dragged me from my maudlin thoughts as it scurried out of some undergrowth to retrieve a nut, taking it in its tiny hands before running off to bury it safe somewhere, its tail bouncing behind.

"Why don't we go on the lake?" Eirlys suggested, and we walked over to hire a rowing boat. As I helped her into the boat, my hands lingered on either side of her narrow ribcage and I felt the warmth of her body radiating through the soft material of her coat. The sensation caused me to shiver involuntarily, which I hoped she hadn't noticed. I rowed the boat away from the shore as Eirlys leaned over and ran her hand through the cool waters, creating ripples which eddied out across the lake. "You've done this before?" she said.

"Yes, since I was little. My brother, Jacek, taught me how to row, how to build rafts, how to do so many things, skills which saved my life on my journey here," I said, before concentrating on the rhythm of the rowing, inviting no further comment from her. Fortunately, Eirlys took the hint and turned her attention back to dragging her hand over the glass-like surface of the water.

"That's the amphitheatre over there." She pointed to a semi-circle of seats arranged around a bandstand. Just then, as though her outstretched finger ordered it, the skies, which had been darkening above us, suddenly opened to release a heavy shower, soaking us in an instant.

"Tad." She shrieked with laughter, the first time she'd called me by my name today. "Row faster, we have to get to the shore to shelter."

As ordered, I pounded the oars as fast as I could, my hair sticking flat to my head, my clothes sodden as I forged ahead. After seemingly an age, the crunch of the bank struck the bottom of the boat and then I was lifting Eirlys out, feather-light in my arms, and we were running hand in hand until we reached the bandstand, dripping wet and out of breath.

There we stood motionless, watching flashes of lightning fork across the sky, claps of thunder resounding in our ears. And then we were laughing, water running down our faces, our hot breath evaporating in clouds which rapidly cooled on the early spring air. Entranced by her eyes, I drew closer until I could feel her breath on my face. I wrapped my arm around her slender waist, pulling her into me until I could sense her heart beating just below mine, fast and strong. And then, my fingers tangling in her loose, wet hair, we were kissing as though we would never be sated.

20

Blackpool, October 2020

Anna leaned against the railings, looking out to sea. The water was dark today, overshadowed by the thick cloud blanketing the sky and she wondered how on earth Second World War pilots had managed to fly planes with their antiquated navigation systems in inclement weather conditions. She thought flying must have been a perilous task for her father long before he'd reached the skies over Germany where he'd run the additional risk of being shot down. How brave he must have been, how much he'd been forced to endure at such a young age! Even though she knew that most of Tad's story would probably forever remain hidden to her, she owed it to him and his memory to take a trip to Poland. She just wished she hadn't waited so long.

Seeing the big hand of her watch move to the twelve brought her crashing back to the present. She was due to meet Barbara at the Cosy Cafe half a mile away on the hour. *Oh God*, she thought, rushing up the stone steps. Passing the cenotaph, a white obelisk soaring up to pierce the sky, she made a mental note to attend the service on Remembrance Sunday, just a few weeks away now. Walking up Talbot Road, she was progressing at a fair lick when she was halted by a red light at the crossing. Calculating she still had another hundred metres to go, she felt her breath quicken, for she hated being late for anybody or anything.

Waiting at the crossing, an intense pain suddenly gripped her chest as though a fist was squeezing her heart. Wincing, she stepped back to lean against a wall, where she took short, sharp breaths as ripples of pain pulsed through her body. Then as suddenly as it had begun, the episode ended, but, zapped of her strength, she was left feeling as though she'd topple over at any moment. Taking tentative steps, she continued on her way, realising she'd never experienced such a brutal pain like that before and she wondered whether she'd just had some sort of mini heart attack. But she'd recently read in a newspaper health supplement that heart attacks, especially in women, were more often than not accompanied by other symptoms, such as nausea or light headedness, and lasted for hours. The duration of hers had been fifteen seconds at the outside, which provided her with some comfort. It was probably just indigestion, brought on by missing breakfast, rushing into town and the stress of everything that was going on in her life at the moment.

"Hi, Barbara." Trying to steady her breathing, Anna walked over to the corner table where her friend was waiting.

"Anna," Barbara leaned over the lacy tablecloth in a cloud of Yardley's Rose to receive a swift kiss on both cheeks from her, "you look a bit peaky, old friend. What's wrong?"

Anna grimaced, taking in Barbara's dark blonde, blow-dried hair, smooth complexion and immaculate makeup, accentuated by a flattering dove-grey polo neck jumper. Like a fine wine, she seemed to get better and better with age, whereas Anna felt some part of her diminish with each passing month.

"I've been quite tired for the past few weeks but, rushing here just now, I had a really odd pain in my chest, totally out of the blue," she sighed, primping her windswept blow-dry back into its heavily lacquered position, her breathing returning to normal. "It was only for a moment, then it passed."

"Maybe indigestion? Or the stress of being late?" her friend said optimistically. "Something similar happened to me last year and after my tests came back negative, my doctor put it down to acid reflux and gave me some medication which sorted the problem. All the same, I'd get it checked out as soon as you can."

"Yes, better to be safe than sorry." Anna nodded as the teenage waitress came to take their order. "I think I'll go all out and have a huge hunk of carrot cake to go with my coffee today. I skipped breakfast so I'm feeling a touch light-headed."

Opting for a conservative tea and toasted teacake, Barbara waited for the young girl to leave them. "Is everything okay, Anna? Is it Sarah or Bella this time?"

"Both," said Anna matter-of-factly, detecting the concern in her friend's frown, "but there won't be a day when I ever stop worrying about them. At the moment, Bella seems to break up and make up and break up again with her current young man at least once a month while not having a clue where she's going with her life and as for Sarah… I know she loves her job, but she works far too hard and has no social life, and I worry that when Bella does eventually leave home, she will be lonely."

"Worries and heartache are just part and parcel of having daughters and granddaughters. Apparently, sons are much lower maintenance!" Barbara laughed.

"Tell the truth, it's not Sarah and Bella who are bothering me any more than usual, it's my father. We are going to Poland in a few weeks to try to find out about him." Anna paused, waiting for her friend's reply.

"Poland? In the depths of winter! Is that wise? You've always said your mum told you everything you needed to know about your father." Barbara eyed her friend suspiciously. "I hope Bella didn't bamboozle you into it? Remember, I know just how manipulative teenage granddaughters can be!"

"Well maybe she did persuade me a little bit." Anna paused as the waitress brought their order. "But in another way I'm looking forward to visiting the country where half of my family came from."

"I'm sensing there's another 'but'." Barbara daintily buttered her teacake.

"But then I was thinking on the way here, what if it's all a waste of time? My father was just twenty-five when he died seventy-five years ago. That is hardly enough time to make any kind of imprint on this earth, let alone one that is likely to have survived all these years. What if we get to Poland and there's simply nothing left of him, no family, no trace? All my life, I've lived with my father's absence. But I think it would make it even more difficult for me if we travelled to his country and turned up nothing about him." She sipped her coffee slowly to stop herself from crying.

"Anna, I think you need to go there with an open mind." Her friend considered for a few moments. "Don't go with the sole aim of finding out anything specific about your dad. Just go with the intention of discovering about your heritage, see the places he may have been, the places where his family came from and lived, soak it all in. If you find anything specific about Tad, that's a bonus after all this time."

"That's what I keep telling myself, but there's also the risk of unearthing something I don't want to," Anna sighed, relieved to finally talk to someone who was impartial, looking in from the outside. "With the war and everything the Polish people went through, I could find something disturbing, that's what I'm most worried about."

"At least you'll know the truth." Barbara raised her eyebrows as she drank her tea. "Just you promise to take care of yourself, Anna."

"I will," she said as they moved onto other topics. Later, outside the teashop despite the chill wind and drizzly rain, the two old friends hugged a little longer than usual. When she arrived home, Anna suddenly felt weary. Drawing the sitting-room curtains, as dusk had already settled over her back garden, she switched on her Tiffany glass lamp. In no mood for a meal after her colossal cake, she made herself a warming cup of tea and some buttered toast and was just about to sit back and watch *Eggheads* when the phone rang.

"Hi, Mum, I was just thinking about you. Is everything okay?" Sometimes Anna thought Sarah possessed a sixth sense for knowing when there was something wrong. But she had no intention of telling her daughter of her chest pain episode earlier, as it would surely jeopardise their trip to Poland. She knew Sarah would insist she seek immediate medical attention for something that was more than likely a one-off caused by all the stress she'd been under these past weeks.

"I went for a walk on the beach earlier and it got me thinking about Tad, how he might have felt when he arrived in England. I was overcome with loneliness." She fiddled with the phone flex.

"Look, Mum, if this is dredging up a bucket load of painful feelings and memories for you that you'd prefer to keep buried, I'll warn Bella off. She's just started her job at the university and, after a few weeks of working nine to five, she might be in need of a complete rest lounging about on the sofa over the Christmas break instead of exploring Krakow. And we've only made a provisional hotel booking on booking.com, which we can easily cancel."

"No, please don't do that." Anna's voice was forceful. "I want to find out more about my father, more than that file of old papers and stash of blurry photos gathering dust upstairs. They only tell half the story, I feel it. I need to see the places he visited, where he lived with his family. *Our family.* I know I've nearly left it too late, but I'm compelled to make this trip back to Poland, to complete the journey that my dad never got the chance to make."

"Well, if you're sure, Mum. I just don't want you to commit to anything you're not comfortable with. You'd tell me if you weren't?" Her daughter's voice was full of concern.

"I would, yes. But it's not even about wanting to go to Poland. *I need to go.*" Their conversation then moved on to gossip about Anna's neighbours, who were having a hot tub installed in their backyard, to making arrangements to get their Christmas shopping done early this year since all their presents would need to be wrapped up and distributed to their friends before they flew out on December 6th.

Even though she didn't tell Sarah of her chest pain episode, on putting down the phone Barbara's concern niggled at the back of Anna's mind, so she booked an appointment with her doctor the following day. Hoping he would put her mind at rest before her Polish holiday by confirming her hopes that it was just stress, she nevertheless fretted over whether she would have to undergo hospital tests and what they'd reveal.

She was determined, however, that her health would not impinge upon her trip to Poland. Wanting to get the most out of her time there, she downloaded an English–Polish translator app onto her mobile phone for occasions when she might want an in-depth conversation with someone over there. Then she took her little black leather notebook from the sideboard drawer, in which she scribbled down page upon page of phrases which would come in useful. She spent the early evening practising enunciating them until they just rolled of her tongue. *Dziękuję* – thank you; *Nie rozumiem* – I don't understand; and *Czy mówisz pan po angielsku?* – Do you speak English? She suspected she'd be using this particular phrase quite frequently! *Jak masz na imię?* – What's your name?; *Jak sie masz* – How are you?; *Przepraszam* – sorry; *Ile to kosztuje?* –How much does it cost? Which, again, might come in handy while shopping in the Christmas market. Time nudging on to 7.30pm or *Coronation Street* time as it was every Monday, Wednesday and Friday, she closed her notebook to lose herself in the current trials and tribulations of life on the cobbles, temporarily forgetting her own in the process.

21

The following Sunday was a warm, sunny day for the time of year and I managed to borrow a car from an affable RAF boy called Joe, recently billeted at the guesthouse, whose childhood spent on a farm in the Lake District sounded very much like my own. I picked Eirlys up at her home, an elegant three-storey redbrick house some way from the promenade and its attractions. She was wearing a light blue dress with white polka dots, similar to the one she'd worn on our first meeting when she'd come to my rescue at the public house. As she lowered herself into the passenger seat, I chastely kissed her on the cheek as her mother watched solemnly from the door. I waved to the older woman in what I hoped was a friendly gesture but saw it was met by a disapproving look. However, as I drove off, Eirlys just smiled sweetly, saying her mother's bark was worse than her bite.

"Pardon me?" I said. Although my English was improving, there still seemed to be many phrases which didn't make any sense at all to me.

"It means that although she looks like a lion, she acts more like a pussy cat," she said as I drove along the prom, my attention divided between the way Eirlys's hair caught the breeze from the open window and the beguiling blue of the sea beyond. "That she will like you when she gets to know you."

"Ahh! I see. Where are we going today?" I smiled back. "I have the car until the evening."

"The countryside, I think." She looked up at the endless blue sky above.

"Perfect." I smiled, remembering the smooth undulations of the Tatras and suddenly wanting to be back there. With Eirlys's clear directions, we soon left behind the buildings of the town, and the countryside was surprisingly green for early spring. Primroses peeped shyly from beneath the hedgerows we passed while in the woods the first bluebells were opening with a promise of the beautiful blue carpet which would emerge in a few weeks time. The landscape was pretty, with its fields, grazing animals and stone cottages dotted around. And yet, while I should have felt at home here, it just re-emphasised what I was missing: rugged hills and mountains where goats ran freely; deep, dense woods where bears brought up their cubs; and, most of all, the carved, wooden houses, their verandas wrapped around them to keep cool in summer, their central fireplaces for families to huddle around in the winter. I noticed Eirlys regarding me thoughtfully. "Thinking of home?"

I told her of how, after my mother's death, my father had found an escape from his grief in the army, leaving Dziadek to raise Jacek and me singlehandedly. I told her of how my grandfather had looked after us both, giving us the love that our parents should have provided, if they'd been able. I told her of my relationship with Dziadek, of how we'd never engaged in deep discussions, that woodworking was our connection, our means of communication. "He can fashion anything he wants from wood," I said. "Each carving is a masterpiece. Warm to the touch, it almost feels alive in your hands."

"And what about Jacek?" she asked. "Tell me about him?"

"We grew up as close as brothers can be, closer than most because of what had happened to us. But Jacek was never interested in woodworking. He is more a practical sort of boy, not an artist at all. He'd rather nail planks together to make a boat and then take it for a sail than spend hours carving something from wood. He's not like me in that way."

"But I get the impression you are a bit in awe of him?" Glancing at her, I saw she was smiling.

"Yes, because he's a few years older than me and I never saw much of our father, I suppose I do admire him a lot. He is everything I've ever wanted to be." I felt myself blush.

"I think you're fine as you are, Tad." She smiled again, and I could tell from the tone of her voice that she was sincere.

"Maybe." I considered before continuing, "I often think some boys might have found a brother four years younger than them troublesome. But Jacek never saw me that way or, if he did, he kept it well hidden." I paused to collect my thoughts. Glancing across the flat landscape which came with being so near to the coast, homesickness suddenly felt like a physical pain in the pit of my stomach.

"That is unusual. My best friend at school, Eve, always had squabbles with her brother, Robert," Eirlys commented. "You and your brother sound as though you have a special closeness not many siblings share."

"Yes, I believe it could be because Jacek lost Mother on the day I was born and our father was away for most of our childhood, as he could not bear to live in a house where each room reminded him of his wife's absence." I paused again, this time in consideration of Eirlys, whose father had died before her birth. "I think Jacek tried to compensate for the absence of our parents by giving me enough love for all three of them."

Eirlys nodded. Considering her close relationship with her mother, she was possibly wondering whether she had done the same for her over the years. But when she offered no comment I didn't feel it right to pry and I used the opportunity to divulge more of my relationship with Jacek. "I've understood for a long time that my brother's fierce protectiveness towards me was motivated by his fear of losing me. One day, when I was nine or ten, I recall I was off playing in the woods on my own and, having lost track of time, I didn't return to the cottage until after dark. That was the first occasion I glimpsed the full force of my brother's anger as he admonished me for being so reckless and thoughtless. I sobbed myself to sleep that night knowing I'd let Jacek down badly and not understanding why. It wasn't until I was older that I realised his anger was merely a mask for a more powerful emotion – fear. After losing his mother – and effectively his father – Dziadek and I were all Jacek had left."

As I drew to a close, Eirlys intimated that I pull over in front of a black-and-white gabled pub, with a beautifully painted sign which read 'The Miller's Arms'. "This building dates back to the sixteenth century, so I thought the architecture might interest you, and it serves good food!"

I followed Eirlys in, the dark wooden beams and white walls of a style I was not accustomed to but the profuse use of wood in the decor and furniture made me feel instantly at home. "I've never been anywhere like this before in my life." I smiled, noticing a few men at the bar giving me curious glances. Probably due to my accent, it was something that I was growing used to. But I sort of regretted wearing my uniform for my outing with Eirlys, even though it was the smartest piece of clothing I owned. We found a table in a quiet corner and I, not understanding the menu, left it to Eirlys to order us food and drinks. When our meal came, I looked at it in a bemused manner.

"It's Sunday lunch. This is what most British people traditionally eat on the Sabbath day. A meat such as beef, pork or chicken served with vegetables and gravy." She smiled. "Try it, Tad. It's delicious, although the portions are smaller than before the war due to the rationing."

I took a tentative mouthful, worrying that I wouldn't like the meal, as had been the case with most of the food I'd tried since my arrival in England. But the beef and vegetables were surprisingly tasty and the accompanying batter creation Eilys called a Yorkshire pudding really delicious.

"Good, isn't it?" Eirlys smiled, wolfing her meal down with such gusto that I wondered whether she just liked her food or whether she hadn't eaten much today. "It's almost as good as my mum's. You must come round and have Sunday lunch with us one day."

"You're really close to your mum, aren't you?" I said as Eirlys gave me a shy smile.

"Yes, we only have each other. She's had to bring me up singlehandedly, providing all the emotional and financial support my father should have shared." She paused before adding, "A bit similar to what you told me about your family."

"Yes, it sounds like it. It must have been difficult for your mother," I said, comparing her situation with that which my father had found himself in. Unable to cope with the absence of my mother, he'd sought an escape in the army, leaving everything concerning the upbringing of Jacek and me to Dziadek, who had cared for us as though we were his own sons, ensuring we wanted for nothing.

"Yes, but she runs a successful boarding house and we have a good life together," she said. "She has not only given me all the love I need but has also provided for me financially. I feel I owe her so much for the sacrifices she made so I could have a good start in life."

"But what about when the time comes for you to leave, Eirlys, when you want to marry and have a family of your own?" I said, instantly wanting to take back my words, fearful I had gone too far.

Watching her face, I saw her emotions were clearly in conflict and that this was indeed territory into which I should not have ventured. Instead, I changed the subject back to food, telling her that in Poland, a typical Sunday lunch consisted of soup, probably borscht, followed by roasted pork or poultry served with cabbage and potatoes, and then dumplings and fruit for dessert.

"Well, Tad, if you're used to eating such copious amounts, I'd better order some treacle pudding. We don't want you wasting away while you are in Blackpool!" She smiled, and I breathed a sigh of relief that she had brought our conversation back to neutral territory. As well as getting to know everything about this girl with the intriguing name and beguiling smile, I wanted to enjoy our time together before it inevitably ended.

Dusk was falling as we drove back to Blackpool that evening, the sunset seemingly setting the sky on fire. The black fretwork of the tower silhouetted against the orange and red streaks, I pulled the car over to take a better look. Slipping my arm around Eirlys, she rested her head on my shoulder as we watched the sun set over the sea. Tentatively our lips came together, gently at first and then with more urgency, my mouth moving slowly down her neck to caress her collarbone. The need to take her completely overwhelmed me as my hands slipped under her coat, a need I know she felt too. But, with supreme self-control, I drew back. I didn't want our first time to be a quick fumble in a car. She was far too precious to me already.

Seeing fleeting emotions of confusion and hurt pass across her face, I whispered, "Eirlys, you're the only girl I've felt this way about, but I'm due to be posted away at any moment and don't know if I'll ever come back. The future's too uncertain and you're far too important to me to give you a false promise."

"But, surely the fact that the future is unpredictable means young people like us have to take what happiness we can." She pulled away, seeing something in my eyes which upset her. "I just ask that you think about it, Tad, that's all."

Over the next few days, I could not think of anything else. But whichever way I twisted and turned it in my mind, I always came to the same conclusion: that, growing up a good Catholic boy as I had, it would be wrong to sleep with a girl I was not married to. Luckily, when I next saw Eirlys, she did not allude to our conversation on the subject. Instead, looking lovely in a rose-pink dress, her dark hair pinned up to reveal the soft, white nape of her neck, she asked me to take her dancing in the Tower Ballroom.

"Before the war, I always danced at the Winter Gardens with my friends but now the RAF uses it for physical exercise." She smiled as we walked along the promenade, attracting the glances of RAF boys.

"Yes, I've heard that they have lecture rooms there and cinemas too," I said, "although isn't that in the day and at night it reverts to being a dance hall?"

"I don't know, I don't go dancing much anymore," Eirlys said, her expression sad. And I pondered whether it was because her job at Vickers Armstrong tired her, as the reason could not be because she was short of suitors. Indeed there had been a recent influx of Americans, who marched through the resort with their caps worn at rakish angles, handing out gum and candy and sweet-talking seemingly every girl they met.

The Tower Ballroom was like nowhere I had ever visited before. As I entered it with Eirlys on my arm, I felt like a Polish king must surely have felt on attending his coronation ball in the splendour of Wawel Castle. I looked up, bewitched by the golden balconies which reached up to an inky blue ceiling painted with a canopy of stars. As I took Eirlys in my arms and we glided around the dance floor together, beneath the crystal chandeliers sparkling above us, I lost myself in a world of elegant charm and refined beauty. Growing up in Poland and then coming over to England to be part of the war, it was a world I'd never dreamed I would glimpse.

After dropping Eirlys off at her home, it was late by the time I returned to the boarding house, but Mrs Matthews was still up, sitting in a pool of lamplight doing her crossword. She made me a cup of cocoa with powdered milk, which, when I first tasted it, made me long for the fresh milk in Poland we fetched from Pan Kowalski's farm every morning. But over the months I'd somehow become accustomed to it. Sipping the steaming drink, Mrs Matthews smiled and said, "Who is this girl you are seeing, Tad?"

Telling her all about Eirlys, I was intrigued to discover how she knew. "Because I've seen the light flash and burn in your eyes these past few days, just as it did with my son, Mark, when he first met his sweetheart," she explained, her expression animated.

"I didn't know you had a son, Mrs Matthews." I saw her eyes cloud over.

"I did. He was a flyer too, but he was killed in the summer of 1940." She took a photo out of her cardigan pocket and smiled at it, lost in thought. "That's why I want to give you and your friends a home. My son is gone, so I try to do what I can for other mother's sons. It makes me feel he's somehow still around – foolish, I know, but it helps me."

"I think you're a very courageous lady." I clasped her hand in mine. "I know my mother would be thankful that I have you to take care of me while I'm so far from home." Finishing my cocoa, its warmth and that of this kind woman gave me comfort as the night fell around us.

22

Lancaster, November 2020

That Saturday, Bella was in work bright and early, having romanticised Eirlys's and Tad's story to such an extent that it had reached fairy-tale status in her mind. Fortified by two black coffees, she'd already restacked six bookshelves when Will made an appearance, his shirt collar snarled up in the neck of his sweater, his eyes half-closed. As Bella had deduced with most academic types she'd come across in her short time at the university, Will was used to burning the midnight oil and consequently most definitely wasn't a morning person.

"Hey you," he said, dumping his red rucksack on his disorganised desk before heading straight for the coffee machine as she had predicted. Smiling, she busied herself piling books onto her trolley until he came back.

"Ah, that's better," he sighed, downing his coffee in one. "Busy night last night, didn't get to bed till half three."

As Will proceeded to shuffle through his rucksack, Bella took the opportunity to study him. Even though he looked a bit rough, he'd managed to take time to cultivate his casually smart look and had artfully arranged his thick dark hair. Glancing up, he caught her unawares and she felt her cheeks redden as she found herself staring into his dark brown eyes. "Looking forward to tonight?" He flashed his brightest smile.

"Yes, I love firework displays." She smiled, relieved that he hadn't been frightened off by her mother when they'd bumped into each other the previous day. The last thing Bella wanted was for her to be proved right about Will at the very first hurdle.

"Good, we'll have a bite to eat after we finish here and then head straight over to Castle Hill because it's sure to be rammed." As he turned to root in a huge cardboard box which had been busted and repaired by brown masking tape so many times it was now principally the tape which held its shape, Bella breathed a sigh of relief. When Will had mentioned he'd had a busy night a few minutes before, she'd found herself wondering whom he'd been with. She knew, from his banter with his colleagues, that he didn't have a special girlfriend, but she supposed that didn't preclude him having casual girlfriends, and the notion made her a little uneasy, if not jealous. But as she watched him carefully remove textbooks from the box, she recalled her mother's advice never to mix work and romantic liaisons. They just didn't work and here she was having unhelpful thoughts about one of her work colleagues. "Grow up," she mumbled to herself.

Leaving the university library that evening, Bella and Will gathered up their jackets, for now, deep into autumn, there was an unmistakable chill in the air. Walking down the campus's south spine, they engaged in a companionable conversation as they negotiated waves of students armed with bulging rucksacks.

"Why don't we try the Jolly Juice Cafe everyone's talking about?" suggested Will, eschewing the uniformly dark frontages of high-street coffee shops for the sunshine yellow one. "Apparently, they have a great salad bar and, of course, fruit juices."

Not admitting she and her mum had already been, Bella joined Will in the queue, filling her biodegradable box with an array of pomegranate-jewelled couscous and sumptuous salads which she topped with pulled pork before being tempted with a Merry Berry smoothie. As they moved to a table in the far corner, Bella couldn't help but notice the admiring glances cast in Will's direction from some of the female students.

"Anyway, I suppose you know all about me now?" Bella swallowed some pulled pork, rolling her eyes as he looked quizzingly at her. "My mum mentioned she saw you yesterday, so I expect you know my shoe size, my teenage crush, everything. But I still know next to nothing about you."

"Well, as you may have guessed from my accent, I hail from Cumbria. Lived with my parents and collie, Fred, in a detached house in a leafy Carlisle suburb, went to secondary school, sixth form etc., etc. until I came down to Lancaster eight years ago. I'd always been interested in history, so I did my degree and then got funding to do my PhD, which I supplement with this job." He grinned, his hair flopping over his face à la Hugh Grant. "That's about it. Family and education just about sum up my life so far."

"Umm," said Bella, seeing his eyes sparkle and knowing full well there were far more exciting things about his life that he wasn't sharing with her. Pushing her mother's warnings to the back of her mind, she decided to play it cool and not appear too eager. "What made you so fascinated with history?" she asked instead, spearing her salad with her fork, hoping to get an insight into how someone actually went about choosing a degree subject.

"I'm interested in people first and foremost, what makes them tick. If I hadn't studied history I probably would have ended up doing psychology. But I'm also riveted by the past, how people lived without all the inventions we rely on, without all the medical advances, how they generally just got on with things in a stoic manner, how we can't judge people who lived in the past with the values of the present." He scraped his salad box clean before sweeping it aside.

"I think I'm definitely in danger of catching that bug," she said, Tad popping into her mind as he often did.

"We'll make a historian of you yet." He looked at her for a long moment and for the first time, Bella thought it was a distinct possibility.

*

After a busy week, Sarah decided to make use of her free Saturday by tackling a mountain of marking, but it didn't go to plan at all. Having had the intention of enjoying a leisurely breakfast of avocado and scrambled eggs, she woke up to discover that, due to a power cut during the night, the freezer and fridge had defrosted, meaning the kitchen floor resembled a swimming pool. After grabbing a quick coffee and toast, it took her the entire morning to mop up and sort out which items could be saved. As a good portion ended up in the bin, she was then forced to do a food shop that afternoon. Not having the inclination to queue in traffic to get to one of the cavernous supermarkets across the city, she shopped at the small artisan supermarket in her neighbourhood. Although twice the price of the others, she consoled herself that, after her disrupted day, she deserved a little treat and found herself tempted by the delights of the deli counter. Later that evening, she laid out the appetising array of cured meats, French cheeses and salads onto the kitchen table, along with a freshly baked baguette and a glass of chilled prosecco. Momentarily she felt her mood lighten, until she remembered her conversation with Bella over dinner the previous night.

"This is lovely," Bella had said, her eyes narrowing as she'd mopped up the lasagne sauce with a hunk of garlic bread, "but what are you after?"

"Nothing," Sarah had said innocently. "Can't a mother treat her daughter without there being an ulterior motive?"

"I suppose so." Bella had smiled, taking another mouthful of pasta.

"So are you looking forward to your date with Will tomorrow night?" Sarah had winced. While preparing the meal she'd rehearsed how to put it to her daughter, deciding that a subtle approach would be best. In her nervousness, however, she'd just blurted it straight out.

Bella had chewed her food rather inelegantly, laughing. "About as subtle as a sledgehammer, Mum."

"I know." Sarah had sipped her wine, unsure where to go next. "I'm just… I spoke to him earlier and I'm just concerned that Will is quite a bit older than you. He's not one of those adolescent boys you led a merry dance in the sixth form."

"Mum! I hope you didn't scare him off!" Bella had whined, raising her eyebrows, clearly embarrassed.

"I didn't, but we can't hide from the fact that he's a twenty-six-year-old man." Sarah had stumbled over her words, realising that she was floundering. "And at the university he has the reputation of a bit of a Casanova."

"So what? Give me more credit than that, Mum," Bella had said, sighing in exasperation. "I'm not about to jump into bed with a man I barely know. I'm not that stupid. And besides, when the time comes, I'll be okay. We've had sex education classes in school for the past few years."

"I didn't mean that… But if you want to talk about it or need any advice, you know I'm here for you." Sarah had winced, hearing her mother's voice in her own and remembering how she had taken no notice of Anna when she was Bella's age.

"I do. Don't worry." Bella had tapped her hand. "Now, can we talk about something else? Will's taking me to watch a firework display along with two thousand other people. He'll be more interested in explaining pyrotechnics to me than trying to get into my knickers!"

"Bella!" Sarah had said, spluttering as a sliver of Parmesan went down the wrong way. "I didn't bring you up to be so vulgar!"

Remembering their terse exchange Sarah decided she wasn't in the mood to eat after all, so, packing away her picnic into the fridge, she made a tomato cup-a-soup and toast instead. Looking at the clock, she saw it was still only 7.17pm, meaning Bella wouldn't be home for hours yet. To distract herself, she puttered around the living room, tidying the magazines on the coffee table into neat piles, plumping cushions and wiping the recently accumulated veil of dust from the bookshelves. Settling in front of the fire, she spent a few moments revelling in the silence and stillness of the room before finally getting round to reading the previous Sunday's newspaper supplement, her mind distracted by thoughts of Bella and Will.

*

At that moment Bella and Will were walking up the steep hill to the castle, whose great gateway was floodlit in all its medieval splendour. Will had firmly taken Bella's hand as soon as they had got out of his car, making it clear this wasn't just two work colleagues going to watch a firework display. Accompanied by crowds of people muffled up in hats, gloves and scarves against the biting cold, Bella began to relax. She saw the joy on children's faces as they whirled sparklers to create patterns of silver and gold in the air and watched as students and locals bit into toffee apples and tried medieval mead at the many stalls lining their route. Bella persuaded

Will to stop to buy some and, warmed by the herbs and spices, they continued their walk up the slope of the field.

"I think here will be a good space to watch the fireworks." Will stopped suddenly as the tide of the crowd moved away from them as though stranding them on their own desert island. "Last year, I went further on and unfortunately all the fireworks exploded behind the priory church spire, although I did have a great view of the tail end of each and every one." He grinned. "Anyway, I have to make sure you come to no harm if I correctly interpret that look your mother shot at me when I saw her yesterday: 'Don't hurt my daughter or else!'"

"That's a terrible impression!" Bella laughed. "But she's just being protective, that's all. I think she has always felt the extra responsibility to look after me and make sure I'm okay because my dad's never been around."

"What's the story with that? If you don't mind my asking, that is?" He grasped her hand a little tighter as strains of Mozart began playing softly in the background.

"My father's American. He met Mum when he was on a year's sabbatical at the university and she was a junior lecturer there. From what I gather, they were instantly attracted to each other, flirting, going out on dates to the cinema, inseparable. Mum is always a bit sketchy on the details but I get the impression it was one of those giddy passionate affairs that burned itself out almost as quickly as it had started." She paused, seeing Will nod even though she suspected he didn't know what on earth she was talking about. Or maybe he did, if his reputation with girls was true.

"Anyway." She raised her voice in order to be heard as the music suddenly grew louder and the first fireworks began exploding above the castle in a myriad of multi-coloured stars. "In September, he returned to Charleston, and my mother and Bradley said goodbye at the airport. She said it was an amicable farewell with no tears or regrets, just a realisation that what they had shared together had run to its natural end. He was looking forward to his new job back in the States and she was waiting to hear whether the application she'd submitted for promotion in the English department of the university had been successful."

She stopped for a moment as the first phase of the music built up to its rousing crescendo, which brought hearty applause from the crowd. Bella and Will then stood enraptured as the second phase began quietly as gold and silver stars rotated through the night sky in time to the music.

"And then, out of the blue, she discovered I was on the way. My grandma and granddad were very supportive through her pregnancy and then provided all the childcare she needed. So, the following autumn she was able to get her senior lectureship and embark upon the career she'd always wanted and had worked so hard for. And she's a good mother who has always been there for me when I've needed someone to talk to or a shoulder to cry on. She has given me so much of herself that I've not really missed having a father, although I often wonder what it would have been like to have had a brother or sister. I always wanted a little brother to give piggyback rides to. All too late now, of course." She paused as a huge firework exploded right above their heads, a shower of green and gold stars falling towards them. "It's magical here," she swooned.

"Yes, it is." Turning, though, she saw that Will wasn't looking up at the sky but was facing her, his expression one of admiration and something else which caused a frisson of excitement to ripple through her. As his face moved towards her, she could feel his hot breath caress her face but then, just as his lips touched hers, he abruptly pulled back. "I'm sorry, I promised your mother I'd look after you. This wouldn't exactly fall under that category."

Seeing that his disappointment mirrored her own, she considered for a moment. They weren't kids. She would be nineteen next birthday, while he was twenty-six. She wasn't beholden to her mother, who, after all, was hardly an example on choosing the right guy. Besides, it would only be a harmless kiss. "It most definitely doesn't." She smiled, cupping Will's face with her cold fingers and pulling him towards her until she felt his warm mouth upon hers as they became lost in their first kiss, blocking out the classical music and the snapping of the fireworks as the show reached its grand finale.

*

Her stomach churning, Sarah checked her watch seeing that it had moved on precisely three minutes since the last time she'd looked to 10.24pm. The fireworks and beacon lighting would long since be over, she thought, but then if they'd stopped off at the food and drink stalls before queuing to get out of the car park, there was the possibility Bella wouldn't be home for another hour. She considered again whether she'd been foolhardy in letting her go out with Will, recalling her mother's misgivings about her dates with Bradley which had turned out pretty accurate in the end. She feared becoming as judgemental as her mother now that Bella was old enough to enter the world of serious relationships. Her head reasoned that she must strike a balance between giving her daughter the freedom to make her own decisions while at the same time being poised to pick her up if those turned out to be the wrong ones. She would do it because she loved her, even though she dreaded making a mistake.

Putting the newspaper down, which she'd read from cover to cover, she picked up that day's post. After opening bills and a bank statement, she came to one with the trademark blue and red border, signalling on first glance that it was airmail. Seeing the exotic stamps and that it had been posted in a place called Hilton Head, South Carolina, she read her name in Bradley's writing, which had become more scrawled as the years passed by but was still unmistakably his.

Ripping it open, she read the letter, which was short and to the point, as though he'd grabbed a few precious minutes of time to write it. Talking of the ins and outs of having his fourth volume of poetry published, most of what he said went over her head, just as it had done during the brief time she'd known him. Eventually she came to the end of his letter where he told her he'd included a cheque for ten thousand pounds in Bella's enclosed eighteenth birthday card. Looking down, she picked up the unopened pink envelope from her knee, tracing her fingers over their daughter's name. Initially she felt rage boil up within her. How dare he believe such an ostentatious present over six months late would in any way make up for being absent from Bella's life? It almost felt like an apology, as though he felt money could replace never being there to tuck Bella in at night, to put a plaster on her bloodied knee, to soothe her tears and fears. But maybe she was complicit too. She'd known Bradley was a free spirit and out of the picture by the time she'd discovered she was pregnant and yet she'd taken the decision to have the child, to be a single parent. Feeling the skin on her neck prickle with anger, she picked up her phone and punched in Cath's number.

"Sarah, long time, no hear," came her friend's Geordie tones on the crackling line. Cath Lowery was Sarah's oldest friend since they'd met over a quarter of a century ago on their first day at university. They'd struck up an instant friendship, even though it was definitely a case of opposites attracting as, during their student days, Sarah had always been in the shadow of the outgoing Cath, with her confident and opinionated views almost as fiery as her red hair. Since then, Cath, happily married to Harry, an economics professor, had become the model housewife, bringing up their three sons while launching a successful jewellery-making business from their ten-bedroom house in a leafy suburb of Oxford, meaning that Sarah still felt in awe of her. Despite that, Cath was the only person in the world in whom she could really confide.

"I know." She stifled a sob. Hearing Cath's voice, she wished she was in the room with her to give her a cuddle, to make everything better. "I've failed, Cath, at being a mother."

For the next hour, she poured her heart out, telling her all about Bella's predicament and Bradley's letter, as well as mentioning Tad and her mum, while barely hearing her friend's encouraging asides. When she'd finished talking through a veil of tears, Cath gave her succinct advice. "Look, Sarah, you're going to Poland in a few weeks and you've got so much going on with your mum and granddad. I would postpone saying anything to Bella about Bradley's letter or the money until you've dealt with all that. And, just remember, Bella is a sensible young woman. With your guidance and support, she'll find her own way. She is made of strong stuff, like her mother."

"It doesn't feel like it," said Sarah, "but rather as though I'm a lone reed being buffeted by winds from every direction."

"No, you've always been the quiet, confident one," said Cath. "The best friend I've always wanted to emulate."

"Really?" She was truly surprised.

"Yes, of course, you daft thing!" she replied. "I couldn't have brought up a child on my own. But what you've done with Bella, well, I just wish you were as proud of yourself as I am."

"Thank you, that means so much. Oh, I think Bella's back," said Sarah, wiping away the tears streaming down her cheeks with the back of her hand. "I'll say bye for now."

"Okay, but if you ever need to chat about anything, give me a bell," said Cath. "Day or night, you know I'm here for you."

Hearing a car pull up outside the house, followed by Bella and Will's excited voices heading up the small front garden, Sarah walked over to the shelf, placed Bradley's letter and cheque carefully between the pages of *Little Women* and just had time to slip the book back into its place as she heard the door open.

23

Blackpool, May 1942

Walking to Eirlys's house that evening, I noticed the roses were coming into bloom, despite it only being the middle of May. It made me think of how, in Poland, after the severe frosts and snows of winter, the spring flowers come a little later. Jacek then entered my mind, as he so often did, and I imagined the dangers he would have faced since the last time I saw him on that dimly lit Krakow street. Was he even alive? It was too painful to even contemplate.

Every night just before I go to sleep, I take out the set of rosary beads Dziadek carved for my first holy communion when I was eight years old. As I incant the mysteries, I pray to my Holy Mother Mary to intercede and keep my brother safe, to wrap him in her protective arms when our birth mother cannot.

I approached Eirlys's front door filled with trepidation, Mrs Watkins having passed on an unexpected invitation to join them for a meal. Surmising that she probably disapproved of my friendship with her daughter, I was anxious to dispel any worries she had about me. Just as I lifted my hand to knock, the door opened, Eirlys's smiling face greeting me. Seeing my surprised expression, she explained she'd been watching from the window for my arrival and, taking me by the hand, she led me through the dark hallway into a brightly lit kitchen.

The kitchen was dominated by a large stove emitting enough heat to warm the entire room even on the coldest of winter mornings, which made it more than a place for cooking and eating food. It was the warm heart of Eirlys's home. In front of the stove stood Eirlys's mother, who this time greeted me with a friendly smile. Wearing a dress in a summery lemon shade, her dark hair was lightly touched with silver and pinned up in a flattering style, and I surmised that, a few decades ago, she would have been the image of her daughter.

"Mummy, I want to introduce you to Tad. Tad, this is my mother." Eirlys smiled, although I noticed her mouth twitched nervously at the corners.

"Hello, Mrs Watkins. I'm very pleased to make your acquaintance," I stammered over the English words as I bowed my head. Taking her hand in mine, I kissed it, hoping she wouldn't detect that I was shaking with nervousness inside and out.

"Oh, Tad, I'm so pleased to finally meet you. Eirlys has told me so much about you." Her voice was deep and authoritative as she studied me curiously with her hazel eyes which were flecked with gold. "And the first thing I need to say is – thank you for coming to England to fight with us, to help us win this dreadful war and defeat Hitler and his Nazis."

Taken aback by her kind words, my nerves calmed. "I didn't really have a choice," I said deferentially. "I mean my country, Poland, had been overrun by invading armies; I had no option but to leave and fight."

"Well, we all appreciate your sacrifice. It still must have been a difficult decision to make." Her comment hung in the air and, as I could not think of a reply, I nodded. "Please, let's make ourselves comfortable in the sitting room?" she continued after a moment, as Eirlys and I followed her through and positioned ourselves on a flowery settee while Mrs Watkins settled into an armchair.

"My Ted fought in the Great War." Mrs Watkins focused her attention on the photograph of the smart-looking young man in uniform angled towards her on the tiny table next to her chair. "But he didn't make it back, unfortunately."

"I'm sorry." I struggled for any words in English to describe how I felt but could find none. My nerves were making me tongue-tied so I tried to breathe slowly.

"Ted was killed a few days before the armistice was signed. He is buried in St Symphorien cemetery near Mons. I've never been able to visit but I hope to see his grave one day." She trailed off to seek refuge in some memory of her husband.

"I'm sure you will, one day, Mrs Watkins, when this war is won." I paused, shifting slightly in my seat while I considered what to say next to this lady who still grieved for her husband. "Your husband served his country well, as I hope to do."

"I told you he was so brave, didn't I, Mummy?" Eirlys, seeing that I was floundering, cut in to rescue me. "Now, why don't we have some tea?"

Despite being on rations, Mrs Watkins had made a real effort, and the table was laid with ham, tomatoes, bread and butter, and pickles, as well as a strange pink and yellow sponge cake wrapped in almond paste which she called Battenberg cake. Despite its distasteful German name, I actually quite liked the almond flavour and helped myself to seconds as Eirlys, her mother and I lost track of time talking about all manner of things, with Mrs Watkins particularly interested in hearing all about my family – Tata, Mama, Jacek and Dziadek. Whether Eirlys sensed I needed to be surrounded by the comforts of home after spending so long away from my own or whether she enjoyed seeing her mother so engrossed in conversation, I don't know, but when I glanced down at my watch, it was already nine o'clock.

"Are we keeping you up?" Mrs Watkins smiled mischievously as, despite fierce attempts to suppress it, I was unable to stifle a huge yawn.

"Yes, I mean, no." I felt my face flush. "I mean I have a 5am start for training tomorrow. We have marching practice on the promenade where the drill sergeant will be on the lookout for any slackers! Late nights are definitely not encouraged."

"I was only joking, Tad, off you go and get a good night's sleep, and come round again soon." She held out my uniform jacket for me to put on. As I eased my arms into the sleeves, Mrs Watkins patted my shoulders, her hands resting there for a moment, and I wondered if she had helped her husband on with his jacket when he had left for the last time. Walking back to my lodgings, I felt a presentiment of dread as if a dark shadow had just crossed my path.

*

In the days that followed, Eirlys and I saw each other as often as we could. The more time I spent with her, the more I knew that she was the girl I wanted to spend the rest of my life with. But the world in which we lived made it impossible to admit to myself, let alone Eirlys, that that could ever happen. Only a few minutes' walk from where she worked and where I trained, we would meet on the sand dunes. I remember one summer afternoon in particular. Sunny but with a brisk breeze blowing off the sea, we lay down on my greatcoat in the shelter of one of the larger dunes.

"Teach me some Polish," Eirlys said, her head resting on my shoulder.

"*Dzień dobry* means hello. *Dziękuję* means thank you. *Dobranoc* means good night." I smiled, stroking her face, trying to commit its contours to memory.

"And what else?" she said excitedly.

"Numbers," I replied. Knowing how complicated the Polish language was, I chose the simplest words I could think of: "*Jeden, dwóch, trzy, cztery, pięć, sześć, siedem, osiem, dziewięć, dziesięć.*" I took my time over each syllable, as Eirlys pulled a funny face.

"It sounds like you are reciting a love poem to me. I never knew counting could sound so lyrical, so romantic. *Dzień dobry*, Tad." Eirlys smiled, and I smiled too, as the words sounded different when spoken by her. Not Polish at all but some other language altogether that I neither spoke nor understood.

"*Kocham Cię*," I said, stroking some stray dark hairs from her forehead.

"*Kocham Cię*," she repeated. "That sounds nice. What does that mean?"

"I love you," I said, bending forward to kiss her lightly on the lips so she could not read the conflicting feelings on my face. Not regretting saying the words exactly but promising a future I increasingly felt I wasn't going to have. Not wanting to invite a response, I pulled her to her feet and, glancing worriedly at my watch, said, "Right, we're both going to be late back to work. We must hurry or we'll be in trouble."

That time was a hiatus for me between what had happened before and what was to occur after. My first war had consisted of watching helplessly as the Nazis invaded my country, their bold black-and-red flags defiling the pale medieval buildings of my beloved Krakow, their jackboots resonating harshly on the ancient cobbled streets, as they arrogantly thought they could erase our thousand-year-old history in an instant. My first war had been saying goodbye to my father as he left Dziadek and I behind. Watching him walk away from us, the thought had formed in my mind that I might never see him again. My first war had been hearing no news of Jacek from the night I last saw him on that Krakow street and fearing for him every minute and hour since. My first war had been witnessing my professors battered and loaded into trucks by the Nazis. My first war had been realising Poland was lost and that I must escape or face being killed like the hundreds of thousands before me. My first war had been putting the survival skills Jacek taught me into practice: shooting and gutting animals and birds, and finding shelter and making fires as I'd made my way across Europe to safety on this island. My first war had been hearing that my childhood friend Antusz had been shot in the back by a Nazi patrol while running over a field, a fate which could so easily have been mine.

But I had survived. I had reached Blackpool, this seaside town where people had been coming for decades to take a rest from their harsh working lives. A brief interlude of peace and enjoyment before returning to reality. The irony wasn't lost on me. Maybe that was what I needed too, if not battle-sore, then foot-sore and weary as I began to grasp just how perilous my journey had been and would continue to be.

The town was now packed with military personnel from all over the globe. After our basic training, things suddenly intensified as the RAF required us rookies to be operational as quickly as possible. We began with a five-mile run on the sand dunes each day before breakfast, which Jerzy despised, but I didn't mind so much, being accustomed to living an outdoors lifestyle. Our officers said it instilled a sense of discipline into us which we would need going forward as they turned my friends and I from enthusiastic but inexperienced boys into able military men. The run was followed by long morning sessions, our RAF colleagues explaining the idiosyncrasies of the aircraft we would have to fly. Following a hurried lunch, we were obliged to go to the gymnasium for more fitness training before briefings in Polish occupied the afternoons. Those were action-filled days, so hectic that I had no time to think.

24

Lancaster, November 2020

Bella scuffed the toes of her cherry-red Doc Martens as she dragged them through piles of dried-up leaves. The tall building looming ahead was blanketed by thick fog in a ghostly eeriness reminiscent of the Dickens novels she was fond of reading as the winter nights drew in. Half an hour ago, she'd been triumphant in the knowledge that she'd tricked her mother into thinking her friend Lulu had returned home from university for a few days and had organised a sleepover, a common occurrence when they'd been revision buddies the previous summer. But now she felt apprehension wash over her.

Five months ago she'd thought that, on completing her A-levels and leaving school, she would make a seamless transition from girlhood to womanhood, but the reality had been quite different. While her schoolfriends had moved on with their lives, Bella was still living with her mum, obeying her house rules as she'd always done. She felt so immature in comparison to them and was determined to finally make the leap into adulthood. Approaching the austere-looking three-storey terrace which housed Will's apartment, she had one thought only in her mind. Tonight was the night she would lose her virginity.

Although her mother had warned her that Will was a philanderer unable to keep his roving eyes and hands, apparently, off every attractive fresher he encountered, Bella hadn't noticed this. In fact, during the weeks that she'd got to know him, he'd been nothing but thoughtful and charming towards her. They'd found that they had a lot in common while talking and laughing over al-fresco lunches, bathed in autumn sunshine on the steps of Princess Alexandra Square, as well as over cosy coffees in campus coffee shops on days when the weather had turned overcast. Then there had been their Bonfire Night kiss, followed by a second a few days later when her mother had been away on a course in Leeds and Will had given her a lift home after work. Other boys with other agendas might have wangled their way into her house, but Will had courteously walked her to her doorstep where he'd kissed her in the rain, leaving the promise of things to come on her lips.

Despite a couple of invitations, Bella had never visited Will's apartment before, and she looked up at the proliferation of buzzers which testified to the many subdivisions of the building. Eventually, she found his smudged name, but as her finger hesitantly hovered over it, a girl in an electric-blue coat rushed up behind her to get out of the rain, letting in Bella in the process. As she climbed the dark stairwell, her heart pumping furiously against her ribcage, Bella imagined what her first time would be like. Being almost a decade older than her and with her mother's assessment of his character, she knew that Will was bound to be an experienced lover who would guide her through it. But would it be the romantic, all-consuming passion she'd seen depicted on films or the sweet meeting of souls she'd imagined Eirlys and Tad had shared all those years ago? Finally, she reached the door to Will's apartment. Licking her dry lips nervously and taking a deep breath, she rapped her knuckles on the peeling white paint three times.

Half opening the door, Will was bare-chested, the look of surprise on his face mirroring Bella's. As he stood motionless and speechless for what seemed like an eternity, Bella literally didn't know where to look but couldn't help her eyes straying to the cramped room behind him. Combining his eating and living quarters, it was far removed from the luxurious apartment she'd pictured him living in whenever he'd described it to her. Just a messy flat filled with second-hand furniture, including a rickety table strewn with the remains of a meal and three empty wine bottles, which, from the glazed expression in Will's eyes, Bella guessed he'd consumed a good portion.

"Bella, I wasn't expecting you," he blurted out in the end, while scooping a black shirt off the floor to cover his modesty.

"No, I thought I'd surprise you." Bella felt a crimson blush creep over her cheeks.

"You certainly have." Will flashed his irresistible smile as Bella's eyes came to focus on the girl dashing from what she presumed was the bedroom to the bathroom. Dressed in just her bra and panties and with her back turned, Bella nevertheless recognised the girl's waist-length auburn hair as belonging to one of the freshers she'd seen hanging around the library that week.

Her mum's stark warnings ringing in her ears, Bella felt sick to the stomach. Looking up at Will, the romantic image she'd conjured of him fell away and she saw the reality of the situation: that he was a rather pathetic man who used his good looks and charm to prey on girls almost a decade his junior. Seeing something harden within her, Will stepped out into the corridor, closing the door to his flat behind him to offer them some privacy. "What you saw just then, Bella, it means nothing. I've had a bit too much to drink and one thing led to another. I like you, Bella. We have such a connection, don't you think?"

"No, we don't," she said calmly, stepping back to lean on the banister, away from his reach. "And don't patronise me by telling me what I saw. I know exactly what I saw and, more importantly, I know what you are."

"Bella, wait! We can sort this out." He grabbed her arm, desperation or self-pity flickering in his eyes.

"No, we can't," she grappled herself free, "because I'm not going to be another notch on your bedpost. Goodbye, Will!"

And with that she rushed down the staircase, Will's pleading voice echoing through the darkness as she let herself out into the November night. Walking home, she felt her emotions see-saw back and forth from one extreme to another as she chastised herself for being so stupid and naive. Over the years she'd been guilty of romanticising her mum and dad's brief relationship just as she had more recently Eirlys and Tad's. Somewhere in the back of her mind, she'd wondered whether she and Will might share something akin to what her great-grandfather and great-grandmother had felt for one another. But she realised now that all she had with Will was a rather one-sided infatuation which had nothing to do with love. Eirlys and Tad's relationship had been so much more than that, a once-in-a-lifetime meeting of souls, something she may never experience, she realised bitterly. She knew that, had she chosen to visit Will on a night when he happened to be alone, all they would have shared was a cheap and rather sordid affair. Playing her foolishness over in her head as she hurried home, she choked back sobs as she realised how close she had come to making the biggest mistake of her life so far.

"Bella, what's wrong?" Her mother's face was etched with concern as she met her in the hall.

"I just had a quarrel with Lulu, that's all," Bella replied, unable to look her mother in the eye. At that moment, she felt she was made of glass and that any sympathetic words would shatter her into a million pieces. "It turns out she was counting on me going to Verbier with her and her family at Christmas but obviously we have the Krakow trip booked." Bella paused, thinking it was better to keep her lie simple. Any attempt to elaborate further would be picked up by her mum, she knew instinctively.

"It can't be helped, Bella. You used to live in each other's pockets when you were at school but now with her away at uni, you're bound to grow apart a bit." Sarah hugged her daughter to her. "How about you take a long, hot shower and get an early night? You can phone her in the morning and sort things out."

"Yes, I think I'll do just that," Bella sighed as her mum dropped a kiss onto her forehead. Smiling at her as she walked upstairs, Bella could see from her mum's expression that she didn't fully believe her explanation but was grateful that she didn't pry any further.

Switching on the shower, the water gushed down her body mingling with an unstoppable flow of salty tears which stung Bella's eyes. For the first time, she saw things as they were; that her mother and father had shared just a brief fling of which she'd been the unexpected result and her dream of a reconciliation between them one day was just that: a dream which had no basis in reality. Turning her attention to her grandma, she saw her marriage with new eyes too. Whenever she talked about George, she always used adjectives like 'dependable', 'caring' and 'a good father to Sarah'. Were these appropriate words to describe the love of your life, the one person your whole world spun around? Drying herself, Bella was too exhausted to think about it any longer, but later that night, as she lay in bed, a certain clarity came to her. Her anger slipping away and replaced by relief, she realised that, inspired by Tad and Eirlys's romance, she'd been trying to rush everything with her own love life. Drifting towards a calm sleep, she saw that it wasn't a man she needed at this moment in time and least of all, Will. She had to find herself first.

25

Following a series of rigorous tests and a medical which I almost didn't pass, as my lungs still bore the after effects of pneumonia, my weeks in Blackpool continued to be occupied from dawn until dusk. Jerzy, my other Polish colleagues and I quickly became acquainted with the ways of the RAF with kitting-out sessions, vaccinations and, of course, continued intensive training. On the beach, the sergeants drilled us at 4.30am every morning to march at one hundred and forty paces per minute, which they ramped up by a further twenty paces within a matter of weeks.

At RAF Squires Gate, they trained us on the bombing and target ranges while we gained practical experience of flying on the surrounding airfield. We were taught how to salute the RAF way, which was very different from the Polish way Father had once demonstrated to Jacek and me.

We were also required to attend a raft of lectures on aircraft recognition, navigation, mathematics and Morse code, which meant our English skills came on in leaps and bounds. Meanwhile, the daily emphasis upon physical training to get our bodies in peak condition and fitness ensured that we were all exhausted by nightfall and slept as soundly as babes back at our lodgings.

On completing our arduous and lengthy training, we finally passed out and so our stay in Blackpool came to an end, meaning we sadly had to bid farewell to Mrs Matthews and her gracious hospitality. Standing on the brightly polished brass front step of her guesthouse, she hugged us all a few moments more than necessary and I knew the tears in her eyes were not only for us but for her son as well, who, although killed three years before in the Battle of Britain, had been in her thoughts constantly as she'd cooked and washed and cleaned for us these past months.

We were assigned to 305 Polish Bomber Squadron and deployed south-east to RAF Ingham in Lincolnshire, an airbase surrounded by the flattest landscape I had ever seen. Separated from Eirlys, the heartache I felt made me realise that I was indeed in love with her. However, I had no choice but to put these feelings to one side now and focus on my job. Initially, we underwent dual flying practice in de Havilland Mosquitoes, twin-engine shoulder-winged combat aircraft, which our RAF colleagues affectionately nicknamed 'Mossies'. They were light fighter bombers with a two-man crew of pilot and navigator and were designed for low-altitude daylight bombing and tactical air strikes on bridges, railway lines and factories. Their big advantage was their speed, nineteen miles per hour faster than Spits because of their lightweight structure, making them, at one point, the fastest aircraft in the world but still able to carry a substantial bomb load.

I made my first practice flight with a cheery chap called Roy, who had a round, red face and a pleasant, encouraging demeanour, which was crucial as nerves tied my stomach in knots. Driven on all this time by a determination to fight back against Nazi Germany for invading my country and brutally assaulting my university professors, it had never occurred to me until that moment when I first sat in the cockpit that my flying skills might be so inferior as to deny me the opportunity. Sweating in my flying jacket, helmet and goggles, I nervously began my take off, bumping a little erratically along the ground. Pulling back on the strangely named 'joystick', I felt the aircraft suddenly weightless beneath me and, looking down, I saw we were indeed rising at a steep angle. I immediately discovered my worries were unfounded as I experienced forty minutes of pure exhilaration and so, driven by the urgency of the war situation and my own emerging skill, I was soon allowed to fly my first mission.

I recall how my body shook with nerves as I sat with my navigator Tomasz in the briefing room before that first mission as Wing Commander Adamczak informed us of anticipated enemy activity and patrols, the bomb load we were to carry, as well as our designated take-off times. The meteorological officer followed him, giving us information about the weather forecasted and alternative routes to follow if conditions were bad on our return to base. Finally, but most vitally, the intelligence officer filled us in on the movements of enemy troops as well as the bomb line, the line separating enemy and Allied troops. With the aid of a topographical map, we all then took time to plan the route for that day.

On the runway before that first mission, nerves bubbled in my stomach as self-doubt set in once more. Just over three years ago I'd been an architecture student at Jagiellonian University, the quiet, studious son not the outgoing, adventurous one. That role had fallen to Jacek, the brave one, the son destined to follow in our father's footsteps. But from the moment I took off that day, I felt at one with my plane as though it was giving me the courage I needed to take control of my life once more. After living in fear during those months after the invasion of Poland followed by my perilous journey across Europe, I felt emboldened and in charge of my own destiny again. Looking down to the green patchwork of fields, intersected here and there by a river, a glade of trees or a building, the world seemed to shrink before my eyes. I was no longer at its mercy but soaring above it towards the heavens.

The flight was truly exhilarating as, without an airspeed indicator, I had to gauge everything by the way it felt. It was both exciting and terrifying! But on the back of these instantaneous, powerful emotions came a whole host of more considered ones. I pondered what Dziadek would think if he'd been able to see me now. Knowing that he wouldn't comprehend what I was doing from the safe confines of his world of wood, I found myself thinking of ways I could explain to him what I was experiencing so that he might share my feelings as I flew. First, that it was entirely up to me to get the aircraft down to the ground in one piece. That the turbulence and updrafts made me realise just how far down my stomach could plummet in my body. That somehow I was able to steer around bumps which weren't even visible. That I was sitting in a metal box five thousand feet up in the sky, held up just by air. That I was simultaneously the most powerful and the most vulnerable I had ever been.

Those early missions always seemed to follow the same pattern. We took off one by one and flew at four thousand feet until we reached behind enemy lines, where we carried out our patrols. Whenever we located something of interest, we dropped down and if it proved to be a train or a formation of tanks, we attacked from low level and discharged our bombs, for which the RAF boys often had amusing nicknames like Angry Ann and Big Bertha. Such operations I found both hair-raising and exciting as swooping down too far risked hitting the ground, trees and power lines. If Tomasz felt we were in any danger, he would shout, "Up!" and I subsequently tried to gain height as quickly possible. After everything I'd endured to get to the UK, the last thing I intended was giving the Nazis a chance to shoot me down.

During those spring months, I managed a few trips back to Blackpool with Jerzy who, by that time, also had a girl, Irene, who lived near RAF Squires Gate. But the occasion that stood out was when Eirlys suggested we visit the Pleasure Beach. I had never been anywhere like it! Even the signs were translated into Polish, as the town's welcome for us extended to its tourist attractions. Though I was, by this time, used to the rush of flying a plane, I screamed with excitement as we went on the Big Dipper and Grand National rides. Strolling around hand in hand with Eirlys as we ate popcorn and chips amongst other people out for fun and frolics, it was easy to forget that we were in the midst of a war. It was only when we were leaving when Eirlys pointed out that a row of sheds, where fairground rides had once been made and repaired, had been recently requisitioned by the Vickers Armstrong Factory to manufacture gun turrets for the Wellingtons, that the spell of the summer's evening was broken.

In August 1943, the squadron moved to RAF Swanton Morley in Norfolk, where it ceased to be heavily affiliated to Bomber Command. Due to my high-level flying skills and successful missions, I was promoted to Pilot Officer and assigned to 303 Squadron; a great honour for me to join the most prestigious Polish fighter squadron of the war. The squadron had just converted to the latest Spitfire MKIX, the most wonderful machine I'd ever flown. Like an extension of my own body, we flew as one.

It felt invigorating to finally come face to face with my enemy as I imagined I was fighting friends and family members of those Nazis who occupied my country and who were killing my people. Our primary role, however, was to escort the missions of the US B-17 Flying Fortresses and B24s over the Channel and on their return from bombing raids over Germany. While some of my colleagues found this rather mundane work, the only thing that concerned me was that we were continuing to down enemy fighters wherever we went, thus helping Allied forces try to win the war.

But whilst my days were an endless stream of duties and dogfights, my nights were empty and desolate. Being separated from my brother was something I hadn't been able to get my head around since Jacek had left Zakopane to undertake his cadet training six years before. Since then, we had been pulled even further apart by war and the need to fight for our country. During the daylight hours with the welcome distractions of my job, I was able to push thoughts of my brother to the dark corners of my mind. My nights, however, were broken by fractured, recurrent dreams of him. In the first one, Jacek was in great danger and I heard him cry out for help before seeing myself as a small boy again, lying on the bank of the Dunajec River spluttering river water as I vowed to repay my brother for saving my life. Despite taking slightly different routes every time, the dream always ended with me snapping awake, never knowing whether I'd managed to save Jacek or not.

Although I sensed Jacek, wherever he was, would be proud of me for reaching the UK to fight with the Polish Air Force, I felt the contradictory pull that every time I put on my flying suit I risked death and the prospect of breaking my promise to my brother. The dilemma weighed heavily upon me until I decided to concentrate on what I could control. The rest was in the Lord's hands.

The second dream, which on waking I dismissed as fantastical, was even more vivid than the first. In it, Jacek and I were flying a Mossie together which had been hit by enemy fire and was plunging wildly though the sky. Desperately attempting to bail out and release our parachutes, the last thing I recalled was Jacek shouting, "*Teraz!*" *Now!* It was at this point, drenched in sweat, that I always woke up to spend the next uneasy hour or so trying but failing to decipher the dream's meaning.

In my waking dream, Eirlys's face appeared in front of me, but as I stretched out my hand to touch her delicate skin, I always found she was just beyond my reach. In fact, the harsh reality was that I had hardly seen her for months, and in November 1943 the squadron was posted to RAF Ballyhalbert in Northern Ireland to fly convoy patrols in the Atlantic, defeating all my plans to steal a few hours with her that Christmas. It wasn't until late spring 1944 that we moved back to England, but even then our location in Horne was thirty miles to the south of London, rendering a lengthy trip to Blackpool impossible on the odd days of leave I was granted. We found time, however, to write to each other every week as we sent letters of love written against a background of war.

26

Bella looked pensively out of the passenger window, the greys and greens of sky and fields rolling by in a blurred smudge as they sped down the motorway that Sunday morning. While she loved the vibrant autumnal colours as well as appreciating the stark monochrome of winter landscapes, she always disliked this in-between time in mid-November when the autumn had discarded its colourful coat of leaves but winter seemed hesitant in launching full-throttle into its first frosts and snowfalls.

She was thinking about her great-grandma, the woman she was just coming to know after all these years. She wondered how it must have felt for the young Eirlys every time Tad had taken to the skies. Had she been able to get on with her day-to-day duties at the factory or had her thoughts been forever bound with him while he'd been gone, worrying that at any moment he could be engaged in a dangerous sortie from which he might not emerge alive? Thinking of the powerlessness of Eirlys's situation, Bella shivered.

"Are you planning on seeing Will again?" Sarah enquired as nonchalantly as she could. Bella had been expecting the question for a few days now and wasn't surprised her mother had waited until this car journey where she had her undivided attention.

"No, I don't think so." Bella smiled, her mind flitting rapidly from one thought to another as she quickly decided upon what exactly she would tell her mother.

"I didn't think he was right for you," Sarah interjected, Bella purposely avoiding her gaze.

"No, he wasn't. We had some interests in common and our Bonfire Night date was okay." Bella paused to consider her lie. "But I think, in the end, the age gap between us is too great. We are at very different stages in our lives so it wouldn't have worked out."

"I did try to warn you about that." Sarah winced inwardly, knowing she sounded very judgemental. "I just worry about you, Bella, that's all. I don't mean to be pushy," she added apologetically.

"Don't worry, Mum, I'm okay." Bella fiddled with the radio frequency to find some music to cut short their discussion. "I've just decided that I really don't need the distraction of a boyfriend at the moment, that's all. I need to focus on getting to know myself rather than someone else, to concentrate on working out what it is I want to do with my life."

Sarah swallowed abruptly, for once lost for words, but deeply relieved that her daughter had seen sense where Will Beckett was concerned. They both fell silent, listening to the music as Bella turned her attention back to the landscape while Sarah focused on the road.

"Do you think Grandma is okay?" Bella broke the silence as the land flattened out on their approach to the coast.

"I think so. She hasn't mentioned anything to you, has she?" Sarah momentarily cast her eyes in her daughter's direction, noting the concern in her voice.

"No, it's just... Well, she's been looking pale and tired recently." Bella took in her mother's anxious expression. "Maybe it's the trip to Poland she's worried about? I'm concerned it might be too much for her, stirring up strong emotions about her father. When we first talked about it, it seemed like a big adventure with sightseeing and Christmas shopping thrown in. But as the trip gets nearer, it feels a much bigger deal than that."

"I've been thinking the same. After the air show in the summer, we all got carried away with it a bit, thinking it would be nice to visit Tad's country of birth and feel connected to him somehow. But what if we find something deeply distressing about him or his family? I know your grandma has coped with his absence all these years by holding it at arm's length, which is how Grandma Eirlys handled it when she was alive. But this past year, she seems to have visibly aged each time we see her." Sarah looked at her daughter, her forehead furrowed with worry lines.

"Yes, I've noticed that too," Bella sighed deeply. "All we can do is ask her whether she's up to the trip, I suppose."

Anna was her usual chirpy self when she answered the door, dressed smartly in a ruby-red linen shift dress which she'd stylishly accessorised with a black bolero, black tights and heeled, knee-length boots. Her hair, which she'd grown into a longer style these past few months, was coiffured in perfect curls at the back, her new long, swept-over fringe giving her a youthful air, which was followed through in her smooth cheekbones and bright blue eyes.

"You look well," Sarah couldn't help but comment, her mother's appearance dispelling the concerns they'd discussed on the journey. "Your new hairstyle has taken years off you."

"Thank you, I feel it." Anna smiled, following them through to the kitchen. Determined to throw them off the track, ten minutes before they'd arrived she'd made sure she'd secreted her hospital appointment letter in-between the pages of *The Winter Folly*, her current read by Lulu Taylor. Dr Duke had been very reassuring when she'd visited him, her blood pressure and heart rate a little high but nothing to worry unduly about. Due to her advancing years, however, he'd referred her for tests in the New Year as a precaution, an appointment she intended on pushing to the furthest corner of her mind during her Polish trip. "Now shall we have some coffee to warm us up before we brave the promenade?" She bustled around, opening cupboards as though she had all the energy in the world.

Grey clouds glowered overhead as the three women walked down to the seafront. Boarding houses were bathed in darkness and would be closed until the Christmas season got into full swing now that the illuminations had been switched off. After a few friendly exchanges with Bella,

Anna fell silent, letting her daughter and granddaughter believe she wanted to be alone with her reflections about her father as the sea came into view. In fact it was an effort to walk and talk at the speed they were setting but she felt she had no option but to continue at their pace. To reveal her discomfort would mean jeopardising the trip to Poland, and with it the chance of discovering anything more about her father. And that was something she could not risk.

The Remembrance Sunday service got underway with a solitary bugler playing the last post. The moving service staged around the cenotaph, a tall white obelisk pointing to the heavens, resonated in its poignant setting on the seafront. As Anna looked out at the grey sea, the waves swelling and falling, she found herself imagining Tad's death. She knew from what her mother had told her that he'd come down in his plane off the Dutch coast just a matter of weeks before the war had ended; she knew the when, the how and the where, the bare, cold facts. But as the crowd around her descended into hushed prayers for the fallen soldiers, she considered what it had been like for Tad on the night he'd been shot down, whether death had been instantaneous and he'd known nothing about it or whether he'd felt his plane spiral beneath him before being engulfed by the cold waters of the North Sea. She wondered whether his life had flashed before him, his home and family life in Poland and the precious time he'd spent with her mother in Blackpool. Brushing away her thoughts and tears, she focused on the minister's prayers.

Sarah felt salty tears sting her cheeks as she delved deep into the pocket of her winter coat and pulled out a scarlet flower. She had always pictured poppies blowing in French fields, their colour coming from the blood of the men who had died there, a romanticised view picked up from the poetry she'd studied in school. As she stood with the other people that November morning, huddled beneath dark umbrellas, she thought of how the demographics of the crowd had changed over the years. Her memories of the first few services she'd attended as a small girl were of extremely old men who had fought on the battlefields of the Somme and Passchendaele. Most of them had been in wheelchairs and had talked to Sarah kindly. Then there had been her schoolfriends' grandfathers who had told her their stories of fighting on the beaches at D-Day. These men had been able to march in the first few years but gradually they had replaced the First World War veterans in wheelchairs as they stopped attending or died. Then, seventeen years ago, new faces had begun to appear. Soldiers in their uniforms in-between tours of Iraq and Afghanistan and the young widows and children of those who had not come home. As the prayers ended, and the laying of the wreaths began, she closed her eyes once more and retreated into her thoughts of Tad.

Turning towards the sea, Anna looked at the poppy laying in the palm of her hand. All of a sudden, a sharp gust of wind whipped it away and she watched as the red flower tumbled through the air and down into the heaving waters of the sea, carried to her father, wherever he was. She momentarily closed her eyes to say a private prayer for the man of whom she had no memories before turning towards the people in dark coats clustered around the cenotaph.

The service concluded, the crowd began to disperse seeking a Full English in one of the many cheery cafes on the promenade to warm up and elevate their sombre mood. Bella suggested the same, but her grandma, not wanting to admit that she was on a health kick in view of her ongoing scare, suggested coffees and croissants in the Beach House Bistro Bar. "We don't want to spoil dinner. It's your favourite, sweetheart."

"Roast beef and Yorkshire pudding followed by treacle sponge and custard?" Bella gabbled excitedly, pulling up the fur-lined hood of her navy puffer jacket as the whipping wind played havoc with her hair.

"Of course." Anna smiled, having decided she'd overload her plate with vegetables before substituting her treacle pudding portion with a mashed-up banana, which she'd smother with custard made with skimmed milk so that neither Sarah nor her eagle-eyed granddaughter would be any the wiser of the dietary advice her doctor had given her.

The wrap-around windows of the Beach House Bistro Bar were steamed up as they entered to find the place crowded out with people who had evidently had the same idea as they had. Bella joined the queue for coffees and pastries while Anna and Sarah retreated to a quiet corner with an unspoiled sea vista. "You would tell me if anything was wrong, wouldn't you, Mother?" Sarah said, her face flushed red as the warmth of the cafe hit her cheeks after braving the bracing sea air for the past hour. "Only I worry about you."

"Of course I would, sweetheart. I'm just tired. I've also been wondering about Dad a lot these past few weeks, whether we'll find any of his family members when we go to Poland." She took her daughter's hand, warming it in her gloved one. "I feel such a responsibility weighing upon me – it's something I need to do, for him, for Mum, for me, for you and for Bella."

"I know you do." Sarah brushed away a tear, thinking of Bella's absentee father and wondering what she'd do when something happened to her mum, to whom she'd always turned for advice and support.

"You're looking tired too, sweetheart. I hope you're not burning the midnight oil," Anna added.

"Oh, you know, the end of term is always manic, and with us going away I won't have my usual prep time for next term during the holidays," Sarah said, feeling snowed under with work and not quite knowing how she'd fit it all into just three weeks.

"I know you're a workaholic, Sarah, and you provide for Bella admirably," Anna sighed. "But you have to be kind to yourself too and make sure you're not absolutely exhausted by the time we board the plane to Krakow."

"They'd run out of croissants so I got us choc-chip and orange muffins instead." Bella breezed over to their table, bearing a tray laden with treats.

"A likely story, Missy," said her mother, passing the coffees around: flat white for her, black for Bella and cafe au lait for Anna.

"So, I'm counting down the days until we go to Poland." Anna smiled at Bella, who was demolishing her muffin. "Have you had any thoughts about what you want to do and see?"

"I've had one or two ideas," Sarah said pensively. "Krakow is such a vibrant city with a rich history that I think we should spend most of our time there. Throughout December there is the Christmas market in the main square, which looks very festive from the pictures I've seen, and then we could do some sightseeing. There's Wawel Castle and Basilica, the old Jewish town of Kazimierz, which has been rejuvenated since *Schindler's List* was filmed there, and then there's the Podgórze ghetto, as well as Oskar Schlinder's former factory, which is now a museum."

"Great minds think alike." Anna clapped her hands. "I've read up on those places and I'd like to visit them all."

"I want to go to Auschwitz too," stated Bella. "We learned about the holocaust in Year 11 and I think it's everyone's duty to remember the people who perished there."

"Yes, I agree. It's a pilgrimage we've got to make," added Anna, "but do you think tour companies will be running trips there in the dead of winter?"

"I'm already on that particular case," said Sarah, digging into the dark depths of her handbag to scroll through her iPhone. "You're right, Mum, most of them do stop taking trips there after the October half-term but I've found a guy who specialises in small mini-bus tours which he tailors to the individual's needs, so I've booked him to take us there."

"What about Zakopane? Can he drive us there too?" Anna interjected, remembering her mother mention that was the town where her dad's family had lived. If she was going to discover anything specific about Tad or his relatives, she had an idea it would be there rather than the city.

Sarah looked at her mother, reading her thoughts as they flipped through her mind. "Yes, he should be able to and I've also given him Grandfather's name so he's going to see if he can find anything out about him, locate a birth certificate or something. Obviously, none of us speaks Polish well enough to find things like that out for ourselves."

"Although, having time on my hands, I've been learning some phrases phonetically these past few weeks. But I'll warn you it's reported to be one of the hardest languages to learn." Bella pulled a face. "And I can certainly vouch for that!"

"Go on then, teach me some words!" said Anna, sipping her steaming coffee. "I'm sure you've got further than I have."

"Okay. *Nazywam się Bella* means I'm called Bella."

"*Nazywam się Anna.*" The old lady clapped her palms together, perfectly copying her granddaughter.

"Nice accent! What else… *Dzień dobry!*"

"That's hello." Sarah smiled. "*Dzień dobry.*"

"*Proszę* is please," Bella went on.

"*Proszę,*" Anna repeated. "That will come in handy in a shop. We can just point to what we want to buy and say *proszę.*"

"*Dziękuję* is thank you." Bella liked the way the language felt on her tongue. In comparison to the harsh German she'd learned in school, Polish sounded almost lyrical.

"*Jen-koo-yea.*" Anna sounded out the syllables phonetically. "I think you'll have to write some of these down for me."

"No, you'll never be able to read them!" Bella laughed. "Then there's *nie rozumiem,* which means I don't understand."

"I've an idea we'll be using that a lot!" Sarah laughed.

"And if all else fails: *Czy mówi pan po angielsku?* Do you speak English?" Bella sighed.

"Just imagine how hard it must have been for Tad and the other Polish flyers to come over here and master English so they could understand and respond to the instructions given by their RAF superiors," commented Anna. "It must have been so daunting."

"That's why we owe it to them to at least attempt their language when we visit their country," Bella said solemnly as Anna vowed to spend as much time as she could in the next three weeks learning her father's language.

Walking home, they took a slower pace, for which Anna was grateful. Back in the kitchen, inhaling the sumptuous smells of the roasting joint of beef, she put on the vegetables. Sarah and Bella safely chatting in the living room, she popped a handful of the tablets her doctor had prescribed. Gulping them down with a glass of cold water, she pondered whether to just come clean about her symptoms to Sarah, fearing that the trip to Poland and the emotions she'd bottled up inside all her life would prove too much for her ageing body. Abruptly, though, she decided against it and snapped shut the kitchen cupboard door, locking the pills and her secret safely inside.

27

On June 6th 1944, I flew with my squadron over the Normandy beaches to provide cover for the thousands of Allied troops disembarking their landing crafts. From the relative safety of the air, I witnessed the bravery of the British, Canadians and Americans as they struggled across the sands, the injured and dead left behind, the sea running red with blood. Joe, the quietly spoken RAF boy, whom I'd got to know quite well sharing as we did a love for the countryside, suffered a great loss, as his brother Oswald was killed on Sword Beach early that first morning. Later that summer, I travelled up to Grasmere with him to attend Oswald's memorial service, the fells and the lakes reminding me of home and lifting my spirits despite the sombre occasion. After D-Day, my squadron remained with the Air Defence of Great Britain for the duration of the summer and by October, the focus of pilots such as us turned to ground attack missions on V-1 and V-2 launch sites in the Netherlands.

At Christmas that year, the war seemed, for us at least, to be on hold for a few days so we were able to take leave to enjoy the festivities. Of course I had heard tales of the Christmas Truce in 1914 with Allied and German troops laying down their weapons that Christmas Eve to join together to sing carols before both sides stepped out onto No Man's Land to exchange food and drink and play games of football. That was not about to happen again, but thirty years later, it felt for a brief moment as though peace had descended from the heavens, filling the earth for a few hours.

Having managed to wangle some leave, Jerzy and I made the long trip to Blackpool where he spent Christmas with his sweetheart Irene and her family while I stayed at Eirlys's house with her mother and three good-natured RAF boys, Stan, Ray and Len, who had been billeted there since the summer. Despite the strict rationing, Mrs Watkins managed to cook us all a traditional English Christmas dinner as we ate two of their chickens, which she and Eirlys had kept in a coop behind the house to provide a steady egg supply. The delicious roast meat was served with potatoes, cabbage, parsnips and carrots picked freshly by Eirlys and me that morning from their vegetable plot, which the government encouraged everyone to have. There were also some strange accompaniments of herb stuffing and bread sauce, which Mrs Watkins proudly served on her best china. Pouring gravy over my meal seemed to meld everything together and I have to say I found it truly delicious.

As I ate, my mind inevitably wandered to previous Christmases spent at Dziadek's cottage, the surrounding pine forest infusing the air with its festive fragrance. Seated around the wooden table, adorned by the magnificent nativity carved by Dziadek's hands, we'd enjoyed our traditional Wigilia meal of fish dishes culminating with carp served in a delicate dill sauce. Helping myself to more of Mrs Watkins' gravy now, I pictured Dziadek sitting on his own at that table the night before, his craggy face bathed in flickering candlelight as he'd prayed for all of us who were absent this year. I wondered whether he had been able to get hold of some fish on the black market or whether he'd had to make do with cooking a soup of vegetables from his garden to mark Christ's birth this year.

"So how do you celebrate Christmas in Poland, Tad?" asked Len, the youngest of the boys who hailed from a long way away in Cornwall and who wrote a letter to his mother every day.

"By eating six different fish dishes!" I laughed, trying to make light of it in front of all these people attempting to enjoy Christmas. Eirlys was the only one to guess my true feelings.

"We eat a lot of crab in Polperro where I come from, but six courses! I think even my neighbours would find that hard going, Tad!" Len laughed, but I saw a cloud pass over his face as he too thought of the people who weren't at his Christmas table this year.

"We eat the meal on Wigilia, on Christmas Eve, rather than Christmas Day. After a day of fasting and, at the appearance of the first star, the Wigilia feast begins. We always set a place at the table for an unexpected guest and spread hay on the tablecloth as a reminder that Christ was born in a manger." I noticed everyone around the table was listening spellbound to my account.

"What a lovely tradition, Tad." Mrs Watkins smiled. "You celebrate the true heart of Christmas, which I think is sometimes sadly forgotten, most especially in times like this."

"Tell them about your Christmas decorations, Tad," Eirlys said, looking forlornly at the puny tree in the corner sparsely furnished with a few homemade trinkets.

"Our cottage is surrounded by a pine forest, so every December my brother and I chop down the biggest tree we can find that will fit into our front room. We then decorate it with wooden carvings made by my grandfather who is a master woodcarver." I paused, wondering whether I still had their attention and saw again they were all enraptured.

"What sort of decorations?" Ray asked. At thirty, he was the most worldly-wise of them but even he was drawn into my stories.

"Everything you can think of to do with Christmas. There are angels with their wings in full flight, nativity scenes, holly bushes, robins, mistletoe, snowflakes and sleighs," I said, my eyes misting as I wondered whether I would ever see Dziadek or the decorated Christmas tree again.

"It sounds like a sight to see," Ray said, and I nodded, unable to say any more.

"Would you like some more chicken?" Mrs Watkins asked, and I smiled, knowing how privileged I was to be a guest at her Christmas table, that the last man to share it had been Eirlys's father. I owed it to Eirlys, Mrs Watkins and the boys to focus on the joy of celebrating Christ's birth together instead of dwelling on the sadness of separation.

"Please, it is delicious." I smiled. After reloading my plate, Eirlys passed it back to me, the candlelight catching the small silver earrings I'd saved up for from my pay and had presented her with that morning. They seemed to perfectly complement her beautiful dark hair and wine-red dress. On finishing the main course, she proudly presented the Christmas pudding which, as she laid it on the table, her mother doused in brandy while I and the others watched, mesmerised as blue flames leaped out in all directions.

"I've been using this same bottle for several years now, as it only gets brought out on Christmas Day. Hopefully it will keep going for a few more Christmases to come," Mrs Watkins joked, and everybody laughed, caught up in the Christmas mood.

"I have never seen anything like this before," I gasped. "In Poland, we set alight glasses of brandy not puddings!"

"You've never lived then, Tad!" Len cheerily slapped me on the back.

"Another tradition we have is to put a silver sixpence in the Christmas pud. Whoever discovers it will have luck bestowed on them for the whole of the next year. But take care and mind your teeth," Eirlys warned as her mother cut the crumbling fruit-encrusted sponge into pieces before handing around a jug of hot nutmeg sauce. "It could be in anyone's slice."

"It's delicious," I commented, the richness of the fruit pudding countered by the sweetness of the sauce. On my fifth mouthful, something hard scraped against my teeth and I pulled it triumphantly from my mouth. "Ah, I think I might have got the silver sixpence."

"The lucky silver sixpence! Well done for finding it, Tad, and not cracking a tooth in the process!" Mrs Watkins clapped her hands together, leading me to suspect she had deliberately given me the piece of pudding containing the coin and the luck.

"I'll make sure I keep it with me at all times." I smiled even though I was not a superstitious man, needing motifs and lucky mascots to fly with as some airmen did. Instead, I believed that God would keep me safe from harm, if that was His will. But I saw from her expectant expression that Eirlys's mother clearly put faith in charms, so I secured it in a safe compartment of my leather wallet.

"Do you have any Christmas traditions like the sixpence to bring the recipient luck, Tad?" the older woman asked, offering me seconds of pudding, which I gratefully accepted for it was very tasty. Looking at her mother in the flickering candlelight as she handed me my dish, I saw how my beloved Eirlys might look in middle age, her dark hair threaded with strands of silver, fine lines around her still lovely eyes and mouth. But I hastily dismissed the picture, not daring to imagine a future twenty-five years hence.

"Not really, although before our Christmas Eve meal we pass around an *opłatek*, a wafer. Everyone breaks off a piece to symbolise forgiveness and letting go of the past. And then, as I told you, we only begin eating when the first star has been spotted in the night sky," I said.

"I think that's a lovely tradition, Tad, maybe we could do it?" Eirlys suggested. "Except we don't have any wafers."

"Perhaps we could use a cracker instead?" I grinned. "So long as it carries the meaning for us, that's the important thing."

So when we'd finished our Christmas pudding, we passed around a cracker, each one of us saying a private prayer before breaking off a piece. Firstly, I asked for God's forgiveness for my inability to feel compassion for the lives I knew I'd taken. I was, however, less successful at leaving the past behind, as Jacek, Dziadek, Tata and Mama stepped to the forefront of my thoughts and remained there for the rest of the evening.

Afterwards, while the boys went to the pub for a celebratory drink, the three of us sat in the living room in the flickering firelight. The darkness infused with the scent of the fir tree, Eirlys and I took the sofa, where we were able to hold hands out of her mother's gaze. Watching the flames light up the older woman's face, I imagined my own mother sitting in Dziadek's house this very night. I wondered whether she would have looked similar to the woman before me with her jade-green dress and slightly greying hair loosely pinned at the nape of her neck or different entirely like the woman who still appeared to me in my dreams, forever young.

The peace of Christmas came to an abrupt end in the New Year when the business of war resumed and the squadron moved yet again to RAF Coltishall in Norfolk to conduct further operations over the Netherlands. On my first sortie that January, as I looked at the straight lines of the Dutch canals and the twists and turns of the rivers far below, my mind rewound to the first time Jacek and I had sailed our raft on the Dunajec River. Thinking how my brother had saved my life that day, I recalled yet again my promise to him and I cried silent tears, wondering how I could possibly return the gesture now, all these years later, all these miles apart.

Returning from this mission, we encountered a fair amount of flak, and although I luckily avoided sustaining any damage to my aircraft, Marek's plane was hit while flying over a gun emplacement, crashing to the ground in flames beneath me. Making my way back to the safety of British shores, my body shook with silent horror, so much so that it was difficult to control the plane. Having known Marek from my adolescent days back in Poland, I relived everything we'd been through together, from bunking off school to go skiing in winter and swimming in summer to hanging around the bars of Zakopane, attempting but often failing to catch the eye of pretty girls. Now he would never see his beloved Poland again, his hopes and dreams, his promising life wiped out in a burning plane tumbling from the sky. Antusz, Marek and I had been part of an unbreakable team, supporting and depending upon each other. Except that now they were both gone and for months afterwards I went to bed each night thinking that if they could die, then what hope was there for me?

Two weeks later, I returned to Blackpool to snatch a few hours with Eirlys at a cafe, overlooking the sea. Dressed in a cheery red coat, she seemed happier than I could ever remember seeing her. Hearing optimistic news of the mounting Allied successes and enemy capitulations on the wireless every evening, she was sure that the war would soon be over. Although I sensed the end of the conflict was indeed coming, I also knew that I was flying into greater danger with every operation, from which the chances of my emerging alive were decreasing by the day.

28

Blackpool, November 2020

Heavy shopping bags strained in Anna's hands as she mooched around the department store searching for the final touches to her gift list. Usually she'd hardly even begun her Christmas shopping by late November let alone almost finished it, but the Polish trip had prompted her to get things in order this year. Browsing the perfume counter, she picked up a large bottle of Rive Gauche she always bought Sarah before locating the aptly named La Vie est Belle fragrance which was her granddaughter's favourite. Witnessing Bella blossoming into a lovely, talented young woman, she felt sure life would indeed be beautiful for her.

Handing the boxes to an elaborately made-up shop assistant to gift wrap, she went through the Polish phrases in her head which she'd require if she bought such items in a Krakow store. *Ile to kosztuje?*– How much is it?; *Proszę*

–Please; and *Dziękuję* –Thank you. Now the countdown of the last few days before their trip to Poland had begun, she'd found herself listening to the language CD she'd borrowed from the library every spare moment she had. Where it had begun out of the necessity of learning a few basic phrases, she'd become intrigued by the softly spoken language of her father and his family to the point that she wanted to hold meaningful conversations when she travelled to his country, not merely exchange pleasantries with shop assistants. But she feared that the language was too complex and the time she had to learn it far too short.

The prettily packaged perfumes added to the rest of her shopping, a wave of tiredness suddenly floored Anna as she made her way through the stuffy precinct. Wanting to avoid a repeat of the health scare she'd experienced on her outing with Barbara, she knew her body was telling her she needed a break so, ducking into M&S, she took the escalator up to the balcony cafe where she enjoyed a cinnamon-sprinkled latte while listening to the Salvation Army band play a medley of Christmas carols. The creamy sweetness of the drink, however, failed to have the desired effect of calming her nerves as she fretted over whether or not her health would withstand the long journey to Eastern Europe in the depths of winter.

Not for the first time, she pondered whether she was being fair to Sarah and Bella. She knew that they were both energetic young women with lots of stamina and she worried that she'd hold them back on the trip. Recalling Sarah had booked a tour guide to ferry them around the city alleviated some of her worries, but she was concerned she wouldn't be able to keep up with their busy itinerary for three weeks or so. She thought maybe she could cry off a couple of outings and stay at the hotel to rest, but she knew that Sarah and Bella, with their razor-sharp instincts, would soon become suspicious if she tried that too many times. On the other hand, if she let Sarah in on her health situation before they went, she knew her daughter would cancel the trip. Nor she thought was it fair to inform her daughter when they arrived when it was too late to do anything about it only worry. A quandary indeed, and one that she had no idea how to resolve.

Stepping out of her taxi, Anna saw a figure, dressed head to toe in black, huddled on her doorstep. She was about to ask the driver to hang around while she ascertained the person's identity before realising who her unexpected visitor was.

"Bella? My god, what are you doing here?" She rushed up the path as her granddaughter stood up from her sitting position on the step, soaked to the skin.

"I quit my job in the library," Bella sobbed, hugging her grandma to her like a warm comfort blanket. "I've been such a bloody fool! Mum will never understand. And our trip to Poland is in a few days! I've ruined everything."

"I'm sure you haven't. Nothing that can't be fixed, anyway," Anna said, twisting the key in the lock while keeping a firm hold of her granddaughter's hand.

Ten minutes later, Bella sat in her grandma's fleecy pink dressing gown at the kitchen table, towel-drying her hair as Anna brought her a steaming cup of tea and huge chunk of Angel cake. "I thought the doctor put you on a healthy, low-fat diet, Gran!"

"What he doesn't know won't hurt him!" Anna winked, biting into the sweet cream and sponge of her slice. "But we're not here to talk about me. What's wrong, Bella? You quit your job? There's no great shame in that. It was only a temporary library job, wasn't it?"

"Yes, it was." Bella shook her head, tears springing to her eyes once more. "There's more to it than that, Gran!"

"Take your time, sweetheart." Anna rubbed her granddaughter's shoulder, somehow guessing where this was going. *Please don't let this be as bad as I'm imagining*, she prayed.

"It wasn't the job. I started dating one of my older colleagues, Will – against Mum's advice, of course. I think that was part of the reason I did it, if I'm honest! And now, it's just so embarrassing." Bella paused, before relating to her grandma everything that had happened the night she'd found Will with the fresher. "I thought I could keep going into work and be civil to him and pretend nothing had happened. But one or other of his conquests is always hanging around and he's started making snide remarks to me, which I find upsetting. I really liked him, Gran, but now I just feel stupid."

"I think you can count yourself fortunate you had a lucky escape. He sounds like a bit of a cad, this Will," Anna said, sipping her steaming tea while feeling light-headed with relief that nothing had happened between Bella and this womaniser.

"He is. Mum had warned me about his reputation, but I thought I knew better. I felt like such an idiot, that night." Bella paused to gather her thoughts. "I know it sounds old-fashioned, but all I could think of as I was walking home afterwards was that I want my first time to be special. I want it to be with a guy I love and who loves me, not because it is the trendy thing to do, or to prove to my mum that I don't need her advice. To think that I almost gave myself to Will for no reason; we didn't even have that much in common to be honest. You won't tell Mum, will you, about what I did? I really couldn't face her knowing how stupid I've been."

"No, I won't, I promise." Anna took another sip of tea, considering. "I hope you will do that yourself, Bella, when you're ready. But I will help you tell her that you've quit your job when she comes to pick you up. We'll be vague, just explain it was making you miserable and that you intend to look for something a bit more challenging in the New Year. I know how tricky she can be! But listen to her advice, sweetheart, she's only hard on you because you're her whole world, Bella."

"Oh, Gran, what would I ever do without your guiding hand?" Bella hugged the old lady to her once again, finding comfort in her touch and her familiar musky perfume.

"That is something you don't have to concern yourself with for a long time yet, I hope," soothed Anna, stroking Bella's fine white-blonde bob before excusing herself to go upstairs. Ten minutes later she returned, clutching a dog-eared envelope in her hand. "I want to show you this letter. My father wrote it to my mother while he was in hospital a few months before the end of the war. It's as though he poured out his heart to her on paper and my mother kept it for the rest of her life, reading it every day. I've never let anyone see it, for it is something very private and intimate between the two of them. But I want you to read it to understand what love can be if you have the courage to pursue it. It's fairly brief, but I think it says pretty much everything."

Bella hung onto every word as her grandmother read aloud Tad's letter. The ink might have faded on the page over time, but the feelings he imparted were as strong and as beautiful as ever. Tad's words to Eirlys were so heartfelt they made both of them weep. When Anna had finished reading, Bella put her arm around her, drawing her near. "You see, Bella, I loved your granddad until the day he died and in the years since, but we never had what my parents shared. A love like Tad's and Eirlys's is worth looking for, worth waiting for. You keep this safe for me." Anna pressed the precious note into her granddaughter's palm.

Bella closed her eyes, picturing Tad. Now she not only knew what he looked like but also the way he spoke. He was coming ever closer to her.

29

One morning in mid-February, I woke feeling extremely unwell. Burning up and shivering simultaneously, I told Jerzy to inform the base that I wouldn't make it in that day. As he clattered out of the dorm in his heavy boots, my head pounded with pain and I pulled the sheets and blankets tightly around me to garner some warmth, hoping that I might sleep off the brunt of whatever illness was afflicting me.

It was four in the afternoon when I came to again, having slept for eight hours straight, something which, being a light sleeper, I'd never done in my life, especially during the daytime. But instead of being refreshed by my substantial slumbers, I felt a hundred times worse. Not only did I have a fever, even more concerning was the pain in my chest, which increased in sharpness every time I inhaled or exhaled. My breathing was rapid and shallow too, as though I'd been for a strenuous run up and down the sand dunes at Blackpool. I knew I was in bad shape as I turned over and resumed my sleep, hoping that whatever strain of flu I'd contracted would soon pass.

When I woke again, I was enveloped by darkness. Feeling that I could barely breathe, I began coughing instead. Although I'd no idea what time it was, Jerzy must have already returned for the night because he flicked on the light, woken by the racket I was making. Blinking as the pain in my eyes intensified in the lamp's bright glare, I guessed it was almost certainly a recurrence of the pneumonia I'd had previously. I got Jerzy to drive me to the base hospital, where two kindly nurses made me comfortable in bed, and eventually I was able to sleep. Later that day, or maybe the next, for I was so disoriented I lost all track of time, a serious-looking doctor confirmed that I was indeed suffering from pneumonia on my left lung. I failed to understand much of what he said after that, as my illness seemed to have diminished my capacity to recall most of the English words I'd learned. He left me alone and I slept again, blinking awake from time to time, wondering momentarily where exactly I was.

Over the next few days, exhausted, I drifted in and out of sleep. Sometimes, I awoke, imagining Eirlys was standing right in front of me, looking pretty in her red coat and emerald hat tilted at a sharp angle on her head to reveal her dark hair pinned neatly beneath it. In my confused state, she was smiling at me in that humorous, twinkly way she sometimes did.

Of course, there was absolutely no possibility Eirlys would have been able to travel across the country to see me. As I lay exhausted, I worried that I would never set my eyes on her lovely face, never touch her silky-soft skin or run my fingers through her hair again. And for the first time since I'd left Poland, I felt fear course through my body at the prospect of never seeing her again. When another doctor, a thickset man with a magnificent moustache who bore more than a passing resemblance to my father, came to see me later that day, I feared the worst.

But then out of the blue, a broad smile spread over the doctor's face. "You're in good company, Tad. You know Winston Churchill suffered from pneumonia a couple of years ago? Well, since then the treatment has improved a lot with the discovery of antibiotic penicillin. You'll get through this, as our venerable prime minister did. You just need to take some time to rest and get your strength back."

I did exactly as the doctor told me. I ate when I didn't feel like eating. I walked in the hospital garden when I could have easily stayed in bed. Even though it hurt me to do so, I breathed fresh air deep into my lungs and felt the sunshine warm my face, imagining it to be healing me from the outside in. I willed myself to get better as quickly as my body would allow me so that I wouldn't have to wait too long to see my beloved girl again. But my need to see Eirlys only grew stronger with each passing day, especially when I received a letter from her in which she poured out all her love for me. Unable to contain everything I was feeling within me a minute or an hour more, I decided to write it all in letter back to her. Sitting at a mildewed table in a quiet corner of the hospital garden, I stared at the blank piece of paper for a long time before I put my pen to it.

My beloved Eirlys,

It seems I have been away from you for so long, even though it is only a few weeks since I last set eyes on your lovely face. Your letter has proved such a tonic for me, Eirlys, you can't imagine. Since I received it, I've felt my health returning to me with each passing hour. You are giving me the strength to fight this pneumonia with all of my spirit, a battle I'm now certain I will win. Even though I already knew how you feel about me, it is lovely to have the words written by your hand on a piece of paper which I can read over and over again. I keep it in my shirt pocket just above my heart and that is where it will always stay.

Although I grew up seeing my father's grief match the depth of his love for my mother, I never imagined what such a love would be like, but now I know. The love I feel for you is higher than the mountains and deeper than the rivers in my homeland. I know that it will burn in my heart forever. Time will not alter it; distance will not weaken it. I am no longer one person now, but a part of you, just as you are a part of me. Always remember that wherever I am, whether here in the south of England or in my plane over Holland or Germany, my heart and soul will always be with you.

Kocham cię, Eirlys, now and forever.
Tad.

30

Manchester, December 2020

A bright December day was dawning as their taxi negotiated the pre-rush hour traffic snarling up the Manchester ring road. All the same, Anna's stomach fluttered with nerves as she saw the sprawl of airport terminal buildings ahead of them. She'd spent a sleepless night tossing and turning in her bed, partly because she knew she'd have to rise at an ungodly hour and consequently didn't want to sleep through the alarm, while a part of her wrestled with the notion that it still wasn't too late to pull out of the trip altogether. Except now it was far too late.

"Are you okay, Mum?" Feeling Sarah's eyes on her, she turned towards her daughter, her best smile painted as brightly as the lipstick on her lips.

"Yes, fine, darling. Just not used to these early starts now I'm a lady of leisure." She undid the top button of her coat to loosen her woollen scarf a notch as the taxi driver had the heating on full blast. Sitting in the middle back seat, it felt as though she had a hair dryer trained right upon her at full throttle.

"Gran, you've got so many peculiar sayings." Bella, who had been dozing for most of the journey with her navy hoodie pulled up over her face, squeezed her arm. "I should write them down before I forget them."

"Yes, you do that, Bella," her mother said. "Maybe you could note them in the back of that sketchpad you carry everywhere?"

As the two chatted across her about e-tickets, Anna pondered their exchange, considering its subconscious undertones. It clearly implied that neither her daughter nor her granddaughter thought she would be around forever to remind them of the oddities which came out of her mouth. Which was fair enough, she supposed. She was seventy-four now and in recent months she'd felt every single day of her advancing years. Even if Bella began her university studies the following September, would she still be around in three and a half years' time to watch her graduate? Would she live to see the day when Bella walked down the aisle, having been through all those Mr Wrongs to finally find her Mr Right? Both Sarah and Bella seemed to live such fast, furious and fractured lives, Anna doubted whether she would ever witness either of them settled and content in her lifetime. Was she destined to miss out on her daughter's and granddaughter's futures just as she'd done with her father in the past? The notion made her feel suddenly older than her years; that she was running out of time to do the things she still wanted.

The airport departure hall was teeming with people hurrying past them with trolleys stacked with suitcases. A swift look around told Anna that they were mainly students eager to get home for the extended Christmas holidays. Luckily, they were mostly French, German and Spanish making the queues to Paris, Munich and Barcelona twice the length of the one to Krakow and in no time the three women were moving through the security check. After warming up with coffees and somewhat tasteless breakfast buns in an overpriced chain cafe, they dropped by WH Smith to pick up a selection of magazines and 'grab'n'go' bags of chocolates and sweets to sustain them for the duration of the flight before heading to their departure gate.

Anna felt Bella grip her hand as the plane raced along the runway before soaring over the vast car parks and terracotta rooftops of the terraced houses which stretched across the Greater Manchester suburbs. Her ears popping as the aircraft continued to climb, she gave her granddaughter a reassuring smile before turning her attention downwards once more. From her bird's eye view, she saw cars as small as ants building up queues on the motorways as commuters made their way to work. It reminded her how insignificant people were in the big scheme of things, of just how small and short life was. And then in an instant the plane swiftly banked into swirling grey cloud and everything below disappeared as though it was never there at all.

"What's the matter, sweetheart?" She saw consternation cloud her granddaughter's face as the plane jolted beneath them. "It's just a spot of turbulence, different air currents meeting, nothing to worry about, Isabella. It's because we're flying in December that there is a bit more than in the summer, that's all."

"That's right, no need to worry, Bella, we'll be Poland in no time," said Sarah, who had her head buried in the sixth magnum opus of Diana Gabaldon's *Outlander* series.

As Bella leaned her head on her grandma's shoulder for reassurance, Anna couldn't decide how such a prospect made her feel, whether she was excited, daunted or a mixture of both that she was finally on her way to Krakow after all these months thinking of it. But as the plane soared up through the cloud to the cerulean blue of the sky above, she was sure of one thing. She'd already waited far too long to visit the homeland of her father.

Closing her eyes, an image of Tad popped into Anna's consciousness as she saw him, handsome in his flying suit, manoeuvring his plane. From what her mother had told her, her father had been an extremely skilled flyer, feeling that his aircraft was an extension of his own body which he controlled with ease on his sorties and raids over the continent during those final years of the war. As the cloud cleared over the sea, she peered down, wondering whether her father had ever done the same. Realising that he would've almost certainly laid his eyes on these calm blue waters, she felt a strange closeness to him as she came ever-nearer to his country.

31

Blinking in the sun, which was high in the watery, winter sky, Sarah emerged from the stainless steel and glass building of Krakow John Paul II Airport. Although the flight had been under two hours, she was relieved to stretch her legs as she supported her mother across the snow-slicked car park, pausing briefly to admire the saint's statue. Bella trailed in their wake, pulling her colossal crimson suitcase which her grandmother had treated her to for the trip, while trying to get a phone signal.

"Last night, Aleksander emailed me to say he'd pick us up in Car Park B," Sarah announced, feeling a frisson of anxiety as she considered that he wouldn't turn up after all, a prospect which would send shockwaves through her plans for their entire stay. She'd spent hours trawling the internet before finally clicking on Aleksander Wiszniewski's professional but friendly web pages. The same age as her at forty-three, he'd spent his twenties and thirties working in the many museums in Krakow, so she surmised he would have a wide knowledge of the city's colourful history to impart to them. Now studying for a PhD in History at Jagiellonian University which he juggled with working part-time as an administrator at the city's record offices and ad-hoc tour guide, she'd also considered the possibility that he could perhaps help them find some information on Tad, either at the record offices or university.

They found Car Park B was jam-packed with empty cars, obviously a long-stay car park, but after a few frantic minutes' search Sarah breathed a sigh of relief as she spotted the eight-seater red mini-bus she'd seen on Aleksander's website with 'Krakow History Tours' emblazoned down the side in tasteful blue writing. "That must be him." She exhaled with relief as she dashed over to the bus before rapping her freezing fingers on the steamed-up driver's window.

"You must be Sarah." Aleksander exited the bus with a smile lighting his face, which on first glance seemed pleasant, open and full of humour. As he proffered his hand in a gentlemanly manner, Sarah noticed the way his hazel eyes were flecked with green behind his rimless glasses, his once-black hair now sprinkled with grey. A day's worth of dark stubble clung to his angular jaw while his lean figure gave credence to the listed hobbies on his website of mountain walking, hiking and canoeing. Her friend Cath would describe him as 'ruggedly handsome', a sentiment with which Sarah would readily concur!

"Yes, that's right, Aleksander." She self-consciously tucked unruly curls of her shoulder-length hair behind her ears in an attempt to remedy her bedraggled appearance, the result of getting up at 4am and travelling for the intervening hours. "And this is my mum, Anna, and my daughter, Bella."

"Ahh, Anna, I'm Aleksander Wiszniewski. *Witamy w Polsce!*" He smiled, lifting her hand to his lips. Anna nodded her acceptance of the old-fashioned gesture before giving Bella a conspiratorial smile as she remembered her grandmother once telling her that Tad had impressed her on their first meeting by kissing her hand in a polite, gentlemanly fashion.

"I think that must mean welcome to Poland! *Dzień dobry!*" Anna said, liking how the language she'd attempted to learn the basics of sounded when spoken by a native. "I've been trying to learn a little Polish these past few weeks. You'll have to write down your name for me, though!"

"*Wiszniewski* means cherry tree. Trees are popular surnames in Polish. In fact, your father's family name *Lewandowski* means lavender," Aleksander smiled. "This is your first visit to Poland?" Seeing his high cheekbones and imposingly tall presence, Anna wondered if her father had possessed these characteristics, guessing from the one grainy photo she'd got of him in his air force uniform that he had. What was more, Aleksander's fur-lined leather jacket and heavy winter boots brought to mind a flyer's garb, as well as confirming her concerns about just how cold it would be in Poland in mid-winter.

"Yes, it is. As I think Sarah told you, my father was born in Zakopane and he escaped to England during the Second

World War, where he joined the air force. My mother was told that he crashed over Holland just a few weeks before VE Day. I believe the official phrase is 'missing presumed dead'. So few words but such a great deal of pain," Anna sighed.

"I'm so very sorry. Sarah gave me your father's name." He nodded, catching Sarah's eye momentarily. "I had hoped to try to find if any records for Tadeusz still exist in Poland but I haven't had the opportunity as yet, as the university term only finished for the Christmas vacation on Friday." He loaded their luggage, even Bella's cavernous case, into the sizeable boot of his mini-bus as though it weighed nothing. "But now I have time on my hands I can devote the next few weeks entirely to you."

"You work at the university?" Anna was suddenly interested.

"I *study* at Jagiellonian University in Krakow," he graciously corrected her as the snow began to fall. "I'm halfway through my PhD thesis. I supplement it with a bit of lecturing, tour guiding and my work at the record offices. You name it, really."

"That is some undertaking. I did my doctorate a few years ago," said Sarah, wedging her Cath Kidston holdall on top of their cases. "It takes a bit of balancing when you're a little more mature."

"It certainly does! You said in your email you were an English lecturer?" he asked, shutting the boot, evidently eager to focus the conversation away from himself.

"Yes, I teach English and Creative Writing at Lancaster University in the north of England." She smiled. For the next few moments, as the two talked about the ins and outs of various research projects they'd undertaken, Anna considered how Aleksander's connection with the university might prove useful when looking for information about her father.

"My father was a student at the Jagiellonian when the war began," she started as Sarah and Aleksander's discussion came to a hiatus, forming her thoughts as she went along. "My mother told me he was studying architecture."

"That might be something we can pursue then. I know that some university records do still exist from that time despite the actions of the Nazis." He smiled. "I'll see if I can talk to someone with access to them."

"Thank you, Aleksander. I read somewhere that the SS imprisoned and executed members of the Polish intelligentsia during the first months of the war?" Sarah commented as they settled into their seat belts.

"Yes, destroying the Polish education system was part of their plan to eradicate our culture. But it wasn't just the SS," he said, his voice tinged with anger as he carefully negotiated the mini-bus out of the car park, "the Wehrmacht and Gestapo killed some sixty thousand government officials, reserve military officers, landowners and clergy. They were murdered region by region in the so-called *Intelligenzaktion*."

"Maybe that's why Tad came over to England then to escape arrest?" suggested Bella as Aleksander briefly slowed down to point out the statue of St John Paul II, the women being too polite to say they'd already seen it before they left the greyness of the airport environs behind.

"Possibly," mused Sarah, having already considered the notion. It seemed inconceivable to think that people, academics like her and her colleagues could be murdered simply for working in an institution of higher education. As Bella twittered away to Aleksander in a disappointingly one-way conversation, Sarah fell silent, contemplating what exactly they would find out in this once war-ravaged country and whether it would be too much and too personal for the three of them. After a twenty-minute drive through a snowy, flat landscape, they passed block after block of tall tenement buildings as the outskirts of the city loomed on the left side of the freeway. In a dilapidated state of disrepair, it brought to Sarah's mind a Holocaust documentary she'd once watched, something which was confirmed by Aleksander. "This area became a sealed Jewish ghetto from '41 when Kazimierz, their ancient township, was cleared and the entire community was moved into the walled and gated area of Podgórze. Two years later the whole ghetto was liquidated and the city cleared of its Jewish citizens. At the other side of these buildings is Ghetto Square, which has been made into a memorial to all the Jewish Krakovians who lived and either perished here or, if they survived the ghetto's privations, were sent to Auschwitz."

"It's a quarter we'd be interested in visiting," commented Sarah, straining to look at the blocks. "And of course Oskar Schindler's DEF factory, which I understand is a museum now?"

"I can arrange it all if you want? I can also take you to see the chemist shop of Tadeusz Pankiewicz, a brave Roman Catholic pharmacist who provided Jews with the medicines they needed while living in the ghetto. Unfortunately conditions were so unsanitary inside the ghetto walls that many of the young and old died anyway. It was a small act of kindness by one man which cut across the tides of evil," Aleksander said as they looked up at the brooding buildings.

A few minutes later, they crossed an iron bridge over the grey River Vistula, and the women had their first view of the seemingly endless church spires soaring above the old town where ochre-roofed buildings huddled together against the biting cold of the December day. For Anna, the city was as she'd always imagined it to be, like something straight from the pages of an enchanting fairytale. But, in a blink of an eye, the scene was behind them as Aleksander sped on, past the bare trees of the famous Planty Park encircling the old town which vied for the women's attention with row upon row of tenement buildings.

Hotel Wyspiański, a fifteen-floor tower block left over from the communist era, was situated just to the north of the Planty. Getting out of the taxi, her ears ringing with the bells of passing trams, Sarah looked up to take in the hulking hotel which made up for in size what it lacked in elegance. It was fronted by a wide expanse of cobbles which she imagined would be a pleasant area to sit and relax as the bar spilled outside on warm summer evenings, with the row of plane trees providing an effective barrier blocking out trams and traffic fumes. Wheeling their cases inside while Aleksander found a space to park, they found the *Recepcja* was warm but functional, with a dark brown carpet and huge polished oak desk, backgrounded by four clocks telling the time in New York, London, Krakow and Sydney.

The pleasant blonde-haired receptionist handing them their keys, Sarah turned around to see Aleksander waiting patiently. Standing upright, she noticed now that he was well over six foot tall, taller than she'd originally thought. He smiled at her before looking over to Anna, whom Bella was dragging over to a small shop crammed to the rafters with tasteful souvenirs, before his attention returned to Sarah. "Right then, I've got a few calls to make." Aleksander hesitated.

"Why don't you join us for lunch?" Sarah suggested, slinging her handbag over her shoulder so she could get more purchase on her suitcase. "We could finalise all our arrangements for our stay here, if that fits in with your schedule?"

"That would suit me." His smile lit up his chiselled features. Nevertheless, Sarah noticed he flipped through his iPhone, a frown momentarily creasing his wide forehead before disappearing. "Yes, that's absolutely fine. I have the rest of the afternoon free."

"We'll just take our luggage to our rooms then and meet you here in half an hour?" She swivelled around. "If I can prise my mother and daughter away from the gift shop, that is."

Having settled into their rooms, where the minimalist brown and cream colour scheme extended, they took the mirrored lift back down to the *Recepcja*, where Aleksander was waiting. Once outside, he negotiated them carefully across the four lanes of traffic and tramways into the dense trees of the Planty. They then slipped down a quiet side street, the pretty mint-green, rose-pink and butterscotch-yellow buildings bathed in winter sunshine. After just a five-minute walk, the narrow alleyway opened out and the three women gasped simultaneously as they were treated to their first sight of the majestic Rynek Główny.

Krakow's market square had been the centre of the city's cultural life since medieval times and, as they looked around that December afternoon, each noticed something distinctively different. The smell of roasting chestnuts, cinnamon, ginger and *glühwien* from the clustered Christmas market stalls cloying in her nostrils, Anna was taken with the pastel-coloured noblemen's townhouses which surrounded the square. Pulling her navy woollen coat tightly to her to ward off the chill, she focused on the spectacular Bonerowski House, wondering whether Tad too had once been captivated by the intricately painted red and blue fresco of the Madonna and Child. An amateur architecture aficionado herself, she noticed how the Gothic seamlessly blended in with the Baroque and Renaissance, with its own distinctive Polish style.

Bella, meanwhile, sharing her grandma's interest in architecture, feasted her eyes on the magnificence of the imposing Cloth Hall, the *Sukiennice*, which dated from the thirteenth century. Following a fire three hundred years later, it had been rebuilt in a curvaceous Renaissance redbrick with an undulating cream hat of a roof, adorned with grotesque stone mask parapets. Sitting proudly at the heart of Krakow's main square, it emphasised the importance of trade in the city's history where the most sought-after goods of the time – cloth and salt – had been traded to make it the richest place in the Polish kingdom. She'd read that the building was still a popular shopping hub, specialising in Polish crafts including embroidery, leatherwork, stained-glass, carved wooden trinkets and Baltic amber and she couldn't wait to buy Christmas presents for her friends as well as bits and bobs for herself during her trip. But, knowing shopping was low down on her grandma's and mum's agendas, she would have to bide her time.

Sarah couldn't help but marvel at the two mismatched redbrick towers of St Mary's, the basilica which rose imperiously above the square to dominate the city skyline. The night before, she'd read in a guidebook that the non-identical towers had been built by warring brothers in an effort to outdo each other and now, standing beneath them, she thought one was indeed very much taller and more ornate than the other. "This takes sibling rivalry to a whole new level," she laughed, "although I think I prefer the shorter, simpler one."

"Yes, it certainly does! Ah, we're just in time for the *Hejnal*," Aleksander declared, his breath leaving icy trails in the cold air. Looking up to the cupola atop the taller tower, they saw a uniformed trumpeter raise his golden instrument as he did every hour on the hour. The square fell silent and still as his mournful melody echoed across it to commemorate the Tatar invasion of the city centuries earlier before coming to an abrupt stop mid-note.

"The man who first played the trumpet did so to warn Krakovians that the Tatars were approaching the city, but the invaders shot him dead in his exposed position before he had the chance to finish playing. So that's why the *Hejnal* always stops so suddenly, to remember the bravery of the man who gave his life trying to protect his city," Aleksander explained before moving them on quickly to seek shelter from the cold in the warmth of Hawełka Restaurant. Overwhelmed by the Polish menu, they deferred to Aleksander, who ordered a selection of traditional dishes for them to share which, when they came, looked extremely appetising.

"These are all typical of Polish cuisine. These are pork tenderloins served with a sheep cheese stuffing, cherry and cranberry sauce and potatoes, *proszę*," he said, pointing to the meat, which was cooked to perfection, the gooey, creamy filling bursting out, before he moved his attention to plates filled with what Bella thought looked like tortellini topped with fried onions. "And these are pierogi, which are traditional handmade Polish dumplings. Here we have ones filled with meat and cheese for you to try. *Na Zdrowie!*" He lifted his glass, clinking it against each of theirs in turn.

"They look delicious." Anna helped herself to one, famished after only pecking at crisps and chocolates on the plane. "And they taste as good as they look; the crispiness of the onions complements the soft dumplings perfectly."

"And that is borscht?" Sarah added, as Aleksander passed her one of the purple-red soups which was seeping into its surrounding bread bowl. "Beetroot soup." She turned to Bella, who, in the throes of a week-long vegan detox, was more than happy to try out the enticing spread.

"Very tasty," Sarah declared, and a bright smile erased Aleksander's pensive look as it became clear the women were enjoying his lunch selection. Over their meal, they flitted across a number of topics, ranging from Tad to their first impressions of Krakow, Bella being the most enthusiastic, caught as she was with the youthful vibe of the city, whereas Sarah and Anna were more taken with the opulent, old buildings. For dessert, they ordered vanilla cheesecake, which was served with hot cherries.

"And I didn't just get these for you because that's my name! You'll find most desserts in Poland contain cherries in some form or another," Aleksander laughed, extracting his iPhone from the inside pocket of his jacket, "but plums come a close runner-up! Now, shall we organise some dates for your trips?"

Over coffee, they made the arrangements for tours to Kazimierz, Auschwitz, Wadowice and Zakopane. "Now I've some time, I'll have a good look in the record offices too, see what I can turn up about Tadeusz." He smiled, gathering his papers into his black, somewhat battered leather zip-around file, before checking his phone, which had beeped a few minutes before. Seeing a deep frown furrow his forehead, Sarah asked him what was wrong. "It's my son's school. He's not very well and needs picking up. I apologise, ladies, but I'll have to dash."

"Oh, I'm sorry," said Sarah, tightly tying her scarf around her neck and pulling up her hood as they prepared to leave. "I hope he's okay."

"Yes, probably just a cold or something. The young ones seem to pick up all manner of bugs during winter." Aleksander stood to help Anna with her coat.

"Yes, tell me about it. A decade or so ago, I was always back and forth to Bella's primary school!" Sarah added, taking in the splendid traditional wooden ceiling and floor of the restaurant as they headed to the till. Even though she'd only been in Krakow a few hours, she already felt at home in the place.

After dividing the tip between the four of them, they exited the restaurant to find the square was buzzing with crowds of expectant children, the festive excitement palpable in the cold, clear air. Noticing Sarah, Anna and Bella's puzzled faces, Aleksander clarified, "It is December 6th, St Nicholas's Day." Before he could add anything more, he was interrupted by cheers and they stood mesmerised as St Nicholas, dressed in his traditional red-and-white robe and golden bishop's mitre, rode through the square on a reindeer-drawn sleigh, a truly magical sight in this city of fairytales.

32

The breakfast room was a scene of tranquillity, the suited business people they'd spotted in the lobby the previous evening having long since headed out as the clock nudged towards half past nine. Two waiters were replenishing the buffet and Bella found it difficult to choose between the array of meats, pâtes, cheeses and breads, cinnamon-soaked plums, sweetened bilberries and freshly squeezed fruit juices, as well as all the enticing pastries and cooked food. After much deliberation, she joined her mum and grandma at a small table overlooking an enclosed courtyard.

"I see you've gone for the continental like me." Anna smiled as her granddaughter, dressed in yet another head-to-toe black ensemble which made her bobbed hair appear almost luminescent white, took the seat next to her. "I can't stomach a cooked breakfast at this early hour any more."

"I suppose all those years spent cooking boarding-house breakfasts would test even the most ardent fried egg and bacon lover?" said Sarah, who had opted for a healthy option of parsley-sprinkled scrambled eggs, which she'd garnished with slivers of smoked salmon.

"A hazard of the job!" Anna laughed merrily as she tucked a white linen serviette beneath her chin. But Bella thought her grandma looked tired this morning and, noticing the dark shadows beneath her eyes, she felt a jolt of anxiety at her frail appearance. Not used to seeing her over breakfast, Bella wondered whether this was the norm or whether her grandma was just recovering from the journey which had indeed tired her too. Bella saw, however, that the old woman had made an effort with her appearance, which was smart in a rollneck sweater with a pretty jade-green scarf and tailored black trousers which accentuated her still slim legs.

"Those look interesting, Bella." Anna pulled a face while sipping her breakfast tea, evidently only half the strength of the Yorkshire Tea she favoured at home.

"They're eggs filled with some kind of vegetarian pâte. Here, do you want to try some? It is delicious with this crusty bread." Bella spooned some onto her grandma's plate as she was eager to get onto the plum and cinnamon pastry which was enticing her from its side plate.

"It's scrummy, sweetheart!" The old woman smiled after tasting it. "I'll get some for myself when I go for my toast. I've already spied a bilberry jam I intend trying."

"I think there is just about everything you could ever want for breakfast," Sarah commented, "and the beds were so comfortable last night. I have to say I couldn't have chosen a better hotel myself."

"That's high praise coming from you, dear." Anna smiled proudly. "But Bella and I did look at a few dozen on the internet before settling on the Wyspiański!"

With Aleksander sorting out their tours to all the places with potential connections to Tad, they decided to spend the day soaking in the atmosphere of the old town's pretty streets. Crossing the tram tracks and the Planty, they found the air was bitingly cold and were glad they'd wrapped up in sweaters, scarves, hats and padded winter coats. "It's not too cold for you, is it, Mum?" Sarah's brow furrowed as she took in her mother's pallor on nearing Krakow's main square.

"No, although it's chillier than I expected. And it's quite a few degrees colder than it ever gets in Blackpool so it will take a bit of acclimatising to," Anna offered. Filled with excitement at the prospect of her first full day in her father's city, she wasn't going to tell her daughter that the icy air was in fact making her chest feel quite sore. Gauging that it was only just past 10.30am, she clung hopefully to the possibility that the mercury might rise a few degrees above freezing before midday.

"Well, lift your scarf up over your nose and mouth to make it into a snood." Sarah helped her mother, pulling up her hood to secure it in place. "There, Mum, you look like Nanook of the North, very fetching."

"Thank you very much!" Anna laughed as she linked her daughter's and granddaughter's arms for support as they negotiated the slushy paving stones.

Reaching the Rynek Główny at the heart of the old town, Sarah decided there was no better place to start than with a walk around Wawel Castle and Basilica but with the mid-morning Mass making the cathedral out of bounds, they opted to explore the former first. Slowly, they approached the royal castle, where, sitting in its commanding position on Wawel Hill in a sheltered bend of the wide Vistula River, the kings of Poland had first taken up residence in the tenth century. But it wasn't until the sixteenth century that King Aleksander and his successor, Zygmunt the Old, had commissioned the palace in Italian Renaissance style which stood proudly today.

As they began their slow ascent up the hill, Bella took in the loveliness of the Wawel's outer buildings in their muted magnolias, creams and browns, topped with their uniformly ochre roofs. She almost could have mistaken the castle for a Tuscan hilltop town, had it not been for the gold dome and bird's egg blue-green of the Basilica's spires which pointed triumphantly towards the heavens. Mesmerised, there was something achingly beautiful about the architecture in this city which touched Bella's soul. Anna was equally taken by the different styles of the buildings and used it as an excuse to keep stopping to admire their craftsmanship and intricacy, hoping her daughter and granddaughter wouldn't notice that she was in fact out of breath and having a hard time as the incline steepened.

Stopping briefly in the arcaded courtyard of the castle, its walls adorned with beautiful frescoes, the women continued through the lusciously decorated royal private apartments at the heart of the Wawel. The sluggishness of the queue allowed them to linger on the various paintings from the Italian schools of Titian, Raphael and Botticelli before admiring the exquisite collection of Brussels' tapestries also on display.

"These are truly lovely," said Anna, the sun streaming through the floor-to-ceiling windows, catching her blonde highlights she'd had done especially for the trip, as well as the paintings' gilt frames. "But wasn't the castle used by the Nazi governor, Hans Frank, as his headquarters during World War II? I wonder how it is that this exquisite artwork remains here today? You'd think the Nazis would have plundered such objects and secreted them into their Swiss bank accounts?"

"I guess the answer might be here, Gran," replied Bella, admiring an ornate gold Szczerbiec ceremonial sword. "It says here that the Poles managed to smuggle this sword and the tapestries to Canada just days before the Nazis turned the castle into their Krakow administrative hub."

"Good forward thinking," remarked Anna proudly.

After a tour of the state rooms, the women huddled beneath glowing heaters and warm blankets in the castle's courtyard cafe. There, they enjoyed mugs of steaming spiced apple juice accompanied by plum crumble cake while looking out over the snowy landscape of medieval buildings in the city below. "It feels just like a holiday." Anna hugged her drink in her hands so that its warmth seeped through her thermal gloves.

"That's exactly what days like this are, Mother," Sarah laughed, "and we need to keep reminding ourselves of it. Whether we find anything out about Tad or not, we have to make the most of our trip, our time together in this beautiful city." Sarah forked a piece of cake, moist with fruit and laced with alcohol, into her mouth. "We are going to have a wonderful time here, whatever happens."

"Yes, I can't remember the last time we all came on holiday together," added Bella, twisting her hair around her index finger in a habit she'd been unable to break since she was a child, "but, I agree, even though we may discover nothing about Great-Granddad or things we find uncomfortable, we should enjoy times like this."

Times like this. A lump lodged in Anna's throat as she mused that such times might be few and far between in the future if her tests showed a deterioration in her health forcing her into a more restricted lifestyle. Later that morning, with music from the Mass they'd caught the end of still playing softly in Anna's mind, they wandered around Wawel Basilica, lingering over the huge, silver tomb of the murdered and venerated St Stanislaus. As Poland's patron saint, his resting place had become a place of pilgrimage and a unifier, as the kings of Poland chose to be crowned and buried next to his relics. On the way out, they paid an extra few złotys to descend to the crypt where they saw some of the ancient kings' tombs for themselves before passing those of the Polish president Lech Kaczynski and his wife, Maria, who had been killed in a plane crash near Smolensk in 2010. They paused to read the inscriptions on the prominent graves, which were festooned with patriotic red and white flowers and ribbons.

"I remember seeing the pictures of the plane wreck on the news," Anna commented as they stepped out into the afternoon sun, which was weak as winter tightened its grip on the city. "Weren't they on their way to or back from a memorial service at Katyn when their plane crashed?"

"Yes, they were travelling from Warsaw to attend an event at Smolensk commemorating the seventieth anniversary of the 1940 massacre of Polish officers. If I remember rightly, there were also members of the Polish parliament and clergy on board the plane, as well as relatives of the victims who perished in the accident," said Sarah. "I seem to recall a thick fog enveloped the airport just as the plane came into land, causing the crash."

"Where is Katyn?" Bella interrupted.

"I think it's in Belorussia now," explained her mother, acting as the anchor between her mother and daughter as they gingerly made their way down the slippery street.

"I've never heard of it before. I think I'll read up about it when we get back to the hotel," Bella announced as snow began to fall once more.

Anna paced herself on the way down by stopping off at the shops on Wawel Hill to browse the traditional Polish craftwork, embroidered blouses and woodcarvings, as well as glass baubles. As a result, it took them well over an hour to wind their way back to the centre of the old town, by which time they were frozen to the bone and in need of hot food. Just off the main square in the shadow of the uneven spires of St Mary's Basilica, they found a cosy corner in a modern cafe, decorated entirely with silver stars and strings of lights in preparation for Christmas. There, they ordered bowls of the traditional beetroot soup they'd enjoyed the previous day mopped up with huge hunks of bread before finishing off with plates of steaming dumplings stuffed with cheese.

"Well, that was our first day as tourists in this city," Anna remarked as plummeting temperatures and clouds threatening more sleet and snow dictated they return to the hotel for the remainder of the afternoon.

As they passed bright cafes and souvenir shops on their way back, Bella found it difficult to imagine this city cowed and under occupation eighty years ago. Now, it possessed a youth and vibrancy, like a veritable phoenix which had emerged from the ashes of war.

33

Krakow, December 2020

In preparation for their trip to Zakopane and the Tatra Mountains, Anna, Sarah and Bella decided to visit the city's Muzeum Etnograficzne. Housed in the Renaissance town hall of Kazimierz, the museum told the stories of the lives and traditions of people who'd lived in the Podhale region and the Tatras for generations, and Sarah, in particular, was desperate to visit. However, seeing how her mother had tired the previous day, she realised they would have to slow down their pace if Anna was to keep up, and so she insisted they catch a cab there which Bella wasn't best pleased about as it was snowing heavily. The child still in her evidently fancied a long walk, catching flurrying snowflakes on her tongue and feeling them melt in her mouth. As they sat in stationary traffic, the tail lights of the car in front infusing their taxi with a red light, Sarah found herself watching her mother. She was relieved to see that after a good night's rest she was looking much brighter this morning. Anna, feeling she was being observed, turned and smiled. "Everything okay, sweetheart?"

"Yes, Mum. I was just thinking how much you and Bella look like one another – the same high cheekbones, bright blue eyes and fair hair." She smiled, hoping she hadn't spotted her concern.

"Slavic features." Bella smiled proudly, clasping her grandma's hand. As the taxi edged forward, Sarah wondered whether they did indeed all resemble Tad in some way, this unknown man's features and personality passed on down the generations, living on today. An intriguing thought.

"I hope Aleksander can discover more about Tad, where he lived and who his family were," pondered Bella, "maybe even trace some of his brother's descendants? They would be your cousins, wouldn't they, Gran?"

"Yes, they would," replied Anna, smiling. "But we mustn't get our hopes up. It was such a long time ago and even Aleksander isn't sure what records have survived. As I told you, Mother said that Tad's brother Jacek was married at the beginning of the war and his wife was expecting a child. My father told her that Jacek was in the Polish Air Force and he was always very concerned for his safety. Beyond that we have no information to go on."

The taxi, reaching its destination, drew up outside the impressive front of the museum. Designed in classical Greek style, the building seemed at odds with the rather dreary surroundings of Wolnica Square. Aleksander hadn't arrived there yet so, as the temperatures had sunk further overnight, Sarah sent her mother and Bella inside while she waited, snowflakes collecting in the dark curls of her hair. Eventually, she spotted him in his greatcoat walking through the blizzard which was obscuring the grey square.

"Sorry, I'm late," he panted, his nose and ears glowing red with cold as he dashed up the six stone steps to plant a kiss on each of her cheeks. Inhaling the musky tones of his aftershave and feeling a little awkward, she was the one to pull away first. "I've no excuse, really, my apartment is only five blocks away, but something always seems to crop up, especially when I'm in a rush! *Przepraszam!*"

"It's okay, Aleksander, we only arrived a few minutes ago." She smiled, suddenly wondering whether he lived in one of the old converted buildings off the main square or in a more functional building from the communist era, picturing him more at home in the former.

"I only moved there last year. It's near the university, so it's very convenient for me…" He smiled, raking his fingers through his dark hair in a vain attempt to tidy it.

"How is your son?" Sarah asked as he wiped his glasses with his coat sleeve before sitting them back on his nose.

"Just a bit off colour, but he was much better this morning and insisted on going into school," Aleksander said, his smile forced. "Kids are resilient little things."

"Don't I know it, living with my one for the past eighteen years!" Sarah smiled but uncharacteristically she felt a small pang of envy. Although Anna had been a willing confidante for Bella since she'd hit her teens, in those early years as a single parent she had had to sort out most problems concerning her daughter more or less on her own. She had never thought about it much; that's just the way things had been. But now she pictured Aleksander's wife phoning him up, knowing that he would immediately drop what he was doing to rush to their son and it brought home to Sarah how alone she had always been. Seeing Aleksander flash a smile brought her back to reality and she smiled back at him. What a strange line of thought, what on earth was the matter with her? This trip must be getting to her more than she imagined.

They followed Aleksander through the numerous rooms of the museum, where they admired faithful reconstructions of the brightly decorated interiors of traditional cottages, with everything from blue and pink baby's cribs to yellow and purple cooking ranges on display. Bella was particularly taken by the walls of each room, which were painted with flowers in every shade of the rainbow, echoing the embroidery on the traditional costumes worn by people of the Podhale region. However, it was the colossal Christmas cribs, some well over a century old, which left the women in awe as they spent well over an hour examining them in intricate detail. About as far removed from a humble stable as it was possible to get, these sublime palaces were adorned with a star of Bethlehem, below which lay the sleeping Prince of Peace in the manger, Mary and Joseph looking on in sumptuous robes of claret and blue.

"I've never seen the nativity depicted in this way," mused Sarah, looking over to Aleksander, who seemed equally taken with these miniature miracles.

"It's a tradition which began in the nineteenth century when the city's master bricklayers and builders formed the Crib Makers' Guild. They stipulated that each crib scene reflects an aspect of the city's ancient architecture," explained Aleksander as they studied a crib standing over two metres tall in regal hues of purple, red and blue. "There are two types, the first one small enough to go beneath the Christmas tree, but ones such as this would probably most likely have been the focal point of a puppet show accompanied by songs. Unfortunately the tradition of putting on Christmas plays died out with World War I."

"That's sad," said Bella, removing her pink mittens to snap a few close-up photos on her iPhone. "So now the cribs are consigned to history and a museum?"

"Not quite." Aleksander smiled. "In 1937, the first contest to find the most beautiful crib in Krakow took place and, from then on, people have built them especially to enter them in the prestigious competition organised by the museum every year. Although during the course of the past eighty years, there have been substantial changes in the materials, lighting, architecture and embossing, as the cribs tended to symbolise the times in which they were made, the stipulation to reflect the city's architecture still gives them their particular character. In the first ones, stylised versions of St Mary's twin towers and the baroque domes of the city's churches were discernible, whereas in latter years, the Barbican, Wawel Castle, city walls, St Florian's Gate and even the Cloth Hall have inspired the makers." Aleksander paused, his cheeks reddening. "Well, I've gone on for far too long. I'll let you ladies admire the cribs in peace, without me boring you with too much detail!"

"You are not doing that at all." Sarah smiled, unloosening her thick scarf. "I think it's fascinating. I'm just happy you're here to explain it all to us, as the information panels seem quite basic."

"And principally in Polish," butted in Bella, capturing a particularly old crib bearing the mismatched twin towers of St Mary's Basilica.

"Oh, that reminds me, I've got some sheets in English." Aleksander took a wad of crumpled, damp papers from his pocket, his expression apologetic as they had almost reached the end of the exhibition.

"I think I'll stick with your version, Aleksander," Sarah said, after glancing through one of the sheets. "Whoever translated these did it quite literally and evidently has a penchant for flowery language."

"Please, call me Alek." He laughed, the corners of his eyes creasing. "I've noticed that about a lot of the English information sheets around the city. It is though they are written in another language entirely, as if whoever compiled them swallowed a dictionary with little understanding of how English actually works, not how I learned it at all."

"When did you learn English, Alek?" Bella enquired, unzipping her jacket as she'd warmed up while walking around the exhibition.

"Way back in elementary school. My brother, who is ten years older than me, had to learn Russian, but luckily I escaped having to learn a whole different alphabet. Although English was no picnic either!" he bent down to retrieve a leaflet Sarah had dropped onto the slatted wooden floor.

"No more difficult than Polish." Sarah tried to mask her shiver as his fingers brushed hers on handing her the glossy paper. Luckily Alek seemed not to notice, but Sarah saw from Bella's cocked eyebrow that she most definitely had. There was nothing that escaped her eagle-eyed daughter.

"Right then, I'm ready for a bowl of steaming borscht." Anna diffused the awkward moment.

"I know just the place." Alek smiled, linking the old woman's arm. "There's a delightful cafe just off the square." He led them out via the museum's extensive gift shop where Bella bought a selection of postcards as well as a canvas bag embroidered with blue, red and white flowers in a traditional design she'd spotted on some of the dresses on display in the museum. Anna and Sarah, with encouragement from the other, each treated themselves to one of the exquisitely embroidered traditional blouses, Anna's in muted shades of mauve and mulberry whilst Sarah's was in a more vibrant red and green design, which she thought would be perfect to wear at Christmas.

Alek then led them down the alleyway at the side of the museum to a traditional restaurant with a wooden veranda, which would have been a lovely place to eat al fresco had the temperature been about twenty-five degrees higher. The carved wooden interior, however, made Sarah feel as though they'd arrived in the Tatra Mountains a few days early and they tucked into bowls of borscht and potato and leek soup accompanied by piping hot cheese toasties. "That soup has definitely renewed my energy for some more sightseeing." Anna smiled as they stepped out into the alleyway later. "Where do you suggest we go this afternoon then, Aleksander?"

"But it's snowing again, Mum," warned Sarah, a frown furrowing her forehead, "and I don't want you getting chilled. We really need to pace ourselves."

"Szeroka Square is just a few blocks away," suggested Alek, tucking his scarf into his greatcoat. "Why don't you take a look and I'll bring the mini-bus round in a short while to take you back to the hotel?"

"Sounds like a good idea." A sightseeing buff, Sarah found herself easily persuaded despite noticing the leaden, frozen skies overhead as they set off back down the alleyway.

"Should I pick you up at 4pm, then, at Szeroka?" Alek smiled as snowflakes began to settle on his salt'n'pepper hair, the dampness curling it at the nape of his neck.

"Yes, if that's okay?" said Sarah, wondering whether the price he'd charged them for the trip today had just included his services for the morning. The last thing she wanted to do was put him out, but his broad smile told her he was more than happy with the arrangement.

The imposing brown brick Old Synagogue dominated Szeroka Square, the main meeting point in the old Jewish quarter of Kazimierz. No longer used for religious purposes, the synagogue was preserved as a memorial to the Jewish people who had practised their faith there for centuries and who had been swept away in a mere handful of years during World War II. Exploring the women's prayer sections, offshoots from the main hall, Anna, Sarah and Bella were interested to learn about the important holidays in the Jewish calendar as well as admiring the display of porcelain and silver plates used for the Passover bread and Kiddush cups used on the Shabbat.

"It's a miracle all this survived the Nazi occupation of the city." Bella studied the intricacies of the craftsmanship of the cups in particular.

"The Nazis were clever. They often didn't destroy objects if they were deemed to be valuable or of great beauty," said her mother matter-of-factly. "The governor in Krakow, Hans Frank, apparently removed the chandeliers from the synagogue before electing to use the building as a warehouse. At the end of 1944 the vaulting collapsed, and although it remained in a ruined state for over a decade, luckily the damage wasn't irrevocable and the synagogue was able to be restored."

Fat flakes of snow were settling over Szeroka Square as the women left the Old Synagogue, bringing to Anna's mind the wintry scenes from *Schindler's List*. Despite the warm, welcoming lights of the cafes and restaurants, the thought of this evil footprint of the past marking the very cobblestones she was standing on made her shiver involuntarily and she was glad to see Aleksander's taxi waiting for them in front of the Ariel Cafe. Stepping into the heated vehicle, she didn't have the inclination to lighten her expression, though.

"Thought-provoking, yes?" he said as Bella pulled shut the door and they proceeded to crawl down the warren of narrow alleyways of Kazimierz.

"Yes, it was, Alek. I was just thinking of all those generations who worshipped and lived their lives on these streets, only to be ordered from their homes, first to the ghetto and then to the camps," sighed Anna, feeling her heart lighten as they left behind the enclosed, hemmed-in streets for a more open road, lined with convenience stores with flashing neon signs. "To think that it happened in the city where my father had lived and studied just a couple of years before, it's so close to home and yet incomprehensible at the same time."

"Yes, it's a dark side to our country's history, for sure," his fists gripped the steering wheel; his eyes focused on the road, "but it wasn't just the Jews in this city who suffered. Of course they bore the sickening brunt of it and tourists who come to Krakow mainly want to visit the places they lived. But most Krakovians lived under adversity during the occupation, as I'm sure your father and others like him could testify."

"It's just unimaginable such things could have happened here or at all," sighed Anna, a profound tiredness creeping into every bone in her body as the lights of the hotel came into view, friendly and inviting.

"Yes, it should have remained that way. In the Nazis' imaginations," Alek said as they hastily exited his mini-bus which he had illegally parked just off the ring-road. "Right then, I hope you have an enjoyable few days continuing your sightseeing in the city. I'll try to unearth something relating to Tad before we meet again on Thursday morning for our trip to the mountains, but I can't promise anything. Many pre-war documents have been destroyed as you can appreciate. *Miłego wieczoru!*"

"Thank you, Alek. Have a lovely evening, too," Anna said, pleased she'd understood his Polish while at the same time observing he was smiling in her daughter's direction, perhaps waiting for a goodbye from her. But Sarah was busy brushing snow off her shoulders and didn't appear to notice.

Leaving her mother and daughter to go in before her, Sarah stood on the steps of the Wyspiański, watching Alek leave. She wistfully thought of him joining his family that evening, sharing a home-cooked meal together and playing with his son before bathing him and putting him to bed. She pictured Alek and his wife sitting by the fire, telling each other snippets of how their day had gone, and felt a pang of jealousy creep up on her. Taken aback, she knew it wasn't just their family life she hankered after, rather it was because of her developing attraction towards Alek. Knowing he was firmly out of bounds, she turned brusquely to follow Anna and Bella into the welcoming warmth of the foyer, trying to put all thoughts of that nature out of her mind.

34

Krakow, December 2020

The following evening, Anna, Sarah and Bella explored the Christmas market in the old market square, the chilly air scented with sausages sizzling on open grills mingling with warming spices of gingerbread and mulled wine. With seasonal music playing in the background, they strolled arm in arm around the wooden stalls, illuminated by strings of red and white lanterns, as they browsed the gifts and treats on offer, side by side with locals and tourists alike. The experience made the three of them remember they were actually on holiday as they lost themselves in the festive atmosphere, leaving their cares and worries, and those of others recently discovered, behind.

Joining a queue at the doughnut stall, Bella found herself bewitched by the tens of thousands of coloured fairy lights twisting their way around the gigantic

Christmas tree standing at the Cloth Hall's entrance. The edifice of the building itself, of which she'd made several sketches in pencil and charcoal back in her hotel room, was illuminated by lights which picked out every crenellation and transformed the already ornate Renaissance building into something truly magical. Sarah, who had visited similar markets on whistle-stop weekends to Luxembourg and Munich with her university colleagues, was enchanted by the choir singing Polish carols as she soaked in the all-encompassing Yuletide ambience and she wanted to try and taste everything the stalls had to offer. Meanwhile, looking over to the stalls selling local craftwork, Anna wondered whether Tad and his brother had ever sampled the delights of the Christmas market here in Krakow, feeling him close by this evening.

"Alek told me that markets like this have always signalled the run-up to Christmas in Poland. In the distant past, local traders set up stalls here, selling Christmas trees and decorations as well as ingredients for the traditional dishes eaten on Christmas Eve." Sarah took a bite of her beignet, the cinnamon-apple filling scorching her tongue, liquid butter oozing onto her fingers. "Wow, that's delicious!"

"Polish people celebrate Christmas on Christmas Eve rather than Christmas Day, don't they?" said Bella, not quite sure where she'd picked up that snippet of information.

"Yes, apparently they have a multi-course meal which consists mostly of fish, so it wouldn't suit you, Bella." Her mother pulled a face.

"No, definitely not!" Bella grimaced, savouring her hot praline-filled doughnut. "I think we might have to look for a restaurant where they serve other food too, rather than just the traditional on the 24th."

"It would be nice to be invited to someone's house to experience a traditional Polish Christmas, though," mused Anna as the woolly-hatted stallholder handed her a plum-filled doughnut.

The doughnuts weighing heavily on their stomachs, they decided it wouldn't be wise to partake in a full-scale restaurant meal. Instead they indulged in some more of the mouth-watering snacks the stalls had to offer, all three having developed a liking for pierogi, the Polish dumplings stuffed with cheese and meat and topped with fried onions and tasty lardons, a warming comfort food to ward off the wintry weather. The aroma of grilled meat enticing them, they then tried *smalec*, an appetiser consisting of hot slices of bread smeared with herb-infused lard and topped with sausage and pickled cucumbers. Although the combination didn't appeal to Bella, after one bite, to her surprise, she found herself hooked, the fusion of flavours creating something incredibly tasty.

Her appetite sated, Bella bought a stash of sweet treats for midnight feasts in her hotel room. Choosing from the colourful array on offer, she settled upon two boxes of cream fudge and cellophane bags of poppy seed cookies and chocolate-covered gooseberries and strawberries, which were a delicious delicacy of these parts. Next, they made their way to the craft stalls displaying all manner of gifts, from handmade plates to Christmas ornaments, exquisitely embroidered pillowcases to painted ceramic figurines and serving dishes. This time it was her mother and grandmother's turn to indulge in some of the beautiful Bolesławiec pottery, which they'd seen in pretty much every gift shop in the city as they each bought cereal bowls, cups and saucers in the traditional blue and white design. Finally, they reached the amber stalls, which resembled Aladdin's caves, the sunshine yellow, fiery orange and seaweed green stones of the necklaces, earrings, bracelets, rings and brooches glistening as the Christmas fairy lights strung overhead shone upon them.

"My mother told me of Polish amber when I was about twelve or thirteen," announced Anna, the warm golden light of the stones reflected in her eyes as she held up a delicate bracelet to inspect it more closely. "It's the native gemstone of Poland."

"Yes, Baltic amber is famous," Bella smiled, studying one of the green teardrop necklaces, "but I didn't realise that it came in so many shades; I always thought it was an orangey colour."

"I read that Poland's coastline supplied the gemstone to the Ancient Greeks and Romans so profusely that they named the trading route between the Mediterranean and the Baltic Sea, the Amber Road," added Sarah, admiring a ring set in silver. "Baltic amber can be as old as ninety million years or as young as thirty million years. It is fossilised tree resin and the most expensive pieces contain an insect or a leaf or tree bark which could be millions of years old. What a thought to hold something in your hand that was alive so long ago!"

"I want you both to choose a piece you like." Anna smiled, putting a hand on her daughter's and granddaughter's shoulders. "An early Christmas present from me."

"Oh, Mother, that's a lovely gesture," Sarah clasped her mother's cold hand, "but some of it is super expensive."

"Oh, don't you worry about cost; in fact, don't even look at the price tags! Either of you." Anna gave them a cheeky wink. "From the moment we decided to come to Poland, I've had it in mind to buy us all something to remember this welcoming country where our roots are. Amber is quintessentially Polish and whenever we wear our pieces in future, it will remind us of this trip and Tad, bringing us closer to him. Just pick the pieces that sing to your soul!" She laughed.

"That's a beautiful idea." Daughter and granddaughter drew Anna into a communal hug before embarking on a search of the stunning array of jewellery before them for their perfect picks. Bella made her mind up instantaneously, selecting a transparent green teardrop to wear next to her cross on the silver chain around her neck, while Sarah took a bit longer to choose a ring with an opaque orange stone set in a cluster of yellow ones, reminding her of a sunflower. It was Anna who dithered indecisively before finally settling upon a silver brooch in the shape of a tree, the tiny brown, orange and yellow stones of amber depicting autumn leaves. Passing the pieces to the young stallholder, who looked just how Anna had always pictured the Snow Queen in her ankle-length, white fur coat and matching hat, she ventured a tentative, *Ile to kosztuje?* But when the young woman replied with a fast flurry of words which sounded like a lyrical Polish poem rather than any of the numbers Anna had painstakingly learned, she resorted to her failsafe question: *Czy mówi pan po angielsku?* And although the woman's spoken English put their attempts at Polish to shame, Anna was pleased with herself that she'd at least attempted to speak her father's language. After paying for her purchases, despite her daughter's protestations to keep them for Christmas presents, Anna insisted they each put on their jewellery there and then.

"I just don't understand why people save things for the future," she declared later as they walked back to the hotel, the twinkling Christmas lights strung along the narrow streets guiding the way. "If I've learned anything from my father and this trip so far, it's that we shouldn't put things off. We need to enjoy the here and now, together."

35

Zakopane, December 2020

Anna was sitting on a wine-red velvet chair next to a huge Christmas tree which infused the air with its pine scent. She was staring out of the floor-to-ceiling windows which wrapped around Hotel Wyspiański's foyer. Hypnotised by the early-morning snowfall, she barely noticed the commuters dashing through it, their heads bowed to avoid the icy sting on their faces. Before the effects of global warming, her memories of growing up in the Fifties were of cold winters, often resulting in heavy snowfalls which she'd always found to be magical. Blown to and fro by wind currents whipped off the sea, she'd watched snowfalls for hours from her attic bedroom window, entranced as fat flakes had scurried and flurried down to the ground as though playing games with the invisible beast chasing them. She recalled the icy shock as she'd leaned out of the window to catch snowflakes on her hand, momentarily retaining their unique, intricate patterns before the heat of her skin had dissolved them to liquid.

Inhaling the pungency of the pine needles, she recalled peeking out of her window in the dead hours of night to watch as the cars, pavements and houses in her street had been gradually obscured by a white blanket, creating a pristine new world awake with possibilities. She remembered her joy on waking after a surprise, overnight snowfall to find her room infused with lavender light and the world outside silent and dazzling. And then there had been all the fun to be had in the snow itself, the days off school when she and her friends had wrapped up in thick coats, fur-lined boots and woolly hats and mittens, and had pulled their sledges through the crunchy snow to the park where they'd embarked on snowball fights and ice-skating on the frozen edges of the lake. Anna thought it all seemed so long ago and yet, in another way, just like yesterday as she stared wistfully at the enchanted blanket covering the Planty.

"Alek's here, Mum." Sarah's deep voice pulled her reluctantly from her reverie. As her daughter approached her, Anna took in her dark curls bouncing on her shoulders, her pale, flawless skin and her belted black ankle-length coat which accentuated her tiny waist. After just a week in Poland away from the daily grind, Sarah possessed a radiance which wasn't there during the fraughtness of term time. Maybe it was the culmination of a few lie-ins, being in the land of their ancestors or something else, Anna couldn't decide.

"You're sure you feel up to the trip today, Mum?" Sarah asked, her forehead suddenly furrowed with worry lines. "It will be a long day."

"I'm fine." Anna smiled as her daughter took her arm, leading her to the sliding doors where Bella was having trouble zipping up her anorak as she had layered up with two hoodies, the bright pink one a deviation from her usual black. "I've wanted to spend a day in the mountains since we arrived. Mother said my dad was always talking about them, how he'd skied and skated there with his brother. I'm so looking forward to finally going there myself."

"Even if we find something out about Tad?" Her daughter's eyes brimmed with concern as they braced themselves against the biting wind.

"That's what we came with the hope of doing, isn't it?" Anna felt a dull pain in her hips as she creaked into motion. "I'd be disappointed if we didn't."

Sarah eyed her mother thoughtfully but offered no comment as they headed out to meet Alek, treading carefully as the snow was already turning to slush on the hotel forecourt, making it slippery underfoot.

"*Dzień dobry*, ladies. Your carriage awaits." Alek bowed slightly, making a flourish with his hand. He was muffled up in a navy-blue parka this morning with fawn fur edging around the hood, his nose red and eyes bright as Anna noticed him looking at Sarah.

"*Cześć*, Alek!" Anna smiled, feeling that she knew him well enough for this more informal greeting of 'hi' now.

"*Cześć*, Anna." His smile was wide. "*Jak tam?*"

"*Dobrze, dziękuję.*" She smiled as she took his offered hand and he helped her to the mini-bus.

"I'm impressed. Polish is really hard to learn." Alek grinned, Anna thinking he looked more relaxed somehow this morning. Maybe it was the prospect of a day in the open air of the mountains, but everyone's mood seemed lighter.

"It must be in my DNA," Anna said proudly as he slid open the back door of the mini-bus. "My mother said Father ended up being pretty much bilingual towards the end..." She trailed off, not wanting to finish her sentence with the words *of the war* and much less *of his life*.

As Bella reached out a hand to help her grandmother onto the plush back seat, Sarah took her place upfront with Alek. The truth was that since their parting a few days before Sarah had often found her thoughts drifting towards Alek as she'd relived their easy conversations and his unforced friendliness, the look in his eye as he'd smiled at her, his clever quips and light, infectious laughter. There was no denying it, she did find him attractive, but it wasn't due to just one thing that was easy to pin down but rather a combination of factors equalling more than the sum of its parts. After so many years spent alone, never finding anyone who'd appealed to her on all these different levels, she thought she might have done now. But he was unavailable to her.

They joined standing traffic coming out of the city once again that morning as locals were starting to make early getaways for the Christmas holidays to ski resorts in the nearby mountains or else warmer climes further afield. Initially, therefore, Alek's full concentration was occupied by the accumulation of traffic snaking its way around the Planty, which eventually gave way to rolling countryside. With the bare branches of the trees reaching up like a layer of black lace pulled over the white, wintry sky, he picked up speed and took up his conversation with Sarah as though there'd been no interlude.

With Bella plugged into her iPhone listening to George Ezra, Anna gazed out of the window at the snowy landscape, her thoughts inevitably turned to where they were headed. Reading her guidebook in bed the previous night, she'd discovered that Zakopane was nicknamed the 'winter capital of Poland' and had been a popular destination for climbing and skiing for more than a century. The scenery becoming increasingly mountainous as they forged ahead, she shivered to think how perilous it must have been for her father to escape from Poland in the dead of winter across such inhospitable countryside, with its dangerous peaks and impenetrable forests. Without modern technology and insulated clothing, she wondered how anyone could have survived taking this route, realising that it must have been by the grace of God that he'd reached Blackpool safely.

Presently Alek pulled off the road, coming to a stop outside a vast wooden building, shadowed by a glade of fir trees. Strings of festive fairy lights hung from the steeply sloping roof while welcoming white lanterns shone in the dozen or so tiny windows. "I thought we might stretch our legs and indulge in a morning coffee." He smiled. As Anna stepped out of the mini-bus, she drew in a deep breath of the fresh mountain air. While it was as bitingly cold as in Krakow, she sensed that it also possessed a renewing, purifying quality as she pictured it inflating her lungs, breathing new life into her tired body.

"This restaurant is typical of the Goral culture in these parts," explained Alek as they stepped inside the low-beamed building, Anna's eyes drawn to the wooden tables set in neat rows and laid with beautifully embroidered tablecloths like those they'd seen on sale in the Cloth Hall in Krakow. She had purchased one with holly and ivy exquisitely depicted in ruby and emerald silken threads for her own Christmas table, but it was here, the carved wooden legs of the tables peeping from beneath the fine fabrics, that they seemed at home. Warmed by a blazing fire and sheepskin-covered seats, they enjoyed marshmallow-topped hot chocolates and, on Alek's recommendation, they shared wedges of spiced plum cake and cream cheese-filled pancakes served with warm apple compote.

As they finished eating, Sarah leaned back in her chair and, turning to her mother, said quietly, "Alek has been trying to discover what he can about Tad for us and told me on the way here he's turned up something that may come in useful." She glanced over to him in acknowledgement of her gratitude that he'd run this information past her first, letting her decide what would be suitable to share with her mother and daughter.

"Have you found his family? Or where he lived?" Anna looked expectantly at Alek as she pictured the prospect of visiting the house where her father had spent his childhood and adolescence that very day.

"No, I haven't. That doesn't mean we won't but, no, not yet." He unfolded a paper he'd extricated from his inside coat pocket, handing it to her. She recognised some of the German words but unfortunately the document was poorly translated into English, which was barely comprehensible.

Der Kommandeur der Sicherheitspolizei und des SD im Distrikt Krakau. Grenzpolizeikommisariat Zakopane – Zakopane, Tatrastraße 7.

Robert Weissmann, 1907 in Neustadt, his father was a tradesman, SS-Hauptsturmführer, Kriminalkommissar, also member NSDAP, he came from Drezno, for October 1939 to 1945 he was a Chief Gestapo in Zakopane, height – 165 cm, black hair, he joined to NSDAP in 1929, in 1932 he joined to SS.

Arnold Sehmisch, 11 March 1905, he joined to police in 30 March 1925, SS-Hauptsturmführer, height – 168 cm, he came from Drezno, he joined to NSDAP 1 May 1937, to SS in 1942/43 as SS-Sturmscharführer, in 9 November 1944 he became SS-Hauptsturmführer.

"I don't understand fully, but does this mean the Gestapo had headquarters in Zakopane, where Tad and his family lived?" Anna stated, the words swimming in an unfathomable black sea before her eyes. "For some reason, I'd always thought the Gestapo were just located in the cities."

"No, they had a strong presence in your father's hometown. They came just a month after the invasion and set up their headquarters here until the end of the war." Alek paused as she passed the paper back to him. "It would have made things very difficult for your father and other young men in his position. I don't know whether you've read anything in your research, but Zakopane served as a focal point for the resistance movement in this area. With Tad's background, I think there is a strong likelihood he was involved in this. This would have made his position increasingly difficult and put his grandfather's life in danger. I think this could have been one of the reasons why he left."

"So you're saying that perhaps witnessing the atrocities happening first in Krakow and then in Zakopane, he tried to fight back with the resistance?" Anna clarified, trying to digest what Alek was telling her. "But as the Gestapo closed in, in order to save his grandfather, he had no alternative but to continue his fight elsewhere?"

"With all my knowledge of events here at that time, if I had to make an educated guess, I'd say that scenario was a very real possibility. In early 1940 when Tad made his escape, representatives of the Soviet NKVD and the Gestapo met for a week in Zakopane's Villa Tadeusz to discuss ways of pacifying resistance in Poland," he said solemnly. "Danger lurked in every corner here, with the probability that young men such as your father would be picked up by the Nazis to work for the Third Reich. Naturally, many men were frightened for their lives and their loved ones, and they saw no option but to risk leaving."

"But for someone who escaped like my grandfather, wouldn't that have had consequences for his family?" Sarah interrupted, having read the document.

"That's what I'm trying to find out," he replied, but from the dark shadow that momentarily passed over his face, both Anna and Sarah could tell he'd already made up his mind about what had happened.

36

Fortified by their hot drinks and sweet treats, Alek had one more stop planned for them before lunch: a visit to the renowned wooden church which sat proudly atop a hill on the outskirts of Zakopane. Set against a backdrop of fir trees, Anna imagined it to be a refuge worthy of a fairy-tale hero attempting to escape from unmentionable terrors in the forest. She thought it resembled a three-tiered wedding cake, its intricate carved details the icing decorating it, so to speak. Approaching it on foot, the snow glinting on its rooftops, it was like no church she'd ever seen. Alek filled them in with details about its construction, explaining that its walls had been built from logs and twisted wood chips to caulk the spaces in-between, giving the impression that the sturdy rope wrapped around it was holding it together. Seeing their awestruck faces, he explained it was a wonderful example of the woodcarving tradition in which the Podhale region was steeped.

While Alek helped Anna negotiate the snow-covered wooden steps, Sarah walked behind with Bella, her heart warmed by the sound of her mother's laughter. Following their successful shopping expedition to purchase the amber jewellery, there was a lightness, almost a frivolity to Anna's mood today, which set Sarah's mind at ease. After admiring the workmanship of the bell tower, Sarah had expected the complexity of the craftsmanship to extend inside the church, but on entering, she was strangely underwhelmed. In place of the exquisitely carved decor she'd envisaged, the interior walls were undecorated log surfaces giving the space a pervading darkness, punctuated only by slim shafts of weak light which squeezed through the windows. She noticed the nave was narrow, the whole space cramped, possibly to retain the heat in the sub-zero winters. Looking up, Sarah admired a portrait of the Black Madonna before her eyes were drawn to a carving of the Last Supper, both of which hung above the main altar.

"The church is named Our Lady of Częstochowa," Alek whispered as the group huddled around the painting. "A place two hundred or so kilometres from here where the icon of the Black Madonna is the focus of pilgrimage for people from all over the world."

"I recall reading about her," said Sarah, admiring the Virgin's lovely face. "Isn't the icon's origin shrouded in mystery but legend traces it to St Luke, who is said to have painted it on a cedar tabletop from the house of the Holy family?"

"Yes, that's right," said Alek, admiration shining in his eyes that she'd recalled such a fact which wasn't widely known among other tourists he'd brought here. "The Last Supper carving is actually quite interesting too. It was carved by a master woodcarver who lived locally. Sadly, his name is not recorded but the plaque beneath it reads that, after the war, it was dedicated to the young men of Podhale who left to fight Nazi Germany but who never came back. I've always thought it a fitting tribute symbolising sacrifice for others."

Taking photographs of the plaque, Bella commented, "What a lovely memorial to my great-grandfather and his generation."

Leaving the church silently, each with their own thoughts, they continued their drive, the snow falling thicker as the incline became ever-steeper. Although the roads were icy and the drop increasingly precipitous, as the mini-bus climbed Alek managed to point out the ski jump on the north slope of Krokiew Mountain, which, he explained, had opened in 1925 when tourism had just begun to become popular in the region. However, despite craning their necks, the women found it was barely discernible in the driving snow.

"The mountains here are very popular for skiing. The cable car to Kasprowy Wierch Mountain was completed in 1936 and the funicular connected Zakopane and the top of Gubałówka Mountain two years later which marked the start of the town's incarnation as a ski resort," Alek explained as the road eventually plateaued out. "There are also a number of cross-country skiing trails in the forests surrounding the town which have been popular for over a century. My friends and I used to follow them every winter but then life took over and I sort of gave it up, unfortunately…" His voice trailed off as though he was pondering exactly why that had happened.

"Has the town ever hosted the Winter Olympics?" Bella asked as Alek slowed down on the approach to the cable car station, a bright-red beacon in the encroaching whiteness.

"No, not as yet! Zakopane made several unsuccessful bids to hold both the Winter Olympics and Alpine World Ski Championships." He brought the mini-bus to a stop in a busy car park. "However, the town hosted the Nordic World Ski Championships on several occasions as well as the Alpine World Ski Championships in 1939, the first outside the Alps and the last official world championships prior to World War II."

"My father's family would have certainly seen something of them, if not Tad, as he would have been at Jagiellonian University at that point," Anna mused ruefully, not allowing herself to consider what misfortunes might have befallen them all just a short time later.

They enjoyed lunch at a small cafe on Krupówki Street, the main thoroughfare in Zakopane which dissected the tourist town into fairly evenly sized halves. Despite the sub-zero temperatures, the street was crowded with tourists, locals and street entertainers. "I really like Alek," Anna whispered in Sarah's ear as they looked over towards him standing in line with Bella at the counter to order their food. "It's a pity he's already spoken for, but the best men always are!"

"Shush, he'll hear you!" Sarah playfully batted her mother's hand with the menu as they sat in a secluded corner next to a Christmas tree adorned with twinkly lights and traditionally carved wooden ornaments of the Podhale region.

Warmed after devouring plates of steaming goulash and thick, locally made bread, followed by yet more crispy pancakes with hot fruit, they braved the snowstorm once more to browse the local market which lined one side of the street. Bypassing the reasonably priced leather jackets, shoes and fur coats, which seemed to be popular purchases among the locals, they bought some exquisitely embroidered scarves and shawls in the vibrant colours of the Goral tradition for themselves and as Christmas stocking fillers for their friends. After buying a selection of beautifully decorated wooden eggs, encouraged by Alek, they sampled the renowned local smoked sheep cheese, Oscypek, which was as delicate as it was delicious. Their final stop before returning to Krakow was the Tatra Museum on the edge of town housed in what appeared to be an enchanting, snow-covered winter palace with majestic windows and verandas, protected against the elements by fir trees reaching above the pointed roof to the white sky.

There in a cosy theatre, they enjoyed a short film about the Goral culture and its distinctive food, architecture, music and costume before perusing cultural and ethnographic artefacts of the Polish Tatras. Photographing the exhibits so she might sketch them on her return to the hotel, Bella's favourites were the everyday, household objects, the historical clothing and furniture as she imagined her ancestors would have once owned similar. She also found herself drawn to the depiction of the interior of a typical nineteenth-century

Podhale wooden cottage with the traditional two rooms and daily life concentrated in the black chamber, so called because its walls were darkened by the smoke from the stove. Walking around, she found herself wondering whether her great-grandfather and his family had lived in such a house and what life had been like for them there.

As it was already growing dark by the time Alek set off back to Krakow, he took due care on the icy roads. While Sarah and Bella huddled together on the back seat, lulled to sleep by the satisfying warmth and hum of the heater, Anna sat up front this time. Chatting to Alek, she wanted to know everything he could tell her about country life here in the Podhale region so she could imagine the lives her ancestors had led. However, despite gaining more understanding of the way of life of Tad, his family and the generations before them, she felt frustrated that these facts were all she may ever know. Entranced by the snowy landscape, she acknowledged her disappointment about not finding any specific leads to her father or his family while visiting his birthplace. If this was the closest she would ever get to him, it was no longer enough for her.

37

Despite the first scratchings of a sore throat, Anna was adamant she felt well enough to visit Jagiellonian University as they'd planned. Ever since their arrival in the city, she'd been desperate to walk the same corridors her father had eighty years before, to sit in the lecture theatres where he'd studied and explore the main hall where he'd prayed, sang and dined alongside his fellow students. "My time here in Krakow is passing so much quicker than I ever imagined it would." She sniffed, looking at the double-digit December date in huge letters behind the main desk in the hotel reception as they sank onto one of the sofas. "We're already a third of the way through our stay and I don't want to waste a single moment."

"But Mother, it might be more prudent to take a day's rest now and nip your cold in the bud before it takes hold of you," pleaded Sarah, a hopeful look playing upon her fine features, even though she knew her mother's stubborn nature would win the day. "Rather than struggle on and maybe make it worse than it would have been."

"I think I'm old enough to know what's best for me," Anna asserted sternly while buttoning her navy frock coat right up to her chin as Sarah and Bella exchanged knowing glances. "I'll tell you if I'm getting too tired or feel too unwell to be out, you don't need to worry yourselves about that."

"Well, alright then," her daughter relented, fastening the belt of her black coat and tucking her unruly hair into her dark green beret. "Bella, can you go up to the room and fetch my thick purple scarf so your grandma can wrap it around her head and bring an extra heat pad for her back?"

"Sure, Mum." Bella smiled, who had layered up in her usual black this morning, accessorising it with a cheery red hat with white reindeers knitted into it and matching gloves which she'd bought in the Christmas market.

"If you think I'm going out with that awful woolly thing over my hair, you need to think again," affirmed Anna. "For one thing it will ruin the shampoo and set I had in the hotel's salon last night and for another, I don't want everyone I walk past today thinking I'm ninety-three."

"Oh, Mother, trust you to put your appearance above your health in these freezing temperatures," Sarah saw her mother's wry smile so decided to play her at her own game, "but I'm afraid, it's either that or we're not going out at all today. I won't be responsible for you catching your death of cold!"

To this, the old woman tutted but didn't offer further comment as Sarah got the fresh-faced receptionist, Agusia, whose her waist-length hair shone like a gold curtain, to phone them a taxi while Bella went to retrieve the scarf. Not feeling like another discussion about her health, Anna decided to let it drop, allowing her daughter to coddle her and claim victory, for once. The scarf draped on Anna's shoulders, rather than over her hair, it took just over ten minutes to reach the Collegium Maius, the young taxi driver keeping up a lively conversation as he asked their impressions of his city so far while driving up ancient alleyways barely wide enough to fit his car through. In faultless English he gave them a potted history of the medieval buildings and baroque churches they passed, explaining that he doubled up as a city tourist guide during the summer season.

"The Collegium Maius is the oldest building in Jagiellonian University, which in turn is one of the most ancient seats of learning in the world. It was founded by King Kazimierz the Great in 1364 and then, in the fifteenth century, they amalgamated a number of town houses to use as lecture rooms and accommodation for professors. It was only at the end of the nineteenth century that the Neo-Gothic style college you see today was built." He paused to negotiate a sharp, very tight, left turn.

"My father studied here in the late 1930s," said Anna as he brought the taxi to a stop outside a grand-looking white building topped with an ochre tiled roof. "According to my mother he was an architecture student here when war broke out. I never got to meet him."

Sarah noticed the driver give her mother a look of something like admiration tinged with sympathy, but he offered no comment. For whatever reason he kept his silence, whether for personal reasons or to guard her mother from talking about her past, she couldn't say. But as the taxi pulled away leaving them on the snow-swept street, Sarah realised that failing to find anything specific out about Tad during their trip to Zakopane had only fanned the flames of her mother's desire to discover something of him before their time in his homeland came to an end.

The 11am guided tour consisted of just the three of them, the bad weather evidently keeping people in the city's warm coffee shops that morning. They were led by a pleasant tour guide, a current second-year Philosophy student named Hanna, whose tall, slim figure was wrapped up in a festive red anorak trimmed with white faux fur and skinny black jeans tucked into knee-length heeled boots. As she pointed out the crystalline vaulting of the arcades surrounding the quad, it reminded Sarah of that in Exeter College, Oxford where she'd stayed whilst attending a linguistics conference the previous spring.

"This place has a monastic feel to it, so peaceful," commented Anna as the snow eddied down over the quadrangle from the grey sky, to softly rest on the group's shoulders.

"It was probably built on a similar design to a monastery or nunnery," the young guide nodded, "for quiet contemplation and learning. I think the academic and ecclesiastical bodies have always had much in common, the same as your Oxbridge colleges, I believe."

They paused briefly beneath the ornate musical clock to admire its intricacies as it chimed the hour before Hanna showed them the famous Jagiellonian globe, which she told them dated back to 1508 and was the first in the world to depict the American continent. As they strolled around, the high walls dulling the noises from the city beyond, Sarah absorbed the air of learning which had always appealed to the studious and academic side of her nature, while Anna felt quietly comforted to think that she was finally following in her father's footsteps.

As expected, the Great Hall was a grand room with glass chandeliers suspended from a gold painted ceiling, which they paused to admire before studying the richly carved stalls wrapped around the walls which in turn were hung with dozens of portraits of intellectual-looking men. "These stalls are still used to this day by the university's senate at ceremonies at which honorary degrees are conferred," explained Hanna, her ice-blue eyes sparkling.

"Who are the men depicted in the portraits?" Anna asked, thinking there was something odd about them; that amidst the centuries-old furniture and decor in this ancient seat of learning the paintings of these venerated souls were strangely modern-looking, dressed as they were in dark suits, shirts and ties.

"They are paintings of professors who the Nazis rounded up and imprisoned at the start of the war," Hanna said abruptly, her blue eyes sombre. "Sonderaktion Krakau was the codename for the operation. The Nazis thought that by eradicating the Polish elite from society, Krakow could then become culturally German."

"When exactly did it take place?" Anna enquired, shivering suddenly despite the welcoming warmth of the hall. Although she'd known of the round up of academics here, she'd never felt brave enough to learn about the specifics of the event before, as she'd imagined her father caught up in this act of brutality, frightened for his life.

"In the late autumn of 1939 when the Gestapo chief in Krakow, SS-Obersturnbannführer Bruno Müller, commanded the university's rector, Professor Tadeusz Lehr-Splawinski, to instruct all his professors to go to his lecture on Germany's plans for Polish education. The rector agreed, scheduling a meeting at Collegium Novum on November 6, 1939. Almost one hundred and fifty eminent professors and lecturers attended, but instead of delivering a lecture, Müller informed them that the university did not have permission to start a new academic year. They were arrested then and there by armed police, who frisked them and escorted them out to waiting trucks." The girl paused for them to absorb what she was saying.

"What happened to the professors?" Anna said, fear coursing through her veins like ice as she knew Tad almost certainly would have witnessed or found himself involved in this terrible event in some way.

"Senior professors were kicked, punched and hit with rifle butts by the heavy-handed Nazis in a most barbaric manner while university students and workers were also arrested. In total, one hundred and eighty-four people were transported to a detention centre in Breslau, Germany, now the Polish city of Wrocław. From there, on the night of November 27, they were loaded onto a train and taken to Sachsenhausen concentration camp near Berlin and in March 1940, they were moved to Dachau concentration camp near Munich," Hanna sighed.

"So they perished?" said Bella, hugging her black puffa jacket to her.

"Unfortunately many of the professors were elderly and they did not survive the roll calls held twice a day in the snow that winter in camps where dysentery was also rife. But not all succumbed to the conditions. In fact, Benito Mussolini and the Vatican voiced their protest to these incarcerations so fervently that, in February 1940, one hundred and one professors were released from Sachsenhausen." Hanna gently ushered them to the edge of the hall to make way for a group of present-day professors, casually dressed in jumpers and jeans now that the autumn term was over.

"It makes me so angry and sad that the Nazis used methods like this to destroy the fabric of this great country," Anna seethed. "How dare they?"

"But they didn't succeed, did they? That's the point. Today, the university has more students than ever of all nationalities, religions and political persuasions. It might be quiet now during the holidays but normally these streets are teeming with bicycles carrying young people to their lectures." Hanna smiled as they continued on to the chapel. "In 1942, those who had gone through Sonderaktion Krakau and the internment that followed formed an underground university in defiance of the punitive edicts of the Nazis. Among the eight hundred students who took part was Karol Wojtyla."

"St John Paul II?" said Anna, the thought crossing her mind that it was possible Tad might have bumped into him on these hallowed corridors, that the two men might have even attended some of the same lectures. Oh, how she wished she could ask him! But of course, it was yet another part of her father's story she would never know.

38

In the Planty, the early-morning sunshine sparkled on freshly fallen snow. Spotting a cluster of snow-covered benches, Anna imagined them packed with locals meeting for lunchtime chats over takeaway sandwiches during the spring and summer months or else tourists taking a breather from sightseeing, cooling down beneath the shady foliage of the trees. Today, however, with the city smothered by yet another heavy overnight snowfall, the pathway was deserted except for the three of them and a handful of well-wrapped up people scurrying to get in somewhere warm.

On the edge of the enclosed warren of streets of the old town, Anna took a moment to glance up to the majestic Wawel Castle standing atop the hill as it proudly surveyed the city below, its green and gold roofs glittering in the sharp December light. Despite being used as an administration centre by the Nazis during World War II, those five years were but a mere footnote in the castle's five-hundred-year history. Inhaling the cold, fresh air, Anna felt an immense pride that her father had been Polish as she imagined that the building's dogged defiance might in some small way reflect the history and character of her family, too.

A vicious wind ripped around the main square, making lingering at the huddled stalls of the Christmas market undesirable, so instead they headed to the lights shining through the stained-glass windows of Bazylika Mariacka, refracting rainbows onto the iced-over pools of snow on the pavement. There in the warmth, fuelled by the heat of hundreds of candles, they whiled away an hour, Anna sitting silently in a front pew, lost in her own thoughts while Sarah, aided by an informative leaflet, gave Bella a tour of the church and crypt. Later, at a nearby coffee shop, accompanied by a few stray students on neighbouring tables who, for some reason, lingered in the city despite being well over a week into their Christmas vacation, they tucked into steaming bowls of lentil soup followed by plates of pierogi: warming winter nourishment.

While Sarah and Bella chatted enthusiastically about the history and architecture of the Basilica, Anna regressed to her thoughts of the previous day, still not quite sure what to make of what she'd encountered and learned on her tour of Jagiellonian University. Warmed by her satisfying lunch, all she knew was that, despite finding nothing specific about him, she felt closer to Tad here than she'd ever done back in Blackpool. It had seemed as though, within the ancient walls of the Jagiellonian, the echoes of the past still resonated in every corridor, cloister and room, that if she had pressed her ear to the cold plaster covering the walls, she would have heard the whispers of former students spanning time itself, speaking in Latin and Polish. She pictured the young, lively man she'd seen in her mother's photograph sitting in the Great Hall listening to a greying professor read out the notices for the day. She saw Tad in the chapel just a few months later after Sonderaktion Krakau, weeping silently as he'd prayed for the souls of his friends and lecturers taken away by the Nazis, asking God for guidance on what to do next.

Is that how it had been? Somehow she felt as though it was. That having escaped this awful act in the autumn of 1939, it had been revenge for the Nazis' brutality against his teachers that had inspired Tad's escape from Poland to an unoccupied country from where he'd been able to mount his fight back. Or maybe it had been something far more idealistic? That he'd decided it was his duty to fight for the future of his homeland and for his family? Or perhaps it had stemmed from a desire to emulate his brother? She wished she could ask him now, feeling frustrated that this trip was unearthing far more questions than it would ever hope to answer.

As the waiter set down three frothy hot chocolates, the whipped cream sprinkled with cinnamon hearts, Bella suddenly announced, "I've made a decision about my future. When we get home, I'm going to apply to do an Architecture degree, just like Tad started but didn't get the chance to complete. It feels right, finally."

Seeing her daughter's disbelieving expression, Anna smiled and filled the awkward silence which stretched between them: "That's wonderful, Isabella and a very fitting way to remember your great-grandfather."

"That's exactly what I thought. I've always been interested in architecture and this way I get to use my creative talents while working towards what could be a fulfilling career." She smiled, her voice brimming with pride. "Last night, I checked on the internet and my A-level subjects would enable me to get on a university course. What do you think, Mum?"

Where on earth had that come from? Sarah suppressed her initial cynical response to Bella's news. "Are you absolutely sure, Bella, or are you caught up in the romantic notion that you're following in Tad's footsteps?"

"This isn't a snap decision I've just made. I've been thinking about it for some time but didn't want to mention anything as I needed to be absolutely sure that's what I want to do with my life. Coming to Krakow has simply strengthened my resolve to work towards this ambition," Bella explained firmly.

"In that case, sweetheart, I couldn't be more delighted." Sarah enfolded her daughter in her arms, kissing the top of her head. "I've hated all the tension between us these past months. All I ever want is your happiness and it makes me so proud that you've not been influenced by pressure from me but have thought this through yourself in a mature way."

"Well, now that's decided, I think we'll celebrate with slices of warm gingerbread," Anna announced. A few minutes later, as a waiter brought their desserts, she watched her daughter and granddaughter tuck in. She was glad for their good moods at this moment, not only for their sakes but because it diverted them away from reading her own, which was still troubled by thoughts of Tad.

After lunch, they headed down Floriańska Street towards St Florian's Gate, majestic against the frosty sky. "This gate is one of the only parts of the ancient city walls that remains. From way back as far as the thirteenth century, moated walls surrounded the city with forty-seven towers and eight fortified gates," Sarah read from her snow-smeared guidebook. "But with the invention of artillery rendering them useless as a defence system, the walls fell into disrepair at the end of the eighteenth century and they were later dismantled and replaced with the Planty. St Florian's managed to survive somehow."

Stopping off at souvenir shops for Bella to purchase a black T-shirt with a city skyline etched in pink neon as well as keyrings, pencils and pens emblazoned with outlines of the Wawel Castle, the Barbican and Bazylika Mariacka, it took them half an hour to reach the gate. From there, they followed the sole remaining section of the city wall, perusing the paintings perched against it, the artists sitting before easels curling their frozen fingers around mugs of hot tea for a moment's respite from the perils of spending the day exposed to sub-zero temperatures. Impressed by the work of a young man, who told them he was a third-year Art History student at Jagiellonian University, Sarah bought one of his paintings which depicted the gate in soft, hazy hues of lavender, rose and ochre, while Anna opted for one in bold tones.

"Right, what do you want to do for the rest of the afternoon?" Bella asked, clearly eager to get back to the shops after feeling left out of her mother and grandmother's deliberations over their paintings.

"Are you feeling okay, Mum?" Sarah asked, her forehead furrowed with concern as she looked at her mother's pale face.

"I can't deny my sore throat is lingering," Anna smiled, trying to keep bright even though it now felt there was a mallet inside her head, pounding away at her skull, "and I do feel rather tired."

"Bella," Sarah exchanged concerned looks with her daughter, "I think we should go back to the hotel."

"But I don't want to spoil your day," Anna implored, wiping her snow-smudged glasses.

"You won't." Sarah took hold of her hand, helping her negotiate the slippery cobblestones. "But if you're feeling unwell, you need to get back to the hotel room, keep warm and rest up."

"Come on, Gran. We've done enough sightseeing and I've bought more than enough souvenirs for one day, or maybe even two!" Her granddaughter held up her carrier bags which, bulging with her purchases, more than proved her point. "And returning to the hotel early will give me another opportunity to beat Mum at Connect 4."

"I wouldn't be so sure about that, Missy." Sarah laughed as they headed through the dark arch of St Florian's Gate and to the fleet of white taxis on the other side.

Hearing her granddaughter squeal with delight on the other side of the bedroom wall as her lucky yellow counters beat her mum's red ones for the third consecutive game, Anna sank her head into her pillows, seeking comfort in their softness. The paracetamol Sarah had given her on their arrival back over an hour ago was indeed beginning to kick in, the heavy hammering in her head somewhat blunted. As that subsided, however, other symptoms were developing. Her throat felt as scratched and raw as sandpaper, making it painful to even swallow, while her blocked nose meant that her breathing was raspy and laboured. The winter sky casting her room in a pale blue hue, she clutched her hot water bottle to her chest, hoping that sleep would claim her soon and rid her body of illness so she could make the most of the remaining days of her trip.

39

Following a surprisingly refreshing night's sleep, Anna felt well enough to go down to breakfast the next morning. However, her sore throat and sore head had bloomed into a full-blown cold overnight, meaning her sense of taste had diminished so she could only stomach orange juice, grapefruit and a bread roll rather than the pâtes and cheeses of the continental counter she'd become accustomed to during their stay. "You're looking quite a bit brighter than you did yesterday, Mum," Sarah ventured, tucking into a plate of steaming scrambled eggs and smoked salmon.

Anna smiled, thinking how she'd spent a good ten minutes applying foundation to her nose, which was as red as Rudolf's. "I actually slept like a baby. Nothing disturbed me at all, which is a rarity as you know what a light sleeper I am, especially with the city traffic moving through the night."

"All the same, I think you should stay indoors today to give yourself time to recover," Sarah braved, knowing that if her mother had set her mind on a particular course, there was no deviating her from it.

"That's exactly what I had in mind." Anna took a bite of her bilberry jam-smeared poppy seed roll, noting the incredulity on Sarah and Bella's faces. "What? I'm not stupid about these things. I know I'm the wrong side of seventy and, believe me, I feel every one of those years today, but I'm also sensible enough to realise when to take care of myself and, more than anything, I want to recover to enjoy the remainder of the break."

"Well, good. We are glad to hear it, Mum!" Sarah's uncertain expression as she sipped her black coffee filled Anna with a frisson of excitement that she was still able to outflank her clever daughter now and again.

"Of course, I still want to go to Wadowice tomorrow as we planned with Alek. Thinking how it's possible my father could have met St John Paul II when they were students, I really want to visit the house where he grew up and look around the museum. My mum once told me that my father's faith was extremely important to him," Anna added, feeling another connection to Tad. "That will give you girls a chance to go your own way today while I rest up here!"

"Can we go Christmas shopping in one of those swanky malls on the outskirts of the city that we drove past the other day, Mum?" Bella interrupted, having abandoned her black outfits in favour of skinny blue jeans and a chunky white knit with a red and blue design which she'd bought from one of the Goral traders in Zakopane. "There's sure to be some smart stores in a city like this!"

"Okay," Sarah relented, buttering her toast, knowing that her daughter's love for brand names more than matched her loathing for them. "If you're alright staying here on your own, Mum? Or we could all just sit around the hotel and have a rest? This is a holiday, after all, and we have had a busy time so far."

"Don't even give me a second thought." Anna waved her hand dismissively. "It'll give me a chance to recharge my batteries and I'll come down to the restaurant for a nice lunch."

Nibbling on a plum-filled pastry, Bella googled the best places to shop in Krakow. Half an hour later, having settled her grandma back in her room reading *The Snow Angel*, she and Sarah braved stinging sleet and slippery pavements to head to the highly recommended Galeria Krakowska, a chic shopping centre whose range of shops, cafes and overall cleanliness more than matched Bella's high expectations. It was indeed the perfect venue for a girly day out with her mum as well as a spot of Christmas shopping. Bella felt she'd died and gone to a big-brand heaven as she insisted on dragging Sarah, somewhat reluctantly, around Guess, Tommy Hilfiger, Michael Kors and Hugo Boss before making a string of purchases at her usual go-to stores of H&M and Mango. There, she stocked up on thick-knit jumpers, corduroy mini-skirts and leggings in rich jewel shades of ruby, emerald and amethyst, which would see her nicely through the winter months. She also purchased a lavender snood for her grandma to keep the cold, Krakow air off her chest when she was finally fit enough to venture outdoors once more.

"This is the most humongous shopping centre I've ever visited," Bella commented, uploading photos of the shiny mall, adorned with sparkling silver and gold swags, to her Facebook page over their lunch in a swanky sushi bar. "Everyone back home will be so jealous when they see these pics."

"Speaking of that, I don't know how we'll get this lot back to England." Sarah glanced beneath their table where a dozen bulging shopping bags were strewn around their feet.

"Perhaps we should buy an extra suitcase?" Bella snapped photos of her meal before uploading them too. "I'm glad we got to spend today together. I've really enjoyed it, although I hope Gran is feeling better soon."

"Yes, I have too, Bella. But we'll have to keep a close eye on Gran over the next few days. I know she was extremely disappointed Alek didn't discover anything specifically about Tad when we went to Zakopane and then she found the tour of the university upsetting, knowing her father may have witnessed the brutal way his professors were treated. This trip is definitely taking an emotional toll on her despite all her efforts to hide it." Sarah toyed with her food, never sure if sushi was really her thing. "I think she set out with a dream of somehow finding where her father had lived and possibly even some of his extended family. But as the days go by and Alek meets one dead end after another, we have to be prepared for the distinct possibility that we might not actually discover anything about Tad or his family."

"Would that be worse for her than unearthing something awful?" Bella commented, switching off her phone to save the battery, as the European adapter she'd been using had made her charger incredibly slow.

"I don't know, but taking into account the background of the Nazi occupation, we have to plan for that eventuality too," Sarah concluded as they finished off their food. After venturing to the third floor of Galeria Krakowska where, in a delightful stationery shop, they splashed out on pretty fountain pens and fancy notebooks, they eventually reluctantly left the shopping centre, the ultra-modern mirrored outer walls catching their reflections. Their winter coats and hoods fastened up against the bitter snow shower, their arms straining with the weight of six shopping bags each, they decided to take a taxi the short distance back to the old town.

As dusk quickly fell, they alighted a few hundred yards from their hotel to call in the local bakers where they purchased some scrumptious-looking cream cakes to share with Anna back in her hotel room. Tram and car lights reflecting on the black, wet pavements, they then hurried back to the Wyspiański, eager to check how Anna was feeling, as well as share their exploits of the day with her.

"I must say you look much brighter, Mother! It was definitely the right decision to stay in and give yourself time to get better." Sarah smiled as she watched her mum tuck into her cream meringue with great gusto. She was pleased to see Anna sitting in the green upholstered chair at the side of her neatly made bed and that she'd dressed in a smart turquoise jumper and black trousers, taking care to do her hair and makeup despite still undoubtedly feeling rotten. "But didn't you have any lunch?"

"Yes, I ordered room service. That lovely girl Agusia brought me up some delicious beef broth and rye bread." She sniffed, her headache and sore throat having mercifully cleared. The cold was all in her nose now.

"We had sushi for lunch," Bella chipped in, removing her new knitted gloves from her frozen fingers and switching on her iPhone. "Don't pull a face, Gran! Look, do you want to see some pics?"

"Now, you can't call me unadventurous, but I draw a line at eating raw fish." The old lady chuckled, licking sweet cream from her fingers. "All I can say is I'm glad you brought me this scrummy cake instead!"

"It was surprisingly nice," Sarah lied to give her daughter some much-needed backup as she took off her beret and titivated her hair with her fingers. "I think there's a sushi bar opening at the university in the New Year. It's meant to be very healthy for you, and the Japanese heart attack rate is supposed to be one of the lowest in the developed world."

"Well, I'll have to take your word for it because I can assure you raw fish will never pass my lips," Anna countered, crunching the flaky meringue. "But my taste and appetite are returning, so I think I'll opt for one of those nice chicken dishes tonight."

"So you feel well enough to go down to the restaurant?" Sarah asked, taking off her coat and kicking off her snow-encrusted boots.

"Of course, stop fussing around me like an old mother hen. I'm fine, fit and raring to go to Wadowice tomorrow to visit St John Paul's childhood home." She raised her eyebrows, an expression of determined defiance on her face.

"Mother, are you sure you're up to it?" Sarah fussed. "I could ask Alek if we can postpone the trip a day or two?"

"Don't even think about it! I need some fresh air to help unblock my nose." She sniffed for effect. "And Wadowice is only a small town, so there won't be that much walking to do."

"Okay, well, if you're sure. All the same, I'll leave it until tomorrow to confirm our pick-up time with Alek." Feeling defeated, Sarah fiddled in the bottom of her bag for her phone.

"Whatever you think is best, Sarah." Anna turned and winked at Bella as her daughter scrolled through her contacts for his number. "Now, are you going to give me a fashion show, featuring all the clothes in those fancy shopping bags?"

40

Hearing Anna's hoarse voice interspersed by a rasping cough, Sarah tried to persuade her mother to have another day's rest in the hotel to properly get over her cold, but predictably Anna was having none of it. "I told you I need to get outdoors. I felt cooped up staying here all day yesterday," she pleaded as they ate breakfast. "The central heating is exacerbating my symptoms and making it hard to breathe. No, a day in the fresh air well wrapped up will be just what the doctor ordered! So, phone Alek or teletext him or whatever you do and ask him to pick us up in an hour, as we originally arranged."

"Well, if you're sure." Sarah dubiously glanced over to Bella, who just rolled her eyes in easy submission. She was too smart to argue with her grandmother when she had a bee in her bonnet, although she did fear that her judgement was somewhat obscured on this occasion by her need to find out about Tad. Well, if she wouldn't look after herself, she and her mother would have to do it for her; it was as simple as that.

The countryside rolled past the misted-up windows as Alek concentrated on the road, which was treacherously icy in parts this morning. Anna was bewitched by the starkness of the bare trees, the only touch of colour in the otherwise monochrome landscape. Occasionally passing wooden farm buildings huddled beneath their blankets of snow as if trying to keep warm, Anna pictured Tad growing up in such a house, an energetic boy, looking up to his brother and grandfather, desperately wanting to be like them. In the cosy warmth of the mini-bus, her eyes eventually grew heavy with sleep as her thoughts became dreams. The next thing she was aware of was someone lightly tugging her coat sleeve as Sarah's voice drew her from her sleep. "Mother, we're here."

"Oh, right." She tidied her hair with the heel of her hand, having no concept of how long she'd been asleep but aware that Alek was drawing the mini-bus to a stop in front of an elegant, magnolia building in a sizeable town square. A crick in her neck testified to the fact that she'd been sleeping in an awkward position, but apart from that, she felt refreshed and ready to explore the town she'd first heard mention of on the day Pope John Paul II had been sworn into the Vatican over forty years before.

It was in 1978 that the town had come to international, including Anna's, attention, when Karol Wojtyla, born just a few months after Tad on 18 May 1920, was elected pope. Anna remembered seeing grainy TV images of the crowded smart market square and the majestic Church of the Presentation of the Virgin Mary, where Karol had been baptised, as Wadowice became a place of mass pilgrimage for Catholics, not just from Poland but all over the world. Stepping out of Alek's mini-bus now, she took a deep breath of the cold air which whipped around them, the sensation of her head clearing for the first time in twenty-four hours most welcome. She saw that the square was vast, framed by pastel-shaded buildings topped by snow-covered roofs and dominated by the ornate white church. Taking in all the details, she pictured the young Karol cutting across the cobblestones on his way to school.

They opted to visit the museum first, housed in the yellow building next to the church, where the Wojtyla family had once lived in an apartment on the second floor. Moving from Karol's sparsely decorated family home to the slick, hi-tech and extremely informative exhibition, they followed the footsteps the future pope had trodden during the first eighteen years of his life. They learned that he'd attended the elementary school just around the corner before continuing his education at the renowned Marcin Wadowita High School where he'd developed his interest in theatre and literature, interpreting leading parts in school plays as well as penning his own poetry. His hometown situated at the foot of the Beskid Mały mountain range, Karol had also developed his passion for hiking, to which he had remained faithful for the rest of his life. Alek told them how Karol's mother and brother had both died when he was a small boy, his mother just a few weeks after his confirmation, and how Holy Mary had become a surrogate mother to him thereafter.

Karol's father, a retired first lieutenant in the army, had also set an example to his young son in his devotion and prayer.

"Growing up in pre-war Wadowice," Alek continued as they climbed a flight of steps to the section of the museum displaying Karol's early ecclesiastical robes, "where Poles and Jews peacefully lived together, was an important experience for Pope John Paul II which influenced him later in life. During his Papacy he worked tirelessly to bring people together."

They continued onto the robe room, seeing the purple vestments he'd worn while Archbishop of Krakow and the black and red cardinal robes he'd donned in the Vatican before they waited their turn in the queue to view his white Papal ones. There they spent a few minutes admiring their simplicity before moving to the next room, their eyes adjusting to the dimmed lighting, as they learned about the pope's miraculous survival of the assassination attempt on 13 May 1981.

"God was definitely protecting him that day," Anna commented, somewhat to Sarah's surprise as her mother had never been strongly religious. But she too had to admit that the story of the miracle of how Pope John Paul II was critically wounded after being shot four times by gunman Mehmet Ali Agca in St Peter's Square, with two of the bullets lodging in his lower intestine, and yet somehow managed to survive, was extremely compelling.

Next, Alek led them to a computer screen where they watched footage of Pope John Paul II's funeral, the wind during the service in Vatican Square so strong that the cardinals' red robes billowed up around their faces. "The cardinals said afterwards that they didn't feel the wind on their faces, which led to speculation that it had been the Holy Spirit moving through the square that day. Indeed, when Pope John Paul II's funeral came to a close, so the wind died down too," Alek explained as they moved on to another room of exhibits.

"What an incredible life he had," Bella commented as they crossed back through the square afterwards, the snow falling heavily once more, "or two lives, really."

"Yes, he did so much, connecting with people all around the world while spreading such happiness, such love." Anna shivered, pulling her new lavender snood up to cover her head. "It makes my little life seem rather selfish, really."

"Nonsense, I sense you've lived a good life. And I'm sure you're nowhere near done yet! You have your beautiful daughter and granddaughter, who clearly think the world of you." Alek paused. "That's not insignificant or self-centred in any way."

"Yes, I suppose. I'm grateful that at least I've had the chance to see my daughter and granddaughter grow up, unlike the unfortunate people who once lived in this town and others nearby." She thought about what the information panels in the museum had said about Karol living in such tempestuous times under Nazi occupation, his Jewish neighbours in constant fear of their lives.

On the same wavelength as Anna, Alek interjected into her gloomy thoughts. "It's true that this town has a chequered history. In fact, under Nazi occupation, it was renamed Frauenstadt and the entire Jewish population, to the last man, woman and child, was either executed here or sent to Auschwitz-Birkenau."

They all paused for a moment's quiet reflection in the centre of the square beneath the rapidly darkening sky as late afternoon approached before Alek lightened the mood: "Well, we could stand here all day in the freezing cold and wait for the fire service to chip us out or we could try one of the famous Pope's cream cakes in one of the cafes here."

"The Pope's cream cake?" Bella pricked up her ears.

"That's right. Its Polish name is Kremówka Papieska. When Pope John Paul II was visiting his hometown in 2001, he said he had fond memories of the cream cake, explaining that, when he was a child, he and his schoolfriends would club together their money to buy one from the bakers on their way home from school." Alek pointed across to a small red-roofed building, its golden light diffusing into the encroaching darkness. "The cake consists of thin layers of pastry, cold custard and cream, and is sprinkled with confectioner's sugar, and I can personally attest that it is delicious!"

"It's making my mouth water merely contemplating it. Just you lead the way, Alek!" Anna linked his arm and they set off for the enticing lights of the bakers, their footprints trailing behind them in a perfect line in the newly fallen snow.

41

"Tell the story, again, Dziadek, *proszę.*" I clambered onto my grandfather's knees, inhaling the familiar scent of freshly filed wood on his scratchy blue overalls. Sitting in his rocking chair in front of the fire, I laid my head in the centre of the old man's chest so I could feel his strong and steady heartbeat, which both reassured and calmed me. "The tale of the Smocza Jama."

It had been my favourite story for as long as I could remember. Perhaps it was because Dziadek had taken me to the dragon's supposed lair beneath Wawel Hill whenever we'd visited Krakow? Exploring the forbidding cave where the fearsome creature had purportedly once lived and breathed fire upon anyone who'd attempted to enter his sanctuary had made the story real for me, while the tales of powerful kings and brave knights which we'd read in books at bedtime only existed in the fantastic realms of my imagination. Perhaps it was because I liked the goriness of the story of the shoemaker who'd made a rancid fleecy ram, smeared with fat and stuffed with sulphur, to trick the dragon? Or maybe it was because it was the tale of an ordinary cobbler, who'd stepped up to be heroic to save the lives of others when no one else had, winning the princess and the kingdom of Krakow for his own? Whichever way, the bravery of the unassuming shoemaker struck a chord with some part deep inside of me.

"Let's begin then. Once upon a time, many years ago…" Dziadek paused dramatically as I sat enraptured. "When people first came to live on the banks the Vistula River, King Krak built a magnificent castle on the hill above it. Little did he know that in one of the limestone caves at the foot of the hill there slept a dragon—"

"What was he like, Dziadek? What was he like?" I jiggled excitedly on the old man's knee, hanging on his every word.

"Well, he was the most terrifying dragon that ever walked the earth. The peasants tried to go about their daily business, but one day the dragon awoke and began stealing livestock and taking young women off to his layer." Dziadek put on his deepest voice, the light from the flames of the fire dancing in his eyes: "The townspeople of Krakow were frightened out of their wits as the dragon terrorised them. So the king offered his daughter's hand in marriage and his kingdom to whoever could kill the terrible creature and so put an end to his people's discontent."

"What happened? What happened?" I pressed my grandfather, even though I'd heard the tale over one hundred times and knew each and every part of it by heart. My teachers, schoolfriends and their mothers had all told me the story. But no one related it like my beloved Dziadek did.

"Many brave men were killed trying to fight the fearsome beast. Then, when almost all hope was lost, a young and brave shoemaker called Skuba stepped into the fray. Unlike the knights who had tried to use their physical strength to slay the dragon, Skuba was clever and devised a plan to rid Krakow of the creature once and for all. So, he sat up all night making a fleecy ram from sheepskins, mutton fat and sulphur, and placed it at the entrance to the dragon's lair." The old man re-enacted the scene with a sheepskin rug, as though he was putting together a mock-up of the ram to trick the dragon, right there and then.

"That must have smelled like the most horrible thing on earth!" I pulled up my nose as I imagined the most disgusting scent possible.

Nodding, the old man continued, "At dawn, the dragon awoke and hungrily ate the fleecy ram, not realising it was rancid. But after a moment or so, the people of Krakow heard him scream out in pain as the sulphurous fire burned deep in his stomach. In agony, the dragon ran down to the river, where he drank and drank to try to extinguish the flames. But it didn't manage to put out the fire in his gut and instead, having consumed so much water, the dragon exploded." The old man made a loud BOOM, making me jump so violently that he had to steady me to prevent me from falling off his knee.

"That must have been some sight to see – a dragon exploding, his guts flying out of him." I pictured the dreadful scene in my mind.

"Yes, it must have been," my grandfather nodded, tickling my chin with his rough-skinned fingers, making me giggle, "and to reward Skuba, the brave little shoemaker, for his ingenuity, the king gave him his kingdom and his daughter's hand in marriage."

I considered for a moment, stroking Dziadek's whiskers which sprouted above his mouth like a cat's. At five years old, I'd been drawn in by the gut-wrenching details of the ram's fleece exploding inside the dragon, but now I was a few years older, I was more taken with the shoemaker's actions and I tried to put my thoughts into words. "Skuba must have been very brave to take on the awful dragon like that," I said at last. "And kill him!"

"He was. Knight after knight had died, remember, trying to slay the fearsome beast. Skuba must have thought there was a good chance he would die too," said Dziadek sanguinely.

"Yes, but he tried anyway and ended up saving everybody in the city." I smiled. "What the shoemaker did was so brave. I think if the people of Krakow were ever in danger, I would want to do something to help them too, just as Skuba did."

Dziadek looked deep into my eyes. And I think he saw the lengths I would go, one day, to protect those I loved as he said in a measured tone. "If such a time comes, you must do what you feel is right, *kochany*."

As we drew to the end of our discussion aromas of baking filled the room, the warm air emanating from the kitchen stove visible in shafts of sunlight which shone through the slats in the shutters. "*Makowiec*," I shouted, jumping up and heading for the oven.

"Watch you don't burn your fingers, *kochany*," the old man said, his back as crooked as a question mark from sitting over his workbench for too many years as he followed me into the kitchen and heaved open the heavy oven door. Sitting side by side at the kitchen table, we ate the warm poppy seed rolls for lunch, savouring each and every mouthful of the rich yeasted dough, baked until golden and wrapped around the sweet filling and dusted with a snow-sprinkling of sugar. "Break the bread in half like this to let some of the heat out," Dziadek warned, blowing down on his. "Or you will burn your mouth."

After I'd finished, I licked my fingers, the smile on my face wide. "This must be what Mama eats in paradise."

The picture of the little boy I'd once been with the wide smile sitting on his grandfather's knee slowly crumbled away, as though the paper they were drawn upon had been crunched up and discarded. Instead of the wooden slats of the kitchen walls and the huge oven billowing out enough warmth to heat the entire house, I saw the faded, flowery wallpaper of Eirlys's front room. Eirlys was in the kitchen making us some tea while her mother was out shopping and my head told me I needed to focus on these precious moments of the present. But then those words returned to me, in my squeaky, childish voice: *This must be what Mama eats in paradise* and tears streamed down my face as I felt the familiar ache in my heart for the loss of my mother, which will never leave me for as long as I live.

42

"It's a pity the dragon's lair is only open in summer, I so wanted to visit it," said Bella. They'd spent the morning snacking around the small Christmas market which had sprouted up overnight in the courtyard of Wawel Castle and, adequately fed and watered, they'd decided on a late evening meal back at the hotel.

"I know, it's a shame," said Sarah, looking dubiously at the steep stone steps leading down to the riverside cave. Unsure that her mother felt as well as she professed to, she made a decision there was no way she was going to let Bella persuade them to go down. "Maybe it's as well that the caves are closed, they could be dark and dangerously slippery underfoot. Long ago they were the focus of criminal activities in this part of the city, with a brothel just down the road, too."

"Yes, I'd rather think about the fairy-tale aspect of the brave shoemaker and the dragon story." Bella nodded, snapping her camera away at the impressive twenty-foot-high bronze statue of the dragon, its ferocious spikes jutting out, its nostrils flared. "I love how a seemingly insignificant man like Skuba the Shoemaker saved everyone in Krakow through his practicality and bravery."

"Yes, that's the part of the story that struck me, too," puffed Anna, leaning against a wall while she caught her breath, "and when I think about it, my father's story has many of the same undertones."

"How do you mean?" Bella paused to link her gran's arm, giving her her undivided attention.

"Well, Tad was just a country boy who had recently moved to Krakow to attend university," Anna managed a deep breath, "but then when the Nazis occupied the city, something within him, some bravery or idealism, call it what you want, made it impossible for him to sit passively by. Some people joined the resistance, deciding to fight the Nazis from within, while others, like Tad, opted to risk a perilous escape to join the Allied forces to fight for their country and the values and freedoms they believed in. Unfortunately for him, he wasn't rewarded like the shoemaker but instead he paid the ultimate price, dying for his cause."

"Maybe someone told Great-Granddad the story of the shoemaker and the dragon when he was little," mused Bella, "and that could have inspired him to go on and fight for his country when it looked like it was beaten?"

"Yes, I think you might be onto something there, Bella."

Anna nodded, gazing at the magnificent model of the dragon fashioned from metal.

Anna and Sarah stood patiently while Bella clicked away to capture sculptor Bronisław Chromy's spiky statue from every conceivable angle. Standing on the rock, the dragon's impressive black claws were unfurled, poised to pounce on its next victim while its mouth was open wide, ready to breathe fire. All of a sudden, it did just that as fearsome orange and red flames leaped from its mouth, making Bella jump so hard, she dropped her precious phone, much to the amusement of her mother and grandmother.

"Well, we knew that the dragon symbolises the fire in the belly of this otherwise studious city." Sarah laughed, picking up and wiping the phone, which mercifully had been cushioned from damage by the soft, newly fallen snow. "Krakow has survived so much from the devastating attacks of the Tatars in the thirteenth century to the Nazi occupation through to communism."

"Yes, the people here most definitely have guts!" A second loud belch of fire interrupted Bella, although it failed to startle her as the first had done.

Seeing the sorry-looking riverboats moored on the banks of the Vistula below them, they decided that the plummeting temperatures made a river trip out of the question today, particularly in the light of the fact that Anna was still recovering from her cold. Instead, they headed for a nearby cafe Bella had found in her guidebook, hoping to spin lunch out over an hour or two to give them ample time to warm up after their walk.

Afterwards, leaving Anna sitting quietly reading with another cup of tea in the cosy corner table they'd acquired, Sarah and Bella took a short stroll along the line of formidable fortifications which curved around the foot of Wawel Hill, enclosing it in their protective grasp. Looking up every now and again, Sarah identified the different towers of the castle, the Clock, Zygmunt and Silver Bells towers of the Basilica dominating the background, while a dozen or so others she couldn't put a name to soared up into the sky, redolent once again, of a half-remembered fairytale, as many buildings in the old city were. After a twenty minutes' saunter, they paused at the Coat of Arms gate, with Bella imagining the townspeople in days gone by entering the castle by ducking below the portcullis. There, she admired and photographed a bronze-mounted statue. "Who is that?" she asked, intrigued by the enormous effigy of a man on a horse, the tops of their heads coated in snow.

"Let's see." Sarah flipped through her guidebook before locating the appropriate page. "It's a statue of the leader of the 1794 Uprising in Poland. Previously having taken part in the American Revolution, he befriended both Jefferson and Washington and was called Tadeusz Kościuszko."

"Tadeusz, like Great-Grandfather?" Bella asked.

"That's right. In fact, I suppose it's reasonable that Grandfather could have been named after him." Sarah read on before summarising: "Kościuszko sounds like an impressive person with whom to share your name, anyway. Oh, here's something interesting – in 1940 the Nazis destroyed the statue and it was only reconstructed twenty years later."

"I don't think it's a coincidence that Tad shared the same name as a celebrated freedom fighter." Bella smiled. Looking up, she beheld the grimly determined expression on the effigy's face, his arm outstretched as he rallied his horse below him and his men behind him into battle. It only took a short step for her imagination to picture Tad in his plane as he crossed the North Sea, leading B24s to some unsuspecting German city. An eye for an eye after what the Nazis had done to his homeland.

Returning to the cafe, they told Anna about what they'd seen, Bella showing her the photos she'd taken of the statue. Noticing her mother was looking pale and tired, Sarah swiped her phone to check the weather forecast predicted for the rest of the afternoon. Seeing that there was a ninety-five per cent likelihood of snow in the next three hours, she suggested they buy three of the cream cakes sitting enticingly in the chilled cabinet and return to Hotel Wyspiański to enjoy them over a pot of tea and a game of cards. To her surprise, neither Bella nor her mother took any persuading.

43

RAF Coltishall, February 1945

By February 1945, good news of mounting Allied victories and German defeats flooded into the base on a daily basis, which helped to keep up morale among the Polish and RAF squadrons alike. It was apparent to us all that 'the end', which we'd only dared dream of up to this point, was well and truly in sight. All we had to do now was finish the job we'd started.

It's a strange thing to think, let alone say, but I dreaded the end of the war just as I prayed for it. I owed it to my brother to return to Poland to discover what had happened to him. I had feared the worst had befallen Jacek since 13 April 1943, when Nazi master of propaganda Joseph Goebbels had broadcast on German radio stations the grim discovery in the Katyn Forest of thousands of bodies of Polish officers whom he claimed had been captured and shot by the Russians early in the war. Whilst there could be no doubt that the men had been killed, as there was plentiful photographic evidence to substantiate the claims, the other inescapable possibility was that it was anti-Bolshevik propaganda on a grand scale, designed to shake the Allied axis to their core. Afterwards the Nazis had apparently sent neutral journalists as well as Polish intellectuals to the spot in German held territory in Russia where they had found pits piled with bodies. When gruesome reports had emerged, the Führer had subsequently made the widest possible use of the propaganda material, with the German press portraying communism as a danger to Western civilisation.

Of course, the Soviet government had immediately denied the German charges, claiming the Polish prisoners of war had been engaged in construction work west of Smolensk and had been captured and executed by 'German-Fascist hangmen' in August 1941. On this occasion, I had no idea who was lying and who was telling the truth. And yet, despite all of this, I had a strong conviction that my brother was still alive somewhere. That Jacek, being Jacek, would have found his way out of whatever dire situation he'd found himself in, evading both the Soviets and the Nazis if he'd so needed. I imagined that if I ever managed to return to my homeland he would be there waiting for me at Dziadek's house with a cold beer and a reassuring slap on the back.

My squadron was now engaged in ground attack missions on V1 and V2 launch sites in the Netherlands. On Valentine's Day, my aircraft was one of twelve Spits which took off in the early afternoon from RAF Coltishall. We crossed the Dutch coast just north of The Hague, where we suffered ever-increasing, although mercifully inaccurate, flak and we pressed on until we pinpointed and attacked our targets south to north. From the cockpit, I spotted multiple clusters of fire bursts as the low-lying surrounding area soon became engulfed by a thick blanket of smoke. It was here I suffered the heartbreak of losing my beloved friend Jerzy.

Unfortunately, Jerzy's plane became disoriented in the smoke and hit a tall tower, immediately bursting into flames. From my vantage point above, it was clear he would have been killed instantly, for there was no chance he had had time to bail out. As I limped back to base, my heart overspilled with grief for my friend who would never see the homeland he'd been fighting for again, never have a wife or children. That was the end for him, the end of his war, the end of his life. Coming in to land safely back on English soil as fog closed in on the airfield, my thoughts were consumed by sadness for the loss of my friend, while I could not escape the strong presentiment that although the war was rapidly reaching its climax, I was not going to survive it either.

The following day, I wrote to Jerzy's girlfriend Irene in Blackpool to break the news of his death to her. It was the hardest letter I'd ever had to write, but I was compelled to carry out my heavy duty in memory of my friend whom I'd been through so much with since those sunny, autumn days in Krakow when we'd met at Jagiellonian University. As I posted the letter I found it unbearable to think of someone breaking the news of my death to Eirlys in this way.

44

Krakow, December 2020

From the taxi window, Anna gazed at the grey waters of
the River Vistula, losing herself in its rapid ebb and flow.
Looking up, the intricate ironwork of the overarching bridge
and the monochrome hues of the landscape momentarily
took her back to the old Odeon picture house in Blackpool,
where she'd watched *Schindler's List* for the first time. She
remembered sitting in her plush red seat in dismay and
disgust as she'd watched the horrors unfold for the Krakow
Jewish population in the early years of the war, her popcorn
left untouched in its red and white striped cardboard box.
Then, an unlikely saviour had entered the frame, confidently
brandishing a cigar in his right hand and a glamorous girl
on his left arm. Oskar Schindler had saved the lives of as
many of the city's Jewish inhabitants as he'd been able, even
paying off the Nazis to turnaround a train misdirected to

the concentration camp Auschwitz, a feat that was otherwise unheard of.

Auschwitz. Her stomach lurched as the harsh consonants of the German name brought to mind images she'd seen on old film reels. Images of heaped suitcases with destinations written on them which their owners would never reach and – most dreadfully – piles of baby shoes and clothes taken from children before they too were cast into the gas chambers. Feeling a tear trace down her cheek as the taxi entered the close confines of the narrow streets of Podgórze, not for the first time, she wondered how she would bear to visit Auschwitz. But she also knew that it was her duty, along with everyone else's, to make the once-in-a-lifetime pilgrimage to remember the millions who'd perished at the hands of barbarians, so that their crime wouldn't be repeated.

"This is Ghetto Square, I drop you here?" the blond-haired taxi driver said as they looked up to read the sign *Plac Bohaterów Getto*. Despite the warmth from the car's fan heater, the words sent an involuntary chill down Anna's back.

"No, Oskar Schindler's Enamel Factory, *proszę*," said Sarah, wishing Alek had been available to take them as the driver continued on through the drab streets. She'd received a text from him late the previous night, saying that an emergency had come up before he'd apologised profusely for letting them down. "After we've been around the museum, we can have lunch in the cafe and then I'll get someone to phone for another taxi back to Ghetto Square," Sarah explained to Anna.

The white building which had once housed Oskar Schindler's Enamelware Factory consisted of three stories with elegant curves and pillars, which gave the impression of a Greek temple. Walking around the exhibition, Anna, Sarah and Bella discovered that it didn't just recount the story of this selfless man and the one thousand-plus Jews he'd saved by paying camp commandant Amon Göth for each of his workers and relocating them and his factory to the Sudetenland. It also painted a vivid picture of what it had been like to live in Krakow under Nazi occupation as it documented the hardships of everyday life, the underground resistance, as well as the degradations inflicted upon the Jewish population.

"I didn't realise that everyone in the city suffered," Bella commented afterwards, flicking through the postcards she'd bought in the bookshop as they ate soup and sandwiches in the museum cafe.

"Krakow was a defeated city," said Anna, taking a bite of the poppy seed bread she'd become so fond of. "In such a situation, everyone lived under hardships with the lack of food and other essentials, as well as the constant curfews. It must have been heart-breaking for people to go from living in freedom to everything being restricted under the Nazis' control. We read about Britain being a haven for those airmen, but Tad must have worried every second of every day about those he'd left behind—"

"I'm worried, Mum, that it's getting a bit too much for you," Sarah sighed, "I'm finding all this information very harrowing and it must be so much worse for you."

"I want to understand the history of this city where my father lived and studied, to feel closer to him," Anna paused, "but the more I see and hear, I don't know if I can bear it or not, particularly as we don't know what happened to Tad's brother and father…"

It was snowing so heavily that the taxi's windscreen wipers had to work doubly hard to push away the collecting snowflakes as they headed back to Plac Bohaterów Getta that afternoon. Taking in her surroundings, the sweet pastel shades of mint-green, rose-pink, apricot and magnolia of the buildings in Ghetto Square reminded Anna of the grander ones in the city's main square. This, however, was Podgórze, a walled ghetto where Jews had been moved to from the surrounding area in 1941 as the Nazis had set in motion the first part of their Final Solution plans. Closing her eyes, Anna thought of the *akcja* which had taken place here on a regular basis and tried to envisage what it had been like for Jewish families with the shadow of fear incessantly hanging over them. She attempted to imagine how people could function day by day knowing that, at any second, they could be ordered out of their cramped apartments and onto the streets. But she found her imagination didn't stretch that far.

Anna saw that at the heart of this smaller square there was no bustling cloth hall or thronging Christmas market but just a stark memorial consisting of dozens and dozens of black chairs nailed to plinths to remember those people who'd perished in the nearby extermination camps. Empty chairs, perhaps symbolising the fact that the rampaging Nazis had flung furniture out of apartment windows during the liquidation of the ghetto in March 1943 or that, afterwards, there was simply no one left to claim them back.

"There's an atmosphere of sadness and abandonment in this place, even now," Bella said as they walked from chair to chair, the cold wind gusting as though the unquiet souls were trying to communicate their stories to them. "It's as though what happened here over seventy-five years ago was so dreadful that it has left an indelible imprint here."

"Yes, to think the Nazis forced over fifteen thousand Jews to live in just three hundred buildings here, subjecting them to forced labour and barely giving them enough food to stay alive, there is no wonder that so many people died here, especially the young and the elderly," Sarah added as they solemnly walked around the poignant memorial, each lost in her own thoughts. "And of course, those who managed to survive this were deported to experience an even greater hell in the concentration camps."

"I know. But as is often the way in the midst of great evil and suffering, a hero stepped forward to make his mark," Anna said, "as well as Oskar Schindler, there was another man, a chemist called Tadeusz Pankiewicz."

"Remember seeing the memorial yesterday to the freedom fighter, Tadeusz Kościuszko? Tadeusz must be a name synonymous with bravery and heroes," Bella said, and Anna chuckled as they looked up at the sign on the building they were standing outside: *Apteka Pod Orłem*, the majestic Polish eagle unfurling its wings above the chemist's name as the sign swung in the wind which whipped around the square.

"The Eagle Pharmacy? I've read about this pharmacist somewhere. Wasn't he a gentile who helped the sick and elderly living in the ghetto?" Sarah shivered. "From what I recall, when the Nazis formed the ghetto he found himself at the very heart of it and, deciding to stay, Pankiewicz and his staff were the only Poles permitted by the Nazis to live and work within the ghetto walls. Pitying the Jews' plight, they risked their lives to acquire food, medicine and falsified documents."

"He helped the Jews resist and escape the Nazis?" Bella grasped the seriousness of the situation.

"Yes, because of his actions he is recognised as one of the Righteous Among the Nations," added Anna as they stepped out of the biting bitterness of Ghetto Square to find themselves enveloped in the warmth of the former chemist shop. Despite the guidebook saying that only fragments of the shop's furnishings still survived, Anna thought the ambience was such that she could picture Tadeusz Pankiewiez with his slicked-back hair, black bow tie, pristine white shirt and chemist's coat standing behind the wooden counter in the dispensing room, the hundreds of medicine bottles stacked on the shelves behind him. Taking time to read about the work of Tadeusz and his assistants, Helena, Irena and Aurelia, who had administered medicine to the sick inhabitants of the ghetto and hidden children in cupboards to escape the Nazis' 'aktions' Anna reflected that maybe it wasn't surprising that a man whose profession it was to help heal the sick had risked his own life to treat others in their time of need. Not surprising and yet unique in Nazi-occupied Krakow.

Entering the prescription room, they lingered briefly at the preparation counter before moving onto a larger chamber dominated by Tadeusz's enormous desk, which they sat behind to watch films featuring harrowing scenes from the 1942 deportations and the ghetto liquidation the following year. After assimilating as much as they could bear, they saw the clock was nudging five and closing time. On Sarah's request, the museum attendant phoned for a return taxi to the hotel and, as she locked the museum behind them, they huddled in the shelter of the doorway out of reach of the driving snow.

"I'm so glad we visited here," Bella said. "What that man did, his bravery and kindness, goes beyond words. Did you read the story about the young girl he saved who went to live in Israel after the war where she had a life and a family of her own?"

"Yes, I did. I think it is wonderful. He probably saved generations of people, just as Schlinder did," Anna said, seeing the square was deserted apart from a group of elderly people, obviously waiting for transport too. "Shall we wait over there? The taxi driver might not spot us hidden here." They thus moved to the centre of the square to within earshot of the other group. As the wind whipped around them, strands of their conversation reached them and Anna recognised they were speaking in Hebrew. Supposing they were doing a pilgrimage rather like she was to find where her father had once lived, she smiled at them in understanding.

After recharging their batteries at the hotel, they hailed a taxi, this time taking the short journey to Kazimierz. It seemed apt that on the day they'd stood in Ghetto Square where the Nazis had tried to erase the Jewish population from the city's past, present and future, that, over seventy years later, they should enjoy a traditional Israeli meal followed by a klezmer concert in a restaurant nearby. Exiting the taxi at the heart of the Jewish town, they found that despite the plunging temperatures which accompanied nightfall, Szeroka Square was awash with festive lights to celebrate Hanukkah and Christmas. Strung from trees, they were pinpricks of colour and light in the wintry darkness as chatter and laughter spilled out from the half a dozen Israeli and Polish restaurants; a new generation breathing life back into this ancient town. Sarah stopped by some railings encircling a tiny green space to read the inscription on the stone, dedicated as it was to the Jewish people rounded up by the Nazis.

"It's all confused." Bella shivered. "This morning, I was thinking about the miseries the Jewish people faced in the ghetto before being deported to their deaths. And contemplating the memorial of the empty chairs in the square, I felt despair and grief envelop me. But here, I don't feel that at all, quite the opposite in fact. People are still here, enjoying themselves. Living life."

Looking around, Bella spotted a handful of Jews, their white yarmulkes gleaming on their heads on this starry night as they left the synagogue. She watched them blend in with the crowds of tourists enjoying a pre-Christmas break and locals celebrating with their work colleagues. And she realised that despite the Nazis' best efforts to rid the city of its Jewish population, they had failed. Just off the square, they wended their way through a garden, the form of the bare branches of the trees outlined in snow, the light and warmth of the Klezmer House welcoming them beyond. Entering, they were led to one of the dining rooms. With just four tables in this particular room, the intimate atmosphere gave off a fussy, dated charm with dark wood-panelled walls crammed with ancient oil paintings, a large sideboard illuminated by a dozen candles and tables adorned with lace tablecloths in the same pattern as the curtains hanging at the windows. Its appearance brought to mind a Victorian sitting room.

Their meal consisted of deliciously hearty food, combining the best of Polish and Jewish traditions. Beginning with a hearty vegetable broth, they moved on to fragrant chicken balls in a light dill sauce, accompanied with hot potatoes and carrot salad, making sure they had each left room for a wedge of the house speciality gateau. The Klezmer Cake was a sumptuous chocolate sponge, sandwiched with cherries and cream which they enjoyed while listening to a girl about Bella's age sing mournful Yiddish songs.

"I'd like to return here in the daylight," Bella said later as they walked towards the end of Szeroka Square which was dominated by the huge Old Synagogue with its vast, flat roof.

"Yes, I think we should," Sarah agreed as they reached the magnolia and white buildings of the Ariel Cafe with their terracotta roofs and climbing ivy, a complex more fitting on a Greek island than the ancient Jewish district of Krakow. "I recall reading that Stephen Spielberg used the outside of this building for the chemist scenes in *Schindler's List*."

"I remember the Nazis shooting an already-injured woman in the head – she fell back on these railings, didn't she? But that building here doesn't look anything like the Eagle Pharmacy," Bella said, thinking how the vast, impersonal corner block they had visited that morning was wildly at odds with the inviting jumble of buildings before her now.

"That's artistic licence for you," said Anna, grateful as their taxi pulled up in front of them. She couldn't wait to get into her warm bed in preparation for the visit to Auschwitz the following day.

"Well, it's confusing!" Bella said. Falling silent as another wave of tiredness washed over her, Anna looked out of the window as the taxi swung down one street, then another. They looked different to the way they did in the day, largely devoid of people and cars, the shops and cafes all shuttered up in darkness, the freshly fallen snow lying untouched on the pavements. Soon the narrow streets opened out to floodlit, perfectly manicured lawns leading up to the steps of the majestic Krakow Opera House, topped with its magnificent bird's egg-blue domed roof.

Watching the people exit it now, the women in their fine gowns and men in dapper suits, she remembered her mother telling her that Tad had once taken her to the opera at the Grand Theatre in Blackpool. As the taxi swung away from the scene in the direction of Hotel Wyspiański, she wondered whether her father had ever come to the opera house here when he'd been a student before the war, whether he'd sat in the audience, entranced by the singing and music. Arriving back, Agusia on the reception desk beckoned them over to give Sarah a big brown envelope which Alek had left for them. "What does it say?" Anna enquired, her voice excited as they sat down beneath the twinkling lights of the Christmas tree, while Sarah carefully eased the flap open.

There was a stunned silence before Sarah slowly lifted her head. "It's Jacek Lewandowski's death certificate; Tad's brother. It says that he died of heart failure on November 30th 2002."

45

On March 15th 1945, I managed to make the journey from RAF Coltishall to Blackpool one final time. Having just a few hours there, I arranged to meet Eirlys at 4pm in Stanley Park, but she was late. Overlooking the mirror-like surface of the ornamental lake, I waited on a bench, the rough splinters catching the soft skin of my clenched hands. The war was drawing hopefully to its close, I knew that, but I still couldn't rid myself of my premonition that I wouldn't survive it. I tried to distract myself from brooding over the loss of Jerzy and the feeling that my fate was to be the same as his by watching as a toddler in a bright-red knitted hat and navy overcoat giggled to his mother as the ducks he was feeding came out of the water and waddled around his feet. I also noticed the first pale green shoots on the bare tree branches while daffodils and crocuses brought splashes of yellow and purple following the drabness of winter. Everything that afternoon seemed somehow brighter; more alive.

Then, suddenly, Eirlys was there and all else faded into the background for me. Her black winter coat was left open to accommodate the early spring weather, revealing a dress the shade of the bluebells which grew behind Dziadek's workshop and which I used to carefully step through, imagining myself walking in the sky itself. As she came nearer, I saw that her dark hair was pinned up to reveal all of her lovely face and the nape of her neck, which I instantly longed to kiss. Coming to sit down beside me, I took her hand, the realisation striking me, as it always did, that this could very well be the last time I saw her.

"I'm sorry I'm late." She smiled, playing with her hair, as she was prone to do when she was nervous.

"No, I was early," I reassured her, drawing her into my arms. As I did, I noticed that despite the warmth of the spring day, she was trembling. Looking into her eyes, I saw my past, present and future. My forever love.

"*Kocham cię.*" I kissed her deeply, not caring whether anyone was close enough to see us. As far as I was concerned, we were the only two people in the world. Thrown together by hate and war, I knew in this moment that we would always belong to each other, body and soul.

"And I love you, Tad, I've missed you so much," she whispered, drawing away to wipe the tears which filled her eyes. "Are you sure you're fully recovered from your pneumonia, though? You look so pale and withdrawn, what's the matter?"

Knowing I couldn't hide anything from her for she was too perceptive for that, I told her of Jerzy's death, sparing her the cruel details of what I'd witnessed. And, for the first time, I was able to release my grief. As Eirlys held me in her arms, I wept for my friend, my family and my country, drawing silent comfort from her. As my sobs subsided, she drew back a little and whispered against my cheek, "You'll come back to me, won't you, Tad?"

I looked at her, wondering what to say. She was an intelligent girl who read the newspapers and listened to the wireless every evening with her mother. She knew that since the Battle of the Bulge, the Nazis had been in full-scale retreat back to Berlin and that now the main task of the Allied air force was to bomb and disrupt enemy transports to bring the war to its end. But whilst she reasoned that my work was potentially less dangerous than escorting bombing raids over German cities, I knew she was haunted by the memory that her father had been killed in early November 1918 just outside the Belgian city of Mons. That less than a week later, church bells had rung out to celebrate the armistice, bells he would never hear.

"Of course I will." I smiled, wiping away the tears springing down her cheeks with the back of my hand. "When the war is over, I will take you to Poland. I want you to see its mountains, its rivers, its villages. I want to show you the fine architecture of Krakow. When we are married, I will take you there."

"Married?" Eirlys said incredulously, her dark eyes wide and full of wonder. Although her pretty features had no doubt attracted the attention of boys since her teens, I knew that she had never thought of herself as someone's wife, that she had never believed me when I'd told her I wanted her to be mine.

"Yes, married! I mean it." I took her hands in mine. "I want to spend the rest of my days on this earth with you."

I detected something like hesitation cloud her eyes and I sought to back off, but luckily she got in first. Tears spilled from her eyes, which I gently wiped away with the back of my hand as she confirmed my surmising. "It's just that my dad didn't return from the Great War and I fear that there is too long to go in this one for us to make any plans."

"I know, but it will be different for us, I promise." I faltered before kissing her, whispering. "We will live happily ever after just like Skuba, the fearless shoemaker, who, according to the legend, saved all the citizens of Krakow by defeating the ferocious dragon who terrorised them from his layer beneath the Wawel Castle."

"I don't think you've told me that story." She pulled me closer. So I recounted the tale Dziadek had told me more than a hundred times, the story of the brave boy who stopped the fire-breathing dragon from destroying the city of Krakow and, in gratitude, the king rewarded him, giving Skuba his kingdom and his daughter's hand in marriage. When I'd finished, Eirlys considered for a moment before lifting my hand to her lips. "You're my Skuba, Tad. My brave boy, who risked your life to fight against evil when it threatened your fellow countrymen."

"Eirlys, I want you to keep this safe for me." I pressed the wooden angel I'd kept with me as a lucky talisman all these years into her hand. "It is the first thing I ever carved with my grandfather and I want you to have it."

After that, we sat on the bench for one, maybe two, hours talking about a thousand and one inconsequential things. There was still so much I wanted to say to Eirlys, but the words cloyed in my throat and so I decided to save them for another day when the war was over and we were both out of harm's reach. Instead, I walked her home in silence, pausing briefly on the back steps of her mother's boarding house. Standing there I had the presentiment that this might well be the last time I saw Eirlys; that everything we'd shared together would ultimately be for nothing. It was a thought that I think crossed her mind too. The house shrouded in darkness, signalling that Mrs Watkins was out visiting her sister, we grasped our one and only opportunity. That evening, in Eirlys's bed, we made love, the moonlight casting its blue shadows over us.

"Take care of yourself, Tad," Eirlys swallowed back her tears, cupping my face in her hands as we stood on the doorstep some time later, "for me."

"For you, my love," I replied.

*

Taking the trains back to RAF Coltishall, as the miles separated Eirlys and me I began to feel guilty that, in a moment of weakness, I'd allowed myself to succumb to my feelings for this precious girl whom I loved dearly. In so many ways what we'd done felt wrong, but in so many others it felt like the most natural thing in the world. One thing was clear to me. My feelings for Eirlys were unlike the love I had for Jacek and Dziadek forged over two decades of supporting one another through the good times and the bad. With no other to rely upon, I realised that this fraternal and paternal love had always made me feel safe, whereas the love I had for Eirlys put me in mind of hurtling to the ground in my Spitfire with neither a parachute nor a net to save me.

46

Auschwitz. The harsh German syllables conjured up disturbing pictures in Anna's mind of skeletal survivors with shaven heads, sunken eyes and ragged clothes hanging off their bony bodies. People stripped of their humanity by people with no humanity. Men, women and children loaded like cattle onto crowded trains and forced to endure arduous journeys across Europe only to arrive on the platform illuminated by the Birkenau searchlights where unimaginable terrors met them in the gas chambers or in the camp beyond. From the day when, as a thirteen-year-old girl, she'd first seen the black-and-white images of the camp's liberation with her mother on their TV set, the sheer horror of it all had rested in the dark recesses of her mind.

However, she'd never actually imagined what it would be like to visit the Nazi extermination camp, had never pictured herself walking through the black iron gates, the *Arbeit Macht Frei* a cruel joke to the innocent men, women and children who had trodden the path before her. Ever since Bella had first mooted a trip to Poland, she'd known it was her duty to visit the memorial to pay her respects to the suffering of so many and yet she hadn't made the leap in her mind to how she would feel actually making a trip there. Perhaps she'd realised that if she did, she might submit to cowardice and protest that the emotions stirred up would prove too much for an old lady like her to handle. But that was not an option.

"I'm apprehensive about today." Bella cupped a mug of hot chocolate as they sat wrapped in warm rugs at a pavement cafe overlooking the Cloth Hall, its ornate arches reminiscent of those found in Arabian palaces. As Alek wasn't picking them up until ten, they'd sandwiched in a morning coffee and were determined to make the most of this pleasant prelude to what they expected would be an otherwise harrowing day. "Even though I feel a compulsion to go to Auschwitz, that it is up to our generations to learn about what the Nazis did there and never forget it, from what I know about the Holocaust I realise it will be extremely difficult to come to grips with."

"I was just having similar thoughts." Anna put her hand on her granddaughter's slender shoulder. "Over the years I've read so much about the Shoah and seen it portrayed on more films than I care to remember. But although I keep telling myself that it all happened so long ago, that Auschwitz is just a museum now, the fact is that in an hour or so we will be walking over the same ground where thousands upon thousands of people were herded to their deaths…"

"I think it's too painful to think about it in those terms." Sarah sipped her coffee, flapping her hand at a posse of pigeons at her feet. "If we can, we should try to look beyond all the misery and focus on the memory of the people who perished while praying that it never happens again. Otherwise today will be too difficult for us to get through, if not impossible."

Alek was late in picking them up behind Bazylika Mariacka and was in a pensive mood as they hit the standing traffic skirting the Planty. "Thanks for dropping off the copy of Jacek's death certificate," Sarah said eventually.

"Yes, I imagine you were as surprised as I was. Everything pointed to the fact that he hadn't survived the war," Alek said, glancing in his rear-view mirror at Anna while scratching his furrowed brow. "And yet he lived to a good age, dying of natural causes. It's a shame though it doesn't give the address of where he resided at the time. But now we know he lived until fairly recently, we might be able to track down his family. You said he had a child, didn't you?"

"Yes, I believe so," said Anna, considering the possibility that her great-uncle might have left descendants, people they'd potentially walked past each day.

As they approached Auschwitz, the snowy drive presented a picturesque landscape with dense woods and fast-flowing rivers running by the side of the road. The scenery, however, failed to lift Anna's mood as she merely found herself thinking of how, for many people, such trees and waterways would have been their last glimpse of freedom as stinking trucks carried them to their deaths. Passing houses with family cars parked in front of neat gardens and a park with a children's playground, she considered how the inhabitants here must be immune to the evil that had happened on their doorstep, or else how could they possibly bear to live in such close proximity? All the same, she wasn't sure whether she could do it.

The local schools not yet having broken up for the Christmas holidays, the ticket queue consisted of groups of Polish children and their teachers interspersed by smatterings of tourists mainly heralding from the US. While Alek purchased their tickets, the women went through an airport-style security check before joining up with him and a small English-speaking tour group beneath the infamous *Arbeit Macht Frei* gates. Walking just behind the guide, a tall, blonde-haired Polish girl in her early twenties with a group of elderly men straggling behind them, Alek helped Anna negotiate the path, which was slippery from the overnight snow, past the kitchens and the spot where the camp orchestra had once played musical accompaniments to the prisoners as they'd marched to work.

From the outset, Block Four struck Anna as harrowing, with sketches of designs for gas chambers held in the vast glass cases alongside empty tins of Zyklon B, forbidding black skulls and crossbones painted on the sides. Walking deeper into the building, they passed walls lined with mug shots of shaven-headed political prisoners with three dates printed below: their date of birth, date of arrival at the camp and date of death. She noticed that often the latter two were only separated by a matter of weeks or, in some cases, days. Expecting it and yet at the same time unprepared, Anna involuntarily covered her mouth with her hand in horror as they walked past cabinets containing huge piles of human hair, the silence of the other people as they shuffled around with them speaking volumes.

In Block Five the three women saw the mountains of personal effects belonging to the people who'd perished, including artificial limbs, spectacles and labelled suitcases to destinations where they would never arrive. Most harrowing of all were the children's shoes and tiny baby clothes displayed behind glass cabinets. The stacks of brightly painted pots and household goods made Anna wonder how the Nazis had tricked people into packing their prized possessions, in hope that they were to be resettled with the promise of a new life. Faded drawings documenting life in the camp were still discernible on the walls of Block Six and Anna squinted in the half-light to see prisoners' sketches of the roll-calls, the back-breaking work and the meagre meals; an attempt to tell the story of what had happened to them in this godforsaken place to future generations. Absorbed in a mural depicting two playful kittens, she felt sobs rise in her and, gasping, she made a hasty exit into the freezing air outside, Sarah, Bella and Alek following in her wake.

"I'll be alright in a moment," she sobbed as snowflakes collected in her hair. Bella put a comforting arm around her and, noticing her grandma was trembling, led her away from the building down a rutted path towards the car park.

"Do you want to proceed to Birkenau or shall I take you back to the hotel?" Alek asked as they settled into the mini-bus. "It's a harrowing place, so I understand if you feel it's too much."

"I think you might be right, Alek," Sarah said, glancing at her mother in an attempt to gauge her mood.

"No, I feel we must go there to complete our pilgrimage in memory of the countless victims," Anna said, her face etched with steely determination.

Alek's mini-bus skirted the snow-covered fields to Birkenau and in a matter of minutes the redbrick tower of the grim gateway straddling the railway line slowly emerged from the snowstorm. Anna shivered as she recalled scenes from films she'd seen of the packed trains coming to a stop here, the Sonderkommando in their blue and white striped uniforms brandishing sticks as people stepped onto the platform, squinting beneath the spotlight glaring from atop the monstrous tower. As Anna alighted Alek's mini-bus to make the short walk to the huts amassed in regimented rows on the other side of the train tracks, she knew this would be the enduring image she'd take away with her from this day.

The snow was unrelenting here, the cold compounding the sadness Anna felt. Huge flakes fell from the wintry sky onto the camp, which was in an exposed position, as apart from the few tourist facilities and houses they'd passed down the road, nothing else had been built nearby since the war. It was understandable why. Anna thought the snow was different from home too, where the warm coastal climate ensured the temperature rarely dropped below freezing, meaning that it always came in a frenzied flurry before quickly reducing to slush on the rain-slicked pavements. But here, the texture was powdery and thick, settling on the infamous railway arch and the row upon row of huts as it enveloped everything in its whiteness in a futile attempt to purify and cleanse.

Walking around the women's camp and mangled remains of the underground network of crematoria and gas chambers, Anna was able to cut herself adrift from it all somewhat, barely believing such events could happen anywhere, let alone on the frozen ground where she walked. Later, as a grey twilight settled over the camp, the four of them stood silently by the train tracks. Alongside them ran boards with photos of people muffled in dark coats crowded onto the very same platform, making it possible for Anna to picture what it would have been like seventy-five years before. Not what it would have been like, she corrected, for that was beyond her comprehension.

Looking into the faces young and old, she thought how seventy per cent of people who'd arrived on this platform had been sent directly to their deaths in the gas chambers and the full force of what had happened beneath these skies suddenly hit Anna with a piercing pain in the centre of her chest. Luckily, Sarah and the others were engrossed in their own contemplations and hadn't seemed to notice. Taking slow, deep breaths, in a moment the pain subsided and Anna managed to make her way back to Alek's mini-bus. Lulled by the lilting movement as they travelled back to Krakow, she soon fell asleep, eager to escape from the nightmare of the day.

47

Off the Netherlands' coast, March 1945

Despite being mid-March, it remained cold with the threat of sleety rain most days. I recall sitting in the cramped, unheated briefing hall with the rest of my squadron that final time as our imposing wing commander gave us the specific details of the mission we were to embark upon that day. My fur-lined flying jacket barely keeping me warm, the truth is I hardly heard a single word he uttered as my thoughts were inevitably bound up with Eirlys.

I saw her as clearly as if she was sitting on the shabby brown leather chair next to me: her beautiful face, her dark hair pinned loosely at the nape of her neck, her radiant smile. How I longed to run my fingers over her skin and feel its silky softness, inhaling her sweet perfume. In my mind, I had been over our last meeting in the park a thousand times and, remembering it, I longed to press my lips to that soft space just above her collarbone one more time. As the commander continued, I pictured Eirlys's neat chin, her smooth cheeks pinkened slightly by the spring breeze and the way her lips pouted ever so slightly as she'd spoken in earnest. Her eyes, which seemed to reflect the shifting light and seasons, had been dark pools that day in which I could have easily drowned.

With a great deal of effort I pulled my mind back to the present, forcing myself to concentrate on what could very well determine my survival. After a lengthy briefing, my squadron took off in our Spitfires at 7.25am. We were headed in the direction of Haarlem, a city which had regularly featured in fairytales Dziadek had once read to me, and it conjured pictures of gabled houses set in neat rows alongside shimmering canals in my mind. That morning, the North Sea was deep blue, the sky washed with the rosy hues of a stunning spring sunrise and I was momentarily caught by the beauty of the world below me.

This was soon forgotten, however, and replaced by an unaccustomed sense of cold dread as we crossed the coast at Katwijk. But, flying onwards, I managed to convince myself that it was just a delayed reaction to Jerzy's death, that the mission would be no different from all the others. Turning south towards Haarlem, we immediately reduced our height to dip below the clouds and sight our first target. Dropping again from five thousand feet to two thousand feet, we attacked with cannon and machinegun fire like seabirds diving for fish. It felt exhilarating and terrifying, and my heart was still hammering in my chest as I flew back to base to refuel in preparation for my second mission of the day.

I was strangely calm on reaching Katwijk that afternoon, my fear from earlier having dispersed. I was doing my job and, after my long day's work, I would return to Blackpool and Eirlys as I'd done hundreds of times before. On crossing the Dutch coast at nine thousand feet, we immediately turned south with the object of dive-bombing the railway line running north-east towards Bremen. I recalled that I'd first heard mention of the German city in the fairytale *The Town Musicians of Bremen* by the Brothers Grimm which Dziadek had recounted to me when I was seven. Manoeuvring the plane from the coast, I went through the story of the donkey, dog, cat and hen in my mind. All past their prime in life, I remembered how the animals were each repaid for a lifetime of hard work by being neglected and mistreated by their former masters. Eventually, they decided to run away to become the town musicians of Bremen, a city known for its freedom. I recalled how they succeeded in tricking and scaring off a band of robbers, capturing their spoils and living happily for the rest of their days.

Approaching our target, I thought of the city now and others like it in Germany, the picturesque old buildings described in the story bombed to empty shells, the inhabitants demoralised and dejected after five and a half long years of war. And in that moment, I realised that to look on what I was doing as a job was to sanitise something that couldn't be sanitised. There was no escape from the facts; these missions, especially those when my squadron accompanied the B24s, killed people. Not the Nazis who had eagerly stormed into my homeland in the autumn of 1939, but ordinary people, including the elderly and women and children just going about their daily lives. How could I justify that as doing my job? How could I tell Dziadek what I'd done, if indeed I ever saw him again?

The mission completed for the day, I managed to banish these maudlin thoughts from my mind. Turning for home, I was relieved that, despite my earlier presentiment of impending doom, I would indeed see Eirlys again, after all. Having reformed with the other Spitfires, we were cruising at four thousand feet to save fuel and were just about to clear the coast when, out of nowhere, our group was attacked by a lone German fighter which accurately aimed cannon fire straight at us. My survival instincts, honed by Jacek and driven by my need to return to Eirlys, kicked in and I immediately retaliated with sustained fire.

As the fighter peeled away, I felt a sense of deliverance that God had spared me to see my beloved once more. With darkness now enveloping the sea, I glanced out of the cockpit window and that is when I noticed angry red flames leaping from the engine. Quickly, I operated the fire extinguisher before feathering the gun propeller to try to bring the fire under control, but with the fighter returning hot on my heels and a further burst of gunfire, I felt the aircraft quickly begin to lose height.

When I'd thought about being killed in the war, I'd always envisaged a quick death in the heat of battle, a split second's worth of pain followed by a descent into peaceful oblivion. But the reality was I felt the cold piercing my body like a thousand needles as my plane plunged into the heaving waves of the North Sea. Momentarily, I was taken back to the day I'd fallen into the Dunajec River, how Jacek had rescued me from its fast-flowing waters and the promise I'd made to him.

Then, suddenly, I felt my brother's presence in the cockpit and I heard Jacek urging me on, pleading with me to save myself where he could not. I sensed him with me as I hovered between earth and heaven, between life and death, wondering which to choose or whether God had already determined that for me. As the black seawater overwhelmed me, I saw Alicja's face before me and it suddenly dawned upon me how I could keep my promise to my brother. Maybe it was God or just my own steely will, but I felt a colossal strength surge in me, propelling me forward, and I managed to smash the hatch above my head. I was able to push myself upwards and out just in the nick of time before my plane was swallowed into a watery grave.

48

Eating in the hotel restaurant later that evening, Anna could hear the whistling tinkle of bells and the muted shuffle of trams on the snowy tracks outside. Chilled from being exposed to the full force of the elements all day and the host of difficult emotions the visit to the former concentration camp had stirred up in her, she found she had little appetite for her meal.

Sarah, Bella and Alek were involved in an animated conversation about how the memories of those who'd perished at Auschwitz and other camps were being kept alive by the British and Polish education systems, bringing their stories to new generations. But Anna deliberately remained silent during this exchange, as she was unable to reflect upon her experiences at Auschwitz. Regarding her granddaughter, she noticed the seriousness in Bella's beautiful blue eyes and realised that, on this trip, she had begun to blossom from an unsure teenager into a young woman who had made a mature decision about her future.

From the moment Bradley had abandoned Sarah and Bella, Anna had always worried that her granddaughter would grow up missing out on something or sense that she was incomplete in some way. Indeed, while in primary school, Bella had constantly asked her mother for a brother or sister as though getting one was as easy as going to the corner shop to buy a loaf of bread and bottle of milk. And Anna had worried that, like Sarah and herself, not having a sibling with whom to share her hopes and fears would have an adverse effect upon her granddaughter's life and view of herself.

But now she saw Bella was slowly shedding the insecurities about her familial status that had plagued her throughout school as she grew into a confident, assured young woman. Whereas Sarah had panicked when her daughter had been unable to settle on what subject to study at university, Anna realised that it was actually a responsible decision on her granddaughter's part to postpone something she was unsure of until she had a clearer direction in mind about where she was headed.

Turning her attention to her daughter, Anna saw her as a babe in arms, her bonny eyes fixed on her in mutual recognition. Recalling Sarah's first day of school, she'd felt her soft dark curls brush against her cheek as she'd kissed her goodbye at the school gates, her heart breaking as she'd watched her toddle off across the playground to join a group of little girls, barely looking back. She saw her in her graduation gown, her plaited hair pinned up beneath her mortarboard as she'd posed for pictures with her friends. She recalled Sarah's sheer happiness when she'd brought Bradley around to the house that first time for a home cooked meal. Even if he had turned out to be the best husband and father on earth, he still wouldn't have been good enough for her daughter. She remembered the night Sarah had cried in her arms, dealing the double blow that she was pregnant and that Bradley hadn't wanted to know about it. Hugging her daughter to her, in that moment, she had made the unequivocal decision to be an enduring support to her and her unborn grandchild, whenever and wherever they needed her. And for the past nineteen years, she'd devoted herself to doing just that.

Watching Sarah chatting animatedly to Alek, Anna could see that after years of avoiding relationships, her daughter had finally opened up to a man and this gave her the hope that maybe one day if Sarah met a man like Alek who wasn't already married, there could be the potential of something lasting. Yes, she smiled. Bella and Sarah were going to be okay, more than okay if they dared to follow their dreams.

Anna looked down at the black-and-white photo cradled in her hand, tracing the outline of his strong cheekbones up to his PAF cap with her index finger. Moving her eyes to meet his, she felt the same frisson of recognition she'd had when she'd first looked into her baby daughter's over forty years before. She was a part of Tad, just as he would always be a part of her. On this trip, she may not have found the house where he'd grown up, nor any family members, but at least now she was acquainted with his homeland. The mere knowledge of that filled her with a peace she'd never known before, bringing a smile to her lips.

The pain was briefer than it had been on the street in Blackpool, just a single stab in the centre of her chest. Quickly subsiding, Sarah's and Bella's faces faded away to be replaced by the handsome face Anna knew as well as her own. Smiling, she stretched out her hand towards her father and as he took it in his and kissed it she leaned forward to whisper in his ear: "*Jestem twoją córką i przez całe życiec zekałem, aż wrócisz do mnie.*"

"I'm your daughter and I've been waiting my whole life for you to come back to me."

49

The waters of the North Sea chilling my bones, I knew I wasn't a strong swimmer like Jacek and that it had only been his intervention that day at the Dunajec River that had saved me from drowning. My arms and legs flailing, I found it difficult to make any progress in the strong sea currents as I felt myself sinking beneath the waves.

Beginning to panic, I once more felt the calming presence of my brother. I held my breath, just as he'd taught me when we were kids, and felt his hands gripping me by the shoulders, propelling me upwards and onwards towards the shore, from which I could see lights twinkling across the dark waters. My beloved brother, whose company I'd missed these past years, was with me once more. Just as that day at the river when he'd saved me from drowning, he helped me safely to the shore.

Later, I was roused by strong, stubby fingers tugging on my soaked sleeve, which proceeded to slap me on the face. My eyes squinting open in the glare of torchlight, I expected to see a German soldier, his expression one of glee as he bound me before roughly taking me away to a work camp or a firing squad. But instead, I beheld a woman's face, her greying hair pinned up, her eyes the shade of the sea on a sunny summer's day, smiling kindly at me. And in that moment, I knew that I owed my brother my life twice, that day at the Dunajec River and that night my plane crashed into the North Sea. I also knew how I could repay that debt to him just as I knew for certain that Jacek was dead.

The woman looked exactly how I imagined my mother to be, had she lived. Despite her advancing years and her slightness, she helped haul me to my feet, which immediately gave way on the soft sand. As I stood, I felt a dart of pain shoot up my right leg, causing me to momentarily catch my breath, and I knew I wouldn't be walking anywhere far. So I raised my hands to the woman in a gesture of surrender, expecting her to run away in fear and tip off the local Gestapo in Ostfriesland, who would inevitably catch up with me later that day and bundle me off to some unspeakable place or, because of my injuries, think that I wasn't worth the trouble and decide to shoot me on the spot instead. But the woman just shook her head. And in that simple gesture, I had hope once more.

Under a merciful cover of darkness, she helped me to the shelter of her stone-built house on the edge of the sands. Stark and cold compared to the wooden cottage Dziadek, Jacek and I had shared in Zakopane, it was nevertheless inviting with a fire burning in the grate and an appetising smell of hot food. After strapping my ankle and foot with a tight bandage, she walked over to the stove where she ladled steaming hot porridge into two bowls from a huge bubbling pot. Setting a bowl before me, she pointed to a pot of black treacle on the table and indicated I should put some on the hot oatmeal.

"*Elske Van Doukje.*" She patted her chest before pointing to my uniform. "*Pools?*"

"Yes, Polish. Tadeusz Lewandowski," I introduced myself, stirring the smooth syrup into the oaty milk pudding, the two melding together in a delicious, chocolate-brown gloop. I swallowed a mouthful and instantly felt its warmth sink to my stomach.

"*Ah, ja. Nazis uitschot.*" She spat on the floor, to which I nodded, my stomach settling further. "*Mijn zoon Caspar vecht in Amsterdam voor het Nederlandse verzet,*" she said proudly, and despite the language barrier I understood that Elske's son Caspar was fighting back against the Nazis with the Dutch resistance in Amsterdam. That night, despite being in a Nazi-occupied country once again and my foot throbbing with pain, I slept soundly, as I knew that Elske would keep me safe just as she would her own son, just as my mother would have done, given the chance.

I spent the next couple of weeks being cared for by Elske while my foot, which she gauged to be badly sprained with ligament damage rather than broken from the impact of crashing into the sea, slowly healed. During our conversations, which veered between Dutch, English and Polish, I discovered that I had in fact washed up on

412

Terschelling, just to the north of the Dutch coast. It was an island of overwhelming beauty which reminded me equally of Zakopane and Blackpool – the former which had always been a part of me, the latter which would be in my heart until the day I died. And so it was here, in this barely inhabited place cut off from mainland Europe by the changing tides that I slowly recuperated.

Growing stronger by the day, I walked in forests full of deer and along the dunes on the arching shoreline, where I explored rare species of butterflies and birds whose habitat was in the tidal marshes. On my seventh morning there, the sun sparkling on the white waves, I spotted a shoal of white-beaked dolphins and, filled with elation and sorrow, I collapsed onto the beach, my body wracked with sobs. I despaired that, in this heavenly place, I was alone once more, that everyone I loved was far away from me and that I might never make it back to them.

As Terschelling was only separated by a shallow sea from a succession of islands which eventually reached Europe to the south, Elske indicated that it was possible to walk to Noord-Holland when the water receded at low tide. So, six weeks after crash-landing on this little coastal haven and wearing her son Caspar's brown jacket, thick jumper and trousers, I said goodbye to this strong and fearless woman to set off on my journey back to the continent, back home, my first step travelling across the mud flats to the neighbouring island of Vlieland. Although nearer to the Dutch coast than Terschelling, the place had a remoteness which I loved. Honeycombed with lush forests and sand flats, that first morning I found myself drawn to the beach. Closing my eyes as I stood on the dunes, I felt the breeze comb its cooling fingers through my hair. I watched the undulating waves, noting the way they appeared to inhale and exhale like living creatures, ebbing and flowing to and from the sandy shore as I returned to Blackpool Beach in my mind, the green Irish Sea gleaming like emeralds in the summer sun. Eirlys's head on my shoulder, scents of the sea in my nostrils, I willed every part of that perfect afternoon we'd spent on the sands together almost nine months before to possess me once more. I remained there for minutes, maybe hours imagining Eirlys was by my side like she had been that day, her delicate hand clasped in mine.

But I had no time to linger, and from there I followed the low tide south to the island of Texel where I walked down mile upon mile of wide beaches. Slipping off my heavy flying boots and the remnants of my bandages, I paddled my bare feet in the sea and, with the cooling waters lapping over my tired skin, I felt refreshed as though with each wave, new life was being breathed into me, preparing me to start again.

I arrived in Noord-Holland on May 5th 1945. Stopping off at a bar in a small town, it was amidst much revelry that I heard the radio broadcaster declare that the Royal Canadian General Charles Foulkes and the German Commander-in-Chief Johannes Blaskowitz had finalised an agreement that morning, resulting in the German surrender. An old man with a pipe hanging from his mouth translated for me as the broadcaster explained in rapid Dutch that Foulkes, accompanied by Prince Bernhard of the Netherlands, had met with Blaskowitz at the Hotel de Wereld in Wageningen. Sitting at a table surrounded by the debris and rubble from fierce fighting just days earlier, Blaskowitz had not questioned a single clause read out by Foulkes in front of the media and press.

"*De oorloq is voorbij.*" My neighbour slapped me on the back. The war is over.

As I sipped my beer, surrounded by men and women kissing and dancing in celebration of the hard-fought victory which had cost everyone so much, one thought made its way to the forefront of my mind: for the first time in over five years, I was free to return home to Poland.

50

Sarah was already aware that Hotel Wyspiański was situated near a hospital, as her nights in Krakow had been punctuated by the screech of sirens and flash of blue lights and she prayed this would work in her mother's favour now. The paramedics loaded Anna onto a stretcher, where she lay motionless and pale, her eyes closed above the oxygen mask and Sarah felt as though she'd stepped into an alternative reality – that this could not be happening here and now.

Aware of Bella crying as she held her grandma's hand tightly, willing her to stay with them, Sarah's heart broke. She wanted to enfold her daughter in her arms to give her some physical comfort but she found she couldn't move a muscle and, as the ambulance set off she felt the enormity of the situation slowly build. A bystander, she could only watch as the terrible scene played out in front of her, not sure how any of them would get through it.

Sensing the ambulance gain speed, Sarah began to feel nauseous as they weaved in and out of the traffic, sirens blaring, lights blazing. Hearing one of the paramedics say quietly, "*Ona nie ma pulsa*," she didn't turn to Alek for a translation for she had no need of one. Instead, perhaps somewhat prematurely, the recriminations and self-blame began to swirl in her mind like thick grey mist. As Sarah had long suspected, she knew for certain now that her mother had been hiding a heart condition from her, or if undiagnosed, at least severe warning signs that something serious had been on its way. Her constant tiredness and breathlessness even when they'd only taken a short, non-strenuous walk, her grimaces in the face of pain she'd all too vehemently denied; she saw it all now. At the very moment when it was too late.

As the ambulance forged ahead, her life with her mother played out in a series of dream-like scenes. She recalled when she'd been three or four, Anna's beautiful long blonde hair falling over her face as she'd carefully removed grit from her cut knee before she'd kissed it better, telling her the story of a brave little girl who'd fallen off her bicycle, only for her to get back in the saddle the very next day. She remembered Anna's hair, greying around the temples, swept back in an elegant chignon as she'd sat in the audience at her graduation ceremony, beaming with the pride and joy of a mother who'd always put her daughter before everything else in her life, more often than not to the detriment of her own needs. Where Sarah had failed sometimes with Bella, having had to arrange for the babysitter to stay a few hours longer when a meeting had overrun or else she'd been forced to miss a school sports day because it had coincided with graduation week, Anna had never let her down in that way. Whereas her dad had always had some pressing work matter, Anna had always been there; a familiar face in the crowd, a helping hand, a knowing smile telling Sarah everything was alright in the world.

Sarah didn't register rushing through the hospital's automatic doors or down the white corridor as she, Bella and Alek followed the paramedics pushing her mother's trolley. And then Anna was gone, the plastic doors to the treatment room slapping shut, and Sarah stifled her sobs into her hand, knowing that the next time she saw her mother, she would have been pronounced dead.

Silence bore down on Sarah, Bella and Alek as they returned to Hotel Wyspiański in the early hours. Sarah was sitting in the middle of the back seat of the taxi, Bella weeping quietly beside her, her head lolling against her shoulder. Alek, on her other side, was staring out of the car window into the inky blackness of the winter night, barely having uttered a word since they'd finalised the arrangements with the grave-faced doctor and coroner for Anna's body to be taken back to the UK.

"Thank you for everything the hospital has done for my mother tonight." Sarah had shaken the doctor's hand even though she knew that by the time Anna had reached him, there had been nothing to do for her, unfortunately.

The young man, with more than a day's worth of stubble on his chin and dark circles beneath his eyes testifying to too many late nights, had nodded silently and she'd exchanged contact details with the middle-aged coroner sitting by his side. And that had been that. Anna's death and transportation back to the UK wrapped up in a little over two hours.

"I just can't believe she's gone." Bella sat on the edge of her bed later that night in the warmth of Sarah's comforting arms, scrunched balls of sodden tissues strewn on the duvet. "I knew she was ill in some way, but I thought that we'd enjoy Christmas together and then we'd return home and in the New Year she'd get some treatment and everything would be alright. Why did we bring her over to Poland in the middle of winter on such an emotional journey? Why didn't I realise it would all be too much for her?"

"Because Gran wanted to come and she was so stubborn we could never have stopped her once she'd made up her mind." Sarah smiled gently. "She knew that if she'd told me how ill she was truly feeling, I would have point blank refused to bring her. She was so determined to visit her father's homeland, I think she knew it would be her last chance, and she wasn't above a little subterfuge to get her own way!"

"Yes, she was stubborn, that's for sure!" Bella laughed before her giggles turned into sobs as fat tears rolled down her cheek once more. "I just can't believe she's gone. So suddenly and quickly, and while we are so far from home! With Christmas just a few days away! Oh God, it's so dreadful I just can't bear it!"

"We've got to be strong for each other now, Bella, like she always was for us." Sarah felt hot tears stream down her face too as she stroked her daughter's cheek as she'd done when she was a child in an attempt to get her to sleep. "Now, try to rest, sweetheart, and may you find the peace you need in your dreams tonight."

"And you too, Mum." Bella hugged her tightly to her, reluctant to let her go. They lay like that for a while in the soft lamplight until Sarah eventually felt her daughter's taut grasp slacken on her hand and her breathing deepen as she drifted off to sleep. Extricating herself, Sarah slid off the bed and unzipped her handbag to take out her phone. Scrolling through her contacts, she came to a stop on Cath's number. Her old friend had always been her first port of call in her hours of desperate need when her dad had died and when Bradley had left her while Sarah had been the first person Cath had got in touch with when she'd suffered a miscarriage. But this time, she didn't call her friend. Switching off her phone, she put it back into her bag and tiptoed across the carpet so as not to wake Bella.

"How is she?" Alek asked as Sarah carefully closed the door to her daughter's adjoining room.

"Asleep, that's about all I can say." Completely spent, Sarah slumped next to him on the olive-green settee, the only light in the room filtering in from the streetlamp outside.

"I'm so sorry for you both. I can't even imagine how you must feel. Such a sudden loss must be a terrible shock." His voice was mellow and deep in the half-darkness.

"Maybe not as much as you think, Alek." Sarah choked back the tears. "All these weeks, I've watched my mother trying to hide her illness from me. Call me irresponsible, but I thought coming on this trip would grant her wish of connecting with her father, but now she's died without being able to do that. It was all a waste of time."

"I don't call that irresponsible." Alek pulled her close so that she could hear the steady beat of his heart in the darkness. "I'd call that the greatest respect and love for a daughter to give her mother her dying wish, even though in the end she didn't find her father." He gently wiped a tear from her cheek.

"I just don't know how I'm going to manage without her, keeping down my job, looking after Bella, along with all the stresses and strains of life. Mother was always my rock, the one person I could always rely upon for help or advice, my port in a storm." She wept silently.

"You will find a way, Sarah. You have the strength inside you to carry on." He hugged her firmly before drawing back and pausing briefly as if considering whether to continue. "But I know how you feel from my own experience. My mother has always been my greatest confidante and help too; she looks after my son Dawid." He paused again, sighing. "I've never spoken to you about my wife because it is still difficult, but..."

"Tell me, Alek," she encouraged, wiping her eyes. "I've said all I can about myself tonight."

"I was married to Anastazja for just over a year. I met my wife in one of those bars we saw in Kazimierz, which all the hip students and trendy business people frequent. Ana was ten years younger than me. Having just graduated with a degree in fashion, she was working for one of the city's up-and-coming fashion houses as a trainee designer." He scratched his chin, considering. "Anyway, she was a pretty girl, vivacious, fun to be with and although as different as two people could be, we began an affair. I was wildly flattered at first, of course, but quickly realised we had absolutely nothing in common. A few months later Ana discovered she was pregnant and for the sake of the coming child we decided to marry."

Sarah silently sat by his side in the darkness as he continued, "When Dawid came along, we shared a few months as a family until the cracks started to deepen. The initial attraction between us had long disappeared, after which there was nothing really left. Ana was desperate to forge ahead with her career, never showing any maternal feelings towards her son, leaving us for days on end on 'business' trips. So I became in effect a single parent caring for Dawid which in turn meant I was unable to take up my PhD at the Jagiellonian for which I'd secured funding. Anyway, I discovered Ana was having an affair with a work colleague and a few months after Dawid turned one, we divorced. That was four years ago." Alek smiled sadly, the moonlight through the window catching his sharp cheekbones and the dark depths of his eyes.

Sarah sighed, Alek's disclosure giving her the opportunity to tell him all about Bradley and their affair, how he'd left her pregnant, how he'd sent her maintenance money out of duty, how she'd come to terms with the fact that he'd never loved her while she loved their daughter so fiercely that, at times, it was physically painful. When there were no words left to speak, Sarah leaned back against Alek's chest and, feeling another tidal wave of grief threatening to overwhelm her, she let herself drift into an uneasy sleep.

When she awoke Sarah found herself alone in the darkness. Her body heavy with sleep, she sought to make sense of the confusion in her brain. The first coherent thoughts that entered her mind were of her mum and the realisation that this was the first day of her life she'd have to face without her. The first day without seeing her smile, feeling her arms around her or hearing her gentle voice as she told her about something she'd done or seen. How could she bear it?

All her life, she had been conscious of her mother's easy presence. She'd just always been there to guide her with a steady hand, giving her courage to get through the tough times as well as the strength and confidence to bring up Bella. With Bradley flitting in and out of her life like a summer bee pollinating a flower but choosing to move on rather than stay to watch it bloom, Anna had stepped in and provided the support she'd needed during the past nineteen years. She'd been the one who had simply always been there for her. On the occasions when Bella had succumbed to one of those worrying childhood fevers, it had been Anna who had held Sarah's shaking hand while waiting in the hospital cubicle until the doctor had arrived and assured them that Bella was out of danger. When Sarah had taken the lecturing job at the university, Anna had been on hand to babysit Bella whenever her busy workload, a training course or a staff night out had left her in a fix. Anna had been there to help Bella through every step of growing up – starting secondary school, puberty, exams and first boyfriends – and had given her another perspective when she'd argued with Sarah. She'd been a doting grandmother and a no-nonsense mother who knew just the right moments to give a home truth or a shoulder to cry on. She'd been a friend, a source of fun and laughter. She'd been a counsellor, building Sarah's confidence brick by brick when she had been unsure as to whether she could hack it in the academic world. She'd been her equal, supporting her through the trials and tribulations of Bella's childhood and adolescence as a partner might have done if he'd stayed around long enough. She'd been so many things to her and the realisation that she'd never see her again broke her heart.

Standing at her hotel window, she gazed out over the frost-encrusted trees of the Planty, the snow-covered pavements glimmering in the golden glare of the streetlamps. Bella must have been sleeping lightly too, for she emerged from the adjoining bedroom, her eyes red-rimmed from crying, her hair tousled and knotted from tossing and turning all night. Breaking down in floods of tears once more, she dashed across the room to the comfort of her mum's arms. "Oh Mum, I can't believe she's gone. I didn't even get to say goodbye."

"I know, I know." Sarah soothed her, careful not to let her emotions get away from her. She must remain strong for her daughter's sake and in turn this meant she could push her own feelings to one side, at least for the time being.

Sarah ordered room service and twenty minutes later one of the waiters from the restaurant appeared with orange juices, plates of scrambled egg on toast and black coffees. Choked with grief, neither had much of an appetite and absently pushed the food from side to side on their plates, eventually having to eat it before it turned stone cold. "My heart breaks that we couldn't find anything about Tad for Gran, at least track down someone who knew the family," Bella said eventually, her cheeks wan and tear-stained.

"It is sad. I know Grandma said she didn't come here with any expectation of discovering anything about her father, but after our trip to Zakopane, I sensed she was disappointed. Alek was still looking into it, of course, and I wish I could have helped him, but the documents being in Polish made it impossible..."

"I know. All too late," Bella sighed, forlornly sipping her coffee, "and then I keep thinking of the emotional strain Gran's been under all these months. Seeing her hopes dashed of finding anything out about Tad, that had to have had an effect on her health?"

"I really think we must stop blaming ourselves, you know, Bella. This is the very last thing she would want us to do. Since the air show in the summer, all she's talked about is coming to Poland to find her father, as it were..."

"Before she died," Bella reluctantly finished her sentence. "And if that's so, at least we gave Gran her dying wish," she continued, tears pouring down her cheeks once again.

"Yes, we did." Sarah hugged her tightly to her, feeling that there still should be something else they could do for her mother before they left this country but unsure what it was.

51

At the end of any war, there are the winners who rejoice in their hard-fought victory while the losers commiserate in the ignominy of defeat. But in the summer of 1945, as millions celebrated on the streets of London, Paris and New York while the inhabitants of Hamburg, Nuremburg and Berlin sorted through the rubble of their wrecked cities and lives, it was too simple to say that the Allied forces had won the war and Nazi Germany had lost. Even those of us on the winning side had all lost something too. So many British cities had to rebuild themselves too as of course did Warsaw which had almost been flattened out of existence. Whilst these were very visible signs, the human cost on all sides was immeasurable.

Before returning to Blackpool to embark upon the life Eirlys and I had planned together, I was drawn to see my beloved Poland one final time. I needed to find out what had happened to Jacek, Tata and Dziadek. But more than that, when my plane had crashed I knew that my brother had saved my life once again and in return had signalled how I could repay him. Knowing in my heart Jacek was dead, I felt he had shown me Alicja's face so that I would ensure her safety and that of their child; that they would be provided for in his absence. My plan was to stay in Zakopane for a few months before making my way back to England so Eirlys and I could spend our first Christmas together in a time of peace. I knew that she would already have found out I was missing and I ached to reassure her but communications were so difficult it was impossible for me to contact her.

Going back to my homeland that summer was bittersweet. Poland might have emerged from the crushing jackboot of Nazi Germany to preserve her history, her culture and her language which, when I'd fled over the mountains into Czechoslovakia that February night in 1940, I had not dreamed would be possible. But although the USSR, Great Britain and the US had come together to defeat Hitler, in the war's aftermath fractures soon began to appear in their uneasy alliance as they each claimed their spoils of war. As the Nazis withdrew west, the Russians pulled the iron curtain of communism over our mountains, valleys and rivers, as impenetrable and inflexible as if it had been actually fashioned from metal. The Soviets considered the Polish Army in the West as enemies which did not bode well for a returning airman like me, who had served in a Polish squadron of the RAF.

On leaving Holland in mid-May, I made my journey east through Germany as warily as I'd escaped through Czechoslovakia, Hungary and Romania five years before. I trod my path back to Poland as carefully as I could, both physically and politically, cognisant of the risk I was taking in returning to my homeland. In hushed conversations in the inns where I stayed overnight, I heard stories of flyers being stripped of their decorations with some of the more vociferous ones being prosecuted.

Realising that could so easily be my fate if I was recognised, I walked those final miles home with a heavy heart. But I was no longer the naive boy who'd left home in the depth of winter with only the clothes I'd stood up in and a day's supply of food. I had survived five long years of war. After everything I'd been through, I had survival ingrained in every bone and sinew of my battered body.

And so I turned south towards the distant Tatras, hoping I may find sanctuary there while I made my final goodbyes to my family. As the countryside became increasingly familiar, I began to recognise the farmhouses of our friends until eventually I spotted the steeply sloping roofs of the Syniaks's farm, our nearest neighbours. And then, suddenly, out of the swirling mountain mist, emerged the low wooden buildings of Dziadek's cottage and workshop, half-hidden by the encroaching dark forest, but mercifully still there. Not having laid eyes upon my home for five and a half years, I realised I'd been dreaming of this moment ever since I'd left Poland.

Dziadek must have heard my heavy footsteps, for he met me at the door and I flung my arms around him, bursting with joy that he was indeed alive. His hair a mass of white curls now, his whiskers tickled my cheeks as we embraced while his faded blue overalls were covered in wood chippings which made me guess he'd broken off from a carving to bid me welcome. But drawing back, I saw that the difficult years of war had aged him tenfold, his skin sallow and etched with lines while his grey eyes had dimmed, no doubt having witnessed things no man his age should see. Whether the change in him was due to the years of rationing and privation he had suffered or the stress of living in an occupied country, I didn't know, but he was no longer the sprightly septuagenarian I'd left behind. He was a frail old man.

Following him into the sitting room where he'd once told Jacek and I stories in front of a roaring fire, I saw that, despite the beautiful furniture carved by Dziadek's skilled hands, there was a general air of unkemptness about the place, with dirty plates and glasses strewn around. It was as though, in the past, he'd kept it homely for my brother and me, but during our prolonged absences from home, he'd seen no reason to make the effort for just himself.

"I didn't know whether you were coming back, Tad," he said at last, his voice rasping and weak as he lifted his hands to feel the contours of my face once more. "All these years, *kochany*, I wasn't sure whether you were even alive, although I sensed that you were."

"I made it to Britain where I trained to be a pilot, Dziadek. I learned to fly planes and carried out raids over Germany for years until I was shot down." I looked at his hands, which were as brown and gnarled as oak. "Luckily I came down near an island off the coast of Holland just a few weeks before the war ended and I was able to bide my time there before returning home."

"I never thought I could feel such happiness again, *kochany*, after all I've been through." He kissed me on both cheeks. "You came back to me, my brave boy. My prayers are answered."

"Have you heard anything of Tata and Jacek?" I asked gently as we sat down, noting how all the light drained from the old man's eyes and knowing what his answer would be.

"No, not since the invasion in '39 when thousands of officers like your father and brother disappeared. German propaganda maintains it was the Russians, but they say it was the Germans who were responsible. Who knows what the truth is; the reality is they're dead," he replied. Although I'd long suspected my brother and father had been captured and killed, the old man's words still tore at my heart as surely as if he'd stuck a knife there. "It's true that nobody I've spoken to witnessed either Jacek's or your father's death, but I know." He patted his heart. "I know they are not of this earth anymore, in the same way that I sensed you were."

"I know it too." Tears spilled over my eyes. "When I crashed into the North Sea, I was trapped in the plane, drowning. Dziadek, I was dying. And then suddenly I felt Jacek's hands grab me and pull me upwards to safety. The next thing I was conscious of was a woman helping me to my feet and, in that moment, I knew my brother had saved my life twice: that day at the Dunajec River when we were kids and that night off the Dutch coast. I also knew for certain that Jacek was dead."

"*Kochany*, you must be so careful now. You are all I have left, but Poland remains a dangerous place for you." He traced his gnarled hand down my face. "The older you get the more you look like your mother, my beloved girl."

"What of Alicja?" I asked, recalling that night when I had stood next to my brother in the candlelight of Bazylika Mariacka and he'd married his childhood sweetheart, so long ago now. I remembered my brother's pride and Alicja's complete love for him as he'd slid Mama's ring onto her finger. Remembering Jacek's joy when he'd told me they were expecting a child made my heart break a little bit more. I knew that nothing on earth would have kept Jacek from seeing his child, the final proof to me that he was dead.

"I visit her and Tomasz every day," My grandfather paused as I digested his words. *Tomasz. Jacek's son.* And it made sense that on the day Dziadek had confirmed my brother's death, I'd also found out that he was living on through his son.

"We must go and see them tomorrow." I smiled, buoyed by the fact that something good had come out of all of this misery; that hope lived on for the future. "Is Alicja still living on her father's farm?"

"Yes, she is, although the old man died in '43," Dziadek stuttered. "But I must warn you, Tad, you will find Alicja much changed. Her grief for your brother has affected her health over the years and the doctor says she has some illness within her which cannot be cured. She carries on going for Tomasz; he is her world, her shining light. He is such a beautiful boy, the image of his father. Anyway, you'll see him for yourself tomorrow."

Later, I didn't even have the energy to remove my boots or clothes as I fell onto my bed. Sleep washing over me in weary waves, I prayed for the souls of my brother and father. I remembered Jacek's adventurous spirit, how he loved nothing more than the mountains and rivers of home, and I couldn't stand to think of him captured, his final moments on earth spent awaiting his fate miles away from all he loved. But I knew my brother was a devout Catholic whose faith burned strongly and I prayed that God had given him the strength and courage he'd needed to embrace death. By the time dawn rose next morning, I had an urge to share my circling thoughts with the one person who would understand and, seeking comfort, I rushed into Dziadek's room.

At first, I thought my grandfather was just in a deep slumber and hesitated to wake him. But as I quietly approached his bed I took in his total stillness and the bluish pallor of his skin. His eyes were open but focused on something far beyond me. And I knew he'd gone; the last person to be taken from me by this dreadful war.

52

The next morning, Sarah was surprised to find Alek waiting in the hotel foyer. As she and Bella dodged a couple with toddler twins in tow, she thought he looked tired and drawn, his hair peppered with more grey than she recalled, his black trench coat making his face appear wan, the same effect her funereal black jumper had upon her, no doubt. There was no denying the heartbreak of losing Anna so suddenly had taken its toll upon Alek as well. After spending well over half an hour discussing the arrangements for her mother beneath the glittering Christmas tree, Alek shifted uncomfortably in his chair.

"What is it?" Sarah said, disconcerted by his uncharacteristically uneasy demeanour.

"I wasn't going to say anything today," Alek sighed, opening his leather zip-around folder to remove a sheaf of papers, "but I know time is short for you in Poland and I've found something in the archives relating to Tad's family. Since presenting you with Jacek's death certificate, I've been doing more research into him and his father, Konrad. Knowing that they were both professional army officers at the beginning of the war, I followed an instinct into what was highly likely to have happened to them."

Noting Alek's grim expression, Bella asked tentatively, "What have you found?"

"I've discovered a document that refutes the validity of the death certificate we assumed was your Jacek's. Lewandowski is a common name in Poland and it sent us off on the wrong track." Alek sorted through the papers, his expression intent and serious. "Have either of you heard about the Katyn massacre?"

"Yes, when we visited Wawel Basilica we saw the graves of the Polish prime minister and his wife who were killed while travelling to Smolensk to attend the ceremony to mark the seventieth anniversary of the massacre in 2010," Bella said. "Didn't Stalin's Secret Police shoot the Polish officers and intellectuals captured during the invasion in 1939?"

"In the spring of 1940, the Soviet Secret Police are believed to have shot thousands of Poles whom they had taken prisoner the previous autumn." Alek nodded. "Many of the victims were army officers while the rest were doctors, lawyers, lecturers, all the people needed for society to function properly. Though the massacre takes its name from the Katyn Forest where the mass graves were discovered, the killings of the Polish officer corps happened in several places. A friend of mine visited Katyn a few years ago and he said the memorial site set among birch and pine trees is an extremely tranquil place. Hopefully the men and women who are buried there are at peace."

"Wasn't there something about the massacre in the film *Enigma*?" Bella struggled to remember. "Didn't the Polish code-breaker betray the British to join the Germans because he'd found that his brother had been shot at Katyn? As Russia was an Allied force, he was compelled to switch his allegiance to Nazi Germany."

"That's right. Although fictional, the story is not beyond the realms of possibility. People fight wars first and foremost to protect those they love as well as for their country. The worst thing about Katyn was that, although there were rumours in Poland for years that the NKVD had committed the killings rather than the Nazis, the families had to wait until 1990 when Mikhail Gorbachev officially acknowledged responsibility." Alek said. "Unfortunately, by the time Gorbachev announced that the NKVD was responsible for the massacre of the Polish officers and elite intelligentsia at Katyn, most of the people directly affected by it had died."

"So you think Tad's brother, Jacek, and their father were shot at Katyn?" Sarah put a hand to her mouth, stifling a sob as Alek nodded. "Oh God!"

"Have you found them named as two of the dead?" Bella, eschewing the emotions her mother was tangled in, got to the point. Alek passed her a wad of papers which she skim-read. Amongst the Polish words, she recognised the word *Katyn* followed by a list of Polish names and accompanying photos. Eventually her eyes – and her heart – stopped on two names: *Jacek Lewandowski, Konrad Lewandowski.*

Bella focused upon the black-and-white photo of Jacek. The handsome face smiling at her bore such a startling resemblance to Tad that she retrieved his photo from her bag and laid it next to his brother's on the table before them. While Jacek and Tad's uniforms were different, there was no denying they were brothers. Jacek's details beneath the photo confirmed his place of birth as Zakopane and his date of birth in 1915, making him five years older than Tad, a fact with which Eirlys had been familiar.

Sarah was choked with emotion seeing these two young brothers reunited, side by side once more. Unable to speak, she gently traced their features with her fingers, wishing her mother was there to see them together.

"At least Tad wouldn't have known anything about his brother's and father's fates, as he'd already left Poland by then. What happened to the men, exactly?" asked Bella.

After checking with Sarah, Alek proceeded cautiously. He told how, according to testimonies he'd read, the Polish officers had been taken from their prison camp and loaded onto a train where they'd endured two days without food or water. He told how the hell had continued as they'd been herded into coaches, the windows smeared with mud so they hadn't been able to see they were being driven deep into the Belorussian forest. He told how in the gloom of the dense trees, the Polish officers had been locked in a huge barbed-wire cage and, from there, taken to the edge of the killing pits.

"The men must have known their death was imminent as they stepped forward," Alek explained, "because before them lay an l-shaped pit already filled with dozens of corpses of Polish officers. The men were then blindfolded and shot in the back of the head. Mercifully, their deaths would have been instantaneous."

Sarah and Bella were rendered speechless as they tried to grasp the horror of what had befallen Jacek and his father. Alek nodded grimly before discreetly leaving them alone to digest the news.

Sarah's thoughts whirled in confusion. She was thankful Anna had been spared learning the terrible fates of her uncle and grandfather. Despite knowing about the horrendous war crimes perpetrated in Poland by the Nazis, Sarah had not for one minute considered that her own family might have been caught up in anything like this. But in her trembling hands she held definitive proof, two names at the bottom of a page telling her that her great-grandfather and great-uncle had been shot in the back of the head. Learning that her family members had been slaughtered like animals turned her stomach and, as a wave of nausea threatened to overcome her, she fled to the bathroom.

53

After Dziadek's death, I was a wreck. Physically, I was a shadow of my former self, the arduous journey from Holland across the north German plains back to Poland having taken its toll on my body which bore the scars of the plane crash. Despite Elske's best efforts, without proper medical intervention my ankle had failed to heal correctly, meaning I was destined to walk with a limp for the rest of my life. But it was the emotional pain which ate deep into my heart and soul. Losing my brother, father and now my grandfather I found myself, for the first time in my life, completely alone. Drowning in grief, I couldn't inflict myself on Alicja and her son, so I stayed away. Alone at the cottage, I endured sleepless nights, the sweet song of a nightingale my only comfort in the all-encompassing darkness as I reached the conclusion that it would have been better if I'd died in the plane crash after all. I saw no one for days, maybe weeks on end. Foraging for food in the forest, I just survived and existed, wanting to continue in a state of limbo forever, for it meant I would not have to contemplate a future without them – Jacek, Tata, Dziadek and Eirlys.

I sat for hours in Dziadek's workshop, unable to carve as he'd taught me all those years ago. Instead, I found myself staring at the two framed pictures on the wall which I'd never noticed before, leading me to think that the old man must have hung them in my absence. The first was of my Babcia Zosia, Dziadek's wife, who'd died many years before I was born. In the portrait was an elegant woman, her pale hair pinned up on top of her head. She was dressed in a folk costume, her blouse and skirt embroidered with intricate flowers in bold reds, blues, yellows and greens. By contrast, the baby sitting contentedly upon her knee wore an elaborate white robe and I guessed the picture had been painted in celebration of my mother's baptism. I thought Babcia and Mama looked radiant and I imagined it was a source of contentment for Dziadek to have had them there with him as he'd worked alone in this room these past years. The second was a photograph of Jacek and me. A river running behind us, Jacek looked about nine, I four or five. Dressed in identical striped jumpers, I stood before my brother, my chest puffed out proudly as I held aloft a trout which was almost as long as I was tall. "*My boys,*" I heard Dziadek's voice whisper through the mists of time. My legs giving way beneath me, I collapsed on the floor, unable to hold back the torrent of tears any longer.

Eventually emerging into calmness conducive to thought, I imagined travelling back to England and what it would be like to see Eirlys again and touch her soft skin, knowing that I'd returned so we could spend the rest of our lives together. But then Dziadek's words came back to me about Alicja's illness and I knew that I had to see her and Jacek's son first before making any decisions about the future. The next morning, gauging that Tomasz would be at school, I followed the dirt track to Alicja's farm, a path I'd trodden with Jacek countless times before. Aged beyond her years, her lustrous beauty gone, she was waiting at the gate as though she'd been expecting me.

"Tad, you came back?" She rushed towards me and, catching her in my arms, it was both comforting and alarming to hold a woman to me once more. As Dziadek had warned me, my sister-in-law was painfully thin and so frail a puff of wind would have blown her away.

"Yes, I did. I flew with the British." I hesitated, feeling guilty that I'd survived when so many hadn't, including my brother. "I was a fighter pilot."

"You were so brave." She released me and I saw the light fade from her eyes. "Just like Jacek."

I gently broke the news of my grandfather's death to her. "I think he was just waiting for me to return," I sighed. Unable to contain my emotions any longer, I broke down sobbing in Alicja's arms as she did in mine as we remembered my brother and all the others we'd lost since that night we'd last seen each other in Krakow.

Inside the farmhouse all was spick and span, a far cry from when Alicja's father lived there. As the sunlight of the early autumn morning filtered through the flowered curtains, I sat at the wooden table while Alicja ladled soup into two dishes from a pot on the stove. With its hearty vegetables of carrots, turnip and cabbage, it tasted like the soups Dziadek had once made for Jacek and I and, instead of reminding me of what I'd lost, I found it comforting that, after all these years, I was able to taste home once again.

"Alicja," I said, breaking a piece of freshly-baked poppy seed bread, "Dziadek told me about Tomasz. He said he looks exactly like Jacek."

"He does, you'll meet him later when he comes home from school. Tomasz is the one thing that keeps me going through all this," she sighed, taking a sip of the soup. "Oh, Tad, these past few months, I've felt weaker by the day as though my illness is slowly eating away at me. I know I have not long left in this world and I lie awake every night wondering what will become of Tomasz. I have no family to care for him and now your grandfather has gone too—"

"You have me, I am your family, and I will look after you and Tomasz," I promised. My decision made there and then.

Later that day, I met the little boy who was to become my pride and joy over the coming years. Shyly peeping out from beneath a thick blond fringe, he was wary at first of the strange man sitting with his mother, but when Alicja introduced me, saying, "Tomasz, this is your father who has returned from the war," the little boy ran into my arms as we struck up an instant bond.

From that day forward, I nursed Alicja like a brother as her sickness got worse and worse until she died the following spring, content in the knowledge that Tomasz had someone to love him and bring him up the way she and Jacek would have done. Following his mother's death, I spent every minute I could with Tomasz as we enjoyed adventures together in the woods, rivers and mountains, just as his father and I had done a lifetime ago. And in doing so, I felt life was being breathed back into me too.

After five gruelling years away from home, the truth was I had aged considerably. However, this worked in my favour. Having grown a beard, I now bore enough resemblance to how people remembered Jacek had looked that they accepted me as him whenever they bumped into Tomasz and I at the market in town or walking by the river. Indeed, if anyone had doubts as to my identity they were never spoken as the small, rural community closed ranks to protect their own.

Knowing that I would have been reported missing believed killed back in Britain, I knew Eirlys would have grieved for me. But I hoped that she would eventually be able to put her sorrow behind her to find a good man to marry, one who loved her as much as I always would. Even though it pained me that she would never bear our children, I hoped her marriage would be blessed with them. But I couldn't forget her and never a day passed when I didn't think of her. At night she often stepped forward in my dreams, smiling as she'd done that time we'd met beneath Blackpool Tower, her eyes sparkling, her hair working free of its clips as it fluttered in the sea breeze, beckoning me to take hold of her hand once more.

What I only learned in the decades that followed was that, as well as personal implications, my decision also had political ones, for after the war Poland was under Soviet control. The Soviets, being distrustful of servicemen of the Polish Armed Forces in the West, barred men like me from flying in the Polish Air Force. One of the most drastic cases was that of Wing Commander Stanisław Skalski, the top Polish fighter ace of the war, who, on returning to Poland, was arrested and spent eight years in prison. So it was a godsend to have the chance to change my identity to Jacek's, a man who had served on Polish soil before being incarcerated as a prisoner of war and then released, rather than an airman who had fought with a Polish squadron in the UK. If only my brother's true fate had been the same as my cover story, all our lives would have been different.

As the years rolled by, I reasoned with myself time and time again whether I did the right thing. My love for my brother was, in the end, so strong that I had no choice but to willingly sacrifice my own happiness. But the issue which still burns into my soul is that when my plane came down off the Netherlands' coast in spring 1945, I could have returned to Eirlys and married her. Why didn't I? It is a question which will haunt me until I draw my final breath.

54

Krakow, December 2020

Later that night, after steeling herself to pack her mother's clothes, toiletries and jewellery, Sarah sat beneath a circle of lamplight and watched from her window as cars and buses competed for road space with the trams tinkling back to the depot along the snow-covered lines. The snow was still falling thickly, a white veil drawn over the world outside. Over dinner with Bella, Sarah had accepted the evidence Alek had found that her great-grandfather and great-uncle had been killed at Katyn as truth. But now, alone with her thoughts, her intuition told her that there was still unfinished business in this sad tale of two brothers.

After answering an email to confirm her attendance at a conference on the assessment and moderation of coursework at the University of Manchester on January 28th, she opened a google search on Katyn and read long into the night. Feverishly making notes as silence descended on the snowy street below, Sarah understood that the Katyn massacre had been beneficial to Nazi Germany in order to discredit the Soviet Union, an Allied force. Reading a disturbing report from Reuters concerning declassified documents released in 2012, she found that during the war Roosevelt and Churchill had apparently hushed up evidence that the massacre had been perpetrated by the Soviet Secret Police for fear of alienating their powerful ally Stalin.

Sarah considered how this would have been cold comfort for the victims' families looking for answers all those years. It was far too late for any perpetrators to be brought to justice for the killings of her Great-Grandfather Konrad and Great-Uncle Jacek.

As she closed her laptop she reflected on the effect this must have had upon the boys' grandfather, the man who had cared for them all their short lives. Both grandsons lost in the war, their fates unknown, never to return home to him. What an unimaginable sorrow he must have endured.

55

Krakow, December 2020

With Anna's body transported back to England ahead of them, Sarah and Bella spent their last morning in Krakow attending a pre-Christmas Mass in Bazylika Mariacka before heading back to Hotel Wyspiański, where Alek picked them up to take them to the airport. The small talk between Sarah and him dried up as the tenement buildings of the city's suburbs petered out and they sat in silence as forests and fields rushed by the window, the bare monochrome landscape reflecting her sombre mood.

Presently, Sarah looked over at Alek, seeing that his face was concentrated on the twists and turns of the snow-slicked road ahead. Although Alek had eaten dinner with her and Bella at the hotel every night since her mother's passing, Sarah didn't know whether it was obligation or kindness that had kept him with them or some deeper feeling. Seeing a sign for the airport looming ahead, did any of it even matter?

Travelling the final few miles, Sarah saw the countryside had been transformed into a veritable winter wonderland since they'd arrived with Anna three weeks before. Thick hoarfrost clung to the branches of the trees while the lakes were now wide, frozen expanses, the sun reflected on their surfaces creating stunning blue phosphorescence. The fields were asleep for the winter beneath soft swathes of glimmering snow, the animals hunkered down in stables, keeping warm beneath blankets of straw and hay. Trying to take it all in, Sarah pondered how the landscape was so changed since her mother had seen it. Somehow, it gave her a strange comfort to see that even when her life had seemingly stopped in the blink of an eye, in the wider world, things just continued as they always had, at their own pace and in their own time.

But Sarah had the sensation that her time with Alek had run its course too as he helped unload their suitcases onto trolleys outside the airport. With Alek parked in a drop-off zone with a five-minute restriction and snow driving in their faces, their farewell was briefer than she'd hoped. Just a tentative hug, the few words which they spoke to each other lost in the Christmas bustle around them. But as Sarah wheeled her case down the icy concourse towards the glass building, she momentarily turned to see Alek offer her a sad half-smile before the stream of people swallowed him up.

For the two-hour flight back to Manchester, the empty seat beside them served as tangible proof of their great loss and was almost too much for Sarah and Bella to bear. Just a few weeks ago, Anna had been sitting between them, chatting excitedly about their plans. Now, as travel tablets made Bella sleepy, Sarah gazed out of the window as the plane soared through the grey cloud to the blue skies above. She couldn't help but think of her grandfather almost eighty years before, flying his plane over the same land, rivers and hills which lay thousands of metres below them. She pictured him crouched in the cockpit, following orders, concentrating upon doing his job properly and trying to stay alive so he might lay eyes on his beloved Eirlys once again. Hoping that one day he would return to Poland to discover what had happened to his brother, Jacek, from whom he hadn't heard for so long.

*

"I am the resurrection and the life, saith the Lord. He that believeth in me, though he were dead, yet shall he live, and whosoever liveth and believeth in me shall never die."

With special permission, Anna's funeral Mass took place at Sacred Heart Church in Blackpool the day after Boxing Day. For all that the church path was slippery with slushy snow, Sarah didn't once cast her eyes down to check her footing. Instead she kept her focus on her mother's coffin, taking in the dark wood and brass ornamentation as four men she didn't know hoisted it high into the air before lowering it ever so slightly to come to rest on their broad shoulders. Leaving behind the whirls of stinging sleet, she felt the warmth of the church welcome them. Following the procession down the aisle, she thought Anna's coffin was too small to contain everything that she had been in life.

"We brought nothing into this world, and it is certain

that we can carry nothing out. The Lord gave, and the Lord hath taken away; blessed be the name of the Lord."

Keeping hold of Bella's arm as she walked, Sarah looked at the faces of the people in the pews around them, grateful that they had taken an hour out in the midst of their Christmas celebrations to pay their respects to Anna.

"Man that is born of woman hath but a short time to live, and is full of misery. He cometh up, and is cut down, like a flower, he fleeth as it were a mere shadow, and never continueth in one stay."

As the Mass commenced, Bella tried to push away the tidal wave of emotions threatening to drown her by focusing on something solid, a trick she'd picked up in her yoga class. Putting her hand into her coat pocket, her frozen fingers gratefully slipped around the wooden angel her grandma had given her in the summer. Feeling the rough grooves of the figure's wings and the waves of her hair contrast with the smooth swathes of her gown, she wondered whether, even back then, with a presentiment that death was coming, Anna was making sure her most prized possession, given to her mother by her father, would end up in her granddaughter's safe hands. To be passed down the family from one generation to another, in accordance with her wishes.

Bella looked across to her mother, who had her arms folded tightly around her, her white, bony fingers gripping the black sleeves of her coat. It was literally as though she was trying to hold herself together as she stared at a point far beyond Anna's coffin which Bella, from her position in the pew, could not see. No tears shone in her eyes, but a silent grief etched itself onto her fine facial features. The chill of the church sent a shiver down Bella's spine, the suddenness with which death had taken her grandmother shaking her to her core.

"In the midst of life we are in death," said the priest as he led the mourners out of the church at the culmination of the service.

Much later, as they neared the crematorium, the sleet began to turn to snow. The snowflakes fell faster and faster, settling gently on Anna's coffin, a reminder of her father's homeland. Cloying Sarah's eyelashes together and straying into her mouth, rather than annoying her, she saw them as a gift from nature to deflect from the grief crushing her heart in its tight fist. But inside, as blue velvet curtains closed around Anna's coffin, Sarah could not contain an anguished cry as the full force hit her in the centre of her chest that her mother, and everything she had been to her, had gone forever.

56

Sarah chewed hard on gum as the plane began its descent into Krakow, the peppermint taste overwhelming. Unsurprisingly, her mind flipped back nine months to the last time she had made the outward journey to Poland, with Anna offering her boiled sweets to combat the effects of the changing air pressure. She recalled how her mother had chatted about visiting the country of her father, excited to follow in his footsteps and learn something of him, his life and his family. Tragically, her health, which Sarah now realised had been deteriorating for a few years, had failed her at the very moment she'd been poised to discover where she'd come from, after a lifetime of not knowing.

So, it felt fitting that they were bringing her back, this time to stay forever. Initially having pondered whether to have Anna's name added to George's plaque in Carlton

Cemetery, Blackpool and have her ashes interred there, once the idea had come to Sarah to bring her mother to Poland, it had been a fait accompli. She had immediately contacted Alek to tell him that she wanted to scatter her mum's ashes somewhere in the mountains, which she'd so loved when they'd visited, and he had been only too happy to make the necessary arrangements.

Diverted from her thoughts by Bella rustling magazines, she glanced over to her daughter. Over the past few months, she'd physically changed so much, her skinny figure broadening out into womanly curves. She'd also grown out her stark-straightened white-blonde bob into delicate honey-tinted waves flowing down past her shoulders as she'd gained a confidence and self-possessed sureness that went with leaving her teenage angst behind. Catching her looking at her, Bella smiled. "What?"

"I was just thinking about when my dad took me to university that first time. I had so much stuff that we had to strap my suitcases onto the roof rack of his Fiat," she sighed, slotting the duty-free magazine into the pouch on the seat in front of her. "Of course, I was only twenty-five miles away in Lancaster."

"And I'll only be a two-hour flight away and remember, Alek will be on hand to help me out if necessary!" Bella smiled, her excitement at becoming a student at Jagiellonian University having reached fever point these past few weeks with her departure imminent.

"I know. But just remember, you can call me any time of the day or night." Sarah hugged Bella to her, glancing at the empty seat. "Your grandma would have been so happy that you've chosen to study architecture at the very university where her father started his degree."

"Yes, as soon as I thought of it, I knew that it was the right thing to do." Bella smiled. "It's almost like I'm finishing what Tad started, as well as entering a new stage of my life."

Sarah nodded as Bella stowed her wad of magazines back into her rucksack while her thoughts made the inevitable jump back to Tad. Over the past few months, she hadn't been able to get over the fact that Alek had found that Tad's older brother, Jacek, had been shot at Katyn, along with their father, Konrad. Indeed, there had been something about her great-uncle's story which had intrigued her ever since her mother had told her of Tad's close relationship with him. Was it the story of a younger brother's idolatry of his elder sibling or was there something more to it than that?

As for Alek, she was more than a little apprehensive about meeting him again. In December, she'd taken an instant liking to him and a friendship of sorts had developed in the weeks they'd spent together, as they'd shared similar values and attitudes to life. In the eight months since, they'd regularly Skyped one another and yet, as the plane touched down, Sarah had absolutely no idea how she would feel about seeing him in the flesh again instead of on a fuzzy computer screen.

One thing she did know was that when she had enquired about staying in one of the ski hotels in Zakopane, which would be quiet between the summer and winter seasons, Alek had been adamant. "No, we're staying at my family's *działka*." A *działka*, he'd explained, was the Polish equivalent of a Russian *dacha*, a house simply constructed from wood.

Alek went on to tell her his parents had bought their *działka* as a summer house to escape the city heat during July and August, and Sarah was looking forward to seeing the garden, allotment and orchard. Before another hectic year commenced at the university, a couple of weeks of chilling out, enjoying barbecues, bathing in the nearby Dunajec River and walking in the surrounding forests was just what Sarah needed.

Sarah spotted his red mini-bus in the car park and felt butterflies fluttering in her stomach as she pulled three huge suitcases of Bella's along with her modest one on a trolley. "Are you sure you didn't fit the kitchen sink in here, Bella?"

"Very funny, Mum." Bella pulled out her tongue as Sarah's eyes were drawn to Alek who was getting out of his mini-bus. He looked exactly the way she'd pictured him all these months and yet different somehow. Used to seeing him muffled in winter coats, his face was tanned from the hot summer Poland had just enjoyed, his figure slender in jeans and T-shirt.

"You look better, you look good, Sarah." He smiled as she sat at the front of the mini-bus with him. "I want to beat the rush hour traffic, so excuse me if I put my foot down."

Sarah wanted to ask him whether he'd discovered anything about Tad or found a suitable spot for Anna's ashes, but she held back. Knowing that her time would come later, she was happy for Alek to chat to Bella about Jagiellonian University, allaying some of her fears as he gave her an idea of what to expect during her weeks as a fresher. After just over an hour, Alek pulled off the road into a lane so narrow that the branches of the trees on either side brushed the roof of the mini-bus, as though bidding them *hello*. Peering through the clustered blue spruce and fir trees, Sarah and Bella gleaned their first sight of Alek's *dziatka*. Built entirely of slats of dark wood rising to the eaves and sloping roof, their eyes were drawn to the ornate porch which arched over the front door. Either side of it were little windows with lace curtains hanging at them and candles burning in a warm welcome. The scene took Sarah back to when, sitting on her mother's knee, Anna had read her stories of mysterious cottages hidden in forbidding forests.

"It's like something out of a fairytale," she enthused to Alek, trying to take in all the intricate bevelling and craftsmanship of the cottage. She half-expected one of the three bears or seven dwarves to open the heavy wooden door and bid them all a hearty welcome.

"It is. My parents bought it in 2006," Alek said, heaving their bags out of the boot before locking up. "My dad had just retired and so they got together the money to buy a summer house. Unfortunately, he passed away soon after, so they didn't get to enjoy it for very long together," he sighed deeply. "Anyway, let's go meet my mother and my son, Dawid."

As the three of them entered the cool parlour, a woman stepped from the adjoining kitchen, her grey hair pinned in a loose bun at the nape of her neck and her glasses perched on her nose as she wiped floury hands on her embroidered apron. Peeping shyly from behind her stood a sweet-looking little boy, bright blue eyes shining under a thatch of dark hair.

"This is my mother, Julia." Alek kissed the old woman on both cheeks. "And this is my son, Dawid. *Mama, Dawid, to jest Sarah i Bella.*"

"*Dzień dobry, Dawid.*" Bella smiled, holding out her hand towards him.

"Hello, Bella." The little boy beamed, and with no further invitation, took hold of her hand and whisked her away to play a game of hungry hippos which was set up on the coffee table in the centre of the sitting room.

"*Witamy, Sarah. Proszę przyjmij moje kondolencje dla twojej matki.*" The woman smiled, proffering her hand to Sarah. Julia continued in Polish, pausing every now and again to enable Alek to translate as his mother offered Sarah her deep condolences for the untimely loss of her mother while welcoming her back to Poland.

"*Dziękuję, dziękuję,*" Sarah whispered in Julia's ear, pulling her into a tight hug. Feeling the woman's arms around her, Sarah closed her eyes and imagined her mother's encircling her once more in a cocoon of love. Finally releasing her, she saw that Alek's mother was overcome with emotion too.

Later that evening, they sat down to a veritable feast laid on by Julia. There were different types of sausages and meats, cabbage and potato salads, peppers stuffed with rice, minced meat and root vegetables, as well as the Polish staples of borscht, pierogi and warm poppy seed rolls. While Bella laughed with Dawid, Sarah was quiet through the meal, overwhelmed that this woman she'd never met before had gone to so much trouble to make their welcome to Poland the second time round a pleasurable experience.

While Dawid insisted on setting up his snakes and ladders board on the kitchen table, alternately challenging Bella and his grandmother to a game, Sarah and Alek retired for a nightcap. Ducking their heads beneath a low wooden beam, they entered the cosy sitting room which was furnished with carved seats, softened with cushions and throws woven in the traditional patterns of the region.

"Dawid's a lovely boy, you must be so proud of him," Sarah commented, relaxing back on the sofa as Alek took his place at her side.

"I am. He was very young when Ana left that in one respect it didn't affect him," Alek sighed. "And my mother simply adores him."

"Yes, I can see that." Sarah nodded, realising there was so much hurt there and also knowing just how it felt. "I've only been here a matter of hours and I can see that the relationship he and his grandmother share is very special."

"And how are you?" His forehead furrowed. "I've been wanting to talk to you on your own since the airport, but there hasn't been an opportunity."

"Getting there, finally, I think. For months, it didn't really hit me. What had happened to Mum, what we'd discovered about my grandfather. Or rather, what we hadn't found out about him." She took a deep breath. "Oh, Alek, it's as difficult as hell. I miss her every single day. It's always in the little things, when I pick up the phone to ask her if she wants anything buying from the supermarket. On Sundays when she always cooked us a roast dinner, that's when it all comes back and I don't know how to cope with it."

"I was the same when my dad died. They say time is a great healer," he said, his voice slow and steady. "I don't know if that's true. The pain just becomes less immediate, maybe."

"Yes, perhaps." Sarah nodded, momentarily distracted by Dawid's squeals of excitement as he evidently beat Bella at another game. "Can we discuss the arrangements you say you've made to scatter Mum's ashes? I know I want her to be in Zakopane and close to where Tad lived." Sarah paused. "I was hoping we could find a place with a specific connection to her father and his family, but I know we probably won't be able to now."

"But I think I just may have," Alek interjected, his expression serious. "I didn't want to raise your hopes until I was sure, but over the past few months, I've been researching the Lewandowski family in this area. I discovered they have a family plot in a cemetery, which is just a five-minute drive away. I took the liberty of talking to the priest and he is willing to do an interment service for your mother at the graveside tomorrow."

"I don't know how to thank you, Alek." She choked back the tears, knowing that, after all these months of deliberation, it would be the perfect place to lay her mother to rest. "Did you manage to find out anything else about Tad?"

"Yes, I did. I tracked down someone who wants to speak to you about him," he said cryptically.

"Who?" Sarah's heart hammered hard in her chest.

"A man called Tomasz Lewandowski, he's coming to Anna's interment." Alek scratched his stubbly chin. "He is Jacek's son."

57

Having barely slept all night as she'd pondered what to ask her cousin, Tomasz, Sarah was a bundle of nerves as Alek drove them to the cemetery. He put his foot down as they followed dried leaves scurrying down the winding lanes, riding the back of a fresh autumnal breeze. Alighting at the traditional wooden church she had visited with Anna in December, birdsong and the calming smell of woodsmoke soothed Sarah's mind as she cradled the urn containing her mother's ashes. Walking up the church path flanked by Bella and Alek, she was prepared for whatever she was about to learn, sensing that it would somehow bring closure to both Tad and Anna's stories.

Cutting around the back of the church, she spotted the priest, his white robes flapping in the wind, and the old man by his side. His silvery hair thick, his blue eyes bright, he was spritely for his age and smartly dressed in a navy suit, pressed white shirt and a respectful black tie. Their flesh and blood standing right before them, a tangible link to Tad, even though Tomasz would have only been a young child when his uncle had been killed at the end of the war.

"You must be Tad's granddaughter and great-granddaughter," Tomasz greeted them in English, presenting a bunch of red roses to Sarah. "I've been looking forward to meeting you since Alek told me your story. I'm so sorry for the great loss of your mother."

"Thank you, you are very kind," replied Sarah, feeling overwhelmed by the man's kind and generous spirit. "We are so pleased and honoured to meet you."

"As I am too." The old man gave Bella a long look as though he recognised family characteristics passed down the generations. Then they all fell silent as the priest commenced the ceremony at the family plot, protected on two sides by the graveyard wall. In English and Polish, he blessed Anna as she carried on her journey in the afterlife before she was interred with her family members. The stillness broken only by the wind whispering through the branches of the surrounding trees, Sarah had the feeling that her mother had finally found the peace she'd so craved and deserved.

After the priest left, Tomasz hovered by the graveside giving Sarah and Bella the opportunity to study the weathered stones. Although obscured by ivy and moss, it was still possible to read the inscriptions on the three graves. Sarah studied the first one carefully. *Krysia Lewandowska 1896–1920. Konrad Lewandowski 1892–1940. Her great-grandparents.* Asking Tomasz to translate the Polish, he told them that while Krysia's remains were there, it was a memorial to Konrad whose body rested somewhere at Katyn. Moving onto the next grave in the plot, they saw it was carved with an ornate Polish eagle spreading its wings above it. Below she read the names *Jacek Lewandowski* and *Alicja Lewandowska* and an inscription in Polish. *Nareszcie razem.*

"What does that mean?" asked Sarah, carefully brushing off some of the lichen which was obscuring the bottom part of the grave before tracing her fingers over Jacek's name.

"It means *together at last,*" Tomasz explained. "They were my parents. Their life together was tragically cut short by the war. Again, my mother's remains lie here while Jacek also rests in the Katyn Forest."

"I'm sorry," said Sarah, resting her hand upon the old man's shoulder as they moved onto the final grave. There, they read the name that had become so familiar to them in the past few months, *Tadeusz Lewandowski*, which had been inscribed beneath *Mateusz Nowakowski*, whom, Sarah knew from what her mother had told them, was Tad's grandfather, his beloved *dziadek*.

"All my family together." Sarah felt a tear escape down her cheek. It was a comforting thought to cling to, even though she knew Jacek and Konrad lay in Belorussia, while her grandfather's grave was at the bottom of the North Sea and their names here were merely memorials to them.

"Yes, that's why I've had their names inscribed on the stones to reunite them, so to speak." Tomasz paused before continuing, "I think we should have Anna's name written beneath her father's name."

"What a lovely idea, my mother would have wanted that," said Sarah, tears welling in her eyes, blurring her vision. "It's fitting she's returned to this place, even though Tad didn't."

"But he did, Sarah," Tomasz said, his voice suddenly elevated. "It's only Jacek and Konrad who aren't interred in this place. Your grandfather Tad is buried here beneath this stone with his *dziadek*."

"What? I don't understand." Sarah suddenly felt weak at the knees.

"Sarah, Tad didn't die during the war," Tomasz clarified. "He returned to Poland, where he lived to be an old man."

Feeling faint with shock, Sarah put her hand upon a nearby gravestone to steady herself. With a supreme effort, she refocused on what Tomasz had just revealed. The notion that Tad had survived the war was something she'd never considered. It was difficult to conceive that he'd survived crashing into the North Sea before somehow navigating the treacherous journey back to Poland. Moreover, Anna had always been so convinced that Tad had been in love with her mother, Eirlys, it seemed impossible that he hadn't at least tried to contact her in the years that had followed. If he had survived and travelled back to Poland somehow, wouldn't he have bided his time before returning to England to find his beloved waiting for him?

58

"But how can that be possible? Eirlys received confirmation that the remnants of Tad's aircraft had been located off the coast of Holland," Bella remarked as they strolled through the woods to Tomasz's *działka*.

"When Tad's plane came down near the Dutch coast in March 1945, he managed to break the cockpit hatch and escape into the water. A few months before he died in 2002, he told me that my father, Jacek, had appeared to him just as he was about to drown and had helped him swim ashore. I'm not sure whether I believed him or not, but Tad was convinced of it as his brother had always been there for him, particularly in moments of great need. Washed up on a Dutch island, a kindly woman called Elske nursed him and it was in this remote sanctuary that he saw out the final days of the war," Tomasz explained.

"I'm glad Tad survived the war. He'd been through far more than anyone should ever have to go through," said Sarah, wiping away a tear. Nevertheless, she wondered how her mother would have coped with this revelation after spending a lifetime believing Tad had perished in his plane.

"I know what you're thinking, Sarah," Tomasz said, leaves rustling and twigs snapping beneath their feet as they walked, "that he abandoned your grandmother? But I can assure you that wasn't the case. When the war ended, Tad returned to Poland to check that his family were okay as well as to find out what had happened to his brother and father. His intention was to see his homeland one final time before returning to England to marry Eirlys. I know this, because when I turned eighteen he told me the truth about my real father, Jacek, and why he'd assumed his identity."

Sarah and Bella listened in stunned silence as he continued, "But Tad had to change his plans when he reached Poland. With the Soviets occupying the country, the situation was so dangerous he was forced to assume my father Jacek's identity because the authorities deemed fighting with the British a treasonable offence." Tomasz paused, seeing the full implications of his uncle's decision register on this woman's face. "His decision to raise me as his son was an unselfish act of love for his brother."

Sarah stifled a sob as Tomasz pressed a photo into her hand. "I've been the custodian of this since Tad died, but now I must give it back to you. It belongs with his family." She looked down at the crumpled image of Eirlys and Tad, their hair windblown, their faces laughing, Blackpool Tower peeking out above them. Their happiness laid bare in the black-and-white picture, Sarah thought of the painful separation they had been forced to endure only a short time later. "I've never seen this photo before. They look so in love."

"Your grandparents." Tomasz smiled, his expression warm.

"Yes, they were," she considered, "and the man who loved you like his own son."

"Yes," the old man nodded gravely, "Tad loved me and cared for me right up until the day he died as my father would have done had he survived. But as you know, Jacek was killed at Katyn." Tomasz paused to allow them to take in the enormity of what he was telling them. "When Tad returned in '45, my mother, Alicja, was extremely ill and died the following spring. Tad told me that he nursed her through her sickness which he blamed on the years of privation she'd been forced to endure, coupled with the heartbreak she'd suffered losing my father." The old man paused as the roof of the wooden *dziatka* peeped out through the trees. "After Mother died, Tad raised me single-handedly in the way his brother would have wanted, instilling in me a love of the outdoors and teaching me how to fish, to hunt and to ski, all the things, he said, Jacek would have done, if he'd had the chance."

"He sounds like a good father," Sarah said, her voice untainted by jealousy or resentment for the love her own mother had missed out on.

As they stepped through a gate and walked up the garden path, Sarah's heart sang that she finally knew the truth. That Anna had been correct all these years in her conviction that her mother and father had shared a deep and enduring love. She only hoped that somehow Anna knew it too, now. Reaching their destination, Tomasz's summer residence, he gestured to the beautiful wooden cottage built in the local style. "Let me present to you the Lewandowski house where Tad was born and died. He lived here all his life, firstly with his grandfather and brother, then with my mother and I, and, finally, when I married and moved to Krakow, he saw out the last decades of his life here by himself."

"Wow! Our ancestral home," Bella gasped. "If only Gran was here to see it."

"Maybe she is." Sarah grasped her daughter's hand. "I've felt her presence since we arrived back in Poland."

Walking from room to room, the house was furnished in the typical Podhale style that they had seen in the museum in Zakopane during their December trip. Her footsteps reverberating on the wooden floorboards, Sarah thought of Tad and Jacek as small boys playing chase or hide and seek, of them sitting on the wooden chairs upholstered in red and white listening to their grandfather's folk tales, the lace curtains closed to keep the wolves in the wood beyond at bay. Observing a framed but faded photo of the three of them, the gregarious old man in the middle with a serious Tad on one arm and a laughing Jacek on the other, she pictured the brothers leaving for war, one destined to return home, the other to be shot in the back of head and buried in a Belorussian forest. Turning to the next photograph, a formal studio portrait of Tad and Jacek's parents – her great-grandparents, Konrad and Krysia were exactly how she'd pictured them, Konrad a handsome, powerfully built man

resplendent in his uniform, while Krysia was a
fragile young woman. But the photo which tru...
her heart was the one of Tad and Tomasz, the yo...
smiling lovingly at the little boy who looked so li...
father, Jacek. She could tell from the expression on Ta...
face that he had indeed fulfilled his promise to his brother
and had been a good father to Tomasz, and her heart ached
again for her mother who'd never known a father's love.

"Come, I have something else to show you. After the
war, Tad became a respected woodcarver in the region just as
his grandfather had been before him." Tomasz ushered them
through the room. "Their workshop is out at the back."

A single light bulb suspended from the ceiling infused
a pale glow over the woodcarver's workshop, the light it
gave out not strong enough to reach into the dark corners
where long-kept secrets could still sleep easily beneath layers
of cobwebs. Walking around, the room looked to Sarah as
though it had been frozen in time. Her grandfather's bench
laid out with carving knives, gouges, chisels and saws, it was
almost as though he had just left to eat his lunch or carry out
an errand and would return imminently to pick up where
he had left off.

"This place is a time capsule. The truth is, I don't come
here often because I always feel I am invading Tad's space,
even though he is long since gone. He spent so much of
his time here quietly carving. Look at these implements,
they're just exquisite. He once explained to me what he
used each one for." Tomasz picked each one up to explain
its properties. "This one is a carving knife, a specialised knife
used to pare, cut and smooth wood, while this is a gouge,

curved cutting edge used for carving hollows, ⌐ sweeping curves. This is a fluter which I think ⌐ to make decorative cuts. Tad has been gone for ⌐st two decades now and yet I could never dismantle ⌐s workshop or use it for another purpose. Look at this, my great-grandfather carved this for Tad when he was a little boy."

Sarah and Bella looked down to see a small wooden chair with the most intricately carved backrest they'd ever seen. "Are they scenes from Polish fairytales?"

"Yes, the Bear in the Forest Hut, the Frog Princess, the Good Ferryman and the Water Nymphs," Tomasz explained. "Tad said his grandfather told him the stories so many times that he knew them by heart. He loved to recount them to me when I was a little boy and carried on even when I was too old to appreciate them."

"To think my grandfather and great-great-grandfather lived and worked here, in this very space," Sarah said as Bella photographed the chair.

"It's more than living and working here. This work is some of the most exquisite I've ever seen," Alek commented, studying the huge tableau of the ascension of Jesus to heaven which dominated the far wall. "Take this piece, to come up with such a complex design is a feat in itself, but then to execute it so brilliantly in such a way that the figures appear to rise out of the wood using just hand tools like chisels and gouges, it is truly amazing. This area of Poland is well-renowned for woodcarving, but this is something else, Tomasz. Have you thought about exhibiting some pieces in a museum?"

"Maybe my children will, after I die. But I'm happy ju.
to leave it here as a collection. I think all the pieces belong
together as a testament to a wonderful woodcarver and
man." He smiled, his voice infused with nostalgia. "Which
reminds me, I have one more piece to show you; it was the
last carving Tad did before his death and it was very precious
to him, so I keep it behind the cupboard to protect it from
damage. Alek, can you help me slide it out?"

Sarah knelt down on the wood chippings on the floor
to take in the tableau's details one by one: the curved
undulating waves of the sea, the familiar shape of Blackpool
Tower, and in the foreground the exquisitely carved figures
of a man and a woman standing side by side, arms entwined.
Tad and Eirlys reunited.

Epilogue

I sit in my studio, the wintry sunlight streaming in through the open window reflecting off the metal of my tools. Having been a skilled master woodcarver for over half a century now, I have, as Dziadek taught me all those years ago, selected the wood the previous night before settling on the size and shape of the figures I wish to create. No doubt a softer wood would be easier to carve for someone with my painful hands, the once-nimble movement of my fingers now somewhat dulled by arthritis. But such woods are also prone to damage and I can't risk that, not on this piece. I know that the hardwood I hold in my hands will not only preserve its lustre but also its longevity. Of all the hundreds of pieces I've produced since the first tiny figure I carved while sitting on Dziadek's knee, I want this one to be preserved for eternity to stand as a testament of Eirlys's and my love.

Possessing the finest grain, the panel will also be ideal for carving the intricate details of Eirlys's lovely face. I've only ever had one photo of her, the one I kept in the inside pocket of my flying jacket over my heart of the two of us standing together in the shadow of Blackpool Tower. The image of Eirlys is too small to really make out her features, but all I have to do is close my eyes and I can see her standing before me once more. I notice the way her dark eyes curve slightly at the corners, the movement of her hair as it falls in loose curls at the nape of her neck, how her bottom lip is slightly fuller than the top. This is how I will carve my beloved.

The nostalgic song 'I'll Be Seeing You' playing on the radio, I am transported back to that precious time we spent together and how we once danced to this music. I set to work. Beginning the general shaping process, I change my gouge twice, settling on one sharpened with strong bevels that I reserve for tricky projects such as this. Happily carving with the grain, it isn't until just before lunchtime that the wood finally reveals to me what it wants to be. Smiling as it silently consents to my plans for it, I pick up the smoked sausage and cheese sandwiches I wrapped in greaseproof paper just before dawn. Sitting on the wooden steps of my workshop, I eat them, flipping the silver sixpence in my fingers, my mind consumed by reminiscences of Eirlys and that one precious Christmas Day we spent together.

Then, as happens more and more these days, Antusz, Marek and Jerzy enter my thoughts, before eventually making way for Jacek. Altered as I am by the passing of sixty-three years with my grey hair and lined face, my brother looks the same as he did the last time I saw him in

.hat Krakow street in October 1939, our mother's crucifix gleaming at the centre of his chest. His blond hair and blue eyes, his muscular build and his reassuring smile. Forever my older brother. Forever my hero. Last night, I walked over to the church to contemplate the Last Supper tableau carved by Dziadek's skilful hands. Twilight encroaching around me, I read the plaque I had put up many years ago and said a silent prayer for all the Podhale men who went away to war and never came back.

When I've crafted the general shape of the piece, I score deep gouges into the surface of the wood before proceeding to carve the more decorative cuts. Once I've added the finer details– the undulating ripples of the Irish Sea, the straight lines of Blackpool Tower soaring into the sky and the wide expanse of the beach – I am able at last to focus my undivided attention on Eirlys. And it is in this moment that I realise the true reason for my undertaking. I've kidded myself into thinking it is to preserve the memory of her in wood forever, seeing now that is just a by-product. For me it is all about the laborious carving process through which I can relive every moment I spent with her; every smile she ever gave me, every expression I saw on her face. In the silence of my workshop, over half a century later, she will be with me once more.

For the next few hours, as afternoon moves imperceptibly into night, my hands deftly finish the surface, the tooled texture created by the shallow gouges breathing life into the picture. Seeing the special meeting with my beloved appear in the wood before me, tears spring to my eyes as I reach for the abrasive paper to complete the polishing. Using large, grained paper with a rough surface first, I then employ fine paper to make the piece silky slick to the touch, just as her skin was, all those years ago.

The next day, after completing the finishing, I seal and colour the wood with walnut and linseed oil to protect it from dirt and moisture. I then lift up the carving, cradling it as carefully as I would a new-born baby and carry it outside to properly view it in the daylight. Propping it up against the wall of my studio, the bright rays of the sun intensifying the browns, I see that the oils I've used impart a delicate sheen on the wood, just as I'd intended. The reflected sunlight helps me read the form as I focus first on the waves in Eirlys's hair, then the soft angles of her forehead, nose and chin, and finally the sensuous curves of her breasts and hips, their definition once known to me by heart.

Drinking in the details of her like a weary traveller denied water for days, months and years, I run my fingers through her dark hair as she becomes real to me once more. Taking her hand in mine, I pull her close and whisper, "I know you've been waiting a while for me. I'm here, Eirlys, I'm here!"

How the mighty have fallen in battle!
Jonathan lies slain on your heights.
I grieve for you, Jonathan my brother,
you were very dear to me.
Your love for me was wonderful.

2 Samuel 1:25–26

Acknowledgements

The Woodcarver of Krakow gave me the opportunity to write about Blackpool, which has always been a second home to me since I grew up visiting my grandma, Sylvia Wynne, every weekend. I first travelled to Poland when I was nineteen and since then I have visited Krakow and Zakopane on many occasions. I am always struck by the stunning architecture and scenery and the warm welcome extended by the Polish people, which I hope I have managed to capture in my novel. Although my characters are fictional, the historical background of the PAF in Blackpool is well documented, despite not being generally well known. It has been a privilege to research their story and bring it to life.

I would like to express my deep gratitude to my mum, Pamela Evans. Thank you for all the time and advice you've given to help me tell this story of courage and love. I couldn't have written it without you. Thank you to my dad, Peter

Evans, for all the support you've given me and for looking after Flora while I've spent hours writing and editing this story.

Thank you to Michael Manton and Jackie Broadley for encouraging me to write my second novel, which, in the end, was much easier and more enjoyable to write than the first. Thank you to Helen Crone and Year Two at St Mary's Catholic Primary School. You are an inspiration every day!

Further Reading:

'Blackpool at War: A History of the Fylde Coast During the Second World War' by John Ellis. Copyright 2013 John Ellis.

'polandinexile.com'. Copyright 2008 polandinexile.com.

About the Author

Rachel gained a BA (Hons) in French/English at Liverpool
Hope University and an MA in Modern Languages Research
at Lancaster University before training to be a journalist.

She now teaches in a primary school. She has enjoyed
writing stories since she was a child and coming runner up in
a *Sunday Express* story competition gave her the confidence
to write her first novel, *Roses of Marrakech*.